I moved from the bed through the darkness, grabbing a red silk robe from a nearby chair. That was when I felt it—vampire energy . . . and it was close. I dropped my hand over my throat to touch over the sapphire jewel necklace that was still lying there. Whoever was coming should not have been able to sense me, but the vampire presence was headed straight for the house, as if they knew exactly where they were going.

My sharp Dhampir gaze searched the dark forest in the direction from which I felt the energy coming, and my eyes widened in surprise when an extremely tall, slender female with platinum blond hair that fell low across her back landed on the roof right in front of the windows to our room, right in front of me. Glass separated us, but that was about it. In spiked heels higher than I had ever seen a woman wear and a barely-there mini-skirt that cut across the very tops of her shapely thighs, she strolled to within a few yards of the window. Her elongated features and pale skin practically glowed against the moonlight. "Well, well, well," she said with an arrogant lift to her chin as she continued to make her way towards me. "I was not expecting to meet Caleb's *little plaything* so soon."

Plaything? I was most certainly *not* a plaything! I had no idea who this woman was, but there was no doubt she was a vampire. Her energy was pulling fiercely inside my chest, which was not surprising because I doubted any human woman could walk so effortlessly on those ridiculous heels. She continued to approach the glass without the slightest bobble or worry that I was a threat to her in any way. And though it was obvious that without the security activated she could break through the glass between us with little effort, she made no move to do so. Instead she waited, as if she wanted me to come to her.

In a decision I probably should have considered a little more thoroughly, I hit the release button to the glass door and walked out onto the roof to confront her.

Book's by Christine Wenrick

Book One: The Charmed
Book Two: The Charmed Souls
Book Three: The Charmed Fates

the CHARMED FATES

Book Three of The Charmed Trilogy

For Toni —
You're simply the best!!!

Christine Wenrick

CHRISTINE WENRICK

PRINT - ISBN 13: 978-0-9882069-5-3

E-BOOK - ISBN 13: 978-0-9882069-2-2

For information, please e-mail Red Tree House Publishing, Seattle, Washington at: christinewenrick@redtreehouse-publishing.com

Cover design by Samantha T. Davis, Mill Creek, Washington Contact e-mail: Samantha.T.Davis@gmail.com

Editorial and interior design by OPA Author Services, Scottsdale, Arizona Contact e-mail: Info@OPAAuthorServices.com

Printed in United States of America

June of 2013

Dedication

For Olivia and Caleb, Two Characters whose love and story inspired me to break out of the routine and try for something new and extraordinary.

Prologue

"How dare he!" Celeste was forced to shout inside her own head because currently she was struggling to draw in even a single breath against the unrelenting chokehold on her throat. Her back was rigid against the cold cavern wall as her long nails clawed at the jagged rock and dirt on each side of her narrow hips. Bright sapphire eyes and razor-sharp fangs gleamed back at her with a mix of dangerous delight and lethal warning . . . and it infuriated her!

"I warned you not to cross into our territory, Celeste," he hissed with an almost eerie calm, but there was no mistaking the threat behind his words. "But, obviously, you did not hear me the first ten times."

Oh, she heard him, all right . . . His blustery order was like a broken record in her head. She just didn't care. What she did care about was the fact that the oversized behemoth responsible for her present discomfort was displaying her in a position of weakness in front of her entire coven. The five women, her coven sisters (who were going to get an earful from her afterwards), were scattered throughout the dim cavern, watching the violent display with almost casual, hooded interest, just waiting for her to respond in some way . . . which was a little difficult to do at the moment. But the scene was nothing new to these women. They had seen *him* threaten her, their leader, many times before. Yet Celeste knew that with only the slightest signal from her, her sisters would attack with unrelenting force. *But damn it!* She would not show them weakness. She had earned her position of leadership over these women and had always demanded fierce loyalty. She had been a vampire for longer than she dared remember, and a damned good one. She knew the game, she knew how to win, and she derived pleasure from taking down those—innocent or not— who were in her fucking way!

"You can imagine my surprise when I smelled your cheap

scent on my property," he continued, tightening his hand even more over her airway as he growled the words. Now he was just pissing her off, but the light giggle that floated from a darkened corner of the cavern was pissing her off *more*.

That bubbly giggle belonged to her coven sister Annabelle, and Celeste wanted to roll her eyes in disgust. The shorthaired strawberry blond wasn't the smartest cookie in the jar. As the newest member of her all-female coven—and the smallest—she was also the least attractive of her sisters. Which explained why she was letting that sleazy Nightwalker (Celeste could never remember his name) feast all over her breasts like a damn banquet, leaving little punctures in her skin from his fangs. "Come on, baby," he panted against her throat while hiking up her skirt with both grubby hands. "Let's go outside. Just for five minutes. I'll make you feel real good in no time."

If Celeste could get any air in her lungs at that moment she would have outwardly snorted at his plea to the woman. *"Yeah, I bet it wouldn't take even two minutes!* Clearly, however, Celeste had more important issues to deal with. Slowly, she concentrated her mesmerizing gaze directly at her attacker, causing her lavender irises to shine with unshed—but very manufactured—tears, then tilted her head to the side in an innocent pose. It was the best she could do, since she couldn't speak. He responded by snapping her head away from him, releasing her from his iron grip and growling with sharp disgust, "You should know by now, that will not work on me."

After several critical breaths, Celeste recovered as a slow, seductive smile spread over her lips, her appreciating gaze appearing to scan the finely honed male form in front of her. "Now, now, Jax," she cooed. "Surely you did not come all this way just because I may—or may not—have crossed onto your land. You worried someone might stop by your little tree-top palace uninvited?"

"Not someone," he replied sharply. " . . . You!"

Celeste scraped her now dirty nails in a deliberate trail across the silk shirt covering his broad chest. Though his wardrobe consisted entirely of one color—black—no one could ever claim that Jax Walker did not have exquisite taste when it came to the cut and feel of the material. It was simply grand to the touch. "But Jax, I am just a harmless female," Celeste somehow managed to say, with batted eyelashes and all, even though she knew every word out of her mouth was a lie. "I mean, I am honored that a powerful vampire such as yourself would spare a single thought for little old me."

Jax snarled, snatching her wrist in one quick motion and twisting her around until her cheek was pinned back against the cold rock wall. His huge, boxer-like form covered her back as his breath, noticeably warmer than her own, closed over her ear. "We both know you are not harmless!" he hissed. "And I will not warn you again. Try to come near Caleb one more time, and I will finish you myself."

Celeste could hear it in his voice. He was not bluffing in the least. "Caleb's my mate!" she replied in outrage. "My fucking mate! You have no right to keep me from him like this."

"He was never your mate!" Jax snapped back. "We both know it." Jax released the woman, smoothly turning on his heels to leave, as if refusing to give her another thought. Celeste was enraged at the Daywalker's arrogance.

"If you really believed that, you would not have wasted time coming here with idle threats. Caleb is mine! So do not threaten me again. Not unless you're prepared to deal with all of us."

Celeste expected to find herself back against the wall, but instead, Jax just turned and carefully swept his gaze around the cavern and its occupants, committing the details of each face to memory. His scrutiny fell lastly on Annabelle in the corner, who was now panting, pleading, her back arched high as that skanky vampire settled between her thighs, preparing to take her with crushing force in front of everyone. Turning back to Celeste with an arched brow, dismissive in its very nature of the raw, brutal world of which he himself was a part, he replied, "They do not seem to be too concerned about my threats at the moment."

Celeste fisted her hands at her side in fury as she watched Jax leave. He had been right, of course. These days, her coven more resembled a pack of lazy, sunbathing coyotes than bloodsucking vampires. *Oh,* how she hated that man, and took out her frustration on the one woman currently pissing her off the most. "Annabelle!" she barked, the sound echoing sharply off the rock walls.

The writhing woman ignored her, instead gasping and begging for more from the bastard now pumping into her like a crude jackhammer. *God,* Celeste would make that bimbo pay later for humiliating her like this. "Oh, yes . . . *Isaac! Isaac!*" Annabelle cried out in fluttered delight. "More, Isaac, more."

Isaac grunted his approval and pumped harder into the woman beneath him, while Celeste inwardly snarled with disgust. *"Isaac!"* That was the name of the mangy coon who had been following Annabelle around for weeks. Didn't he have his own coven to worry about?

Without warning, Celeste swung around on them both. "Take that shit outside before I fucking vomit!"

Chapter One

When you have succeeded and failed enough in this life to own your own path, what are the odds that fate will come in and force a change of course?
The truth is, the odds don't matter...
Fate is just fickle that way.

***

"Well boys, this is certainly unexpected," I said with a derisive smile directed toward the three male Dhampirs—human-vampire hybrids like me, only nasty—who had just dropped from the forested canopy above me and now stood in my direct path. One appeared about the size of a WWF fighter who moonlighted on weekends as a bouncer at the nearest biker bar, while the next, beside him, was exactly the opposite—thin and pale, with long, straight hair, projecting his best Orlando Bloom 'elfin' impersonation. But the third Dhampir was the most disturbing because he looked like an average teenage boy who could have just strolled in from second period math class.

Given the ferocious scowls warping all of their facial expressions, the eclectic group obviously had no intention of letting me continue up the mountain trail in peace, which was confirmed when the larger one growled rather inarticulately, "You're coming with us, Charmer."

"Oh really," I replied. Then, with a sigh, I set the grocery bag I had hauled halfway up the mountain on the ground and turned back to them with my hands at my hips. "Davin's boys, huh? I guess I shouldn't be too surprised, since I haven't run into any of you for a few weeks. But seriously ... can't a girl go out for a few groceries without some vampire soldiers hassling her?"

The responding chorus of grunts and snarls said they were in no mood for my sarcasm. And really, why should they be? It was too damn hot outside today—mid July in the Cascades, in fact. As a Dhampir myself, I knew from experience that the only reason a Dhampir was out on a scorching day like this was that they had to be . . . or they were ordered to be by a deranged and obsessed Nightwalker, the man I knew as Luther Davin, vampire baddie. One glance at these guys and I knew they were a good three-quarters vampire, except maybe for the math whiz. He had such an innocent expression about him that, for a moment, I thought he might have only recently been turned. But his eyes weren't black, like those of a new vampire. Well, I judged, their tolerance to the sun would be much less than mine, since I was only one-quarter vampire. "Boys, you obviously know who I am . . . what I can do? You might want to rethink this situation, because I really don't think this is going to end well for you."

The Elfin wannabe laughed, reminding me of a cackling chicken. "You think the three of us are afraid of one small woman?"

I blinked back at him in amazement. "What? Is Davin not even warning you guys anymore what you're in for? He just sends you in, fangs out? Or are you simply that stupid?"

The beefy one took one ground-eating stride forward without actually moving any ground, while the math-wiz laughed, "Look at this—the Charmer wants to play."

"Not if it's going to take long," I replied, becoming impatient. "In case you hadn't noticed, it's hot out here. I've some sun tea in the bag, though, and I'd be more than willing to share if you'd like something refreshing before we get on with this little throw-down." The three of them only stared back at me as if I were daft, while I swiftly twirled my long hair into a tight bun in preparation to fight. I knew I was pushing my luck with the sun tea remark. In truth, this was not the best situation to find myself in on a Monday morning when I knew someone back home needed my help now. In many ways Dhampirs could be more dangerous than plain old nasty vampires—mostly because they *did* have at least some tolerance for the sun, which enabled this bunch to interrupt me on a perfectly beautiful summer morning.

"This is going to be fun," the teenager said as he flashed his sharp fangs for effect and stalked towards me. Of course, he would be the first to approach. It almost wasn't a fair fight.

"Seriously," I continued, " . . . is Davin recruiting you guys out of junior high now?" In response, the boy came at me with little strategy other than bombing forward with the directness of a bullet. Lucky for me, I happened to be almost as fast as a bullet, so I was able to duck underneath his charge. As he whirled back around, I dropped over the grocery bag and pulled out two sharp pointed hawthorn stakes. "You can never be too prepared," I smiled before giving a quick twirl of my wrists and launching right back up, thrusting one wooden stake straight into his shoulder while at the same time tripping him below the knees with a swift kick that completely took him by surprise. His weight fell underneath him as I drove him back to the ground, burying the pointed tip through his shoulder and into the hard earth. Then I followed with the second stake into his other shoulder, pinning him tightly. He snarled at the pain of the hawthorn wood and blaring sun now directly on him as I declared, "That should hold you for a bit."

Now I sensed the oversized bully coming at me from behind. Evidently the other two had finally decided they would have to put some effort into this kidnapping attempt. Locking his arms around me in a crushing bear hug to keep my dangerous Charmer touch under control, my only recourse was to snap my head back, smacking his chin so hard I was sure his fangs would dig into his lip and draw his own blood. It gave me the time I needed to slip free from his grasp, but my freedom didn't last long. He grabbed at my arms again and yanked me back to him. It felt as though he was nearly pulling my arms from their sockets. But the contact of his hands on my uncovered forearms was all that was needed to unleash horrible images and incite a tremendous amount of pain throughout his body. The Dhampir quickly released me, stumbling several steps back. "Shit!" he cursed.

"Uh-oh," I replied with deliberate sarcasm. "Someone has been a very, very bad Dhampir. You're really not going to want to touch my skin, then—though that may not be so easy, considering all I have on is a tank top and shorts."

"You smart-ass bitch," he snarled, driving his booted heel into my stomach before I had a chance to respond. The resulting impact launched me into the air and I crashed onto the forest floor about twenty feet away, with a hard thump to my rump. *Ouch*, that was going to leave a mark . . . or more like several.

With no time to regain my breath because the big guy was coming right back at me, I shot back to my feet just as he charged, with the third thug right behind him. I blocked his descending fist with a tight grip that stunned him for a precious second while I used every ounce of force I had to crack-block his knee with the heel of my foot. The bone-jarring crack as the limb broke and his enormous weight collapsed out from under him made me flinch. He fell to the ground, cursing, while I swung around and started running the other direction. The remaining Dhampir, the Orlando look-alike, was hot on my tail when I spotted a conveniently located tree branch and bounded onto it, then to another, then another, but not without smacking into several limbs along the way.

I was moving fast but my pursuer was equally fast. He was right on my heels! It was only by a mere fraction of a second that I was able to spring to the next nearby branch to escape him, then to drop back to the ground a safe distance from the other. Man, this guy, Orlando was fast! And crafty. He was actually smart, making me lead so I was doing all the hard work.

As I circled back through the open clearing where this all started, I knew I had to make my stand or he would be on me. Busted knee guy was probably down for the count, but there was no telling how many seconds I had before the math whiz was able to withstand the pain of pulling the stakes out of his shoulder. I swung around on Orlando, obviously holding my ground now, and he halted right in front of me with a menacing smile. He believed he had me cornered. "So what's in it for you guys, anyway? I mean, Davin has the easy part . . . relaxing back in a nice, cool cave somewhere while he sends all of you out to do the heavy lifting. That hardly seems fair."

"You talk too much," he growled irritably.

"Really? I like to think of it as getting to know you, Orlando" I said with a wink just before I vaulted at him. He met me step for step and we collided in mid air with brutal force, but I was somehow able to latch on to his temples before we came crashing back to the ground. The focused contact had him rolling away from me in tremendous pain, but that didn't stop him for long. He shook off my effect and almost instantly was back on me. But he had slowed down a little, just enough so that he cursed as I pushed him back, latching onto his face with my fingers and holding him in a vise grip. Soon, my touch induced searing images of all the evil he had done in his Dhampir life. I could almost see them racing through his head like a demonic slideshow. He crumbled to his knees in pain, and he was not the only one. Though I had spent the last nine months trying hard to work on controlling the horrific images that would seep through to me while I was making contact, I was still only able to block some of them . . . but it was an all important some because it kept me from being in as much pain as the bad guy I was fighting. I held on to the Dhampir beneath me until his dark eyes were completely dilated, his mind now flooded in so much agony he was held motionless against the ground. When I finally did release him, he rolled clumsily to his side, moaning, his hands clawing at his temples. I had held onto him longer than I had done with most I had fought, and I could only imagine that it felt to him a bit like having a lobotomy.

Rising to my feet, I slapped the excess dirt off my hands and clothes then took in the scene around me, which appeared as if I had just whipped a bunch of thugs in a bar brawl. "There," I sighed, reaching for the grocery bag once again. "I did warn you. But you'll get yourselves out of this mess soon enough, I'm sure. But Davin's definitely not going to be happy that you guys flubbed this up." I started to take off but then stopped and turned back to the cursing and moaning group. "Oh, and I wouldn't follow me up the mountain if I were you. You think I'm a bitch to deal with? You should see my mate and my grandfather. Unlike me, they have tempers."

My triumphant laugh echoed through the forest as I raced with Dhampir speed up the mountain. This little distraction had made me late!

It was summertime in the high Cascade Mountains, and over nine months had passed since Caleb, Jax, Gemma and I had returned from our battle at The Oracle—The Brethren's North American site in Alberta Canada. That also meant I had nine months of solid training to add to my already expanding repertoire of skills. Soon, I would be twenty-eight and I felt like a completely different person from the naïve woman who learned over a year ago that she was destined to battle vampires for the rest of her life . . . but different in a good way. I was much stronger now, more empowered, able to defend myself quite capably on my own. But I rarely got the chance to prove it as I did today. Mostly because my very skilled, very protective vampire mate, Caleb Wolfe, was always putting himself in between me and whoever or whatever was threatening me. He did it because he loved me and didn't want to see me get hurt, but I understood that because he was a vampire who could not be out in the sun, it was not possible for him to always be there. Trying to get Caleb to realize that, however, was another thing entirely.

"Olivia!" came a familiar booming voice right on cue. "Get your sweet *ass* up here, now!"

"Ahh," I sighed, "the sounds of love." Even nine months after I mated the man—the vampire equivalent to being married—he still held the power to make me positively giddy with love. When I glanced up at the tree house, our wonderful home literally built among the tree tops in the middle of the Cascade Mountains, the glass doors to the house were open high above me to release and amplify his booming voice. With a small running start, I jumped up to the midway perch Caleb had built for me in the trees, which got me up the first fifteen feet, and then bounced the last fifteen feet up to and through the glass doors. I landed on walnut planked floors in a pool of sunlight that washed across the cozy, but empty, entry hall, then walked over to a cantilevered arm that was bolted directly to the floor a few feet inside the doors. I turned the handle that would return the five glass panels to their closed position.

The second the sun was blocked again by the filtered glass, a whoosh of air hit my back and several hard breaths pushed from some very large vampire lungs. I turned to face my clearly worried mate, who was standing there in all of his six-foot-four rugged glory. Man, was he yummy, with his slightly longer dark hair and stunning gray eyes. His body was built like a swimmer's—wide shoulders, narrow at the hips. Seeing him standing there dressed in dark jeans and a navy sport shirt that cut him just right, I wondered how I ever got so lucky. Caleb Wolfe breathed alpha male confidence. And at the moment he was breathing it pretty hard. "Are you all right?"

The way he said that, I wasn't quite sure if it was a question, but regardless, I shrugged innocently. "Yes, I'm fine."

Caleb then stared back at me with an incredulous glare before throwing his arms up high then slapping them back against his pant legs. "Well, then, are you out of your *goddamn* mind?" That definitely was a question. "You were attacked again, weren't you? And you knew I wouldn't be able to help you with the sun out." When I merely smiled at him, he added, "Olivia, this isn't funny. I felt the blow to your stomach and when your arm was nearly twisted to its limit!"

Even when he seemed to be authentically angry it was hard to take his growly temper seriously when it was so obvious he was simply worried. Though it had been nine months since I had started to get used to the idea of how powerful I was becoming in my Charmer gifts, Caleb was still trying to adjust to the fact that I could handle myself. I knew in time he would come around. But it was taking a lot of reassurance and patience on my part. "Then you also felt how I kicked ass down there, didn't you? I barely broke a sweat." His gray eyes narrowed with doubt, but then I saw just the smallest hint of a smile at the one corner of his mouth. These were the moments, whether he would admit to them or not, that showed he was gradually accepting that I knew how to handle myself. He still did not like it, because he was a warrior at heart and every primal instinct in him screamed at him to protect what he loved, but he was handling it.

Caleb's gaze scanned my dirty and rumpled clothing, and then the torn tank top and scratches on my shoulder. Reaching out to examine the shoulder nearly yanked out of its socket during the fight, his touch felt as gentle as his expression. He could *feel* the swelling, the stiffness underneath. Sometimes his little gift—to be able to feel any heightened emotion in a human, like my pain, for instance—was inconvenient because it made my telling even the slightest little white lie nearly impossible. "Ok, so maybe I broke a little sweat," I corrected.

He removed the grocery bag from my arms and searched its contents. "This was what was so important for you to sneak out of here this morning and risk your life?"

I blinked back at him, surprised he didn't agree with the items' importance. "We're going to need these. We weren't expecting things to happen this quickly. And I didn't sneak out. Didn't you get my note?"

He blinked back at me as if he were truly stunned. "*Note?*" he questioned.

"Yes. It took me about an hour to find a scrap of paper around this place."

The scowl returned to his face. "I'm a vampire, Olivia. We *feel* everything. We don't look for notes!" Caleb then mumbled something additional under his breath and pinched the bridge of his nose, his unconscious habit that signaled he was trying to push back his growing stress or anger. I tried to conceal my guilty smile over a moment that he considered a 'seriousness situation.' Stress definitely had him worried this morning, but in part he couldn't help it. For Daywalkers, good vampires, anger was part of his vampire world, and it was tied directly to his blood thirst—a thirst that had to be controlled at all times, but mostly especially during times of stress . . . like when your mate slipped out on you while the sun was bright in the sky and you could not follow her. "I'm trying here, Olivia. I swear I'm trying . . . But you're going to give me a heart attack. And that would be saying something, since I'm a damn vampire!"

I was just about to say the perfect thing to reassure him when he shot a concerned glance upstairs. "You and I will have to figure this out later. Right now Gemma needs you. But just so we're clear, we're not done with this conversation." He then cupped his hand around my cheek, his eyes filled with sincere emotion as he added, "*I* need us to figure this out, all right?"

I placed my small hand over his large one and smiled gently. "I understand." Then I glanced upstairs toward the room Gemma and my recently discovered grandfather, Jax Walker, shared. "Is she OK?"

Caleb's lips pulled into a tight line. "You better get up there. I think Jax could use your help."

Wasting no time springing up to the second floor ledge, I sensed Caleb was right behind me. We were both nearly at Gemma's door when it was suddenly hurled open and Jax jumped out backwards onto the balls of his feet. "Get out!" Gemma shouted right before a tea mug hurtled through the doorway with such velocity that it missed Jax only because he ducked at the last fraction of a second. The mug smashed against the wall of his study, breaking into dozens of tiny pieces. "Don't you ever touch me again!"

Jax, a handsome, muscled giant of a man with an absolute heart of gold, turned to me in complete wide-eyed bewilderment and said, "She has gone mad."

Chapter Two

Standing there in the narrow hallway, I shifted my gaze between an equally stunned Caleb and a rarely flustered Jax. To see these two giant warriors frozen in place as if they didn't have the slightest clue how to handle a five-foot-four redheaded ball of fire was, at the very least, unusual—more accurately, bordering on amusing.

"Jax," I began carefully, "There probably isn't much reasoning with her at this point. You know how, uh . . . stubborn she can be."

Jax was quiet as he smoothed his open palm over his forehead and the long hair tied back at his nape with a leather strap. His jaw was tight, his expression twisting with worry. "For the first time since I have known her, I do not know how to help her."

"Let me try," I offered, my hand brushing lightly over his forearm.

He nodded. "Thank you."

I turned to meet Caleb's gaze, which had already been fixed on me. His fingers were hitched at his jean pockets, making his shoulders even more broad than usual. He gave me a reassuring nod. "We'll wait out here until you call us in."

"Tell her that I love her," Jax added just before I opened the door carefully.

"It's me, Gemma," I said once inside the room with the door closed behind me. The normally exuberant and happy redhead was sitting up in her bed, but she was pale as a sheet and sweating profusely. I could see why Jax was so worried, but my concern eased a bit as soon as she spoke. "Oh, thank God you're here!" she began with a sharp finger pointed towards the door. "That brute is never touching me again!" Then she let out a loud wail of pain. I rushed to her side, taking her hand in my own. "Easy, Gemma, just breathe," I said calmly, trying to conceal the smile on my lips. I knew she didn't mean what she was saying at that moment. "You know, you've never seemed to mind Jax's touch before this. In fact, I do believe you've made a comment or two about . . ."—I cleared my throat a bit uncomfortably —"and believe me this is weird for me to say as his granddaughter . . . appreciating his rather extensive experience."

She managed one wicked laugh, really more of a grunting sound, just before another contraction hit and she reached for my arm to squeeze till I thought the blood circulation had stopped. "Oh, God, oh, God, *oh, God!*" she squealed, then shot me a warning glare just before hissing in a sharp breath between her teeth. "Yeah, well, now that I'm trying to push a baby the size of a watermelon through my cervix, I have some objections. I have *big* objections. God, look at me, Livy," she said miserably. "I'm the size of a car!"

I bit back my laugh. "You're not the size of a car . . . maybe a Mini Cooper," I teased.

"That's not funny, Livy!"

"OK, OK . . . how long ago did the contractions start?"

"A couple hours . . . but Chay says things are progressing fast."

"Where is Chay?"

"He's downstairs getting things ready." Gemma's expression grimaced as she closed her eyes and shook her head. "Honestly, what's there to get ready? This baby's gonna come screaming out of me either way."

"It means this will all be over soon," I reassured her. "Just do as he instructs. You know Jax trust him completely or he wouldn't let him near you."

Chayton "Chay" Red Feather was also a vampire and Jax's long time friend . . . and by that I do mean *a long time.* Chay, which is Sioux for "falcon," had taught Jax how to live in peace with who and what he was—how to become a Daywalker—how to live without killing humans and control his vampire thirst, which he, in turn, taught Caleb.

In the early seventeen hundreds his tribe had recently migrated down from central Canada to settle in the Dakotas when he was attacked by a rogue vampire. He had been thirty-one at the time he was turned, leaving behind a cherished wife and son for a cursed life he had no choice about. He survived at first by living among the small coven that had turned him, but, like Jax and Caleb, he hated the demon he had become. Born a man of nature, he chose to leave the coven to live a solitary life off the land, where he fought everyday to feed his thirst without killing humans. Chay didn't know it at the time, but he was part of a select few vampires spread all across the globe who fought the nature of what they were, looking for a better way to live their immortal life. Chay was part of the first group of Daywalkers, and nearly two centuries later he had taken Jax in after he was turned and taught the young vampire how to live as he did. They had been close as brothers ever since.

Over time, Chay became a brilliant self-educated physician to the vampire world, and Gemma was certainly not his first Dhampir childbirth, although there was no telling her that at the moment. "It's so hot in here, and the pain is getting worse. Where the hell is he?"

"I'm sure he'll be here soon," I said while administering soothing strokes with a towel over her forehead. "He left some ice chips here. Would you like some?"

"Forget the damn ice chips," she growled. "Just get this thing out of me!"

"Now Gemma, you know you don't mean that."

"*Oh, God*," she said, leaning forward with a gasp. "Don't bet on that." Wincing, she looked down desperately at her hugely rounded stomach. "Look at what he's done to me. There must be five babies in there. I'll never fit into my clothes again."

When another contraction hit she screamed out, then bit her lip as she crushed my hand. I glanced downward to see her white-knuckled grip over my fingers and worried about how much pain she was already experiencing. The contractions were getting closer together, and as I continued to help her breathe through them I was startled to notice she was crying. Gemma rarely cried. With a fresh, cool cloth I wiped the tears from her cheeks. "What is it, Gemma? Are you OK? Is something wrong?"

Her weak olive gaze lifted to me, red and swollen. She looked utterly defeated in that moment. "Were you able to get the milk and diapers this morning," she asked. "The baby just came so fast, I didn't have time—"

"Shhh," I said, continuing to wipe her forehead. "I've got everything. You don't need to worry."

"Did you get the other thing I asked for?"

I nodded, pulling out of my pocket a small, pink, little girl's notepad—with matching sparkle pen. Gemma glanced up at the still closed door to the room and then reached for the pad and pen to scribble something down. She didn't have to explain why. In a house full of vampires who can overhear your slightest breath and feel your every heightened emotion—such as fear—it was hard to find privacy sometimes. Something Gemma and I as Dhampirs, and more importantly, *women*, needed once in a while. But we couldn't really explain that to the two over-protective men standing outside the room, guys who loved us and wanted to take care of everything.

She turned the notepad back to me, on which she had written:

I'm scared!

My heart ached for Gemma. Giving birth to a vampire's child was difficult at best, even for a Dhampir mother because of the strength the baby possessed in its infancy . . . and Gemma knew it.

Staring into her fragile face, I could see the fear and understood why she had chosen to say nothing to Jax. Seventy years ago Jax had lost his first wife, Isabeau, my grandmother, after she went into labor with my mother, Eve. He had been away overnight helping Chay's coven to the north when Lycans had attacked them, and he never forgave himself for not being able to return to Isabeau in time to save her.

Isabeau was human. You're a Dhampir.
You're stronger. You're going to do just fine.

She scribbled back:

It would destroy him if me or the baby didn't make it.

I don't want him to ever have to live with that.

That was not an option. There was no doubt Jax would be destroyed by the loss of either Gemma or the baby. He loved and cared for Gemma more than his own life, constantly spoiling her with affection and gifts. The same would hold true for any child that was created between them.

That's not going to happen.

You don't know that.

I do. He told me to tell you just now that he loves you!
He wants to help you, be with you for this.
Let him.

Tears fell from Gemma's eyes a moment before another contraction hit, sending her screaming out in pain. The contractions were now practically on top of each other. I held her securely at her shoulders. "I want you to concentrate only on this," I ordered. "Get the rest of that stuff out of your head. Nothing is going to happen to you!"

Gemma practically grunted as she grabbed the notepad and pen and scribbled:

Please don't tell him!

Just then the door flew open and Chay entered the room, while Jax called out to her from the hallway beyond. I hurriedly slipped the notepad and pen back in my pocket as Chay took a place beside Gemma and began examining her. "Everything is prepared. Are you ready to become a mother?"

"I'm ready for this to be done," she screeched.

His instructions were calm, giving her an empathetic nod. "We have a little ways to go before you are there . . . but you will get through this just fine." He then laughed lightly and added, "You have to, because Jax looks as if he will come through that wall any second if your cries get any louder."

Gemma's body seized as another contraction hit her. She sucked in her breath and tried to brace herself against the pain, her features strained to their very limits as she cried out, "I need him! I need Jax!"

I didn't even have a chance to stand to my feet to go get him when Jax blew through the door, rigid worry plastered over his face. He came to her side, taking her hand and placing several kisses on the backs of her fingers and cheeks. "I am here, angel. We will do this together, OK?"

A look of pure relief crossed her face as she nestled her head against his shoulder. "Together," she murmured back to him.

After *a lot* more screaming and several more hours of labor, Gemma did make it. She and Jax had brought a child into this world together. Gemma was completely exhausted as she watched Jax with happy tears in her eyes. He held his little girl for the first time, his face alight with a look of complete wonder. Jax never had this moment with my mother, his first and only child up to this point, because she had been stolen from him the night Isabeau had died. "Our little girl," he murmured, holding her little pink feet between his large fingers. "She is perfect . . . an angel, just like her mother."

"Sophie . . . ," Gemma whispered tiredly.

"Sophie," Jax agreed. "Our beautiful little Sophie."

Vampires didn't cry, but if they did, they would display Jax's current fragile and humbled expression. He held the tiny little brunette so lightly, so gently, it was as if someone had just given him the most precious gift in the world . . . and indeed Gemma had.

He worriedly glanced from baby Sophie to Gemma, noting how exhausted she was. "Chay, will she be all right?"

Chay patted him on the shoulder. "Your mate came through it fine. I have cleaned and stitched her up and she is already beginning to heal."

Relieved, Jax dropped his head towards Gemma until their foreheads touched with baby Sophie between them. "I love you, Gemma," he whispered. "And I promise you will never have to go through this again if you do not want to."

Gemma made an odd sound, somewhere between a laugh and a snort. "Oh that. I've already forgiven you for getting me knocked up. We can have another. Just give me a little time to recover."

Jax's smile was positively beaming as he kissed her on the lips. I stood back in the room with Caleb, leaning back against him with tears in my eyes as he wrapped his arms around me from behind, his head resting over my shoulder. Watching Jax already fuss over his new little girl was truly moving. I couldn't think of another couple who deserved this happiness as much as he and Gemma. "Come," Caleb murmured. "Let's give the new family some time alone."

With the sun set for the day, Caleb led us outside to the rooftop of the tree house through our master suite. The night was crystal clear, with a bit of a chill, and it seemed every star in the sky was within reach of my fingertips. I assumed I was about to get the ass chewing I knew I deserved for scaring him earlier in the day, even if I had left a note, but instead he took a seat near the edge of the roof and settled me in front of him, pulling me back against his chest and wrapping his arms around me as he stared up towards the sky. Snuggled quietly with him like this was almost perfect, but I was not quite sure what to make of his introspective mood. It almost seemed he was waiting for me to say something . . . which I did. "I'm sorry for disappearing on you this morning," I began. "I know you were worried. Gemma just knew the baby was coming, and she was scared. She needed to know that she had the items ready."

"I know," he replied, to my surprise, then reached into his pocket and pulled out the small notepad Gemma and I had been using to scribble messages back and forth, still flipped open to the last page we had been writing on. Caleb set it beside his hip as I blinked up at him in question. "You dropped it from your pocket in the room," he answered without my having to ask. There was also no need to ask him if he had seen the last entries. His quiet, heavy expression said he had. "I won't say anything to Jax," he answered with a frown. "You know I hate keeping things from him . . . but it would bring back too many painful memories to know she feared for her life as Isabeau had."

"She just needed reassurance," I replied, "a way to talk about it without worrying him. And I knew if I told you what I was doing you wouldn't have wanted me to go—"

"Of course I wouldn't have wanted you to go," he replied calmly . . . a little too calmly, actually. "At least not alone—not without some kind of backup plan." He sighed heavily. "I realize you are getting stronger in your gifts. But Davin has only gotten bolder in his attempts to capture you. He's obsessed, which makes him even more dangerous. We can't afford to be giving him easy opportunities like this."

I snorted rather indelicately. "The way I left those Dhampirs this morning, I definitely wouldn't call that easy."

Caleb laughed lightly at that, and it felt good to hear him laugh. "Took them all down, did ya?"

"You betcha. You know the little crack-block to the knee you showed me? It worked perfectly," I smiled, tipping my head back on his chest 'til my lips were right there for him to kiss, and he didn't squander the opportunity. He kissed me gently at first, then more deeply as I responded to him. "That's my girl," he breathed as his hand brushed over the teardrop-shaped sapphire hanging around my throat. The decorative jewel held sacred ground inside and kept me blurred to his vampire world, and to him unless I was close. "But you had the necklace on and they still found you, didn't they?"

I nodded quietly, realizing his point. Being alone without the others knowing where I was going had made it easy for Davin . . . and very hard on Caleb. "I hate this time of year," he grumbled. "I can't stand feeling so trapped within these walls—especially when you need me."

My heart reached out for him in that moment. Caleb was such a free spirit, a lover of the outdoors. Yet even in Seattle, July and August were considered summertime. As a Daywalker, he was a vampire with more tolerance for the sun, but this time of year still kept him mostly trapped inside, and it was definitely hard on him. "Yes, but the summer nights are beautiful, aren't they? Look at the stars tonight."

"Yes they are," he laughed in a quiet rumble as he felt me roll my head back and forth on his chest. "What're you doing?"

"I'm trying to find . . . There!" I said, pointing my finger towards a cluster of stars. "The Big Dipper—seven stars that form a ladle." Smiling up at him I added, "I bet you didn't know your mate was an astronomy wiz." I said this knowing full well that the Big Dipper was the only pattern I could recognize in the stars.

"Well, you are *something*," he replied with a smirk. "But an astronomy wiz . . . I'm afraid not. That's the Little Dipper. You can tell because the highest star on the handle is Polaris, the North Star. If you draw a line down from Polaris you'll see the two stars that make up the front bowl of the Big Dipper. See?" see he said, pointing his finger and drawing his hand down.

Now it was my turn to be impressed. "I do. I see it." Quickly I swung my head around to scan the other side of the sky, pointing to a random grouping of stars. "What about those?"

Caleb tightened his big arms around me as he laughed quietly at my ear. "Testing me, huh? Let's see here . . . That's Andromeda. Just to the left, there is Perseus. And see those five stars that form a W?" I nodded with interest. "That's Cassiopeia."

"I'm impressed."

"Well prepare to be more impressed, mate," he smiled. "In Greek Mythology, Andromeda was the daughter of Cassiopeia and King Cepheus. She was a very beautiful young woman, but jealously prompted Cassiopeia to declare herself more beautiful than Andromeda or any of the Sea God Poseidon's daughters."

"And was Cassiopeia that beautiful?"

"Poseidon certainly didn't think so. To punish Cassiopeia for her arrogance he ordered Andromeda to be chained naked to a rock and sacrificed to the sea monster Cetus."

"That's terrible," I replied. "Did the sea monster kill her?"

"Rest easy, sweet," he chuckled. "She was saved at the last second by a very heroic Perseus, who came flying in on his winged shoes—fresh off his beheading of the evil Medusa. He used her petrified head to defeat the sea monster. And it wasn't long before Perseus became so enchanted with Andromeda that he asked for her hand in marriage."

I snuggled in tighter to his shoulder. "Well that's better. Did they live happily ever after?"

"Of course."

"That's a beautiful story," I said, turning my chin up to face him.

He smiled, reaching down to kiss me softly on the lips, nibbling with such gentle playfulness it made my stomach tingle. "It's our story," he murmured.

"Really?" I smirked. "I don't remember being naked when you rescued me from Isaac after the train crash."

He laughed in a deep, sexy sound that brushed right over the senses. "Oh, I assure you . . . I already had the full picture in my head." I blinked back at him in surprise as he squeezed his arms around me, holding on tight. "It's our story because I knew from the first moment I saw you again that I wanted you to be mine. In my heart, I claimed you the same way Perseus claimed Andromeda. And I will fight any monsters that try to hurt you."

"I love you, Caleb Wolfe."

"Come here," he said, threading his fingers through my hair and bringing my chin upward to face him. "I love you, too, my sweet." He descended over my lips, his hand supporting me behind my neck so his mouth could capture mine fully. Licking over my bottom lip, he tempted, he teased—sliding his tongue inside my mouth to coax me with gentle exploration until my whole body fell soft and breathless against him. When he kissed me like that the whole world seemed to spin around me. Even if I had wanted to play hard to get (which I really didn't) there was no way I could deny him anything. I was simply his.

We sat there under the night sky like that for several hours, just enjoying kisses and each others company under the stars.

It was a perfect night.

Chapter Three

Late the next morning I was working inside the rooftop greenhouse Caleb had constructed for me, filling a basket with some fresh summer squash, onions, peppers and tomatoes to bring in for dinner later. It was a beautiful day outside, sunny and warm, the scents of evergreen and earth a wonderful reminder that I was home. I was definitely more on guard after my encounter with the Dhampirs the day before, so I kept my eyes open and my senses alert for any sign that there might be trouble, but everything seemed fine.

When I re-entered the house through the entry to our master suite, Caleb was quietly waiting for me, his long, lean body relaxed in an oversized chair in the shaded corner of the room. "You look a little tired this morning, sweet."

It was true after my battle with the Dhampirs, the arrival of baby Sophie, and staying up late with Caleb to watch the stars, I had felt a little tired. He had to practically carry me inside to bed, where I fell asleep in his arms in an instant . . . but strangely I didn't stay asleep. I was restless, tossing and turning non-stop until Caleb's reassuring voice at my ear had soothed me back to sleep. "Well, a woman never likes to be told she looks tired," I replied with a light smile as I crossed the room towards him. "I am a little tired today. I wanted to get dinner started early for Gemma. She's feeding for two now."

"Come," Caleb said as he reached for my hand. I set my basket beside the chair and crawled into his lap, sinking easily into his strength. Resting my head against his chest, I inhaled a deep breath, absorbing the wonderful scents of fir and sage—his scents. "What kept you so restless last night," he asked.

"It was nothing serious. I just kept waking with the baby."

"Having a baby in the house is going to take some getting used to, isn't it?"

"It is, but having Sophie is such a blessing."

Caleb squeezed his arms around me. "I don't like when you

can't sleep," he continued. "It means you're over-thinking something." He was quiet then, as if he expected me to add comment. When I didn't, he stroked his hand ever so gently along the side of my face, the motion so relaxing I thought I would fall asleep right there in his arms. "Olivia, is the baby upsetting you? Because we can't have a child of our own, I mean?"

I hated being reminded that I could not have a child—could not give Caleb a child. The parents who had raised me, The Greysons, had tubal implants surgically placed by a doctor in an effort to protect me from a future they feared for me—a future that could include rape from the vampires drawn to my gifts. Ironically, the Greysons could have never imagined that instead I would fall in love with one—a vampire who I very much wanted to create a child with.

I had gone back to see Dr. Li at The Oracle and asked him to remove the implants, but he'd been very clear that the chances of me ever conceiving a child were unlikely at best. And so far he'd been right. Caleb and I had tried with not even a hint of success, and it bothered me to no end. I loved him so much—I loved us, what we had together. I wanted this for both of us.

"It's true; I wish we could have our own child. But how can I be upset at having a baby brought into our life in any capacity? She's so cute—with all that thick, black hair and that little button nose."

Caleb kissed the top of my head, his lips gentle, soothing, as if he wanted to take away any pain that would touch me. "We'll keep trying for our own little one. I promise."

I glanced up into his relaxed expression. He meant every word. Caleb truly believed a baby would happen for us one day, and I didn't want to damper his hope. I hugged him close and we stayed like that for several quiet minutes, until his next words interrupted the peaceful calm we'd found. "I need to talk to you about something," he began. "I've made a decision . . . and you're not going to like it."

My relaxed state seemed to disappear almost instantly.

"I've had more time to think about what happened yesterday with the Dhampirs. I won't let these attacks on you continue. I'm going to take care of Davin once and for all."

I flew out of his arms and the chair so fast, for a moment I felt dizzy. "I told you I'm all right. I only have a few scrapes and bruises to show for the whole event. Why can't you let this go?"

Caleb came to his feet and walked towards the windows to stare out at the forested views, his fingers raking roughly through his hair. "Because you shouldn't have to live this way! Always wondering if you're going to be attacked. I can't continue to live like this, either . . . worried every second that you're out of my sight that he might have you. That thought makes me crazy. I finally have the life with you that I want, and I'm not going to let this obsessed lunatic take it away from us."

"Caleb, do you hear yourself? This concern that someone is going to come in and take everything away from you because you somehow deserve it . . . this is an old demon you're fighting."

He finally turned back around to face me. "I know you don't like it, but I'm going to do this. I need to know that you are safe."

"No, you're not just '*going to do this,*' we're going to discuss it," I replied sharply. "If the situation were reversed, there'd be no way you would agree to a decision like this if it threatened my life."

"You mean like the decision you made yesterday to go out for groceries alone, making yourself bait for Davin's soldiers?"

I blinked back at him, stunned, unable to believe I had walked right into that.

"I will leave in a few days," he continued, as if not even giving a second thought to my argument, "after Jax and Gem have had a chance to get the baby settled."

"No!" I blurted, so stunned I didn't know what else to say. "He could kill you!"

"Chay and his coven have agreed to help. Jax will stay here with you, Gem and the baby."

"I don't need a babysitter!" I snapped. "And you can't expect me to stay here and wait patiently to find out if you've gotten yourself killed. I'll—"

Caleb whirled around on me so fast it swept the breath from my lungs, his gray eyes storming. "Don't you dare finish that sentence," he warned. "You are my life! The love of my life! And you'll do everything in your power to keep yourself safe. Everything! Do you understand?"

I swung away from him, trying to get control of the anger and worry for him that felt as if it were eating me alive at that moment. If I had to look at him just then I thought I might cry. Caleb must have been able to feel the war going on inside me because the room suddenly settled into a disturbing quiet. "Olivia?"

"I love you," I finally said in a barely-there voice. "We are happy . . . I can defend myself. And I can deal with Davin's threats—his attempts to capture me . . . as long as we're fighting him together. But if something happens to you, then I . . ." I couldn't finish the thought. It was too awful to think about losing Caleb.

In two strides he was behind me, his arms coming around me and hugging in a fierce grip as he tucked my head under his chin. "I swear, I won't fail you. I'll take care of Davin and come back here to you. We will put this behind us and live our life without this threat hanging over us."

"And what about the next threat—the next Davin? This is my life as a Charmer. You can't just run off on your own to take care of every threat there is to me. You need to let me fight with you."

He shook his head. "There won't be another Davin. Most are mindlessly drawn to you, but Luther Davin is organized. He has a specific goal in mind—he has a purpose. Olivia, I'm not sure you're really ready to do what it takes to defend yourself against a man like Davin. He won't stop until you stop him. Are you really ready for that? Think about it. You've grown up in a beautiful world of music—been given an amazing gift of music—and I love you for adapting to all of this supernatural shit that we've heaped on you. But ask yourself: "Are you really prepared to destroy—to kill—a man like Luther Davin?"

I was struck silent. In all of my training and learning of my gifts I never had really stopped to think about where this path I was on with Davin would lead. It was about doing what I needed to survive. When I didn't respond, Caleb turned me around to face him, his intense gaze trying to convince me as his palm stroked my cheek. "You've talked to me about feeling trapped at times. How nice it would before you to be able to complete your masters and to perform again. None of that is going to happen if you have to constantly worry about Davin trying to capture you. Your life—our future—has been on hold for too long. I won't let him continue to do this to us."

I did want those things, but I could live without them if it meant keeping Caleb safe with me. But he wasn't giving me a choice, and I knew there was no stopping him once he decided he *had* to do something. His determination was part of that warrior inside him that was afraid of nothing. Dropping my forehead to his chest in defeat, I asked, "How long will you be gone?"

"It'll take some time to track his location and come up with a plan," he said quietly, "... probably a month."

Chapter Four

"A month?"

We were all gathered the next evening for a coven conference in the kitchen. Caleb had just outlined his and Jax's plan for destroying Davin, and predictably, Gemma wasn't biting. "That is a completely ridiculous idea," she continued, her disapproving tone capturing everyone's attention while she simultaneously prepared some warm milk for Sophie. " . . . the obvious brain child of two vampires with way too much testosterone mucking up their common sense."

Caleb hitched his hands at his hips and lowered his head with an audible sigh, knowing what was coming next. Delightedly, I bit back my smile of outright glee at how the small Dhampir had these fierce men quaking in their boots. Her green-eyed gaze then flared at Chay, who had been trying to carefully get out of the line of fire behind Jax's shoulder, but it didn't work. "Make that three vampires," she declared, trapping him in her sights. "And you should know better. You'll be pushing the back side of four centuries before you know it."

Now I had to fight back my laugh. Chay was no dummy. He had learned when to stay clear of an unhappy Gemma. At first he teased Jax about how she had him wrapped around her little finger, but Chay soon discovered that he was no better at defending himself against the fiery redhead's temper. "You'll be completely outnumbered," Gemma barked in general at all three men.

"Angel, calm down," Jax intoned softly. Then, his voice hardening, he said, "This is the right time to do this. We cannot allow Davin to keep coming after Olivia as he has been, and now we have Sophie's well being to consider."

Gemma slammed the warm bottle of milk hard against the counter, and some of the frothy liquid spilled out onto the stone surface. "Oh, I see . . . so it's in Sophie's best interest to have her father and uncles charging after a madman like boys who need to play war just because they can?"

Caleb frowned at her, obviously not happy with her analogy. "That's not what we're doing, Gem—"

"That's exactly what you're doing, Caleb, and you know it! You're happy with Olivia—finally happy," she added, throwing her hands up in frustration. "But you can't let yourself just *be happy!* So you're going to charge in after him with both barrels cocked and the first half-baked plan you can come up with—"

"And if I do nothing," Caleb spoke through his teeth, "he *will* eventually succeed in his plan to take her. I won't sit back on my ass and allow that to happen."

Caleb's raw expression revealed his true fears, the worry he'd been living with every single day for the entire nine months since we'd returned from The Oracle. He quickly reverted from a snarly facial expression to a more neutral one, obviously trying not to worry me, but it was too late. I didn't want Caleb anywhere near Luther Davin, the one person who had the power to take away what I loved most in this world.

"Do Olivia and I even get a say in this?" Gemma pressed. "I can't imagine she's thrilled with this idea of you risking your life." She then turned to me, expectantly, for confirmation.

"I'm not," I replied, practically wanting to shout it from the rooftop.

Caleb stepped behind me and rubbed his hands down my arms in gentle coaxing. "But she understands why I need to do this." He was trying to smooth things over, placate the simmering redhead who was as close to him as a sister while not–so subtly reminding me how important it was for him to do this.

Gemma harrumphed and Jax's face pinched in a grimace, as if he foresaw the blistering response that was about to come. "Bugger that, Caleb Wolfe!" she spat out, her normally faded English accent from her childhood in London coming through full bore with those words. "That is just code for 'I didn't give her a choice.'" She swiped her hand dismissively through the air. "I thought after finding Olivia you'd finally learned to stop chasing death. But noooo . . . you can't just stop and be happy."

Her words sent a harsh jolt through me as I realized that was exactly what was going on here. The restless warrior I had fallen in love with was back, and he wanted Davin's head. In that moment, thoughts just kept swirling in my mind of possibly losing him and it felt like my heart was being torn right from my chest.

"Gemma, enough!" Jax warned. "This is not easy for any—"

"Oh you don't like it, mate?" Gemma warned with false sweetness, screwing the plastic cap onto the baby's bottle like she was screwing a lug nut onto a tire with her bare hands. "Well, guess what else you won't like? Sleeping alone!"

She jerked her head once for me to follow her, and I didn't hesitate. I was all for a joint protest if it had any chance of stopping Caleb from actually leaving.

"Olivia?" Caleb called, startled that I was pulling away from his side.

I turned back to face him, my words seeming stuck in my throat for a long moment, but finally I was able to say, "I don't want you to do this. It's too dangerous. *Davin* is too dangerous. I don't want to lose you."

"You're not going to lose me," he replied instantly, his voice tender as he reached for my hand. But Gemma continued to pull me out of the room with her and out of his grasp. When he continued forward, Gemma swung back around and shoved her open palm against his chest to halt him.

"You two can take your buddy, Chay over there, and enjoy your chilled room tonight. Because that's all the warmth you're going to get." Gemma then slid her narrowed gaze to Jax. "And don't even think about crossing that door to *my* room. You're not welcome."

"Our room!" Jax snapped back as she proceeded to march out of the kitchen with me in tow, but it certainly didn't feel like any kind of victory.

✱✱✱

Later that night, Gemma fell back, exhausted, onto the bed after finally getting Sophie to sleep in her crib. She feared the little girl already missed her father, who would normally watch over her while she and her mother slept, almost as if he were afraid to lose his good fortune in life.

I was slipping into my not-so-sexy blue polka-dotted boy

shorts and a sleeveless white tank top, and couldn't help but frown at my reflection in the mirror. I usually liked to wear the sexy stuff for Caleb, mostly in his favorite color, red. But since I was sleeping apart from him tonight—something I hadn't done since I'd been mated to him—I decided that this outfit would work fine. As I smoothed my hands over the comfy cotton fabric I couldn't help but think of how much I would miss not lying beside him tonight. Sleeping beside Caleb Wolfe had become as natural and easy for me as breathing . . . and just as vital.

"I'm sorry, Olivia," Gemma whispered with a heavy sigh while I crawled under the covers beside her. She was trying to speak as softly as possible so she wouldn't wake the baby, and because we both knew the vampires would have no trouble hearing us if they chose to listen in. "I tried. But you should prepare yourself that my little tirade won't alter Caleb's thinking on this matter one bit. I recognize this restless energy in him."

"I know," I replied sadly, bunching the covers up to my neck. "His strength and fearlessness were some of the very reasons I fell in love with him. But I really don't think he understands how devastating it would be to me if I lost him."

"He does," Gemma assured me. "Because he knows it would be almost as painful as if he lost you. That fear is what's driving him to do this."

"Then what can I do? I love him. I don't want to fight with him . . . especially not the last nights we have together before he leaves. But I don't like that he's giving me no choice in this."

Gemma's lips pressed tight in a sympathetic smile. "I'll tell you what you're going to do. You're going to teach him a lesson by sleeping apart from him tonight. Teach him that if he makes these kinds of decisions without regard for your feelings, there will be consequences for him." She then sighed dreamily. "Then, just like me, you will forgive him and spend every precious minute you have together . . . because—darn it—I already miss my own stubborn hunk of male sexiness myself. I'm such a sucker for muscles. Gees!" She then smiled up almost apologetically and added, "Not that I mind sleeping with you."

"Me, either," I laughed quietly.

Gemma yawned and closed her eyes that very next moment. "Yes, this will definitely teach them," she murmured, her soft words falling away as her breathing became heavy and she found her dreams.

But I lay there for quite a while, staring through the skylight at the brilliant stars above, thinking about the wonderful story Caleb had told me the previous night of Andromeda and Perseus. I loved that he thought it was our story, and I wanted to go to him right then and have him hold me in his arms and tell it to me all over again. But inside the incredible silence of the house my head won the battle with my heart, and I finally rolled onto my side and fell into sleep, but once again it was a restless sleep.

When Caleb was not beside me, my dreams tended to rush around. I would toss and turn until I was practically sweltering under my own anxiousness. The only way to escape was to bring him into my dreams with me, and those dreams were so vivid it was like I could feel his cool, whispering breath right over the shell of my ear. "Forgive me."

I turned towards his voice, needing to feel close to him. The tension eased from my limbs when I could feel his open palm smooth across my sweat-misted forehead, then a lofty breeze blew over my skin and I suddenly felt as if I were floating. It was as if some troublesome itch had been soothed and I was able to relax against a solid wall of strength. Before I knew it, I was being set in a familiar place, sensing my lover's long form stretched out beside me. For me, this was heaven, and I wanted to curl myself into the luxury of it. "Caleb?" I heard myself call.

"Shhh. Just rest, my sweet," he whispered as soft kisses pressed tenderly into my cheeks and throat. "You're safe and you're where you're supposed to be . . . right here with me."

But Sophie's loud wails interrupted my heavenly dreams once again. Hearing her high-pitched cries, so full of innocent emotion, stirred something inside of me I that had trouble understanding. "The baby's crying," I said pushing back the covers to go to her. But the familiar feel of Caleb's skin, his taut muscles, and dusting of hair over his arms and legs, wrapped around me and held me there with him on the mattress. "It's all right, Olivia. The baby's fine. Just stay here with me. Let me hold you while you sleep."

And I did.

***

Sometime later, I woke. Dawn was still a little ways from rising, which I could tell—not from the glass skylight in Gemma's room, but by the dark, forested views from my own room. It was not surprising that Jax wouldn't allow Gemma or Sophie to sleep apart from him, or that Caleb had moved me during the night to our room. Both men could be equally stubborn when it came to *being told* where they would sleep. What did surprise me, however, was the fact that the space on the bed beside me was now empty. I wondered if sensing that Caleb was no longer with me caused me to wake. It was then that I vaguely remembered him whispering to me that he and Jax needed to check something out, and that he would return shortly. I wasn't sure how much time had passed since then, but it had me worried that he wasn't back. It wasn't like Caleb or Jax to leave like that. But neither had they brought up the security for the house—several bright, neon-green bands of ultra-violet lasers that protected all the possible entries into the house from vampires who would be burned to a crisp by the focused light. How worried could they be if they'd leave the house unsecured?

I moved from the bed through the darkness, grabbing a red silk robe from a nearby chair. That was when I felt it—vampire energy . . . and it was close. I dropped my hand over my throat to touch over the sapphire jewel necklace that was still lying there. Whoever was coming should not have been able to sense me, but the vampire presence was headed straight for the house, as if they knew exactly where they were going.

My sharp Dhampir gaze searched the dark forest in the direction from which I felt the energy coming, and my eyes widened in surprise when an extremely tall, slender female with platinum blond hair that fell low across her back landed on the roof right in front of the windows to our room, right in front of me. Glass separated us, but that was about it. In spiked heels higher than I had ever seen a woman wear and a barely-there mini-skirt that cut across the very tops of her shapely thighs, she strolled to within a few yards of the window. Her elongated features and pale skin practically glowed against the moonlight. "Well, well, well," she said with an arrogant lift to her chin as she continued to make her way towards me. "I was not expecting to meet Caleb's *little plaything* so soon."

Plaything? I was most certainly *not* a plaything! I had no idea who this woman was, but there was no doubt she was a vampire. Her energy was pulling fiercely inside my chest, which was not surprising because I doubted any human woman could walk so effortlessly on those ridiculous heels. She continued to approach the glass without the slightest bobble or worry that I was a threat to her in any way. And though it was obvious that without the security activated she could break through the glass between us with little effort, she made no move to do so. Instead she waited, as if she wanted me to come to her.

In a decision I probably should have considered a little more thoroughly, I hit the release button to the glass door and walked out onto the roof to confront her. "I'm not his plaything. I'm his mate."

A slow smile crossed her blood red lips and she narrowed her gaze. "No," she said in a low, warning voice. "That title belongs solely to me."

In that moment I felt like biting off my own tongue. *Celeste* —Caleb's first mate—was standing not five yards in front of me with spiked heels and what felt like eighteen extra inches in height (though in reality it was probably only a little more than the height of her shoes). Everything about her screamed 'confident woman!'—and I do mean *woman*—in the tall, Amazon Goddess-like sense of the word. She looked at me as if I were about as interesting as a gnat squashed under one of those heels. But despite how completely thrown off guard I was feeling at the moment, there was no way I was going to let this woman intimidate me. "I guess he didn't get the memo."

Celeste continued to smile in an easy way that was completely irritating. Her eyes, a strikingly pale shade of blue that was so bright they flickered with red, making the overall color of them appear lavender. "He doesn't need a memo. He feels it in his blood, in his body. Whatever kind of house you are playing with him right now will not last. And it will never be recognized by our world."

She was wrong! I had felt the connection created between Caleb and I when we mated, exchanged our blood. I was now part of this world—part of him. In fact it had been so earth-shatteringly powerful that there was no way she would convince me otherwise. "Interesting declaration for someone who has not seen him in ten years," I replied back calmly. "Because any vampire with a nose can smell that I'm Caleb's mate, not you. Your scents don't match." *Er . . .* I was kind of going out on a limb with that one because I couldn't actually smell the scent myself. I was trusting that what Caleb had told me regarding our scents matching would be obvious to other vampires . . . namely her.

Evidently there was some truth to it because her eyes seemed to darken with anger, becoming even more unique in their unusual lavender color. She took one long step forward on those very long legs. "Careful, little girl," she warned in a very intentionally degrading remark, and I could see by her dilated eyes that my gift was drawing her to me as she came closer. "You are out of your league here. I had that man coming between my thighs when you were no more than a pimple-faced high school virgin. I created him."

Oh, I already hated this woman. I may have still been a virgin at sixteen, yes, but I was definitely not pimple-faced! And I loved Caleb. Celeste, on the other hand, had *turned* him, tricked him into mating her. That was not love, so why was she here now? I felt so hot with anger at that moment that I wanted to hold her down under my painful gift of touch and pull all that platinum hair of hers out by its roots. "What you turned him into is something he has fought to not despise for the last ten years. You can take all the pride in that you want, but he'll never want you, or want you back."

"Care to bet on that?" she came back, confident, and that confidence made me uneasy.

"I'll take that bet, you platinum blond ho!" It was Gemma, barging into the room and coming to stand beside me, pitching one hand on her slim hip as she glanced at me for a brief second with a questioning look that said, '*What in the world are you doing challenging Caleb's ex with a silk robe and bare feet?*'

"Caleb would never leave Olivia for you."

Celeste's whole expression seemed to flicker with delight. "Why, Gemma May, you do look like you have gained a few pounds. Really, sweetie, why not lay off the donuts and add a few more sit ups to your routine."

I nearly gasped at the outrageous comment. Gemma just had a baby a few days ago and looked as if she were only a few pounds away from her normal tiny shape. Gemma, however, just offered a bored, almost amused smiled back to Celeste. "It's Gemma Walker now."

Celeste cocked her brow with barely feigned interest. "Really? That walking fortress of brawn finally found a woman stupid enough play second fiddle to Isabeau. Surprising."

"*Oh!* That's it, you tramp!" Gemma growled as she started to reach for the woman, but I held her back just in time. "Give me one shot at her," she argued, but Gemma had just had a baby, and even though she might be feeling like her old, sassy self, it was no time for her to be fighting vampires.

Celeste didn't even flinch. She was about as threatened by Gemma as she was by me. Yet she continued to make her way closer to me, completely unaware that she was being drawn by my gift. Was she even aware that I was a Charmer? I could see she wanted to reach for me, but showed remarkable restraint for a vampire in not doing so. Gemma appeared to notice as well, and nudged ever so closer to me in a protective gesture. "Humans!" Celeste's voice dripped with disgust. "It's so like you to be proud of a silly surname." She stopped right in front of me, her six-foot-plus, statuesque frame dwarfing me. "So are you claiming to be Olivia Wolfe now? Has he asked you to take his last name?"

I stiffened at that. Caleb and I had never actually talked about me taking his last name after we mated. It hadn't bothered me up to this point, but now I wished we had. Before I could even utter a reply, four women appeared to drop from nowhere and surrounded Gemma and me on the roof. All four were dressed in similar, tight clothing and spiked heels, like Celeste, and collectively they resembled a female rock band, one you would never want to find yourself a groupie of because it would more than likely cost you your life. "I thought not,"

Celeste laughed, wickedly. "Taking his last name would imply commitment on his part, something Caleb does not do well. He has a nasty habit of abandoning his mates, you see. You are a fool if you think he will not be bored with you by the next moon cycle."

This woman was *really* starting to piss me off! I had three or four blistering replies all worked up in my head (that more than likely sounded fiercer in my head than they really were), but before I could even test one, several sharp growls sounded through the predawn darkness a moment before Caleb, Jax and Chay flew up over the edge of the roof, landing only a few steps behind Celeste. Caleb looked furious, his body stiff and his muscles flexed with a barely controlled anger. When he finally shot a quick glance at me, I could see the intensity in his eyes. He wanted to know I was all right, and I gave a quick nod to reassure him. He then refocused his attention on Celeste. "I'll give you precisely one warning. Step away from her now."

Celeste turned smoothly towards him, a smile coming to her lips as if someone had just given her an early Christmas present. This was what she wanted—it was all she wanted . . . his attention. "So, sensitive these days, mate? Ahh, but you still look good—delicious, in fact."

Her use of the term 'mate' brought a scowl to his face, and I was glad to see it. I didn't like how she talked to him as if there had been no ten-year separation between them. "I'm not in the mood for your games, Celeste, or chasing your little pack of kittens around this mountain. Why are you here?"

"Oh, darling . . . ,"—*Darling? God, I hated her*—"of course I am here to see you. I was hoping you would invite me in for a lovely sampling of that stale refrigerated blood you seem so fond of."

"Not on your life. Now go," he dismissed her blandly. But Celeste didn't move, and that's when I noticed Jax was glaring at her with an expression that said he wanted to rip her head off. I had seen Jax in battle, seen the heights of his vampire anger, but I had never seen it on such display toward a woman, even if the woman was a vampire.

"I would reconsider that if I were you," Celeste warned. "I think you will want to hear what I have to say. Believe it or not,

I am here to help you."

Caleb crossed his arms over his wide chest, his expression remaining bland. "I don't believe it. You never do anything unless it suits your purpose."

With a lusty sway of her hips, Celeste strolled towards him, running her finger over the line of his shirt collar when she reached him. "Well, perhaps I've changed. It has been ten years, lover."

With a quick flick of his wrist Caleb snatched her hand in a fierce grip, but his eyes refused to look directly at her. In all the time I had known Caleb I had never seen him back down from any challenge. By not meeting her gaze directly, he was doing just that. It wasn't like him. I inhaled deeply as he cast another quick glance at me. This time I didn't know how to give him reassurance, because I didn't understand his response to her. "I said I'm not interested," he growled.

"I think you are," she added, her suggestive gaze scanning the length of his body in slow increments. " . . . In more ways than one, I would say."

My hands involuntarily fisted at my sides. I'd had enough of her overtly sexual comments right in front of me, as if I weren't even there. I may have some nagging doubt in my own mind about truly being recognized as his mate, but I could not let that doubt show in front of Celeste. I stepped forward, deciding it was time to do something about it, but Gemma halted me by jerking hard on my arm. "Stay here," she ordered under her breath. "Celeste is dangerous. She's been a vampire —"

"For six centuries," Celeste finished, swinging back around to come towards me. "Give or take a decade or two. Do not be so stupid as to think you can take me, little girl. I taught Joan of Arc the art of battle when she was little more than a peasant. That voice of God that implored her to fight? Not quite so divine." She laughed wickedly then, as if enjoying the direction of her own thoughts. "Though . . . my given name is Caelestis, which does mean '*coming from heaven.*' Maybe there's something to it?"

"Enough!" Caleb growled, trying to draw her attention off of me and back to him, but even his fierce warning wasn't working. She was being drawn to me again. I had seen it enough times in the eyes of the Nightwalkers who had challenged. It was rather like looking at someone staring at you without blinking. Their eyes would dilate until they were dark like a storm, and the color never moved once they were focused in on me. Celeste, however, seemed to have a little more control, similar to Chay, which lead me to assume my drawing power was not as strong on vampires who had lived for many centuries. That was rather important fact to know going forward.

"Oh, so protective of your newest little cupcake," she replied to Caleb but still staring right at me. "How adorable. Does not change the fact that we both know she is nothing more than a sweet lick of frosting."

That was it! I didn't care if she was born before Christ. She was going down. I barely moved a half step when Caleb's ice-hard gaze sliced over to me and halted me in place. There was no mistaking the warning in his eyes. I was not to move another muscle. *Oh,* he and I were so going to have to have a serious discussion later about when he chose to go all 'extreme alpha' on me.

"Well, we can either stand out here all day while the sun comes up over the horizon and turns us all into charcoal briquettes . . . ," Celeste added, taking a lengthy pause while she carefully glanced over the three men, "or you can provide us shelter for the day. You may be Daywalkers, but I do believe you have to avoid the direct sun, just like the rest of us. And it really is the least you can do, darling, since that little whore over there got me into this mess with Davin in the first place."

Whore? I didn't know how I was still managing to keep my feet in place. But Caleb's furious gaze slid back to her in a flash at mention of Davin's name. She had him and she knew it! And unfortunately there wasn't a lot of time to debate the subject, since the sun was about two minutes from coming over the horizon. "Gem," Caleb called. "Take Olivia inside and open the glass doors for us downstairs." He then looked at me, his voice softer, more like the familiar lover that I knew. "Olivia, I want you to remain in our room until I get Celeste and her coven locked in the basement, all right?"

Jax growled his disapproval at Caleb's obvious decision to give shelter to Celeste and her coven. Caleb turned to him as if reading his coven leader's mind. "We have no choice. If she has information on Davin, we need to hear her out."

I was about to argue that point, but Gemma grabbed my hand and practically dragged me towards our room. Before we made it to the door, one of Celeste's coven sisters stepped between the room and us. A striking Asian woman who was closer to my height, she studied me with piqued interest. "Let her pass, Sherra!" Caleb ordered.

"I can handle her," I replied, getting right up in the woman's face, but she merely laughed in response. My ego was starting to take quite a bruising at how little these women were intimidated by me. Gemma stepped between us, trying to keep Sherra at a distance.

"So I see the intelligence requirement for your women really bottomed out after me," Celeste said with amusement. That caught my attention causing my head to snap around.

"Olivia, get inside!" Caleb growled.

"There's a familial link between her and Jax," Sherra announced, looking from me to Celeste. "I smell it in her blood."

Celeste smiled wickedly, then turned to face Jax, who looked about ready to strike at her like a snake. "Really, how interesting . . . Sherra has an extraordinary gift for smelling the scents that lie underneath. And in this case, Jax, that explains why you have threatened me repeatedly with my life for the past ten years to keep me away from my mate. You wanted him with your Granddaughter."

Caleb seemed to stall for a moment at something Celeste had said, but I wasn't quite sure which part. It was obvious that Celeste did not realize that Jax and I had only known we were related for less than a year. That gave Jax time to strike. He launched at Celeste. "I warned you!" he hissed. But Caleb was on him in a split second, pulling Jax back before he even reached her.

"We can't do this now," Caleb growled as we all saw the first glimmers of light begin to creep over the horizon. "We need to get inside."

After pulling me around Sherra, Gemma rushed me inside,

closed the glass door in front of me, then disappeared downstairs. I stared back, dumbfounded, at Caleb as I watched him lead Celeste and her coven over the side of the roof towards the glass door entry to the house. They would make it inside in time, but the realization that he had just defended Celeste, his ex-mate, against Jax, his own coven leader, was all I could focus on.

Chapter Five

After a quick change into some more appropriate clothes, I found myself stretched as far as I could possibly be out the doorway to our bedroom, feeling compelled to eavesdrop on the conversation happening right then on the main floor. I mean, technically, I was doing exactly as Caleb had asked. I was waiting for him in our room. But there was no way I was missing a single word of the goods that Celeste was trying to sell everyone. I suppose that as a Dhampir I didn't need to hang over the doorframe; I could probably have heard their conversation just as well in the far corner of the bedroom. But the human woman side of me, the side that was feeling a bit . . . *something* . . . something between uneasy and pissed off at having Caleb's ex-mate now right here inside our home, simply couldn't help it.

"Well, it's nice to see you still know the meaning of common courtesy" Celeste began with an arrogance that was truly irritating. "I didn't believe for one moment that you would let me burn."

With absolutely no emotion in his voice, Caleb responded, "You have one minute to tell me why you're here. And if it's not a good enough reason, then I'll let Jax decide if he feels courteous enough to let you stay."

"Oh, come now," Celeste responded softly. "Don't be so frosty, mate. You remember how good it was between us, don't you. You can have it again . . . here . . . now. The girls won't mind. And I remember how much you appreciated an audience."

With a gasp, I blinked hard. *Audience?*

"You now have fifty seconds," was Caleb's only reply, uttered in a flat monotone.

"She's listening, is she not? Tell me, does she know about your preferences? Does that young thing really know how to satisfy your hunger? I quite doubt it."

"Caleb, if you do not shut her up now, I will," Jax warned.

Next, Celeste made an odd, breathy sound that seemed to indicate she was struggling in some way. "If the next sentence out of your mouth doesn't explain why you're here, I *will* toss you outside and let you roast."

"Oh, how I like it when you are rough," she replied in her sexiest voice, openly defiant.

"I warned you," Caleb said, and a clamoring began to break out below.

I was about to race down and offer my whole-hearted assistance to booting her outside on her ass, but Celeste suddenly shouted, "Fine! Maybe it will interest you to know that Davin killed Annabelle last week. He tortured her, for Christ's sake—all because of that gutless whore upstairs."

My audible gasp could be heard the same moment it sounded like Caleb growled through his teeth, and it wasn't completely clear if that growl indicated his displeasure at Celeste . . . or me for eavesdropping. "What possible reason would Davin have for killing Annabelle? That makes no sense. He is obsessed with Olivia. You're the one with the connection to her through me, not Annabelle."

"You think he needs a reason? Do not be so naïve. Nightwalkers like Davin don't need justification for killing. They just do." I couldn't help but arch my brow at her comment. Celeste was acting as though Davin belonged in another category of vampire than her. I'd only known her twenty minutes, but I highly doubted that was true. "Annabelle was going to be mated to Isaac before you destroyed him last year." There was an audible silence in the room, and I wondered if the others were as stunned as I was. *Isaac was going to be mated?* The filthy, disgusting leech that couldn't keep his hands off me when he kidnapped me was to be mated to another woman. A sour taste welled up in my mouth at the thought of it.

"She speaks the truth," Jax spoke up in a tight voice. "I saw the two together a few months before Olivia came to us."

"Yes," Celeste replied with displeasure, "when Jax came to deliver one of his yearly death threats."

"I don't care if Jax threatened you. You probably deserved it,"

Caleb came back quickly, but I could hear in his voice he had been caught off guard by the information. It was subtle, but not for someone who knew intimately the tones of how he spoke. Caleb would not like being kept in the dark about his coven leader confronting his ex-mate on his behalf. The two of them would probably be having a not-so-quiet conversation about it later, but right now Caleb seemed determined to let it pass and stay on subject.

"Tell yourself whatever you like," Celeste replied, "But perhaps you might care about this . . . At the time of Isaac's death Annabelle knew of three secret locations where Davin had been hiding out with Isaac—locations that the rest of the coven didn't even know about. And she also knew from Isaac which of these locations Davin had prepared to hold your whore once he had her. My guess is that Davin didn't find this out until recently. Tying up loose ends so she couldn't tell anyone sounds like a pretty good motive for getting rid of her, don't you think?"

Caleb let out a rough growl filled with anger, frustration and emotion, and then everything downstairs suddenly went quiet. It was not easy being reminded that Davin had come very close to capturing me, and that he would certainly want to keep me someplace where Caleb would never be able to find me. I was guessing by the silence downstairs that all this information was not resting easy within Caleb, either. "I appreciate you warning me of this," he said in his steeliest voice. "You may stay here today and we'll escort you down the mountain tonight."

"Oh, Caleb . . . ," she sighed. "You are still not seeing the bigger picture here. It's disappointing really. I never said she didn't tell *anyone*. . ."

Suddenly, Celeste's voice sounded choked, and I heard a loud, pounding sound against the wall. "Enough with your games!" Caleb roared. "I need those locations, and I need them now."

In the absolute silence that followed, once again I could hear Celeste's deep, slow breaths. She wasn't sounding like someone who feared for her life; in fact, quite the opposite. "Well, well . . . rough and with an audience. Even better."

Gritting my teeth, I nearly fell forward because I was leaning so far out of the bedroom door. Gemma came through Caleb's study below, a disapproving frown twisting her delicate features. "What are you doing?" she whispered. I'm sure I must have looked ridiculous, but regardless, I waved a dismissive hand at her and braced myself against the doorframe once again, continuing to listen as she came up the stairs toward me.

"I'm not going to play games with you," Caleb warned, "and I'll not ask you again. What do you want in exchange for the locations?"

"I want Davin by the balls for killing Annabelle. I never agreed with her being with that mongrel, Isaac, but she was our sister. She did not deserve what happened to her. Especially not because of that whore—"

Celeste's next words were cut off as she once again seemed choked for breath. "Stop calling her that or you'll have much bigger problems to deal with than Jax or Davin. Now get to the fucking point!"

"Very well," she rasped, then recovered her voice as if the pressure had been released. "I have a proposal for you." There was a long silence while my nails curled against the doorframe, their moon-shaped edges digging deeper into the wood with every additional second that went by. What the heck was wrong with me? I was acting as if my whole future rode on this woman's next words . . . which was ridiculous. *Right?*

"My coven cannot take Davin out alone. His forces are too many and too strong. At this rate, he will become the most powerful vampire I have come up against in quite a while, and that *is* saying something after six centuries."

"Yes, we can!" came an angry female voice. "We do not need this selfish bastard who has not shown one ounce of loyalty to you or this coven. We took him in!"

"That's enough, Sherra," Celeste responded coolly. "Jax here is responsible for my mate's shift in loyalties. Which is something I intend to fix—?"

"I make my own choices, Celeste!" Caleb interrupted, angrily, as a low growl from Jax sounded beside him. "I left you because I hated you—hated what you made me!"

"It's a thin line between love and hate, Caleb. Are you sure what you felt for me was hate?"

"How many soldiers does Davin have?" Jax asked, also sounding fed up with Celeste's games and trying to keep the conversation on track. "We need to understand what we are up against."

"At least six dozen . . . But if you and Chay agree to team up with us, along with your covens—as well as a few other covens who owe me favors—I believe that together we can come up with a plan to take him out. And in exchange, I will give you the locations."

"Fine, I agree," Caleb responded quickly. "Now tell me the locations."

Celeste let out an odd sound that sort of resembled a snort. "I realize that I am a platinum blonde, but do not treat me like I am an idiot, mate. I will lead you to the locations."

I marched back into the bedroom and straight out the glass door to the roof. Gemma followed right behind me. "You knew you weren't going to like what you heard. So why did you listen in?"

"Isn't it obvious? I needed to know what she's up to," I replied, continuing to stomp towards the greenhouse, knowing it would not be far enough away to escape Caleb's ears, but at least he couldn't follow me outside into the sun while I was so upset.

"Well that's a given. It's Celeste. She's always up to something." Gemma then reached for my arm and swung me around to face her, her voice nothing more than a whisper. "She's trying to get to you, Olivia. Caleb's chosen you. He's made that very clear. Celeste has to be able to feel that in his heart, and she knows there's nothing she can do about it unless she can get to you. Don't let her."

"Easy for you to say," I replied sourly. "Apparently she knows some *preferences* about my mate that I didn't, and she intends to use them. You heard her throwing herself at him. And it's going to make things a lot easier for her if she's traipsing him around the countryside after Davin while I'm stuck here."

Gemma's olive-colored eyes narrowed with disapproval. "Are you forgetting that Caleb has to be a willing participant for her little seduction plot to work? There wasn't anything about that exchange that said he had even a sliver of interest. And she may have just provided the solution to getting Davin out of your life permanently."

"I don't trust her."

"And you think I do? That's like saying you trust the Grim Reaper—only he probably dresses better. Of course, I don't like that they're going after Davin any more than you do. But we've already established that Caleb was going to do this with or without anyone's blessing. Now he will have the numbers to make things a little more even. In a less than even battle, I'll take Caleb any day of the week."

I didn't say anything to that. I couldn't. I was too scared with the thought of losing him to Davin, I wasn't thinking clearly. Gemma placed a reassuring arm over my shoulder. "Why has Jax kept Celeste away from Caleb all these years?" I asked with a quiet voice, raising my eyes to meet hers. "He's been protecting him. Why?"

"That is something you should discuss with either Caleb or Jax."

"I thought you were my friend, Gemma. I'm asking you."

"I am your friend. You know I'm your friend. This just isn't my story to tell."

Quietly, I turned back toward the greenhouse, deciding I needed to work off my own restless energy in my gardening. "Olivia?" Gemma called after me. "You know Caleb isn't going to like you hiding from him out here while all this is going on."

I shrugged my shoulders at her. "No, he won't."

✱✱✱

I spent the next couple of hours pruning, shearing, and then I cleaned the greenhouse until it practically gleamed, but I didn't feel any better. I knew that this situation with Celeste was something I needed to come to terms with because I didn't want Caleb to think I did not trust him . . . but that didn't mean I had to like it!

My hands were carrying a basket full of fresh cucumbers and tomatoes for salad and sandwiches when I heard unhappy cries off in the distance. *Sophie?* Had anyone thought about the danger the infant would be in with Celeste and her coven in the house? Suddenly, I felt this need—this compulsion, really, to go to her, to protect her and make sure she was all right. I set the basket down on the table and rushed out the greenhouse door, headed for the rooftop skylight that looked down into Jax and Gemma's room. There I crouched down on my knees and saw that Jax was already there, holding Sophie in his big arms and trying to calm her tears while Gemma prepared a bottle. The newborn was hungry. Everything was fine. Jax would never let anything happen to his little girl.

I sat back on my heels and took in a deep breath, sensing immediately that I was being watched. Glancing over my left shoulder towards our room, I saw Caleb standing quietly behind the glass with his arms crossed over his chest, his stance wide as he watched me with a scrunched brow. For some reason that brought me back the words he whispered to me the night before. "*It's all right, Olivia. The baby's fine. Just stay here with me . . .*"

I could see the concern in his eyes, the strained lines in his forehead. He wanted me to come to him, but he wouldn't demand it. He was asking silently.

I returned to the greenhouse.

Later, when I did come back inside, forced by nature really since I needed to use the bathroom, I heard Jax and Caleb's tense whispers downstairs. I suspected they were discussing why Jax had been keeping Celeste away from Caleb for the last ten years. I wanted to know the answer to that myself so I was tempted to listen in, but they had all ready heard my noisy entrance back into the house and had cut off their conversation.

I grabbed a quick shower then, needing to wash off all the dirt from my gardening, and I was not at all surprised when Caleb was waiting for me in our room once I finished. "Does this mean you've decided to stop avoiding me?" he asked with a sour expression.

I saw no reason to mince words at this point. "Are you going to go along with her plan?"

"Yes," he replied without hesitation, which surprised me. He wasn't even trying to ease me into it. "I believe this will work— that it will give you your freedom and your life back."

"I have a life!" I snapped at him, " . . . with *you*, in case you had forgotten. Right here and now. But instead of enjoying *this* life together, you would rather go chasing after Davin—with *her*." As I tried to move past him he pulled me to him, his arms holding me firm against his body. His breath coolly flooded my cheek and I could feel the hard tension in every one of his muscles. "Let go of me!"

His brows were drawn tight, his voice and expression filled with injured surprise. "Do you honestly believe I'm doing this to be with her? That I have any sort of feelings for her? Because if you do, I need to know that right now."

I hesitated for only a brief moment because I knew the answer. "No," I whispered weakly. "I think you're doing this because you believe it will be best for me—best for us."

There was visible relief in his expression as his thumb stroked back and forth over the ridge of my cheek. "Do you trust me?" he asked with so much emotion in his gray eyes it pulled at my heart. "Do you trust in the promises I made to you the day I mated you? To love and cherish only you?"

"Of course I do."

"Then let me do this," he coaxed, pleading this in nothing more than a soft whisper. "So I can come home to you and you can know what it feels like to live free again." He lowered his head and brushed his lips against my cheek, kissing a path lower over the column of my throat. I wanted to give some persuasive argument about how it would be better to wait a few days and really think this plan through, but I was too busy responding to the tingling sensation happening in my knees, which seemed like such an odd place to have any kind of sensation. Soon his breathing affected me more and more as he moved his lips tenderly over my skin. That was what I loved most about Caleb Wolfe, his capacity for tenderness, especially for such a strong and powerful man. His kisses were so wonderful; it felt as if he were trying to commit every inch he touched to memory while simultaneously setting the whole of my body on fire. My fingers curled into his shirt as we both became more excited and his lips, teeth and tongue worked over my skin in both gentle and not so gentle nibbles.

A small purr-like growl rumbled in his throat as he hauled me up and fully into his arms. "I need you," he murmured, carrying me to the bed and stretching me out flat against the mattress. Never moving his eyes from mine, he put my up-stretched hands together, surrounding them strongly with one hand, while the other toyed with the red silk sash around my waist that would expose all of my shower-warmed skin to him. A coy smile lit up his face as he slowly pulled the silky fabric open and began caressing my skin beneath. Then he was kissing me again, drawing his body lower until I spread and lifted my legs around him, entangling his hips with mine.

Responding to the strength of him, feeling his skin on mine, my breaths came slower and deeper. There was no way for me to resists this man when I knew he was about to take me. Because my body was his, always his, just as my heart was. "You're so beautiful," he whispered, his voice brushing over me like his softest caress as he stretched my wrists even further upward, causing my breasts to round and lift higher, the already hardened tips rising until they were right there for the taking. "Let me touch you. *Let me* . . . have you."

Lowering his head, he took the cherry-tipped mound of my left breast into his mouth, suckling it on his tongue until I thought the sensation would become unbearable. I let out a soft cry, feeling the rougher texture of his oral caress. The sensation was heaven. Then my soft cry turned into full-blown squeal as he bit over the tip and then, almost instantly, he transferred his attention to the other breast, further intensifying the sensation. I arched higher toward him, pleading for him to stop—no, to continue, to never stop. His deep, pleasing chuckle vibrated against every square inch of my skin and left me feeling weak to my toes. "Caleb," I murmured.

"Vanilla and oranges," he breathed. "I have never wanted a scent so carved into my brain. It's your scent, and I will carry it with me every day I'm apart from you."

My hands raked through his hair, fisting at the tips to hold him there against my breast as he continued to work his lips and tongue on them. "Please don't go," I murmured so quietly I wasn't sure if I actually vocalized it. "I can't lose you."

"You won't lose me, sweet girl," he said, pushing the robe wider and moving lower to kiss over my stomach. As he licked circles around my navel, I cried out with such pleasure it seemed to echo around my head.

Then another cry.

After a moment of clarity I realized that last one wasn't mine. This was more an angry howl of warning.

Celeste.

She was yelling out her displeasure from down in the chilled room, her loud cries echoing throughout the house. Caleb let out a fierce growl that vibrated my stomach just before I stiffened and rolled away from him onto my side. He followed me, his teeth nibbling gently at my hip, trying to coax me back into submission while his hand rubbed between the seam of my thighs, but Celeste wouldn't stop. "Don't, Caleb. I can't do this while she's listening."

"*Damnit!*" he cursed under his breath, rolling his body away from me onto his back. "I'll take care of it," he grumbled as he left our bed.

Chapter Six

After Celeste's rude interruption earlier in the day, darkness was slow to fall that night. I had barely seen Caleb in the meantime, because his *ex-mate* had continued to howl and make demands of him, keeping him at his wits end trying to keep her quiet and away from me. Celeste didn't fool me, though. She had accomplished exactly what she set out to do, keeping Caleb and me separated from each other . . . and I let her do it! I should have taken him inside me and howled my pleasure to the heavens, letting her choke on it. But I couldn't. It wouldn't have been lovemaking at that point. It would have been trying to prove something and come from a place of frustration, not tenderness. That was the last thing Caleb and I needed.

That afternoon I had listened as the three men agreed to Celeste's plans and finalized details on how they were going to destroy Davin. Considering I was the one who Davin was crazed to capture, you would think I'd love the idea that he could soon be out of my life . . . but I didn't. Caleb had asked me if I was truly prepared to do what it would take to get Davin out of my life for good. The truth was, I didn't know. Even after all of my training, and no matter how relentlessly he came after me, I wasn't sure if I could destroy him. But I knew I didn't want any more scars left on Caleb's soul from protecting me. He had already fought so hard against that darker half of himself.

The plan was for Caleb, Chay and Celeste to leave in two days. Of course, the whole time they had been discussing this Celeste had already been throwing herself at Caleb, and when she wasn't, she and Caleb were arguing. Jax kept stepping in and warning Celeste to back off, and I could tell from Caleb's harsh tone that he was getting frustrated with his coven leader. There was something going on there that I didn't understand; a tension that was unspoken between the two men.

I fell asleep later that night and was aware when Caleb moved into bed beside me. I slept a little easier and breathed a little deeper, literally sinking into the comfort of his body as he brought me against him. Inside my dreams he was whispering sweet words at my ear as he caressed me, words so heavenly I felt like I was floating on a cloud. It was some time later that I felt a chill run through me and I sensed immediately that Caleb was no longer at my side. Sophie was crying again. Her exhausted little wails were full of tears, and she sounded so close.

Coming to my feet, I grabbed my robe and headed downstairs, stopping right in front of the closed door to Jax's study. I didn't enter, just stood there with my ear against the door, listening as little Sophie calmed down to Jax's gentle cooing sounds. Then I heard soft suckling sounds.

Everything was fine.

"Olivia?" Caleb whispered, and I jumped back with a start, turning to face him. "Are you here because you heard the baby crying again?"

I didn't get a chance to answer because Jax called us into the room. I waited for Caleb to lead us through the door and saw Jax feeding Sophie a bottle. Her tiny fingers tried unsuccessfully to clutch at the bottle in his hand as she suckled on the little rubber tip with a smile on her lips. "I'm sorry if we disturbed you," Caleb said, wrapping his arm around my waist and pulling me in with him.

Jax's amber eyes were literally soft as honey, happier than I had ever seen him. "I should be saying the same to you," he said, looking straight at me. "It has been an adjustment to have a new little one in the house, has it not, Granddaughter?"

"She's beautiful, Jax. It's a welcome adjustment."

"She is perfect," he sighed contentedly. "I do not believe you have had a chance to hold her yet. Would you like to feed her?"

I tightened my hold around Caleb as I looked up at him. He had a questioning pull to his brow, like he was trying to understand the emotions that were rolling through me in that instant. "I . . . I . . . I don't want to hurt her. If she touches me, I mean."

"You will not hurt her," Jax assured me. "She shares the same blood as you." He stood to his feet and nodded for me to take a seat on the sofa behind me, then brought the baby over and set her gently in my lap. Jax knelt in front of us and continued to hold the bottle. "It is all right. Touch her." I licked my lips nervously and looked back at Caleb, who was leaning, relaxed, against the doorframe. His face was expressionless, but he nodded at me in encouragement. I touched my index finger to one of her tiny hands. She immediately responded by trying to grip my finger. I laughed with relief. She seemed to like my touch, a huge smile pulling over her rounded cheeks while she was still trying to suckle at the bottle.

"She likes you," Jax smiled. "I can *feel* her already. She responds when you are near her."

"Would it be all right if I make a connection with her?" I asked. "I'd like to know what it feels like to touch such a pure soul. I promise I won't hurt her."

"Go ahead," he nodded.

Gently I touched three fingers to her temple and took in a slow, deep breath. Sophie was absolutely perfect inside, her inner light brighter than anything I had ever touched before. She was pure innocence, free of all the violence that would surely surface at some point in her life because of the world she was born into. She held no darkness inside her, and the longer I stayed connected to her, the more her light seemed to wrap around me from the inside. I almost giggled from the warmth, the sensation of love flowing through me. "She's so per—"

Suddenly I froze, blinking back an image that just popped into my head. It was an image that didn't belong there, one from a nightmare, really. I could see a woman on her knees, surrounded by nothing but darkness. She was hunched forward with her back to me, her arms and legs shivering so hard I could almost feel the bone-deep chill she was experiencing at that moment. Sophie was practically screaming at the top of her lungs but I couldn't see her, only hear her. Then a second image flashed . . . The woman's head was being yanked back by the roots of her hair. The force of it was so great that it almost appeared as if her neck was broken in the process. The image scared me and I couldn't quite breathe right, a chocking sensation closing the back of my throat.

"Olivia?" Caleb's voice was there beside me when the image finally let go. I blinked my eyes several times to focus on his worried expression as he held my face in his hands. "What's happening? Talk to me."

My own thundering heartbeat was blasting like a drum in my ear as I turned to see Jax carrying Sophie across the room. It was odd how I didn't even remember him removing her from my arms. The infant was screaming just as loudly as she had been in my image, but it surprised me to see her reach one of her tiny, outstretched hands back towards me. "She is not injured," Jax said with a start, " . . . she is scared."

Just then Gemma raced into the room, clearly startled from sleep but anxious to reach her daughter. "What's wrong?"

"I am not sure," Jax replied.

"Sweet," Caleb said, pulling my chin back around to face him, "focus right here on me. Are you all right?"

"Yes," I nodded and then pulled away from Caleb to stand to my feet. "I'm sorry. I didn't mean to upset her."

I then turned and rushed out of Jax's study and back towards our own room, debating the entire way whether I wanted to keep running out into the pitch-blackness of night to escape this sinking feeling that had come over me. Perhaps the night breeze would blow it all away. I stopped short of the glass and felt Caleb right there behind me. He wrapped his arm around my waist and pulled me back against him, where he held me in a tight embrace with both arms. "No," he said calmly but firmly at my ear. "Tell me what happened."

"I don't know," I replied as he turned me in his arms, my voice sounding a bit lost then. "I just saw images—violent images . . . but they didn't make any sense."

"Have you had images like this before?"

"I guess," I answered. " . . . When I have touched a bad soul. But these images were different. I can't explain it." I could see the worry in Caleb's eyes, and I wanted to reassure him that I was all right, just startled. "Perhaps it's that my gift is getting stronger. I'm sorry. I didn't mean to hurt her."

"You didn't hurt her. You heard Jax. Sophie was scared." His tone was emphatic, his expression absolutely driven to understand what was happening. "Did you see what scared her?"

"Caleb?" Chay interrupted from downstairs in Caleb's study. "Celeste and the Rockettes are back from feeding. We need to get them locked down before the sun rises."

Caleb curled me into his body, hugging me fiercely as he stroked his hand through my hair and spoke to Chay over my shoulder. "I'll be right down." Pulling back to look at me, he said, "Lie down and get some rest. I'll be back to join you in a little while."

***

Throughout most of the next day I sat at the piano in our room and played until I thought my fingers were going to bleed. I hadn't been able to sleep very well after the incident with Sophie, and was frustrated that this was my last night with Caleb before he would leave with Chay and Celeste to hunt for Davin. They had decided that Jax would stay behind, just in case there was any sign of trouble. In truth, I think he was worried about his little girl and wouldn't consider leaving her or Gemma right now.

The more I thought about the images I had seen the night before, the more I was convinced there was something familiar about them, but I couldn't quite place why. That's when I decided to work my frustration out on the keys, hoping it would eventually come to me. It hadn't, but I loved playing, and hoped—*really, really hoped*—that Celeste hated piano music! That it drove her frickin' insane to be forced to stay in a locked room and listen to me play for hours on end.

About an hour after sunset I wandered downstairs from our room. I was actually surprised how quiet the house was. Chay was keeping guard outside, while Jax and Gemma were spending some much needed alone time together on the roof, Sophie sleeping just below. I sensed Caleb was downstairs, though my senses seemed more muddled with all this different vampire energy floating through the house.

Hopping down from the second floor ledge, I went to find him in the kitchen and was stopped dead in my tracks as soon as I crossed the threshold. Caleb was perched on a kitchen stool, his elbows supporting his weight against the island's granite top as Celeste's stood between his parted legs, her body leaning into him and her hands roaming everywhere!

What . . . the . . . hell!

That alone had been enough to make me feel as if someone had ripped my heart from my chest, but then I realized Celeste had her fangs sunk in his throat. She was drinking from him— drinking his blood! I blinked several times and still couldn't believe what I was seeing. Worse yet was the fact that Caleb didn't seem to care that I was standing there. He had to sense that I was there, but he made no effort to pull away from her. A lost glaze filled his sapphire blue eyes as he stared up at the ceiling, his breaths calm as he stretched back to give her more room. The sight sickened me.

Her roaming hands came around to the front of his jeans and started tearing at them beneath his sport shirt, and still Caleb did nothing to stop her. "Caleb!" I called, but before I could even blink Celeste was on me with a loud, wild cry, shoving me back against the kitchen wall. My hands gripped over her temples just as she was about to sink her fangs into my throat. Almost immediately dozens upon dozens of images flashed through my head at what seemed to be warp speed. They were the lives of the innocent she had taken, and she desperately wanted to add me to that list.

But Jax, who had practically flown into the room, ripped her off of me just in time. He now had Celeste shoved against the kitchen wall, his forearm braced against her throat. He inhaled a quick scent of the blood dripping from her fangs and then swung around to Caleb who was standing there absently shaking his head. "Caleb!" Jax barked.

Caleb's head shot up and he blinked several times at Jax, then followed his gaze over to my shocked form backed against the wall. Tears burned my eyes as I looked at him, realizing this man I loved with all my heart had just hurt me more deeply than I thought possible.

"Get off me Jax!" Celeste snarled. "He is my fucking mate! I was just taking back what belongs to me."

Chay and Gemma came rushing into the kitchen at the same moment I knew I had to leave or I would forget how to breathe.

The betrayal inside my heart felt as if it would double me over right there. I had been such a fool to agree to be mated to Caleb without fully understanding what was still left between him and Celeste. She made me feel petty with jealousy and I hated it. "Olivia, wait!" Caleb called to me as I pushed passed Gemma and headed straight for the glass doors. Behind me I heard Caleb bark, "*Goddamnit, Chay! Let go of me!*"

"Hold him there!" Jax ordered. "Gemma, go!"

I jumped through the glass doors to the thirty foot drop below, landed hard and then kept running through the forest, not caring that it was pitch dark—the most dangerous time for me to be out alone. I could hear Gemma right behind me but I refused to stop, or even slow down. When I realized I had run right to Caleb's favorite rock perch that overlooked the mountain valley, I was stopped by my own shock that I would choose this place—a place that was so important to him. What on earth was wrong with me that I would instinctively come here?

Feeling as though I was about to be sick, I fell to my hands and knees on the rock, breathing so hard my limbs were shaking. That's when I felt a small, reassuring arm stretched across my shoulders, bracing me against the wave of pain that seemed to want to rip me completely in half. "I swear it's not what it seems," Gemma said quietly.

"Don't!" I said roughly. "I know what I saw. Don't defend him to me." For a moment there I felt as if I were going to hyperventilate, which was definitely not normal for a Dhampir. "I need my friend Gemma. I need you to take me down the mountain—back to Seattle."

"Tonight?" Gemma asked, startled.

I nodded, sitting back on my heels and holding my hands over my chest as if trying to keep my heart from leaping right out. "You can't leave until you first speak with Jax." I was shaking my head at her when she came around me and grabbed my tear-soaked face in her hands. "Listen to me. What you saw was not what it looked like."

"I'm leaving!" I said shooting to my feet.

I swung around to do just that when a wave of cold air hit me and Jax was suddenly blocking my path. "You are not going anywhere, Granddaughter, until you first hear what I have to say. If, when I am finished you still want to return to Seattle, I will take you there myself."

"Listen to what?" I challenged bitterly. "More excuses? We're all down *here* right now. Which means she is back there, doing God knows—"

"Enough!" Jax warned. "Caleb would never willingly do anything to hurt you like this. He loves you."

"Well, he looked pretty willing, all bent over the kitchen island like that."

Jax scraped his hand roughly through his hair. "It is not like that. Celeste is trapping him."

"Oh, so now he's being forced," I snapped angrily. "How stupid do you think I am? Nobody forces Caleb to do anything."

"You are not stupid," Jax came back quickly, " . . . but you are being played. Celeste has the gift to entrance, and her gift is more powerful than just about any other I have come across."

"What? Is this some kind of joke?"

"It's true," Gemma insisted. "If she focuses on you with her eyes she can lull you into a state of semi-consciousness—like hypnosis. Once there, the person is no longer aware of everything happening around them. They are more open to suggestion. To them it only feels like losing bits of time."

I blinked back at both of them, remembering that night when Celeste first appeared. "That's why Caleb wouldn't look her directly in the eyes?"

Jax nodded. "When Gemma and I met Caleb, Celeste had him convinced he was mated to her. He believed it to be true because of the connection she had forced on him—a connection to this day he can feel. But I sensed right away, that though they were connected, they were not mated. Caleb would have realized it himself, but she was using her gift to keep him tied to her."

I swung away from both of them, unable to believe what I was hearing. I wanted to throw my arms up and scream at the sky but settled for a loud unladylike grunt of frustration. "First she turns him . . . then she lies to him and claims to mate him . . . then she keeps him connected to her against his will. But he does nothing about it!" I marched back to Jax, getting right in his face . . . or sort of in his face, given his size. "Caleb has been a fighter since the first day I met him. Yet he lets this woman control him like he was some sort of mindless puppet. Why?"

"He cannot harm her. He is connected to her, and that connection pulls at him to protect her, even when he does not wish to. It is a connection that will not be broken until one of them dies. Only then will he be completely free of her."

Standing before Jax, I blurted out an odd sounding laugh, something between a snort and a cry, but there was absolutely no humor in it. "Is that why you took him into your coven? Is it why you've been protecting him from her all these years?"

"Yes," Jax answered simply.

"So if you hadn't interceded," I began, "would he still be with her now?"

"Probably," Jax responded quietly. "But it would never have been his choice. He would be no more than a prisoner."

I dropped my head in my hands, shaking it back and forth as a shocking revelation hit me. "Wow. How he must have hated me when he thought I trapped him under my illusion. In his mind, I must have been no better than Celeste."

"There was no comparison!" Jax came back quickly, " . . . and he saw that. Unlike Celeste, you never tried to trap him with your gift. I could see the doubt and pain in him that next day after you had left with Alec to train at The Oracle. He could feel in every fiber of his being that your love was real because you had let him go. Celeste would never have done anything so selfless. Since the day she turned him it has only ever been about what *she* wanted. She has lived so long she believes herself equal to a God."

"She doesn't know how to love, only how to take," Gemma added somberly. "But you do. And Caleb wants that love with you. It's why he's so determined not to let Davin destroy what you have."

"Why didn't he just tell me this? If he had told me when she showed up here I think I would've understood. I could have been better prepared for the game she was playing with me. I could've supported him instead of doubting him. Why's he not down here telling me this himself?"

"He wanted to be," Jax replied. "It is taking all the strength

Chay has to hold him back right now at my insistence."

"Why did you do that?"

"I wanted you to hear this from us first—so you would know it was the truth. You have to understand that this is something that shames him down to his very core, and yet he can do nothing to change it. Instead he has focused on moving forward and living the life he wants for himself. That life is with you. And at this moment there are two things I am quite certain of. *One*—he is scared to death that he has lost you. *Two*—he is scared to death that something will happen to you out here while he is waiting to see if you will come back to him."

There was a long silence between us while I tried to digest how this was all possible. Why had Caleb lived with this all this time and not shared it with me? Did he not trust that I would see the truth of what she was doing?

"So what's it going to be, Olivia?" Gemma asked. "Do we take you back to Seattle . . . or will you come home and talk with him?"

My body was flowing with so much raw anger, I almost felt sorry for the person who now had to face me. "Neither," I replied coolly, surprising them both. "I want you to send Celeste out here to me. Alone. No interference from any of you. Understood?"

"Not going to happen," Jax replied. "She is too dangerous."

"He's right," Gemma agreed. "All it would take is for her to lock eyes with you and before you knew what was happening, it would be over. Caleb would never allow you to do something so dangerous."

"Caleb will agree—"

"No, he will not," Jax growled, not appreciating my stubbornness on this subject. "He will say that you are insane." That was certainly true enough with regard to facing a six-hundred-year-old vampire alone. But it probably wasn't the first or last time Caleb would question my sanity. "Celeste is threatened by you, and she has made no secret of why she is here. She believes she can get Caleb back. And she will have no issue with killing *you* in order to do it."

"Well, then she's going to get her shot—or you will take me back to Seattle right now. One or the other. If Caleb wants any hope of me staying—of me forgive him . . . he'll give me fifteen minutes alone with her."

Jax had a fierce scowl on his face, not at all liking my ultimatum.

"This is my battle, Jax. If I don't stand up to her now she will just continue to come at me. You and Caleb can't protect me from this."

"Yes we can!" he barked, but I calmly stood my ground in front of him, and he knew I wasn't going to back down.

"You tell Caleb it's his choice."

Chapter Seven

When I saw Celeste clear the tree line and spring up on her booted heels, light as air, to meet me on the rock ledge, I had to admit I was surprised. Part of me believed Caleb would rather have me leave him and go back to Seattle than taking on the danger of confronting her. The other part of me expected him to show up blustering something about how I was insane and to get my butt back to the house. So as the statuesque woman glided towards me with her long legs and barely-there skirt, a lethal smile displaying her intent to get me out of her way once and for all, I decided it *was* quite possible that I was insane. But I knew I had to take a stand with her. She was a fighter and had earned the respect of those around her. Even Caleb, Jax and Chay respected her in that they all saw her as someone not to be trifled with.

"Sure this is a good idea?" she drawled, her snowy white hair swinging low across her back and her hips swaying as she came towards me. "I don't need an excuse to kill you out here."

My gaze followed her movements carefully, half expecting she would charge me at any moment. I had no doubt that this could be exactly the opportunity she was waiting for. "You go right ahead and take your best shot," I replied calmly, taking a deliberate step towards her in an effort to show I was not afraid. "Because killing me is the only chance you'll ever have of getting Caleb back."

She snorted at that, propping one hand on her hip. "My, someone is full of herself today. I should remind you that I have killed weak-willed sluts such as yourself for nothing more than a bloody, late night cocktail . . . pun intended," she said, stretching her hand through her long, platinum hair until the ends floated from her fingertips. "I cannot imagine even breaking a finger nail sucking you dry." "Well this slut," I said wickedly to her through my lashed, not really minding if she envisioned Caleb and me humping as frequently as rabbits, "just might surprise you."

Celeste responded by coming even closer, those lavender eyes of hers appearing luminous in the moonlight, their violaceous color literally jumping off her face. She was trying to lock me into them, trap me in the extraordinary color. It took all the concentration I had to focus on the features from her nose down. It didn't feel natural to look at a person this way, of course, but I certainly wasn't going to make things easy for her. "Why, Caleb?" I suddenly asked her, my voice losing a bit of strength. "Why did you wait six centuries to mate and then choose a man who didn't choose you?"

She laughed loudly in reply. "Oh, I have been mated before—twelve times in fact. Caleb's lucky number thirteen. But none of them satisfied me "in the sack," shall we say, like he did. I don't know what he's told you to spare that fragile half-human ego of yours, but he enjoyed every moment he spent fucking my brains out."

I felt my face scrunch with disgust at her crude description. It was clear to me that although there may have been chemistry between them, which I couldn't stand to think about, there was never any love. I knew because Caleb had shown me day in and day out for the last nine months that there was much more to being mated than just fucking. There was laughter and tenderness—there was real emotion and trust . . . and even pain. And there was love—real love, something Celeste did not have time for because she was too busy loving herself. "So where are all of these other mates?"

"Dead," she replied matter-of-factly. "Funny the run of bad luck . . ."

Bad luck or boredom I wondered. "You really do see yourself as a God, don't you?"

"Why yes I do. And if you were smart, you would high-tail it back to Seattle while you still have your life. But you are not smart. That is the rather sad truth. You're too stupid to know to be afraid of me."

"So I'm supposed to believe you would let me walk out of here alive?"

She snorted. "No."

I now understood why Caleb and Jax were so protective of

me ever meeting Celeste. This woman had zero conscience, a wealth of hate and an abundance of self-love. That made for one very dangerous combination. "OK, so let's say you do manage to get me out of the way tonight . . ." Celeste's entire expression seemed to light up at the prospect. "What then? Will you eventually grow bored of Caleb? Will he have the same bad run of fate as your other twelve mates?"

Celeste smirked as she began to circle around me, forcing me to have to turn with her to keep her in my sights. "I love Caleb," she began and I could see on her face how much it delighted her to dig at me like that. "I want him around for a very long time. I dare say there are few who are more handsome—and even fewer with the appetite for sex he has." She stopped her circling right in front of me and bit enticingly into her lower lip while dragging her long fingernails along the length of her thigh. "You see, I understand what he likes . . . the desires he does not speak of. A naive woman like you could not possibly keep a man like that satisfied."

I really hated how she kept implying that Caleb had sexual needs that I was clueless about. It was true I came to him with little experience, but our sexual chemistry seemed to click right from the get go . . . at least I thought it did. He had never mentioned wanting an audience for our lovemaking, as Celeste kept implying. But then again, I'd never asked. Maybe I wasn't totally satisfying him. I certainly didn't have six hundred years of experience to draw from.

Celeste took another step toward me, and I realized she was maneuvering me toward the edge of the rock. One false step and I would fall about the distance of the Space Needle into the canyon below. If I fell, Celeste could claim my own clumsiness killed me. That would certainly be a lame way to go out.

"You hope that's true, don't you? So I will make things easy and play the insecure mate."

"You are not his mate," she corrected.

"Yes I am," I came back, giving her my best smile. "I know it —he knows it . . . and most importantly, deep down in that arrogant head of yours, you know it. That's what brought you barging back into his life. You can feel the connection we have and you know you've run out of time. So you go right on ahead and play your little mind games, flaunt those long legs of yours —but it won't work. He loves me. I *know* he loves me."

"You are kidding, right? I was about to mount him tonight when you so rudely interrupted us. Another ten minutes and we both would have been coming."

I cringed as she said those words, and fought off the images of what I had walked in on. "The only person you screwed tonight was yourself," I replied calmly. "You showed your hand, and now that Caleb knows what you're up to, he'll never let you close to him again."

A flash of recognition shown through her eyes, which quickly turned to fury. She knew I was right. And more importantly, I knew I was right. I would not let this woman manipulate me. "Just know if he still leaves with you tomorrow to track Davin, I'll support him. I trust him. And I'll be waiting right here for him when he returns."

"I think not," Celeste came back, her eyes locking with mine before I had a chance to realize what had just happened. I had made a critical error, letting my eyes come back to hers in a show of strength. But the blue and red mixed into a color that was so bright it was mesmerizing, as if they were charged with electricity, making them pop like a 3D cartoon. I couldn't seem to take my eyes off hers and I knew this was what Jax had warned me about.

Celeste launched at me like a cannonball. My arms came up in instant reflex to meet the force of her collision against me but it felt like a truck had hit me! She was incredibly strong and confident in her ability to kill in an instant. The air was completely blown from my lungs and my arms felt unsteady as she pushed harder against me, but somehow I managed to hold my ground. That's when I realized that I was not entranced as I should be—and even had full control over all my responses. This, however, had caught Celeste off guard. Her head snapped up once she realized her gift had not worked. She tried to lock on me a second time. Once again I seemed to be able to look directly at the incredible color and not be paralyzed by her gift. My gift was protecting me, shielding me from hers.

She came at me again, shoving me backward, and this time I was taken to the ground. With her physical strength, this is where Celeste would have the advantage. Soon, my arms and legs were pinned beneath her and she hissed above me, her lethal fangs ready to sink into my throat any second. "I can't wait to kill you," she snarled as she lowered her fangs to my neck.

But then she stopped . . . The forest around us was deathly quiet for a long moment before that silence was shattered by Celeste's loud cry. It held such raw violence that shook me almost as much as it shook her body. She was desperate to drink from me but it was as if her hands burned where she had them gripped over my bare skin and she couldn't pull them back.

Taking advantage of her pain, I was able to pull one hand from her grasp, then I latched onto her face with a firm hold and focused all the energy I had to that one little spot. Almost instantly her grip loosened and she was reaching her free hand to her temple. It was as if I could feel the power in my hand surging through her like a lightning bolt that shot straight at the darkness within her soul, conjuring up hundreds of images of her past victims, visualizations that wracked her mind with pain at warp speed. Over the last nine months I had trained myself to block out most of the images that I could also see as a result of my touch, but with Celeste there were so many victims spread over six centuries, blocking even most of them was not nearly enough. As the images continued to stack one on top of the other, I heard my own shrill cry in response to the pain, almost in unison with Celeste's above me. But I continued to hold on.

She started to collapse under the pain of my hold, bringing her weight down on top of me until it partially restricted my breathing, but I still didn't stop. I had gained a critical edge on her and didn't want to take a chance on her recovering and coming back at me if I let up. The next thing I knew, several angry growls were sounding above me, and suddenly her weight was lifted as easily as a feather, my breath quickly restored. Once free, I rolled to my side and came up on my knees preparing to defend myself again in an instant.

"Olivia?" Caleb questioned worriedly as he came over me like a shadow and shielded me from her with his body.

"I'm all right, Caleb," I said, pushing away from him and reaching my hand to my throbbing temple.

"Don't tell me you're all right," he said incredulously. "I *feel* your pain."

Where I found the strength to push aside the pain and come back to my feet I wasn't sure . . . but I did. Inside that moment I was thinking a bit irrationally. I wanted to be held by him—I almost always wanted to be held by him—but I was still hurt that he hadn't told me the truth about her in the first place, and that he was coddling me in front of her. I couldn't let Celeste see any weakness in me or she would never relent.

Caleb, on the other hand, was so tense it appeared he wasn't breathing. He tried again to come to me, but I put my arm out protectively to keep him at a distance. His frustration showed in his expression as he did not understand what I was trying to do, and he was bewildered as to how to coax me into letting him help.

I looked over to see Jax and Chay holding Celeste down, but it wasn't taking any effort. That's when I realized it was because she was still crumpled against the ground in a crippling amount of pain. I blinked back, unable to believe what I was seeing. I raised my hands and saw they were shaking. Only then did it strike me what had actually happened. My gift wielded enough power in that moment to bring a six-hundred-year-old vampire crying to her knees . . . and it frightened me because there was nothing *human* about what I had done.

"Release me—now!" Celeste bit out angrily as she forced herself to her feet, then turned to me with a hate that I had never seen from another being before—human or vampire. "We are not done," was all she said before disappearing in a whoosh of air that left me standing there on the rock with the three men. Make that two men and one very angry grandfather.

"What were you thinking?" Jax yelled as his head snapped around. "She could have killed you just as easily as breathe on you."

But Jax had not seen everything, or he refused to see how his granddaughter had turned a very powerful vampire's mind into silly putty for several crucial moments. "Thanks for the vote of confidence, Grandfather."

"Do not *Grandfather* me. When we showed up here you were screaming out in pain!"

I stepped forward towards him, now feeling somewhat defensive—and I had no idea why, because my heart was still beating a million miles a minute in my throat. With a certain sense of self-justification, I ventured, "In case you hadn't noticed, she was also screaming out in pain."

Jax looked at me as if I were the most stubborn person on the face of the earth. I could see he was about to give me a blistering response, but surprisingly, Caleb stopped him. "Jax," he began calmly, "can you and Chay give me some time with Olivia?"

Chapter Eight

As I watched Jax and Chay depart through the forest in the direction they came from, I inhaled a slow, deep breath, feeling Caleb's energy right behind me, all around me in the suddenly tense night air. It reached out like little sparks of electricity, prickling over my skin, refusing to let me forget how utterly aware of him I was at any given moment. "Look at me," he intoned softly.

"I need a minute." I was trying to stop the shaking in my hands by squeezing them together. I remembered the power I had felt beneath my fingers when I held Celeste in my grasp, and it terrified me. If I hadn't stopped would I have had the power to kill her? Could she, a six-hundred-year-old vampire, fail to feel that I had that kind of power?

Caleb slid his hands over my forearms until he closed them over my own in an effort to try and stop their shaking. After applying his own gentle, reassuring squeeze, he pulled me back to rest against his chest, and I swear, the strength of him saved me from the embarrassment of having my knees collapse beneath me. "Are you all right?" he asked.

When I didn't answer he turned me around in the circle of his arms, his hand tilting my chin up until I met his gaze. "Please look at me."

I did, and his expression was visibly upset, as if it were taking every ounce of energy he had to hold himself still. "Why didn't you just tell me?" I asked him quietly. "Why didn't you trust me to tell me the truth of what she was doing?"

"God, I'm sorry," he rushed out, as if the breath he had been holding came with it. "I never meant to hurt you . . . I thought I could handle the situation so that it would never touch you. It was never about my trust in you."

"But it is. It's exactly about that. Instead of trusting that I would believe you—that I would see the truth of what she was doing—you chose to say nothing. You let me doubt you—doubt us." Caleb was about to respond, but I didn't give him a chance. "Do you even know what feelings are real for you?" He quirked his brow strangely at me. "I mean . . . between Celeste entrancing you, and me trapping you in my illusion—"

"You never trapped me, and you damn well know it," he growled. "What I feel for you is real. It always has been!"

"Then why?" I shouted, unwilling to accept that answer. "You had to have felt that she still wanted you when she showed up here . . . that it was only a matter of time before she tried something like this."

"I did," he answered truthfully, " . . . but I thought I could handle it. Jax warned me, and I still . . ." Then Caleb Wolfe, one of the strongest, most confident men I had ever known, hesitated. He seemed at a loss for words more than at any point I could remember since I met him. "I don't want to believe . . . that as strong as I am . . . I can't control this."

"Is that why things between you and Jax have been so strained?"

He nodded as he tipped his head down. "Olivia . . . ," he began and left the thought unfinished.

"What do you feel for her?" I questioned him. "That part of you that is still connected to her must feel something? Does she excite you—?"

"Stop!" he said, and I was glad he stopped me. As soon as I had asked the question I wanted to take it back. Celeste had succeeded in causing me to doubt for a moment that what we had was strong enough to withstand anything. His gaze then locked on mine once again, and there was incredible determination in his eyes. "Have you seen or sensed my body responding to her in any way since she's been here?"

"Are you really asking me that?" I blinked back at him. "I just watched her drink from your throat while she had you bent over the kitchen island."

"Was I responding to her?" he pressed. "Was I touching her? Think about what you saw."

I didn't have to think about it long. Even when Celeste was tearing into his pants I saw there was no physical response in him. It wasn't there physically, nor did it emanate from him in his masculine scent—the scent that I was now so familiar with.

Instead he had appeared distant, glazed, and unfocused. He had been entranced—held trapped—just as Jax and Gemma had described. For all of Celeste's bragging that she was about to mount him, there had been no response on his part. Maybe he had felt something for her at one time, but he didn't in that moment.

"I feel a connection with her," he offered quietly when I didn't respond, and I could hear the raw honesty in his voice. "It's a connection that I cannot break . . . but it's not love. I don't want to feel her heart or know her mind. I don't want to lie with her and hold her while she sleeps—to protect her from all the bad dreams. And I've no desire to be lost inside her body as I make love to her. I only want those things with you."

He reached for me, bringing me carefully against him as if he feared I would push away from him again. But I wouldn't—not this time. Instead, I could feel myself trembling within his arms as I leaned harder into him. My current tremors weren't caused from the lofty night breeze that had crept in around us, or contact with his cool skin, but rather an exposure to my heart that had my emotions spiraling all over the place. "Stay with me," he whispered, like a promise, his breath tingling over the shell of my ear. "I was wrong to not tell you the truth . . . for hurting you like this. I was trying to protect you. But please don't pull away from me now when I need to feel you the most."

Those words were all it took for me to sink into his chest, to surrender against his body. This was what I had missed most since Celeste had intruded into our lives—the closeness, the unspoken intimacy with this man that I cherished so much and he seemed to feel it had returned as well. "My sweet," he murmured. "Just let me hold you."

Standing there in his arms, my heart beat a little faster and my breathing became a little deeper. The moment felt so genuine and pure. I opened my palms and slid them up along his chest and over the broad expanse of his shoulders and could see how my touch was affecting him. His shoulders tightened behind my fingers as he fisted his hand into my hair, drawing my head back to capture my lips in a soft, tender kiss that asked for forgiveness. "Caleb . . ."

"Come," he murmured, lowering himself—me with him—till

he was seated on the rock. I found myself straddled over his hips as he wrapped his arms around my back to pull me close— so close I was pressed tight against him. The strength of his body was an amazing thing to feel. It was impossible to think anything could penetrate it, yet he held me with such gentleness sometimes I would forget that he wasn't human.

I kissed him—lightly—like I really didn't want to admit to myself that I was initiating it. Then I pulled back. But he followed me, his rough bristle nuzzling at my cheek until he was in a position to capture my lips once again. And capture he did, taking his next kiss without asking, without apology. When he kissed me like that he was making it clear—I was his and nothing would change that fact. "I'm sorry I hurt you," he whispered.

Again with the gentleness . . . There was such sincerity it was almost unnerving.

I stared up into his eyes and the world seemed to stop for both of us. The tension with Jax, the problems with Celeste, they all seemed to disappear in that moment, and it was just me and Caleb . . . Caleb and me. "Can you forgive me?" he asked into the quiet.

"Yes," I nodded against his shoulder which seemed to draw a relieving breath from him, then I smiled against his skin, "But you're gonna have to earn it."

He laughed at that. "I will earn it, my sweet," he said, drawing back with a soft glow in his gray eyes as he began tugging at my sundress to pull it up on my hips. "But right now I need to feel you all soft and sexy around me."

My breath suddenly drew in quicker at his words and I felt my own fingers gripping at his shirt. "To feel your warmth pulling at me," he said as we continued to stare at each other and his large thumbs traced back and forth across my hip under the little strings at the sides of my bikini. "Will you let me have you, Olivia?" he growled softly against my collarbone.

Although it was pretty obvious by the way my body curled around him that he could do pretty much whatever he wanted, I shook my head at him with a smile. "Convince me more . . ."

He laughed quietly at that, his thumbs ripped apart the strings at my hips with ease. "Convincing you is my favorite part," he murmured as one hand slid lower and his deft fingers sought out the silky heat already easing from my body.

"Caleb," I whispered as my grip tightened on his shirt and he found that sweet spot that controlled the whole mass of sensitive nerves endings throughout my body. He began to circle in a smooth, unhurried motion that revealed he would take all the time in the world to do with me as he pleased. But in no time at all he had my back arching deep and my hips lifting in response. I thought I would bounce right out of his arms just as he cinched an arm around my low back to hold me in place, then increased the pace and pressure of his strokes. Small whimpers turned into larger cries as my fingers dug into his shoulders and my head fell back.

"Do you know you are at your most beautiful when you surrender," he offered as a statement of fact while easing two long fingers inside my warm flesh, at first almost tauntingly, then more evenly. I inhaled a gasping breath as he stroked with such ease that I was literally becoming putty in his hand. "You have such a look of wonder about you, pleading. That is such a turn-on," he said with heat in his eyes. "That moment you release. The beauty in your face as you accept the pleasure I give you."

He continued to whisper even more sweet words as his fingers increased their pace and my grip tightened on his shirt at his shoulders. All the nerve endings in my body felt as if they were swirling up into one, giant ball that was about to unfurl. At that moment I was hanging on by a very thin thread, as we were practically nose-to-nose, exchanging a mix of each other's heavy breaths right above our lips. When I saw his eyes transform in front of me to the most brilliant shade of blue and his large fangs lengthen to their lethal form, I became even more excited. This was the moment when the man became so aroused he was lost to the vampire—the warrior taking over from within him. "Caleb," I moaned desperately against his chin and grasped the sides of his face in my hands. "Please . . . Please . . ."

And still he spoke as if he was trying to seduce me. Didn't he realize I was already seduced? "Nothing makes me harder than watching you accept pleasure. Those beautiful eyes of yours tell me how close you are. Even if I couldn't *feel* you, I would know. Your body talks to me. It whispers what it wants. You're mine . . . all mine."

My hips lifted higher and all I could do was try to hold on as I stared into his beautiful eyes and his fingers quickened their pace inside me. Moving my whole body to match his strokes, lust seemed to overwhelm me for a moment, then the world blew up in front of me. My satisfied cries echoed through the canyons below us as my thighs locked my man in a fierce grip.

What had just happened? One minute I was determined to keep some distance while he explained what had happened with Celeste, and the next I was screaming out through the canyons as if I had never experienced such an earth shattering orgasm with him before. Resting there languid and soft within Caleb's embrace, the most wonderful sense of peace floated through me. His palm held my cheek as he stared into me with a smoky, lust-filled gaze that asked a single question. *Would I let him make love to me?*

The answer, without a doubt, was yes. I wanted to claim my mate—*my mate,* not Celeste's—and refuse to give in to my fears that she may somehow come between us. "Yes," I breathily replied to his silent question. "I want this. I want to be close to you."

Wasting no time, his large hands gripped around my hips to lift me into place above him and then worked at freeing himself from his jeans. My heart was beating so fast it felt as if it were skipping several of them, and I counted the seconds until I would feel connected with him in the most intimate way. He must have been feeling the same way because I wasn't sure if he realized how loudly he was growling at that moment. It was a deep throated gnarl that . . .

Suddenly his head snapped over his shoulder and his growl became one of true warning. I followed the direction of his gaze to see Celeste emerging from the trees, the moonlight catching her pale face full of fury. "You had better get off of him now," she snarled, "because you are not going to mount him right here in front of me."

Trying to decide if I was more mortified, angry, or pained by unfulfilled need at another unwelcome interruption, I stiffened against Caleb's body. How had this woman managed to do this to us again? Come between us at the most intimate moment. Caleb turned my head into his shoulder, as if trying to shield me from the rage currently pouring through him. "You have three seconds to get the hell out of here!" Caleb gnashed through his teeth, the lethal tone in his voice unmistakable.

I moved to lift myself away from him, but his arm snagged around my low back and rooted me in place, notching his swollen flesh into my sex to serve as a reminder that we weren't finished yet.

"There is no way I am leaving here with that whore spread all over you," Celeste hissed. "I can smell her lust from here. It sickens me!"

Caleb roared out in rage as he moved me off of him, refastened his clothes with lightening fast efficiency and was in front of her before I could think to utter a word. He clamped a gripping hand over her jaw as her back stiffened with anger. "Go," he said with terrifying calm. "Before I change my mind and kill you right here."

Celeste's lips curled in a coy smile, her eyes moving to catch his. She was trying to draw him in, lock her gaze on him once more. This was how she had managed to gain control over him in the kitchen. It would not happen again. Not while I could do something about it. Ready to charge at her myself, I was stopped short at seeing Caleb crank her chin around so she could not look at him directly. He knew exactly what she was trying to do and he had her under control.

Unfortunately, it didn't stop her from speaking. "Who are you trying to convince?" she laughed. "You will not kill me . . . we both know it. And I am not about to let you find satisfaction in that little tart's body. She has the sexual prowess of a beet worm."

A beet worm? Oh, how I hated this woman.

"Of course, if you want to find satisfaction in mine," she purred. "I am more than willing. I'll even let her watch. She might learn a thing or two . . . or a dozen."

Caleb snarled out as he released his grip of her chin and turned his back on her. "Our deal is off! You can hunt for Davin on your own."

She blinked back as if she actually had the nerve to be surprised that she had pushed him too far. "Don't be a fool! You want Davin as badly as I do."

"More, actually," he replied as he came over to help lift me to my feet. "But I'll find a way without your help."

"You need me and my coven . . . the Rogues I bring with me!"

Caleb swung around on her hard. "Wrong! I would *use* your coven and the Rogues. But I don't need you."

Celeste let out a nasty snarl. "Fine! I will leave! But when you're ready to stop being manipulated by your dick, you know where to find me."

Before I could blink Celeste was gone, and the awkward silence left in her absence was suffocating. Caleb lowered his head, shaking it back and forth just before his fingers pinched over the bridge of his nose. "I'm sorry," he began. "You shouldn't have to be dealing with this . . . this mess I have brought into our lives."

But once he met my gaze again I could see the resolve in his eyes and I blinked up at him with surprise. "You still have every intention of going with her, don't you? Even after everything she's done—knowing full well she will try to trap you again."

His expression was quiet and he didn't deny it.

"Why can't you let go of this obsession you have with destroying Davin? At least for a little while . . . Why does it have to be right now?"

"I told you; I want you free of him," he replied calmly. "I don't want my life with you—our life together—to be on hold any longer."

I laughed bitterly. "We aren't going to have a life together if —and we'll just set aside for now the very real possibility that Davin could kill you—Celeste succeeds in her plans to trap you."

"Celeste won't succeed. I won't let that happen."

"Really? And exactly how are you planning to stop her? If she entrances you, she'll try to keep you tied to her. She won't let you return to me."

Caleb's hands reached for me, holding me at my shoulders as he spoke. "Listen to me. She won't succeed. Right now it's more important that we take Davin out before he gets even more powerful. If we wait, his forces will continue to grow exponentially and we may never get another chance to fight him with a force of this size. I spoke the truth when I said I don't need Celeste, but I do need the fighters she brings with her. She knows that."

"It's still an obsession, Caleb."

"You can call it whatever you like, but Davin won't stop coming for you, and I'll be damned if I sit back on my hands and allow that to happen." He then pulled me back into his arms and kissed me on the top of my head, whispering his next words as if to give them more, not less, emphasis. "After what happened tonight I know I don't deserve it, but I'm asking you to trust me. I know what she's trying to do. It's not going to happen. I swear that to you on my life."

Slowly, I stepped towards him, resting my head against his chest. I knew there would be nothing I could say to keep him from going once he made his mind up. He was a warrior. Warriors went into battle when challenged, and Davin had practically been challenging him from day one. I looked up at him with watery eyes. "I love you, Caleb Wolfe . . . and I trust you. But if you do this and don't come back to me, I swear I'll never forgive you."

A quiet laugh escaped him. "I'll be back, my sweet. That I promise you. I'll be back."

Chapter Nine

Sitting alone under the stars in our favorite spot on the roof of the tree house, I felt the sting of how much I missed Caleb. He had been gone for two long weeks, but my discomfort was especially poignant in this moment because I was seeing his beautiful smile . . . in my mind, that is. We were connecting to each other through our gifts—my gift to see him, reach for him over great distances, which I inherited from my mother, and his vampire gift to feel my emotions, stresses and pain, though, I had to remove my protective necklace filled with sacred ground to share these precious moments with him. And even though it meant the world to me to have this, it wasn't the same as feeling him beside me as I slept, or touching his wonderful skin, or hearing the deep, velvet brush of his voice. I missed him so much.

This morning, after cleaning the linens to our bed—something I had been putting off doing because I knew I would lose all traces of his scent left behind—I missed him more than ever. Connecting with him now, I felt him as he mouthed the words '*I love you, my sweet*' and I couldn't seem to stop the huge smile that split my cheeks as I giggled into the night air, wishing he were here so he could tell me the story of Andromeda and Perseus all over again as we looked at the stars.

"Spending time with your mate again?" Jax asked with a soft chuckle as he came to join me.

I nodded quickly. "I can't tell how things are going in their hunt for Davin, but just knowing he's all right . . . that means the world."

"Things are going fine," Jax assured me. "I can *feel* him. He is not unduly stressed or anxious about things."

"Would you tell me if he was?" I challenged him. Jax returned only a crooked smirk. "Clever girl," he replied, appearing to look straight through the trees that surrounded the tree house rooftop. "You should come inside. Andie has some dinner ready, and the weather is shifting. A storm will be moving in and it will be very cold tonight."

Andie Stevenson was the new love of Chay's life. She was a kind and lovely woman—a human woman—with the most gorgeous naturally-curly, chocolate-colored hair I had ever seen on any woman. She had come to stay with us while Caleb and Chay were away hunting Davin. The pair met only recently and had to deal with the constant strain of Andie being discovered living with him in this world. In the supernatural world, a vampire was not allowed to let humans know of their existence unless they planned on turning the human. It was the only way to keep the two worlds cleanly separated. But after much deliberation, Chay and Andie decided together that he would turn her so that she could remain with him in his world, a decision Jax disapproved of very much, believing Andie did not truly understand what she was committing to. But out of respect for his longtime friend he kept his opinions to himself and was nothing but a gentleman to Andie.

"I'll be in soon," I replied. Jax nodded and turned back towards the house. "Jax?" I called back. "Is everything alright with Sophie? She seemed pretty upset last night."

Jax stopped, and looked off into the distance as if he were considering something. "Yes, she was," he sighed. "My little girl is afraid of something. I can feel it in her." I could see the concern in his expression. "She is too young to already know fear in her life. I hate it . . . and I do not know how to help her."

"You are helping," I assured him. "You watch over her when she's sleeping and walk with her in your arms during the night when she's upset. That little girl already knows so much love from both you and Gemma. Love will take away the fear."

Jax replied with a smile that didn't really come close to reaching his eyes. "Granddaughter, I've been meaning to ask you something. I felt the same fear in her that day in my study . . . while you were connecting with her. Do you have any idea what is frightening her so?"

I paused, remembering the jumbled array of dark images that I saw when I touched Sophie—images an innocent newborn should never have. Then again, I couldn't be certain that I wasn't somehow projecting those images to her from what was being projected to me when I battled the Dhampirs. But they weren't images that were even the least bit familiar to me. Still, I didn't want to worry Jax until I better understood what I saw. "I did see images . . . ," I began, carefully. "But I didn't understand them."

"Do you think, if you connected with her again, you could focus in and understand what you are seeing?"

I blinked back at him in surprise. "J—Jax . . . I don't want to hurt her. I'm not confident that I'm not somehow hurting her when I touch her."

Jax shook his head in response. "I do not believe you are. She responds when you are near because I believe she senses you have an ability to communicate with her that none of the rest of us have. You may be able to help her in a way that I cannot. I am just asking you to try one more time. If it does not work, it does not work."

I could see the determination on Jax's face. He was indeed worried for his daughter, and who could really blame him? "Of course, Jax. I'll help in any way I can."

"Thank you," he replied with a relieved sigh, and then he smiled down at me. "Sophie senses your good heart, you know. I have said this to you before, but you so remind me of your grandmother, Isabeau."

I smiled back at him, a little sadly. "I wish I could've met her." I paused for a moment to consider something, then returned my gaze to him. "Jax . . . I know you haven't been separated from Gemma since you've been mated. But were you ever apart from my grandmother for any length of time?"

Jax inhaled a deep breath as his eyes seemed to glance off into the distance. "A couple of times."

"Did you miss her when you were gone?"

"Of course," came his quick response. "When you find the person you want to spend the rest of your life with, it is difficult to be separated from them for any length of time." He frowned down at me then, as if a thought had just occurred to him. "Are you asking because you believe Caleb does not miss you?"

"No. It's nothing like that," I replied, playing with the edges of my shirt between my fingers. "Some days I think I miss *him* too much. You know, like . . . more than what's healthy. I wonder if it's a bad thing that he is such a big part of my life. Maybe I should figure out what I want to do with the rest of my life. Like finish school, or maybe get a job—"

I was interrupted by a sound rarely heard around the tree house—the distant ringing of a cell phone. *My* cell phone to be exact, which was probably a good thing, because it looked like Jax was about to disapprove of the job suggestion on many different levels. Why I was surprised I didn't know. Both Jax and Caleb were notoriously against any decisions that were a risk they deemed unnecessary. "Better get that," I said, jumping to my feet, knowing it was probably Maya or Lucas calling from The Oracle, since it was a Brethren provided cell phone.

As I raced back into our room I heard Jax's trailing voice say, "We will finish this *job* discussion later." *Oh, yeah*, he definitely had an opinion about the job.

Several more rings sounded while I searched through a pile of clothing on top of the built-in dresser in my walk-in closet. "There you are," I mumbled, sliding my thumb over the touch screen to answer the call. "Hello?"

I had barely gotten the word out before a gruff voice came back at me on the other end of the line. "What the hell took you so long to answer?" Lucas grumbled, though I could hear the underlying amusement in his voice. "This could have been and emergency."

Lucas Rayner was the current Brethren Guardian assigned to me by my former Guardian, Alec Lambert, after he became the Elder in charge of The Oracle. A Guardian was basically what the name implied. They were to look after me—which meant checking in regularly—making sure Caleb and Jax were doing their job and keeping me safe from the vampires drawn to me. And he could be just as over-concerned and over-protective as Caleb, Jax or Alec ever were. I suspected that's why Alec chose him. "Well . . . is it an emergency?"

"No," he said flatly. "I said it *could* be an emergency."

At that I rolled my eyes with an exaggerated sigh. "Let me guess . . . Alec wants you to check in on me."

"Alec, I'm sure, will be interested to hear how things are going," he began almost coyly. "But actually I was just checking in myself."

"Everything's fine," I replied, carefully leaving out the important detail that Caleb was off hunting Davin instead of being here guarding me. Lucas and The Brethren were a little particular on those sorts of details, since I had chosen to live with Caleb and Jax and have them protect me instead of The Brethren. "I had a small skirmish a few weeks ago with some Dhampirs, but I took care of them."

"Lord, help me," he mumbled, "don't make me fucking have to go back and tell Alec that you had another *skirmish*. You know how he hates it when you try to downplay things with that word . . . if that even is a fucking word."

"It's a word, and I thought you were working on your cursing?"

"What?" he asked with genuine surprise, not really even noticing when he said a curse word anymore, he was so use to them. "What did I say?"

"Never mind," I sighed, hearing Maya's chirping voice in the background asking to speak with me.

"Just a second," Lucas grumbled at her before returning his attention to me. "I wanted to let you know that our tracking parties on Davin are picking up some abnormal movement. He's been covering a much larger territory the last couple of weeks —making fewer stops. Almost as if he's on the run. You wouldn't happen to know anything about that, would you?"

"Hmm," I replied coyly. "Let me check into it and get back to you."

"Olivia?" he questioned hard, and I thought I would have to confess what I knew, but I was saved at the last second by Maya, who must have grabbed the cell phone out of his hand.

"My turn," she declared.

"Women," Lucas could be heard muttering as his voice trailed off in the background.

"Olivia?" Maya cheered.

"Maya! It's so good to hear from you."

"You, too. I wanted to let you know I'm going to Victoria next month to visit my aunt. I'd like to come down afterwards and see you, if you're not busy."

"I'd love that! Of course," I cried. "Maybe I can bring you up the mountain so you can see the tree house. You'd love this place."

"Oh, that sounds like fun! And I have so much to update you on regarding me and Phin."

"I hope things are still going well," I said although I could tell that they were by the happy tone of her voice.

"They are," she said, practically beaming through the phone line, "but I'll fill you in on all that when I see you."

"Sounds good. I'll see you then."

✱✱✱

The next morning I was startled out of my sleep by the fierce cries of baby Sophie. There was an urgency to her outbursts that seemed to rattle through the entire house. Jumping from my bed, I grabbed my silk robe and headed straight for Jax and Gemma's room. "Come in," Gemma replied frantically to my knocking. She was pacing the room, with Sophie screaming over her shoulder, and no amount of cooing or rocking seemed to help. "I'm sorry she woke you," Gemma sighed.

"Is everything all right?"

"I'm not sure. She slept soundly, and I just changed her. I even offered her a bottle, but she won't take it."

"Where's Jax?" I asked. "He can feel what's wrong."

Gemma's expression seemed to freeze for a moment. "He left about an hour ago to check on a Rogue that was passing through."

"Why do you look so worried?" I questioned, seeing her crinkled brow.

"I can't sense him," she said with complete focus on her expression. "He's gone out of my range."

A jolt shot through my heart. "Gemma, the sun's going to be up shortly."

"I know," she replied, calmly, going to her dresser to grab a tee shirt and pair of jeans while holding Sophie in her other arm. "It's all right. He knows how to hide himself from the sun if he's caught in it." But I could hear the worry underneath her voice. She hadn't been convincing herself anymore than she was convincing me. "Will you stay with Sophie while I go out and find him?"

"No, I'm coming with you." Before she even had a chance to argue with me I rushed out of the room. "I'll get Andie," I called over my shoulder. "She can watch Sophie while we go look for him."

Both Gemma and I were dressed and downstairs ready to go in about two minutes. Andie was waiting at the glass doors, still in her robe and slippers as she took an even more upset Sophie from Gemma's arms. The little girl tried to grab onto her long, curly hair while Andie tried to coo and calm her, but the infant would have none of it.

After explaining to Andie how to activate the security lasers for the house, Gemma kissed her daughter on her forehead and glanced with some intensity back at Andie. "I want you to turn the security on after we leave, and keep all of it up until we return," she instructed.

"Gemma, what if something happens to you both? I won't be able to help you."

"It'll be fine, Andie. Even if something were to happen, Chay and Caleb will be able to sense it. They'll come back here. Please just keep my daughter safe."

"Of course," she replied. "Chay should have turned me before he left. Then I could be of more use to you both."

"Don't be ridiculous, Andie," Gemma scolded. "Turning doesn't work that way. You would be unrecognizable to those around you for weeks. Your only concern would be finding fresh blood." Even as Gemma said this, Sophie was screaming herself red, and I feared that this little girl somehow knew that her daddy was in trouble, which made knots begin to twist in my stomach. "We'll save the rest of this discussion for when we return," Gemma said, seeming to pick up on my very thought. "We have to go."

Dropping the thirty-foot drop to the forest floor below, Gemma and I waited only long enough to make sure Andie got the security up before we took off down the mountain. I glanced towards the eastern horizon line and knew that in a matter of minutes dawn would be cracking over the mountains, and might already be showing down at the lower elevations where we were headed. "Gemma?" I called.

"I know," she replied, continuing to run full speed even over the rough terrain. "He's going to be all right. He's had to deal with being trapped out in the sun before."

Of course, she was right. You didn't get to be a two-hundred-year-old vampire without knowing how to deal with some tight situations. "Did you sense which way he went this morning?"

She nodded. "Southwest, toward the plateau . . . This way," she said, making a slight turn and hurtling over some giant fallen pine trees directly in our way. A few minutes later we reached the high mountain meadow, but there was still no sign of him.

Gemma was now visibly worried as she quickly scanned every shades area in her vision. "It's all right, Gemma," I said. Just relax and try to sense him. He will be able to feel you are near and will reach out to you." She stopped long enough to focus, pouring every ounce of concentration into this one task. But she was his mate. She would be able to sense him more strongly than anyone else.

Suddenly her eyes popped open with a gasp. "He's down near the vehicles! *Oh. God,* that's still ten minutes away on foot," she cried.

"Let's go," I said, then rushed off at a Dhampir pace that, to a human, would appear more like flying. We were pushing our bodies to their absolute limits, not a word spoken between us as the sun began to crest over the horizon. When we finally broke through the tree line, deep, guttural cries of a man in terrible pain were heard a moment before we saw him. My breath drew in sharply as I came to a sudden stop and stared in disbelief at seeing Jax on his knees tied, to the base of a tree by layers of thick, silver chains.

"Jax!" Gemma cried as she rushed toward him.

The silver had weakened him terribly—to the point he was folded over on his knees against the ground, the sun now blaring straight at him. His skin was blackening so quickly, so deeply, that his flesh was starting to burn away. For a split second I was so choked by fear and shock, I seemed rooted in place. Someone had purposely done this to him!

Gemma, however, responded without hesitation. She was over him, covering him against the sun while frantically tearing at the silver bonds lashing his body to the tree. When I finally shook off my shock, I raced over to help pull the silver chains from around his neck. The amount of silver was so large it was burning my own hand as I tried to remove it.

"Get out of here!" Jax yelled in an unrecognizable, threaded rasp. Gemma ignored him, while his howls of pain continued to cut through the air, his skin now charred to the point his face was no longer recognizable.

Once she had him free of the trunk, he roughly pushed away from both of us and began crawling farther into the shaded area of the forest. "I said get away!" he snapped loudly, though he was so weak he could barely move.

"Jax?" Gemma whispered in astonishment as she watched him with tears filling her eyes. She was watching the man she loved, *her mate*, dying right in front of her. There was an almost desperate despair that washed over her expression. So it startled me when she blinked it all back and turned to me with absolute resolve in her eyes. "Stay back, Olivia," she commanded. "No matter what happens, you don't go near him! Understood?"

"Gemma, what're you—?"

But she never let me finish. She grabbed my hand and squeezed, her olive-colored eyes glistening with her unshed tears. "Tell him that I love him. That I've always loved him." Then, unbelievably, she lunged herself towards him.

Before I could even process what was happening, Gemma had dragged his enormous body deeper into the shade and curled herself around the front of him. Jax fought to push her back with what little strength he had left, but he couldn't. He simply had no strength left. His normally vivid blue eyes were now pale and held a rabid mix of anger and pain, but they still stood out dramatically against his fire-blackened skin.

Wrapping her arms around his wide shoulders, Gemma took in the fire raging against his body on her own skin. Dropping her head to his ear, she positioned her tender throat right at his fangs. "Take it, Jax!" she ordered as he shook violently against her body. He knew what she was trying to do and fought with everything he had inside him not to give in to the thirst ravaging his throat in that moment. "Do it!"

Suddenly he roared out in torturous rage and his mouth opened wide as his knife-like fangs snapped into her throat as quickly as a snake. He drank from her like a man starved, possessed—a man whose very life depended on it. Gemma held back her cries but clung to him rigidly as she just sat there and let him feed on the blood that would sustain him—save him. He clutched her so tightly in his grasp that I thought he would suffocate her right there in his arms.

"Jax!" I finally screamed, trying to fight off my own stunned disbelief at what was happening too quickly. "Stop! It's Gemma! You're going to kill her!" But Jax didn't hear me. He was too far gone in his rabid thirst.

Completely ignoring Gemma's warning to stay back, I ran to them, knowing I had to be quick or in Jax's uncontrolled state he would turn on me, as well. Dropping to my knees behind him, I clamped my finger over his charred temples and focused quickly, because if I didn't stop him soon he would drain Gemma of all of her blood.

When he didn't respond, I suddenly remembered that since we were related by blood my mirroring gift did not have the same effect on him, but I kept trying, refusing to give up. I had to make him *see* what he was doing.

I focused my touch on the fragile light inside him that the darkness was trying take over. Stretching my touch deeper, I pressed to make contact—to do anything to make him aware and come back to the present moment. And suddenly I felt him pause. "Jax! Look at what you're doing," I cried. "It's Gemma—your mate. Look at her!"

He stilled then, retracting his fangs from her throat, letting the unmoving woman slip in his arms a bit as he stared down at her in wide-eyed shock. Awareness dawned on him that this woman, who meant the entire world to him, lay motionless in his arms, and the knowledge appeared to rip a hole right through his horrified expression. Jax roared through the forest with such anguish as he hugged her to him that the branches in the trees around us seemed to shiver in response. He rocked Gemma back and forth in his arms. "Olivia, please . . . ," he rasped out in a voice that was not his own. "Get her back to the house. Secure her in the chilled room. She will need blood when she wakes—lots of it. You will not be able to go near her when that happens."

"But, Jax, I need to get you—"

"Go! Now!" he snapped angrily. "I will be fine."

I knew he was lying. I didn't have to have the ability to feel to know he was in great physical pain. Even under shade, if he stayed out here all day in the heat, as badly burned as he was . . . he would die.

Chapter Ten

I searched around us and then focused a little farther down the trail. "Wait right here," I said jumping to my feet. "I'll be right back."

As I raced down the trail I could hear Jax yelling behind me, "Olivia, get back here!" He didn't give a damn about his own life at the moment. All he cared about was getting Gemma back to the tree house as quickly as possible. But in less than a minute I had reached the vehicles parked in the landing below. Caleb had taken his X-Terra, but Jax's enormous metallic gray H2 Hummer was still there. Like all the vehicles, it was prepped with provisions for a vampire's survival, and most importantly it was unlocked . . . but I still needed keys to drive it.

I rushed over to a nearby grouping of rocks and dug at the secret spot that held the metal box with all the keys for the vehicles. Jax and Caleb believed in keeping an extra set of keys by the vehicles at all times, never knowing what the circumstances might force them to use them . . . and right now I was really glad they did.

Springing up into the high driver's seat, I jammed the key into the ignition, started up the engine and gunned the off-road vehicle wildly through tree limbs and rocky terrain until I reached Jax and Gemma. I kept the vehicle running so the air conditioning would keep it nice and cool, then grabbed two blankets from the back. The always-stocked ice chest was ready to go with several bags of blood, and the extra thick insulation made sure that ice could last up to six days at a time, which meant that Caleb and Jax didn't have to change it as often in the summertime. I made sure the lid was open and ready; Jax would need the blood.

"Olivia! Get over here—now!" Jax barked

I raced back to his side, his face so badly burned it was terrifying. He was nearly unrecognizable. There was no time to focus on that, however. Wrapping the blanket around Gemma,

I knew even in its infancy the virus working inside her made her more sensitive to the sun. She needed to be covered for the trip back up the mountain. Picking her up in my arms, I looked to Jax, intensely aware of how his blue eyes stood out from his charred face and stared back at me with a mix of anger, pain and fear. "Use the second blanket to get into the vehicle," I instructed. "It's cool, and the ice chest is open."

"Just go!" he snapped. "I will be fine."

"I'll come back down—"

"No! You stay with her," he replied sharply. "No matter what! Do you understand?"

"But Jax, you're so badly burned . . . you can barely walk."

"Go, Granddaughter! I will meet you back up at the house tonight."

I turned away from him, not at all convinced he could get himself back, but I headed up the hill, regardless, with Gemma in my arms. I tried not to think how I just left my only biological family stranded down by a car to possibly die.

It took about forty-five minutes before I was standing at the base of the tree house. This would take some doing to get her up the thirty feet. I was not able to make the jump on my own like the others without a middle perch. And right now I could really use Gemma's gift to levitate.

After flipping the secret switch to lower the lasers from below, I got a running start and lunged with great effort to the middle perch, barely making it. From there I could hear Sophie's hard wails above me, and I knew the baby girl understood on some level that both of her parents were in serious trouble. With another huge jump that took all the remaining energy out of me, I landed just inside the glass doors and found Andie waiting for me with Sophie in her arms. Wordlessly, she asked with her wide brown eyes, "What happened?" as she gently bounced the crying girl in her arms. "Where's Jax?"

"He's still down the mountain, but he's under cover. He's safe for now."

"But the heat—"

"Gemma's been bitten," I interjected, as if to emphasize that we did not have time for a discussion on what had just happened. And I definitely didn't want point out that Jax was the one who had bitten her. "I need to get her downstairs."

Andie seemed to accept that—more than likely putting two and two together—and she was smart enough to understand that now was not the time for questions. "Let me put Sophie down and I'll help you," she offered.

Fiercely, I shook my head at her. "You can't. You're human. If Gemma wakes while I'm getting her settled she will attack, and more than likely she'll go for the weaker one of us."

She blinked back at me as if surprised by what I had just said, and while still trying to calm Sophie, who was still crying. "I'm going to be *turned* anyway—"

"No!" I cut off sharply. "As far as I'm concerned, the only person you will be turned by is Chay. There is no way I'll let it happen like this. There would be no guarantee I could stop her once she's started drinking from you." I didn't actually wait for her to respond and headed for Caleb and Jax's chilled room beneath the kitchen.

"But what about you?" Andie said, following me. "She can attack you, as well. There's no way Caleb would want you taking a chance like this."

"I'm the only one who *can* do this," I replied, gently lowering Gemma's limp form to the kitchen floor while I lifted the heavy door to the dark, refrigerated room below. "Stay with Sophie. Try to keep her as calm as you can."

"She hasn't stopped crying since you both left this morning. It's weird. It's like she knows something has happened to both of them."

"I think she does," I replied just before jumping down into the dark room with Gemma. Placing her on one of the two metal tables that were topped with white cushions, I removed the blanket from around her and brushed my hand over her face. She appeared cold, frozen, her olive-colored eyes unblinking, and yet, somehow, they showed just the slightest sense of life. "I know you can hear me," I whispered. "Caleb said he could hear everything that was going on around him when . . ."

Suddenly, I lost the words. "Oh, Gemma . . . that was an incredibly brave thing you did to save Jax. I wish you were not lying here like this, but thank you for saving him." Grabbing some blood containers from the refrigeration unit there in the room, I set them on the other bed, close beside her. "I just realized I don't know if it's still too cold for you down here. I wish Caleb or Jax were here to tell me how to do this right. I will stay with you as long as I can. Caleb said it took twenty-four hours for the virus to work through his system."

Several tears welled up in my eyes and I quickly swiped the wetness away with my hand. "I don't want you to worry about anything. We'll take care of Sophie and Jax. The burns will heal and he'll be as good as new—I promise. I just want you to think about getting through this. Your beautiful little girl needs her mother."

I stayed with her like that for most of the day, checking her regularly to make sure she did not feel too cold, and talking to her so she wouldn't feel alone. I knew from what Caleb had told me that she would be in an incredible amount of pain as the virus transitioned her to full vampire. I could only pray that because she was already half vampire that the transition would not be as painful as it was for a human. But her life would never be the same. Jax knew that the second he pulled his fangs from her delicate throat. Which begged the question: even if they both survived this, would Jax ever forgive himself?

Long after midnight, when I finally felt it was too risky to stay with Gemma any longer, I closed and locked her down in the pantry and then went to check on Andie and the baby. Sophie had finally cried herself into complete exhaustion and was sleeping. "You haven't eaten all day," Andie noted, clearly worried. "I'm making you a sandwich."

I shook my head with a tight-lipped smile in reply. "I'm not hungry."

"You are going to need your strength if we're going to get through this," she reminded gently. "Gemma and Jax are counting on us right now."

"You're right," I sighed, rubbing my hand through my dirty, bloody hair. "I'll go downstairs and grab something after I take a quick shower. And I want you and the baby to sleep up in my room tonight. I need to make sure you both are kept as far away from Gemma as possible."

"Surely Jax will return soon to help," Andie said, with surprise and concern in her voice.

"I'm sure he will," I replied, not knowing if that was even close to the truth. I had seen the look on Jax's face once he realized what he had done. He looked like a man who had seen the devil. Only this time, the devil was him.

***

After a warm shower and some hearty food I was still unable to sleep. It was nearly dawn and Jax had not returned. I worried endlessly that his injuries may have been too severe for him to survive in the back of a tinted-windowed vehicle with a few bags of blood in an ice chest. He had promised to return tonight, but could his absence into the wee hours of the morning also mean he didn't want to come home to face what he had done?

Sprawled over the downstairs sofa while Andie and Sophie were sleeping in our upstairs bedroom, I listened for the slightest sounds of stirring from the pantry below. The virus would soon be complete, so Gemma would be coming out of her motionless, pain-filled hell at any time.

God, how had this day gone so wrong? I kept praying that we could take it back and start over again. I wished Caleb were here to reassure me that everything was going to be all right. Of course, he would be devastated to learn what had happened to his family—to the woman as close to him as a sister, and the even worse devastation it would certainly bring to the man responsible for turning her, a man who was like a brother to him. I wondered if Caleb had already sensed yet that something was terribly wrong.

I decided I wanted to try to connect with him so he would feel what had happened and come home. But then, within the deathly silence of the house, I heard heavy breathing right above me. A chill shot down my spine as I glanced up to see Gemma standing over me, her skin pale and her coal black eyes appearing almost feral in their thirst. And her scream was grating in my ears as she lunged for me.

Chapter Eleven

From the force Gemma used to crush me into the sofa cushions it was clear she was fully in the clutches of her now *dark half* and had no intention of letting me out of her grasp anytime soon. Her eyes, normally a rich and lusty shade of green, were coal black and utterly detached from any emotion or awareness of what she was doing. Typical of any new vampire, her thirst came first and I happened to be the closest person around to satisfy it.

I was able to hold her off of me for the first few seconds but was soon losing my tenuous grip as she continued to push down against me with an almost desperate need to sink her teeth into my throat. The adrenaline was pumping so fast into my system that Gemma was catching my responding scent, and it was causing her to frenzy above me.

"Gemma! It's me . . . Olivia!" I squealed as my arms finally started to give way and she fell forward towards me.

I closed my eyes, certain I would feel the cold slice of her fangs into my neck, but instead I felt her weight instantly being lifted from me. When I opened my eyes again, I blinked at seeing a still severely burned Jax holding Gemma back from me with her arms pinned to each of her sides. Gemma always appeared tiny next to Jax's stout form, but now it was magnified as he hugged her in a tight embrace that had him fighting off clear and painful emotion on his face. "It is all right, Gemma," he murmured quietly in her ear as she fought wildly against him. "I understand the pain you feel in your thirst. I will help you feed it." He then glanced at me sharply, a fierce glare that ordered me not to question him. "Go upstairs to your room —now. And do not come out until I tell you. Keep Sophie with you."

Of course, I was never very good at following orders. "But I want to help—"

"Now!" he snapped, and this time the dark tone of his voice

kicked me into high gear. I ran around the corner and sprung to the second floor ledge. Once inside Caleb's study, I remembered that Andie and the baby were already upstairs, asleep in our room. So I curled myself on the leather sofa and let myself give into the tears that were rushing into my eyes. "Tomorrow will be a better day," I whispered to myself.

Because it had to be.

***

A few hours later I woke to the startling sounds of crashing objects, loud guttural roars of anger, and high-pitched crying. Normally, any one of these would be enough to bring me right out of a sound sleep, but all three combined nearly jolted me from the sofa. Andie was at the top of the stairs above me, trying to calm a screaming Sophie down, her eyes focused on the wall across from us that separated Caleb and Jax's studies —the direction the loud crashing noises were coming from.

"Stay up there with Sophie," I said as I turned back to her.

A worried looked tugged at her brows. "You can't go in there right now. He's too upset."

"I'll be fine. He won't hurt me," I replied, hoping I was right about that.

When I opened the door to Jax's room, I sucked in a quick breath at the chaos he had inflicted on his normally meticulously organized study. Another loud crash signaled the impact of a chair thrown against the wall, shattering several picture frames into nothing more than shards of glass. The room appeared completely destroyed—as though a tornado had blown through it. There were only one or two pieces of furniture left undamaged. Books and endless numbers of their torn pages were sprayed all over, and every photo and memorabilia item from his long life had been stripped from their rightful place and smashed against a wall or onto the floor.

His head snapped around toward me, enormous anger creasing his face. "I told you not to come out until I called for you!" he exploded.

"I'm not a servant for you to order around," I replied, shutting the door behind me. Though his badly charred skin made it difficult for me to face him unflinchingly, I did, standing my ground against this huge giant of a man. He was showing some signs of healing, but he was still barely recognizable and had to be in intense pain. But whatever pain he felt, it was nothing compared to the pain he was evidently experiencing on the inside. "I won't just stand by and watch while you destroy yourself. We all need to be strong for Gemma right now."

Jax let out another ear-splitting growl and sent a hardbound book slicing into the sheetrock on the other side of the room, where it stayed lodged in the wall. "*We* are not going to do anything. *You* are leaving."

"I think I made it clear . . . I'm not leaving this room—"

"Not only this room," he returned fiercely, " . . . this house!"

"W—what?" I stuttered back, believing I hadn't heard him correctly. "What're you talking about? This is my home. I'm not going anywhere."

"Oh yes you are, Granddaughter," he yelled, his anger so shocking I was literally stunned in place. "You are going back to Seattle—today!"

I could feel the anger gripping at me. This had nothing to do with me and *everything* to do with him trying to accept what he had done to Gemma. "That's not your decision to make."

He was inches from my face in an instant. Using the mass of his muscled body to loom over me with intimidation, his eyes widened in anger while intense heat radiated from his skin like the sun. "You do not get it, do you? You were this close to ending up just like her," he snarled, pointing his finger downstairs toward where Gemma had once again been locked up. "For a moment there I wanted your blood so badly, I did not give a damn about the fact that you were my granddaughter."

He then whirled around on his feet as if he could no longer stand to look at me, while I just stood there, completely speechless. My heart felt as though it had just been crushed inside a meat grinder.

"Gemma . . . ," he continued, " . . . my own g*oddamn* mate came second to my thirst."

I blinked instinctively at hearing Jax utter this curse. No matter how upset I'd seen him in the past, he had *never* cursed.

"I attacked her and drank from her like the *sick monster* that I am—with no regard for the fact that I almost *killed* her."

"That's not true!" I came back at him once I had found my voice again. "You didn't attack her. You tried to push yourself away. Gemma is the one who pushed you to drink from her. She made the decision. She knew it could save you, and she knew what she was doing."

I stepped close to his rigid back, feeling the heat and anger radiating from him. "And she did it because she loves you. You were dying, and she simply refused to stand by and watch it happen when she knew there was a way to save you. I would've done exactly the same thing if Caleb—"

"Do not dare finish that sentence!" he warned, swinging around on his feet. "Do you think Caleb would ever want that? It would destroy him to have to live with that."

"But we're not talking about Caleb, are we? *You're* the one who believes he can't live with what he's done. But you can!"

Jax whirled back around, shoving the only remaining intact chair into the wall then coming right back with a sharp finger pointed in my face. He was so large, so imposing, that I should have been completely terrified of him, but I wasn't. I was scared *for* him—scared of losing the grandfather I had grown so close to. "It is not a matter of *if*," he growled out, "but *when* one of us turns you. We may like to walk around under the clouds and pretend there is some humanity left in us—that we are better than the Davin's of the world—but we are not. What happened yesterday proved that. And I will damn myself to the fires of hell before I watch it happen to my granddaughter. Isabeau would never forgive me."

"Well, you're going to have to find a way to deal with it because I'm not leav—"

Without warning Jax grabbed me at my shoulders and shook me, as if wanting me to see reason. Just when I was about to push him off me, the door blew open behind us, and before I knew it Caleb had shoved his tall body between us, the veins literally bulging from his neck as he pushed Jax back from me. "Back off!" he warned.

I tried to move around Caleb, but he held me behind him with his arm until Jax took a small but distinct step back. Still,

I could see Caleb trying to process the destruction to the room and the fact that the man as close to him as a brother was burned almost beyond recognition. He then turned to me, his mouth crackling dry and his gaze unblinking as he asked, "Are you all right?"

I nodded silently in reply, hugging my arms around him as I lay my cheek against his chest, so grateful that he was home.

"What has happened, brother?" Chay asked as he stepped towards Jax.

Jax remained silent, unable to verbalize what he had done to these two men he respected above all others . . . but he didn't have to. Caleb's shoulders stiffened and I glanced up at him to see his face frozen in disbelief. It was as if the air had stopped moving in his lungs and I knew at that moment he was *feeling* Gemma. His fingertips gently reached to stroke over my temple as he gazed back at me with such a bottomless sadness. "Wait for me in our room," he said. When I moved my lips to challenge him, he placed his thumb over my mouth to stop me. "Please," he added gently as he bent down to kiss the top of my head.

I nodded, taking one last look at Jax before leaving the room and closing the door behind me. He looked totally abject and completely defeated. He knew he would have to confess everything about what had happened, and the dread I saw so plainly in his eyes pulled at my own guts.

Returning to our room, I saw Andie had eventually been able to get Sophie back to sleep, and now she seemed anxious, wanting to see Chay. Though she hadn't showed it until now, I knew she had been scared by all the events of the last twenty-four hours . . . and I couldn't blame her. She was human, utterly defenseless, and unable to leave of her own accord from the trappings of our thirty-foot-high tree house.

"The answer is no," she said, and I stared at her blankly. " . . . To your next question. No, I've not changed my mind about Chay turning me."

I nearly laughed in response even though it definitely was not a time for humor, nor did she mean anything funny by her heartfelt statement. But I had been thinking exactly that a moment before. "I would have done the same thing were I in

Gemma's shoes," she continued, "if it had been Chay burning in the sun."

I nodded in agreement but kept the words to myself, realizing they would easily be overheard.

For the next hour I listened from the other room as Jax explained how he had been ambushed by four of what he suspected were Davin's soldiers. He had fought them off for a time, but ultimately he was overrun and left tied to a tree with silver to burn to death, as we found him. Self-loathing and shamed anger vibrated in his voice as he reluctantly recited the account of what happened when Gemma and I reached the plateau. An unnatural silence permeated the room, and I knew that couldn't be good . . . and it only got worse. Jax went on to explain that when he reached the house a few minutes before dawn this morning Gemma had me beneath her and was about to sink her fangs into my throat—which was definitely not helpful *at all* in keeping Caleb calm. "Damn it!" Caleb responded in a low, guttural curse. "Did Gem hurt her?"

"Not this time. But there are no guarantees next time. You know that. You know she cannot stay here, Caleb," Jax continued, and there was no question he was talking about me. "Not while Gemma is transitioning. It will be only a matter of time—"

"She's my mate, Jax!" Caleb returned sharply. "Her place is with me. Exactly what are you asking me to do?"

"I am asking you to put my granddaughter's safety first. How will you feel on the day you find yourself in my place," Jax challenged, " . . . when you must live with the guilt of knowing you could have prevented what happened if you had only chosen differently?"

"It is not that simple," Chay interjected calmly, "In this immortal world it is rare to find true love with a woman. More often than not, the connections we make are those of animals. It is about blood thirst and lust—not love. You and Caleb have found love with two extraordinary women. Do not ask him, or yourself, to forsake that. Gemma loves you. She will remember that love and hold onto it. And she will return to you once she has finished her transition."

"And what am I supposed to do when that day comes?" Jax

bit back. "Just pretend that everything is normal? That *I* was not the one responsible for stripping her of her humanness?"

"You accept her love," Chay pressed, "and you let it heal the pain of this day."

Jax growled irritably in reply. "I no longer deserve her love . . . or her forgiveness."

There was a long silence in the room before Caleb finally spoke up. "Jax, you are upset right now. You're not thinking clearly. Give yourself some time to heal and accept this."

"He is right, my brother," Chay added. "Gemma was prepared for the consequences when she made the decision to offer her blood to you."

"You need that to be true. Right, Chay?" Jax snarled. "You need to justify in your own mind what you will soon be taking away from Andie."

"Andie and I are at peace with our decision," Chay responded in a harsher voice. "She will be my mate and we will be together. It was not a decision either of us made lightly. And I will let no man—not even you, my longtime friend—interfere with that. You forget I have lived much longer than you. I know what I am speaking of when I say that you cannot deny yourself love in this life."

"Fine. Do what you wish. But I will not stand by and watch this happen to Olivia—my granddaughter."

"And you think I will?" Caleb questioned sharply. "You think I've not had nightmares about this very thing? Cause I assure you I have. But in the end I know I love her too much to ever hurt her like that."

Jax snorted in disbelief. "*Love* did not stop me when I needed Gemma's blood to survive yesterday. In fact, Olivia stood before me in this very room and told me she would have done the same for you. If you think this choice is yours then you are a fool . . . just like me."

Hearing Caleb defend me to Jax made me feel better, but I was still worried. I understood why Jax was so scared for me, but I was not about to leave my family or my home. I was just grateful that Caleb agreed with me. But their arguing continued for what seemed like hours. After a while, an exhausted Andie was taking advantage Sophie's rest period by catching a little sleep of her own, while I went to the greenhouse for a quiet place to think. Jax wanting me to leave here had been upsetting, even though I knew he was only trying to protect me. When would he learn—there's protecting the people you love, and then there's trying to control fate? In my short life I had already learned that fate usually won that battle. *Did I want Gemma to be a vampire?* No. But fate had different plans. And Gemma had made a decision. I knew her. She would live by that decision if it meant she could still be with Jax, and she would not look back.

Caleb was right. Jax just needed to give himself time to heal and think more rationally.

I was so sharply focused on my thoughts that I didn't even realize Caleb had entered the greenhouse. The sky was finally overcast enough for him to be outside, and I could see in his relaxed demeanor that he loved every second of it. There was always an easiness about him when he could spend time outdoors versus being trapped behind walls of separation from the natural environment. His connection to the nature around him, how he used it in his architectural designs, was one of the things I loved most about him.

Wrapping his arms around my waist and curling his shoulders into mine, he closed his hands over my own. It felt wonderful to be alone with him like this in the quiet, after missing him for two weeks. He nuzzled his stubbly cheek against my neck and inhaled the scent of my hair. "It feels good to be holding my sweet beauty again," he smiled against my skin. "I have missed you."

"I missed you, too," I replied, allowing my head to drop back against his chest and sinking into his embrace. "Is it wrong that I want to keep you here, all to myself?"

"That day will be here soon."

"I hope so . . ."

I could hear his deeper breaths at my neck, sensed the peace within him as he breathed out with a long sigh. "You know . . . challenging Jax when he's upset like that may not have been the smartest idea. He didn't have control of his anger just then."

"Well, somebody has to," I practically snorted. "The man is more stubborn than a mule."

"Yes, and I'm starting to think it runs in the family," he laughed quietly, a not-so-subtle reference to my own tendency toward stubbornness at times—though I was pretty well convinced that mine was all warranted.

"He's hurting himself more than anyone, you know."

"Yes, he is. Chay's still trying to talk some sense into him. But Jax can be particularly ornery when he's trying to punish himself . . . as if the world has not punished him enough already."

"Did you go see Gemma?" Caleb nodded silently over my shoulder, and there was plenty of pain to be interpreted in that silence. Gemma was as close to him as a sister. I knew what she was going through had to weigh on him heavily. I was hoping he might talk about it; instead, he remained silent.

"She did it to save him, you know." I crossed his hands around me even tighter, so that his arms could brace me with his strength. "You've seen him. He's so badly burned. He would've died, and Gemma knew that. No one could have expected her to just stand by and watch it happen."

"It's going to be OK," he whispered, pressing several sweet, tender kisses on my neck while his fingers deftly slid my sundress and bra strap over the edge of my shoulder, where it fell slack on my arm. That allowed him to kiss lower over the fleshy part of my neck and follow the line of my shoulder outward, then still lower, his tongue teasing over my collarbone. *God*, his tongue was magic. "He's weak, though," his deep voice murmured. "I can feel it in him. He needs to be regenerating downstairs, but I don't think he can bring himself to face her."

"He will—you'll see." I was trying to reassure myself as much as Caleb. "I know Gemma. She loves him too much. She would want to be with him, even like this, if the other choice was to be without him. Any woman in her shoes would."

My subtext had not been subtle. It was obvious we were no longer talking only about Gemma and Jax. There was nothing but silence between us for a long while, and I worried what he might be thinking, so I changed the subject. "So how did your search for Davin go with your ex-mate?" I hated how the tone of my voice lifted on the word 'mate,' betraying the forced casualness of my effort. A low chuckle rumbled from him across my freshly kissed skin. "What?" I questioned.

"Oh, nothing," he said as his voice drifted off. "It's just that my *one and only* mate is pretty adorable when she's trying to pretend that she's not jealous."

"*Jealous?* I don't think so. Curious maybe . . ." But then, of course, I couldn't help but ask, "Did you give me a reason to be jealous?"

He pressed his body forward, pinning me against the edge of the work table as his erection swelled against my low back, his fingers lightly massaging over my hips through the thin material of my dress. It was definitely clear how Caleb Wolfe intended to spend the afternoon. "None," he replied, as his hands bunched the thin fabric up in his fingers and he pulled the dress higher on my legs. "But God, I've missed you."

"Are you saying, then, that she didn't try to seduce you?"

"Oh, she tried," he almost laughed. "She just didn't succeed. There is only one woman I have thought about—one woman I want. And I intend to prove that, right now."

"Really? Sounds fun," I teased him, though still stuck on the previous subject. "But I don't trust that this isn't all some kind of game to Celeste. I'm starting to think—being six hundred years old—she's bored with life and likes to play games just to see how miserable she can make other people."

"That does sound like her," he readily agreed, his voice light and playful.

"Do you really believe she knows where Davin is?" I asked in all seriousness, but at the moment, Caleb seemed distracted and more interested in fiddling with my clothing than answering my question.

"You know, I may be giving summer a bad rap," he suddenly said.

"What?" I replied to the random change of subject.

"These little sun dresses of yours are going to drive me insane."

"Oh, so you likey," I laughed.

His hand slipped under the pretty floral fabric and gently began to tease back and forth across the lacy lingerie beneath his fingers. Back and forth, back and forth, the thoroughness of his strokes dizzying to the point I had to brace myself against my hands on the table. "Mmm-hmm," he murmured. "I like very much." Laying my head back against his shoulder, I moaned softly as his fingers began to caress their way lower over the delicate fabric, stroking with such gentleness that I could feel the tingling begin throughout my stomach. Then, without warning, he playfully he flipped up the edge of my dress to my surprised squeak, causing a rush of air to hit my thighs before letting the dress fall back down into place. "Is that red lace you're wearing under there?"

"I know what you're doing," I smiled. "You're trying to distract me from the subject of Celeste."

"Not at all," he insisted. "The color of your underwear is vitally important to my concentration at this moment."

"Caleb . . ."

His chuckle was deep, more like a purr. "I thought the same thing about Celeste after her little stunt here. But we're both wrong. She led us to two of Davin's current sites. With her help we were able to take out several of his soldiers."

"And then you felt what had happened here?"

"Yes," he breathed a little rougher. "I got back here as quickly as I could." I sighed then as his hand slipped beneath the stretchy lace and moved tenderly along my skin until I felt his long fingers slowly sink into the warm, wet flesh that was waiting for him, all for him. Carefully, deliberately, expertly, he stroked, and I suddenly felt as if I had been catapulted into heaven. How had I made it a day, let alone *two weeks*, without feeling his touch? Longer than that, when I thought about how Celeste had kept interrupting us those last few days before he left. I moaned in response to his stroking fingers, arching my back and sighing in pure contentment. "Feel how wet you are. My sweet has missed me, haven't you?"

"Maybe a little," I replied with a strange lift to my voice as I came up on my tippy-toes. My palms went flat on the table to brace me against all of the wild sensations that were rolling through me at the moment as his fingers began to circle, faster and faster. "Caleb, please . . ."

"Just a little, huh?" he questioned right there above my ear. "So you didn't miss feeling my body beside you as you slept?"

OK, he wasn't playing fair. He knew I didn't sleep as well when he wasn't beside me.

"You didn't miss the feeling of me being inside you? Maybe you thought of me just a little when you were composing some of that beautiful music of yours?"

"I did," I murmured softly. "I've some new music for you."

"Oh, sweet, I want to hear it," he breathed harder against my skin. "And I want to be inside you while you're playing it for me. The music feels good, doesn't it? Do you remember how it felt to have me inside you as you played?"

Remember it? The vibrations I experienced while the music channeled through his body was one of the greatest sexual experiences of my life. "You are definitely trying to distract me, Caleb Wolfe, and it's not fair," I sort of complained, but not really.

"Come here," he said roughly, lifting away from the table to turn me in his arms, then hoisted me up off my feet and onto the work bench. Before I could get past the sweeping dizziness of it all, he had my legs propped across the narrow greenhouse aisle against the other table behind us. I now caged his hips between my thighs as I prepared for him to take me. But instead he fell to his knees in front of me, his hands pushing my dress all the way up on my thighs. He stared back up at me with a boyishly devilish look in his eyes that made my breath seem to suddenly race out of control. "Brace your legs," he instructed.

"Caleb, Andie's just inside," I said with nothing but breath. She's human, you know. She doesn't have the great hearing to warn her that we might be fooling around in here."

The way Caleb disposed of what was left of my lace panties and cupped my hips firm in his large hands, I wondered whether he was even paying attention to what I was saying. He positioned his head between my thighs, his mouth so close I gasped at feeling his cool breaths tickle over my wet, aching flesh. "Not going to happen," he said.

"How do you know?"

"Because Chay missed his woman, as much as I did. My guess is she'll be occupied for some time, just like you'll be."

He then stopped talking.

At the first contact of his tongue on my flesh, I thought my hips were going to bolt right from the table. Caleb just laughed and hooked his arms around the outside of my thighs to keep me fixed in place. His eyes closed then and he seemed to relax, taking his fill of the sweet juices easing from my body for him. It was torture. It was heaven. It was out of control. And in the very moment when I thought I would die of ecstasy, he stalled, and then slid his tongue higher to swirl over the little knot that seemed to be the key to my very existence at that moment. I was gasping for breath and couldn't seem to hold onto the table hard enough with the little strength I had left in my fingers. "Keep your legs braced," he growled just before his fingers opened my flesh wider to him, allowing his tongue to work deeper. .

My legs were braced, all right, the muscles in my thighs tense as they stretched across the narrow aisle. I was coming apart at the seams, unable to believe how good he had gotten at controlling his vampire change—the warrior inside him that came with some very sharp fangs—long enough to bring me so close to pure ecstasy. In fact, if I didn't know any better, I'd say he intended to topple me right over. Almost there . . . almost there . . ."Caleb!" I squealed. "*Oh God*, please!"

Suddenly, he stopped, and a long rolling growl escaped him as he lifted his head from between my thighs. His eyes became the most brilliant blue, while long fangs lengthened and pushed at his lips. "Do you trust me," he asked, and I was amazed that I could understand English at the moment.

I blinked back at him, unsure what he was thinking. "Yes," was all I could manage to say.

My legs tightened as his head came forward slowly. His smoldering gaze remaining locked with mine just before his fingers parted my flesh and, *slowly*, his tongue slipped forward between those sharp fangs, the very tip swirling as if he were enjoying the sweetest honey. *Lord*, it was too much. The tip of his tongue was all it took. If his other arm hadn't been holding me down, my hips would have bounced right off the table like a soccer ball. I exploded in a sky of light and a sea of warmth, all at the same time. Powerful tingles shot out in all directions from the very spot where his tongue continued to move. I was floating, swaying, falling—unaware of how much time had passed when I finally sensed he had came to his feet once again and was tearing at the front of his jeans.

With one hand he pulled free the thick flesh that stood long and erect from his body, stroked over the length of it from base to tip and then lined himself up with my hips. "*God,* I've missed you," he said as his hands cupped under the curves of my bottom, protecting my soft skin from the splintered wood tabletop. I hadn't even had a chance to come down from my blissful high when I felt the heavy size of him part my flesh in one slow, deep push that filled me, then seemed to split me in half. All the breath left my lungs in an instant as my inner walls adjusted to accept his size. "Damn, you feel good. We're going to take this nice and slow . . . so slow," he breathed as his fingers gripped into my rounded bottom, angling me high against him so that I would have to take him deeper. "I want you screaming to the heavens."

Small sounds that I had never heard myself utter before left my throat in a sort of verbal plea. The muscles in my thighs and lower legs flexed as my toes curled deliciously over the edge of the work bench. Right then I really didn't care if someone walked in on us. Nothing was going to stop either one of us from reaching that climactic high that had been so long denied to us because of Celeste's interference. I grabbed onto his shoulders as he positioned me beneath him, continuing to work his body inside me. "That's it, just relax. You've got me now," he said, murmuring just above my lips, close enough to kiss me . . . but he didn't—no, couldn't—with his dangerous fangs.

He reared back then thrust forward, the motion so powerful it jolted me upward, the very breath in my lungs thrown with it. I dropped my head back and closed my eyes, the fresh garden scents of the greenhouse filling my senses as he fell into an even rhythm. My leg muscles tightened with each consecutive thrust, to the point that I feared I would kick the other work bench right through the back wall. "Caleb!"

He always knew how to please me, how to take my body to the highest point of pleasure. But then I had a strange thought. My mind jumped back to the words Celeste had taunted me with on the rock ledge. "*. . . I understand what he likes . . . the* *desires he does not speak of . . ."* Was Celeste right? Were there things Caleb wanted sexually that he had not told me about? Should I have asked? "Would it excite you, Caleb," I asked breathily over his ear, "if someone walked in on us? If they watched us?"

"*God, yes,*" he replied from some place very deep inside him. And if my body wasn't right at the edge of another cataclysmic explosion I would have taken time to digest what it all meant. Instead, my breath became trapped as my sharp nails dug into his shoulders and my inner muscles contracted over his flesh. My mind was preparing for another blistering explosion that would surely dissolve me into him. "Stay with me," he said as he brought my head up to face him. "Look right here—right into my eyes. Let me watch you as you come."

"I love you!" I squealed, my legs lifting from the bench to curl around his waist as the balls of my heels pressed into his low back. My body let go under a soundless scream. Huge waves of pleasure rolled through me like the pattern of the sea, one right after the other.

Caleb shuttered forward in his own release, his eyes never breaking contact with mine as I felt him explode inside me. He seemed to blink at the initial force of it, then he braced his hand against the work bench and came a second time.

For several moments I lay there like jelly, my every muscle slack with pleasure as I stared into his handsome face. His breathing slowed and his body relaxed, while his head dropped into the curve of my neck. "I love you, too, sweet," he murmured. "Only you . . ."

Chapter Twelve

Later that afternoon Caleb lay sprawled with me among the messy bed covers as I began to wake from a deep sleep, my eyes blinking up at him from the crook of his shoulder. He had carried me in from the greenhouse and made love to me a second time before I collapsed against his chest from exhaustion, the few hours of sleep I lost the night before having caught up with me. He brushed his finger over the tip of my nose with a smile. "You're finally awake. I thought for a minute there you might've slipped into a coma."

"No. Just a really good kind of exhaustion," I sighed happily.

He snuggled in closer. "Well I like to hear that."

"I'm sure you do," I smiled, then glanced around the quiet bedroom. "Where's Sophie?"

"She's in her crib in her room," he said, stroking his fingers through my hair. "Andie and Chay are watching her."

"We should go check on her," I said with a quick kiss to his cheek, then I rolled away from him to the other side of the bed. But he followed me and hooked his leg over mine, bringing me back and keeping me pinned to the bed beneath his long body.

"Are you worried about her?" he asked with a slight pull to his brows. "She's fine. She's sleeping right now."

"Aren't you?" I asked in reply. "The poor girl must miss Gemma and Jax terribly. Has he even been to see her yet?"

Caleb shook his head. "I don't think he will until he recovers from his burns. He doesn't want to frighten her. But even then . . . ," he began, seeming to be lost for a moment in his thoughts. "I'm not sure his current frame of mind would allow him."

Just then I reached for him, simply because I had to. I wrapped my arms around his neck and curled my head into his shoulder, holding on as if it would be the last time I could for a while. "Hey, what's this?" he asked, his embrace tightening around me. "What's wrong?"

"Will you be leaving again?"

"I'm not going anywhere," he assured me. "I have to help with Gem's transition. Jax is certainly in no condition to do it."

"What about your hunt for Davin?"

Caleb drew himself back, his hand stroking the side of my face. "My family needs me right now. That comes first." I was so relieved to hear him say the words that I literally felt myself sink into his chest. I wasn't sure how I would've felt if he had said he was leaving us again right now for this unrelenting quest he had undertaken to destroy Davin. "Celeste and her coven can continue to drive Davin north . . . away from here. Chay's coven is still with her, and he'll be returning to them soon. He'll update Celeste on what's happened."

"I'm sure she'll be thrilled," I half snorted. "She can't seduce you if you're here."

"And I know that just breaks your heart," he teased as he speared his fingers into my side to tickle me. I giggled out loudly, rolling away from him on the bed, only to have him follow and catch me in his grasp again.

As I stared up into his thoughtful gaze, I couldn't help but wonder how much time we had before he *would* eventually leave. "Gemma's transition . . . how long will it take?"

Caleb sighed as he shook his head and glanced distantly through the windows. "In some ways, the easy part is over, as crazy as that sounds after what she's been through with the virus. In the next couple of weeks she will be able to get past her painful thirst long enough to understand what has happened. With the females, the process is usually slower. It will probably take her at least a month—maybe more—to regain whatever parts of herself that will cross over. Until then she will be very dangerous—wild . . . completely driven by thirst. She'll not be in control. You need to stay away from that room. Understood?"

I remained quiet, my heart breaking trying to imagine what Gemma must be going through, and knowing there was nothing I could do nothing to help her. "Olivia?" Caleb pressed.

"I'll stay away. I don't want to do anything that will make it harder for her. But what about Jax? He was so insistent that I leave."

"I'll handle Jax," he assured, then lowered his head to bring his lips gently over mine. "I need you here with me."

"Really?" I smiled. "What *exactly* do you need me for?"

"Well definitely for more of what we did this afternoon," he teased with wagging brows. "And I'd love to hear the new music you composed."

"I think I can manage that," I said as my voice and smile faded slowly. Lying in bed with him like this was always so intimate, so perfect. I didn't want to sour the moment, but I very much had a question on my mind. "Caleb, now that I know you're going to be staying for a little while—that we will have more time to be together like this—well, there is something I want to ask you, something with regard to Celeste?"

"Am I going to regret saying yes to this?"

"No," I replied quietly. "I just hope you feel that you can be completely honest with me."

His dark brows pulled into a frown. "What are you talking about? Of course I can be honest with you."

"I . . ." I began slowly, not quite sure what was the right way to ask without sounding like an insecure idiot. "It's just that . . . she's lived for so long. She's had twelve mates . . . Well, twelve-and-a-half if she counts you."

"Olivia, why are we in bed together counting Celeste's ex-mates?"

I knew I must have had a pained but ridiculous look on my face. "I'm only pointing out that she has *a lot* of experience." *Could this be any more awkward?*

His hand curled forward several times as if calling for more information. "Yes . . . experience living, killing, turning . . ."

Nope. He wasn't going to make this easy for me. "Sexual experience," I clarified. "A lot of it . . . About five hundred and eighty years more of it, in fact. Experience that I don't have."

He was staring back at me then in almost stunned silence, as if he wasn't quite sure what to say in response to that. And that really wasn't making things any easier. "I'm saying," I continued on, "that you can be honest with me if you need something more . . . more from me."

When he still didn't say anything, I started to wish I could pull the whole question back, but I knew I couldn't because it was already out there. "What I'm trying to say—and not very well—is that I can learn—"

"Stop!" he said, placing his fingers over my lips. "Stop right there. Olivia, is this why you asked me if I wanted someone to watch us in the greenhouse while we made love?" I nodded my chin beneath his fingers, staring up at him completely unsure as to what he was going to say next. But instead he rolled over on the bed so his body was directly over me, his eyes projecting complete sincerity. "I want you to hear me on this," he began carefully. "Yes, I would find it erotic if someone watched us while we made love. But I would find making love to you on *bales of hay* erotic."

I frowned back at him. "Ouch, that doesn't sound comfortable at all."

"My point is," he continued, "it's about being with you—you and me. That's all we need. I want us to discover how to please each other—what we like and don't like—together. What you're comfortable with and what you're not comfortable with."

"Well, so far I've been very comfortable with everything."

He laughed. One of those laughs that you could tell caught him completely by surprise. Those were my favorite laughs from him. "I'm glad to hear that."

"But still . . . There must be other things you like."

"Olivia, are you asking me what my sexual fantasies are?"

I nodded quickly. "Yes. I guess I am."

Now he laughed fully, in that deep, masculine voice of his as he rolled me on the bed till I was lying atop his chest. He looked amazingly handsome, happy, his breaths relaxed as a mischievous smile curled his lips. "You know what my fantasy is? What I think about—dream about when I'm with you." I shook my head and held my breath. "To be able to kiss you as you come," he said. "To inhale your cries as you explode around me. To hold every part of you in that moment as you let go."

I was rather surprised at that answer. Kissing during orgasm seemed a simple enough thing for most couples when compared to the whole list of things we could be talking about when it came to sexual fantasies. But for a Dhampir and a vampire, it was nearly impossible. With his fangs in the heat of that moment it was altogether too dangerous to kiss me. If they broke my skin, caused it to bleed and mix with his saliva, it would begin the turning process for me. That was a risk that was unacceptable to Caleb. But his next words surprised me even more.

"I want to learn how to control my change so I can be completely with you in that moment. Just like a normal human man . . . instead of the monster."

"Caleb," I answered with feeling, stroking my palm over the rough bristle of his cheek. "You know that I love all of you, right? Both sides of you, equally? Your change doesn't matter to me."

A half-hearted smile crossed his lips. "I know," he replied. "But you asked me for my fantasy."

"Well, you've certainly been lasting longer—"

I stopped my clumsy words under a veil of complete mortification. "*Oh, God,* that didn't come out right at all! What I meant to say was that I've noticed you are controlling your change much longer than you used to be able to. Not anything else . . ." I felt my cheeks warming as I continued to fight my way out of the awkward moment. "What I mean is, I didn't know that the change . . . that moment . . . was something you could control."

I was surprised when I looked up again to see his shoulders shaking with hard laughter. Thank God he had a sense of humor about these things. Who else could be with a woman who put her foot in her mouth as often as I did? "It's not something I can control right now," he said, " . . . but I'm getting better. Jax has been teaching me how to focus my energy—how to relax, which can help me control when I change."

"So then Jax doesn't . . . ?"

Caleb shook his head then looked at me questioningly. "I guess I kind of assumed Gem might have mentioned something to you about this."

"No," I came back sourly. "She's obviously been holding out on me. How can she leave me in the dark about such important details? She needs to tell me these things." I then felt guilty about my self-centered babbling when I remembered what she was going through right now. I cleared my throat. "When she gets better, I mean."

"Well she may be holding back . . . *some details* . . . as you call it, because she is talking about your grandfather."

"That is true," I replied as I snuggled closer to him. "I'm excited for that day though . . . to be with you like that. But just know, whether its tomorrow or ten years from now, I can wait."

"Hopefully it won't be ten years," he laughed, leaning down to nibble playfully on my bottom lip, drawing it into his mouth. "But I do feel like I'm gaining more control. That's why I wanted to try a mini test-run there in the greenhouse."

My cheeks warmed again as I remembered panting from his tongue swirling on my clit, something that was also normally a no-no when we were both that close to exploding. "Uh, yes, that was quite nice," I replied with a smile. "I'm hoping we can do that again soon."

"Let's take things carefully," he laughed. "And until then I guess we'll just have to discover other fantasies. In fact . . . I think I'd like to do some more discovering right now."

"OK," I sighed dreamily.

***

A few days later, after I had finished playing for Caleb some new music I had composed, he left our room to go check on Gemma. In this initial week, he spent most evenings with her and made sure throughout the day that she had enough blood to feed her seemingly endless thirst, but it wasn't an easy task. Sadly, she had grown more violent, so Jax and Caleb refused to let me anywhere near her. As her mate, Jax should have been the one taking care of her, but he was still despondent, preferring that Caleb watch over her while he sat alone in his trashed study, the destruction in that room seeming to mirror his mood.

Jax's severe burns were healing but he was still punishing himself. There was no doubt about it. And with each day that went by Caleb was becoming increasingly worried about his coven leader. There was no question my grandfather had known heavy heartache in his life, but what happened with Gemma seemed to break his spirit in a way from which I worried he would never recover. It was as if he could no longer face the world around him. He couldn't look his little girl in the eye and hadn't even tried to hold her since that fateful morning. But there were many times I caught him watching her from a distance, and I could tell he longed to hold her, to rock her to sleep as he had many nights before things with Gemma had happened.

To make matters worse, Chay, the only other person besides Caleb who I thought stood any chance of reaching Jax, had left to take Andie to one of his homes outside of Victoria. Understandably, he believed that Andie would be safer there with the other women of his coven while he moved on to connect with the rest of his coven members and Celeste to let them know what was happening. That left me to be a poor substitute for Sophie's mother and father at the moment.

The infant struggled daily from missing both of her parents. In the short time she had been with them, she clearly knew who they were and was as attached to them as any baby could be. Often it was difficult for her to sleep. That just could not be good for the little girl, not to mention it seemed to affect her appetite. I did the best I could and celebrated on this morning when I finally was able to get her to close her eyes and nap soundly for a little while. It was also the perfect time to take advantage of getting some sleep myself.

At first, my dreams were restless, but eventually I settled into a calmer sleep once I felt Caleb curl behind me and pull me securely against his body. Some time later, however, I saw an image in my dream of Sophie crying. She was in a dark, scary place, wrapped tightly in several blankets, screaming at the top of her lungs. I went to reach for her, but I couldn't move. My hands felt trapped somehow, and I couldn't quite make sense of it through the darkness around me. I became anxious and fought harder to reach her. That's when a familiar voice invaded my dreams. "Olivia? Wake up, sweet."

"Sophie!" I cried, jolting up from the bed and away from Caleb.

"Shhh," he sounded, bringing me gently into his arms. "She's fine, everything's OK. You're just having a bad dream."

"I heard her crying," I murmured into his throat. "She was so scared."

"Sophie's sleeping peacefully. I can feel her. She's not upset."

He speared his fingers through my hair as he pulled back and palmed my cheek, his gray eyes staring into mine with obvious concern. "Why does the baby affect you so? Is it because you want to have a child of our own?"

Shaking my head, I replied, "I've accepted that we can't have a child. I simply want to protect her—help her through this until Gemma can be with her again."

He kissed me gently on my forehead. "Gemma will be with her again soon."

"Caleb . . ." I began carefully. "Gemma once told me that it's not in a female vampire's nature to be a mother. Will Gemma still *feel* connected to her daughter? I mean afterwards . . ."

I could see the hesitation in his eyes as he looked away for a moment then returned his gaze to me. "We'll have to see what parts of her nature she brings into this world. I'm hoping, since she was already half vampire—and a mother—that the changes will not be as significant." He drew in a deep sigh. "He hasn't said it, but I know Jax is hoping for that, as well."

"He's in so much pain," I replied sadly. "He won't talk to me. It's like every time he looks at me he remembers that horrible day."

"He loves you, Olivia. You're his granddaughter. He can't face what he's done right now, that's all."

"Will he ever forgive himself?"

"I don't know," Caleb replied. "I don't know if I ever would, had I done the same to you."

***

Several more days had passed and very little had changed. Gemma was suffering some of the worst bouts with her thirst. Her body naturally craved fresh human blood, rejecting the chilled packages of blood Caleb kept trying to force feed her. One encouraging sign, however, was that Jax had fully recovered from his burns and had been looking in on Gemma and Sophie more frequently, though remaining at a distance. It was, at least, something, but it made me sad because he obviously still didn't feel he had the right to be with them. Yet he had every right! He was their family and they needed him.

That night, I spent the evening in our room, composing at the piano. I had a playful little tune running through my head that I really had to get out on paper—something around an allegretto but with a slightly faster tempo—light and happy. As more notes came together, the developing melody brought a smile to my face, and that's when I knew . . . I called the piece Sophie's Lullaby. And I decided I would play it for her every night before bedtime to help guard her in her dreams while she slept. I just couldn't quite get the last two bars to come off as I wanted. It was important that they came off right. They couldn't leave the listener hanging, but rather they needed to bring with them a sense of finality, fulfillment, which I seemed to be struggling with.

While trying a couple of different combinations, I paused for a second, suddenly feeling the hair on the back of my neck stand up stock straight. A loud, shrill cry came from downstairs and rolled through the house like a cannonball, straight towards our room. I had only enough time to swing up from the piano bench and throw my arms out in front of me before Gemma slammed into me with the force of a Mack truck. Her coal-black eyes narrowed in rage, shoving me back against the sharp edge of the piano, where I heard ribs immediately crack under the pressure of being wedged between her and the upright piano being crunched against the unyielding wall.

Though struggling to breathe, I still had strength in my arms. If I could hold her in place long enough, I could try to calm her down with my gift of touch. In theory, her nature was still good, and this was certainly an excellent time to find out if I could reach the light inside her to calm her quickly.

But I didn't get a chance.

Gemma's slight weight was jerked away from me by Jax. Once free of her iron grip, my arms fell forward until they connected with the bench for support, unfortunately causing more jarring pressure against my ribs. Gasping several short breaths, I tried to relax, and that's when the gust of air hit me and Caleb was suddenly in front of me. "Olivia?" he questioned in just a breath as he carefully ran his hand along my side, knowing straight where to go because he could feel my pain.

"Hold still."

"Is she all right?" Jax asked while controlling a kicking and screaming Gemma in his oversized arms. She didn't look at all like herself. Large, dark shadows had appeared under her eyes and rabid anger seemed to swallow her whole expression.

Caleb pressed into my side where the ribs felt like they were on fire. I held back a painful cry in response, but he could *feel* when he reached the spot. "Damn it. She's fractured two ribs," Caleb replied. "I'll have to move her carefully."

"I warned you," Jax growled. "Gemma is drawn to her. It will only be a matter of time—"

"I'm all right," I interjected. "It's not like I haven't had broken ribs before," I added, referencing the first time Caleb brought me back to the tree house after the train crash.

"Take Gem downstairs!" Caleb snapped at Jax, and I blinked up at him, surprised by his sudden temper. Without another word, Jax left the room with Gemma while Caleb slowly led me over to our bed. He positioned me gently, placing a pillow under my head, then he sat beside me on the mattress and checked the ribs again. "Lie still," he said quietly. But there was something in his eyes . . . something had changed just that fast.

"Caleb . . . ?"

"We'll talk about this later."

Chapter Thirteen

Two more days had passed and Caleb and I still had not talked about what had happened. Chay and Andie had returned once Chay had sensed something was wrong, which was good because with me hauled up in bed with broken ribs, Caleb seemed to be taking care of everyone, including baby Sophie. Now that Andie was back, she could help.

Though I felt healed, Caleb did not want to hear me even utter the words that I was moving from our bed until he was convinced I was completely healed. That morning, I was walking around the room comfortably when both Caleb and Jax entered. I smiled up at them both. "I think I'm nearly good as new. I can help with Sophie again." But I could see from the stoic looks on their faces that they were not here to congratulate me on my speedy recovery.

"Take a seat," Caleb said, motioning towards the bed with his hand. I did just that while he pulled a chair in front of me, taking my hand while Jax stood behind him.

Something was terribly wrong. I could see it in both of their expressions. "Is everything OK with Gemma?"

"She's doing as well as can be expected. But we need to talk to you about what happened the other day." Caleb then seemed to struggle with his next words as his gray gaze moved away from me. "Gem could have killed you. She nearly did. I was a fool to think you'd be safe here with her drawn to your Charmer gifts as she is. I won't let her have the opportunity again."

I blinked back at him, completely stunned. "What're you saying?"

"I'm saying I need to take you someplace where I know you'll be safe."

"Y—you want me to leave here?" I replied with quiet disbelief. "Leave my home?" Caleb saw how upset I was and tried to reassure me by clutching his hand more tightly over mine. But that did little to soften the crushing blow he had dealt me, and I pulled my hand away from him.

He suddenly looked worried and then went into 'convincing mode.' "Just give us enough time to get Gemma through her transition and evaluate how strongly she will be drawn to your gifts. Now that she's a vampire, she'll have a much more difficult time controlling it."

I immediately came to my feet. "I can't believe this! You are my mate—my partner. You're supposed to want me with you."

"You know I want you with me," he suddenly gritted through his teeth. "And you will be. Jax and I will figure this out. We'll find a way to help Gemma with this and then bring you back here where you belong."

"And how long will that take? A month? Six months?"

Neither of them answered, and I realized it was because they didn't know the answer. Caleb and Jax were the only vampires who were not drawn to my gifts to some degree or another, since Caleb was my true love and Jax was my blood family. Being a Dhampir, Gemma had an easier time learning how to control her attraction to my gifts by never touching my skin. But now, with her full transition to vampire, that was all changing. Even Chay, a Daywalker for over three centuries, who prided himself on his great discipline and control, had to be reminded by Jax or Caleb when he was getting too close to me. There were some days I saw my gift as a curse, and this was definitely one of them.

"What about Sophie? It's also dangerous for her—"

"I agree," Jax replied evenly. "My daughter is entirely innocent of this mess I have created, yet she will pay the highest price. I have decided to keep her at the condo downtown with Andie for a while. Chay will get them both settled and then join back up with the tracking party."

Flabbergasted, I stared back at them hoping this was some kind of joke. "You want Sophie to stay with Andie? Then where am I staying?"

"I want you to stay at your condo," Caleb replied, trying once again to reach for my hand—but I wouldn't let him. "It's the only place where I know you will be safe. Davin can't get to you there. And I need to know you're someplace where he can't get to you, or I'll go insane."

I turned away from them both, my heart feeling as if it were being weighted down inside my chest with concrete. *Caleb was sending me away?* I swung around on them, unable to control the overwhelming sense of betrayal and anger I felt towards both men—but focusing only on one. "This is your doing!" I snapped at Jax with a sharp finger. "You don't want me here."

"I do not," he said, and the crushing of my heart was complete. "Not when it puts you in so much danger. This is about keeping you safe, Granddaughter. Nothing else."

"Bullshit!" I snapped back, trying to control the breaking in my voice that was threatening to pop with tears. "This is about you not being able to live with your guilt. Every time you look at me now that day replays in your head. I'm just a walking reminder of it, aren't I?"

Jax stared back at me in shocked silence.

"Olivia, this was not Jax's decision alone," Caleb started as he reached for me, but I pulled away from him, as well.

"Let go of me!" I snapped, feeling like I was going to explode within my own skin. "You think I'll be safer at my condo? What about Davin's Dhampir soldiers?"

"We've already figured that out," Caleb explained. "Chay, Celeste and the others are going to keep pushing Davin and his soldiers to the north for the next few weeks while we deal with Gem. If Chay feels they can take him out before I can join them, they will. Regardless, Davin and his army will be too busy fleeing to be tracking you. And he won't know where you are as long as you continue to wear the necklace."

I threw my hands up. "Are you kidding me? You think your *ex-mate* is going to lift one finger protect me? She wants me dead. How clueless are you both?"

"Celeste will not know you have left the house or our protection," Jax replied. "Only Chay will . . . and it will remain that way."

"Well, you've thought of everything, haven't you?" I snapped at Jax. "And you prefer Andie to take care of Sophie rather than me." That thought bothered me most of all. "I'm her family. Do you not trust me to take care of her?"

"Of course I trust you," Jax replied, " . . . but she has been upsetting you. And I believe you are holding something back about that day you touched her—"

"I would never hurt her!"

"We know that," Caleb replied quickly. "But are you going to stand there and tell us that you have no idea what has her so frightened? Because I think you do. I think you saw something in those images that frightened you, too."

"I told you, the images didn't make any sense."

"What were the images, Olivia? Let us determine if they make any sense."

My heart was thumping inside my throat. They were right and I knew it. Somewhere deep inside me I knew I didn't want to examine what I saw too closely, but I wasn't exactly sure why. "Get out!" I cried. "Get out, both of you!"

"Olivia . . ." Caleb again tried to reach for me, but I pushed him away.

"I'll leave in the morning. But get out of here this instant before I kick both of your over-protective asses!"

Caleb's eyes narrowed in a stern warning. "I'll give you some time. But I'll be back to discuss this with you when you're more rational."

"Don't bother!" I drew in a hard breath, drawing in my courage, as well. "You know . . . I'm not that scared woman anymore you saved that night of the train crash . . . the one who didn't understand who or what she was. I've grown—changed. I know how to protect myself. But you both keep treating me like I'm some defenseless kitten that you need to hide away every time it gets dangerous."

"For the love of God, Olivia," Caleb said with exasperation, "Gemma nearly killed you. She would have, if we hadn't of stopped her."

"No, she wouldn't! I would've gotten out of it! And I would've done it without hurting her. You are my mate. You're supposed to have faith in me. You're supposed to stand by me." Then I turned to Jax, the anger seeming to pour out of me with each passing second. "And you should know better. Did you not learn anything from Isabeau and Eve?" Jax suddenly looked as if I had cut through him with a sword. I knew better than to use the loss of my grandmother and mother against him, but I was so angry, even that taboo subject didn't stop me. "You never had the chance to know my mother. She was stolen from you. But you have the chance to be with me—to get to know me—to love *me* . . . but you are sending me away. You are a two-hundred-plus-year-old vampire and still you have not learned that you can't control fate—mine or anybody else's!"

"That's enough, Olivia!" Caleb warned. "Jax and I are doing the best we can, given the situation. We are trying to keep you safe—because we *both* love you. You're going to have to find a way to deal with that."

Caleb then pushed a still stunned Jax towards the door, but Jax swung around, the normally proud, handsome set of his face distorted by a quiet sadness. "I love you, Granddaughter. Do not ever doubt that."

"It doesn't matter," I said turning away from him. "I won't forgive you for this. I've lost so many people in my life . . . I had no one. Then I thought I'd finally found a home—found a family."

"Listen to me," Caleb growled as he swung me around and held me at my shoulders. "This *is* your home. We are your family! Don't make this about something that it isn't."

I pushed away from him, not stopping until I was through the glass door and onto the rooftop garden, under the sun's direct rays, where he could not reach me. I was breathing hard and knew I needed space from him just then or I would suffocate from the pain that was squeezing over my heart. I glanced back to see Caleb standing at the window, looking as if he were about to barrel through the glass, regardless of the sun. Turning my back to him I murmured, "If you truly believed that, then you wouldn't send me away."

Chapter Fourteen

I was being stubborn and I knew it. Not to mention, Caleb would throw a fit equivalent to another eruption of Mount Saint Helens if he had any idea what I was up to while standing in the small lobby of the Walker Foundation Blood Clinic.

Actually, Jax would, too, for that matter . . . but I didn't care.

After Caleb had driven me to my condo on Lake Union, I had spent the first hour arguing with him, then the next humoring him with placating smiles and oh-so-sweet promises that I'd be "*on my best behavior*" till he came back down to see me on Saturday.

Yeah, right.

Caleb wasn't easily fooled, however. His expression reflected his disbelief practically the whole time. That's why I was so surprised when he actually walked out the front door, and hours later I didn't sense him anywhere nearby. The only thing I could attribute it to was the fact that it had been a rough forty-eight hours for both of us and he wanted to show me a little trust.

Big mistake. *Huge.*

I was angry. No, I was furious. And I was hurt, sad and lonely. After two days of deliberately breaking things around my condo, I decided to get over it and make myself useful. I refused to let those two '*over-protective sods,*" as Gemma always called them, break my spirit with their lack of faith in my ability to protect myself. Being here was step one in that plan.

I watched as Christian Nichols, Gemma's second-in-charge at the clinic, came to the small front lobby to greet me. He was a nursing student from the University of Washington who had been at the clinic with Gemma for nearly two years-which was quite a while, considering how often Gemma shuffled people in and out of there so no one could tell she was not aging. Very friendly and sharp as a whip, he had a most wonderful sparkle to his hazel colored eyes, one that would catch any woman's notice. But a woman would never catch his. Christian's sexual preference was for the male gender, and Gemma adored him.

"I'm afraid we're not open yet," he called. For seven-thirty on a Tuesday morning, Christian's pearly-white smile was way too cheery. It practically beamed at me from across the clinic. But as he came closer, his forehead wrinkled with the recognition of trying to place me. "Wait . . . Aren't you . . . ?"

"I'm Gemma's friend, Olivia Greyson," I replied, offering my hand in greeting. "I've been in here a couple times with her."

"Oh, yeah, right . . . Olivia. I thought I recognized you. What can I do for you?"

I bit my lip nervously, then remembered that if I was going to pull this off I had to act like I knew exactly what I was doing. "Well, as you know, Gemma's taking a leave of absence."

"Yeah, that sucks," he replied, raking a hand through his dark blond hair as he hitched the other in his pant pocket. "It won't be the same without her around here. That woman knows how to have fun."

"Yes, she does," I laughed. "And I assure you she will miss you, too. She mentions you all the time and told me that you were the man to talk to when I got here."

Though nothing but polite, he was obviously not quite sure what to make of my surprise visit. "I'm not sure I understand. Are you here to give blood today?"

That certainly wouldn't be happening. Dhampir blood was a mixture of bloods that could be potentially toxic to a human, so allowing it to be tested and mixed with the human blood supply was not an option. "No. You see, in her absence she has asked me to look after things here at the clinic. I'm surprised she hasn't called already and let you know I was coming."

I spilled that fib so lightly, I almost had myself convinced.

"I'm familiar with how some things work, but I was hoping you could show me the ropes a bit. I'll also need someone I can rely on steadily, since I'll be juggling this with some other obligations."

His face lit up, obviously pleased that he was seen as valuable to the day-to-day operations of the clinic, and he was. I hadn't been lying when I said I needed someone I could trust to handle things when I wasn't around—which would be often if I didn't want to get my ass caught by Caleb or Jax. They would, no doubt, disapprove of my working here. But with everything going on, I was sure neither of them had thought far enough ahead to realize that with Gemma no longer working at the clinic, a crucial lifeline had been cut as far as bringing blood home for the family was concerned. I could solve that problem while keeping myself busy at the same time. It was a perfect plan. And, Lord knows, after they'd get over their initial shock of the idea they had better be grateful, because they certainly didn't deserve my help after practically booting me from the family in one afternoon.

I meant what I had said to Jax. I wasn't going to forgive him. Both Jax and Caleb had hurt me with their refusal to listen to reason, but that didn't mean I wanted to see him starve to death from lack of blood. He was still my grandfather, my only blood family, besides Sophie . . . even if he didn't act like it at the moment.

"There would be a nice pay increase, of course," I added to tempt the—I was guessing—starving college student.

He offered his hand with an even broader smile. "I'm your man, Miss Greyson. Where do you want to start?"

"You can start by calling me, Olivia."

***

After being shown around the clinic and meeting some of the staff as they arrived, it was time for a little upstairs visit to the Walker condo . . . another thing on the agenda that Caleb and Jax would never approve of. But after a successful first day in my new life, where I refused to sit around and hide, I was in a particularly rebellious mood.

Stepping outside, I glanced over at the horizon. At most, I would have a couple hours before I needed to be safely tucked inside before sunset. I pulled from my pocket the elevator key Caleb had given me last winter and pressed the button that called down the cab that serviced the penthouse. When the 'ding' announced my arrival on the penthouse floor, I stepped off to see a startled Andie with Sophie in her arms. "Olivia, you scared me. I wasn't expecting anyone. Chay didn't mention—"

"He didn't know I was coming," I interjected, as a smiling Sophie gurgled. "So how's she doing?" I asked in a child-like voice as I touched my nose to her soft cheek.

"She misses both of them," Andie sighed sadly. "Even though she's only a few weeks old, she knows exactly who her parents are."

"Oh," I cooed to the wriggling bundle, "do you miss them, sweetheart?" I glanced up at Andie, whose golden brown eyes were weighed down by a tense smile. She looked tired, like a woman who had been on her own and responsible for a crying newborn for the last week. Yet her fabulous long, winding curls —her best feature, I thought—sat perfectly in place just over her shoulder, aside from the drop of milk that was splattered in it. "May I," I asked, motioning that I wanted to hold her.

"Of course," Andie replied.

Rocking her gently back and forth in my arms it felt good to hold her as I tried to give her comfort. "Your momma's going to be better before you know it. And she can't wait to see her beautiful little girl. No, she can't."

"Do I dare ask if Jax and Caleb know you're here?" Andie questioned with a smirking grin.

I rolled my eyes with a rather ungraceful snort. "If it were up to them, I'd be locked inside my condo twenty-four seven, which I have no intention of doing."

"And exactly how do you plan to keep it from them that you're prancing around the city as if you don't have a care in the world?"

"I'm being careful," I defended. "It's not like I'm running around after the sun goes down."

"Small distinction. You know to them it won't make a bit of difference."

My next words came out in googly baby talk right above Sophie's wide smile. And I swore she had the capability to understand every word I was saying as her tiny fingers reached up to touch my nose. "Well, too bad for them that they can't feel me this far away when I have the necklace on. No, they can't. I just have to make sure I'm back in place, like an obedient mate, before Saturday morning."

I glanced back up at a frowning Andie. "I'm managing the

clinic downstairs for Gemma a few days a week. So, I can come see Sophie after my shift."

"You're what?" Andie blurted in disbelief. "Oh, man, you're so going to get busted. Working at a *blood* clinic was not exactly what Caleb and Jax had in mind when they gave you the whole '*keep yourself safe from vampires*' lecture."

I scowled back at her, remembering that particular argument the morning I left. "Of course, I know I can't keep it from Caleb for long—"

"Or Jax," Andie interjected. "After all, he does own the clinic."

"Yes, I know that. I just might not mention it for a couple weeks until I get settled in a bit."

"Good luck with that," Andie snickered, and then it finally struck me to be concerned.

"You're not going to tell anyone, are you?"

She laughed further, and I had to say I suddenly didn't find this situation nearly as funny as she did. "I'm not going to have to say anything. They're going to figure it out—and soon. If I were you, I would come clean."

I gave her my most pleading look, hoping to guilt her into not blowing my cover until I was ready. She shook her head under a knowing smirk. "I won't lie to any of them if asked directly, especially not Chay. But I won't offer, either." She then held her finger up to qualify her statement. "For a little while . . . You need to tell them soon."

"Thanks," I replied. "I just need to keep myself busy for a little while. And working at the clinic is something that will help the family." I then sighed heavily as I stared down into Sophie's innocent face. "And I want to be able to spend time with this little angel. I can't believe how much I've already missed her."

"You don't have to explain it to me. She's an attention stealer, much like her mother." She winked at Sophie then glanced back up at me. "But you're still going to get busted long before two weeks . . . and I don't want to be anywhere near when the shit hits the fan."

I stared back at her under a narrowed gaze, surprised when her teasing smile faded from her face. "They're over-protective, and they may not be handling this situation right, but they're doing it because they love you. You do know that, right?"

"Yes," I said with exasperation. "But I didn't feel particularly loved when they kicked me out of the house."

"They don't see it that way. They see it as protecting you. If there has been one thing I've learned since observing Chay and his coven, it's that sometimes Daywalkers are not logical when it comes to protecting their women. Once they find real love—something that is not common in their world—their primal instincts take over. It becomes all about what they can lose—what can be taken away from them. I'm not sure Caleb or Jax could handle it if something were to happen to you."

Handing Sophie back to Andie, I replied, "I get that . . . but they can't keep me locked behind glass like some pretty little object they treasure. I can defend myself. I could have handled Gemma if they would have just given me a chance."

"You're asking them to stand back and watch a new vampire that they love attack you—someone they also love—and trust that you will be able to handle the situation without hurting her or yourself. That's never going to happen. But there is a middle ground, *I'm sure of that.* You just need to find a way to make them see it."

***

The rest of the week had actually ticked by pretty fast, since I was keeping myself busy at the clinic. By Friday night, I was more relaxed and on the terrace of my condo overlooking the view to the lake and enjoying a glass of *sweet wine*—which was Caleb's and my code word for blood. I was feeling pretty good about what I had learned and accomplished at the clinic during the week, while finally finishing the last couple bars of Sophie's Lullaby. An arrangement had just popped into my head earlier that day, stayed stuck there, and I needed to get it worked out and down on paper. It was funny how things worked like that. I took it as a good sign that my inner musician was free enough to let the music come to me. And now the last few bars to the sweet infant's lullaby were perfect —light, happy and hopeful, just as I wanted them to be.

"Your gift to see music in your head always amazes me,"

Caleb spoke, startling me from behind. I swung around to see his tall body leaning against the door frame of the glass atrium, his arms crossed over his chest and a soft smile setting easily on his handsome face. I had been so focused on my playing, I hadn't paid attention to the fact that my chest had tightened, letting me know that he was near. In the beginning, when I was discovering my gifts, the sensation had been so jarring it was distracting. But now that I was used to it, it seemed more like the norm rather than the unusual.

"I thought you weren't coming until tomorrow."

Caleb glided over to the bench and smoothly took a seat beside me. "I've missed my sweet girl and wanted to see you. Is that all right?" He leaned in to give me a gentle kiss on my cheek, not my lips, since I had been drinking blood. When any blood mixed with Caleb's saliva the combination was dangerous and had the potential to turn a human or a Dhampir like myself. When I didn't say anything in response he added, "I was kind of hoping you might've missed me, too."

"You know the answer to that," I said quietly, trying to fight back the firestorm of emotions it brought over me just to be near him again. His body touched mine at the hips and shoulders as he sat next to me on the bench, and that was all it took for me to wonder how I was going to continue to be separated from him for weeks while Gemma recovered. I feared it might truly break my heart. "I never wanted to leave you in the first place. That was your doing."

He was quiet, though I could see the tension that had tightened in his shoulders in response to my comment. Then he reached for the empty wine glass I had sitting on top of the piano and closed his eyes, inhaling deeply near the rim. He was taking in all the subtle scents of the blood left behind on the glass. Just as quickly his whole body seemed to relax, as if he were absorbing the most luscious, the most exotic fragrance in the whole world. It was intriguing to me that his inherent need for the blood was something I had always found so captivating about him. He wanted it with such passion. That kind of passion crossed over to how he lived his life—how he fought those who threatened that life. And was part of what made him so beautiful in my eyes. "I can take the glass back inside if the scent bothers you."

Caleb shook his head. "It's all right. I just fed. But this scent is so . . ." His words dropped off and at first I didn't think he was going to finish. "Complex, I guess, is the word I'm looking for. It smells fresh. Where did you get this?"

Ooops! Andie was right. At this rate I wasn't going to make it two days until Caleb would find out about the clinic, let alone two weeks. My chest braced itself against the hard and fast pitter-patters my heart was bashing against it. Of course, a vampire would recognize the scent of *fresh* blood. Fresh from the donations made this afternoon at the clinic. I shrugged it off, not wanting to directly lie to him, even though I knew by omitting the truth I was doing exactly that.

"You're still upset with me," he said, setting the glass back down in its place.

"Yes. But you can change that." His brows rose with his interest. "Tell me you're here early because you and Jax have wised up and decided to let me come home?"

In response his lips pressed into a thin line and my hopes were dashed—that quickly. I rose from the bench and stepped away from him, needing to maintain some distance so I could get my mind off how distractingly handsome he was under the moonlight. "You know what hurts the most?" I began sadly. "That you could send me away so easily . . . That you can be OK with me living apart from you."

"You think this is easy for me?" he growled, springing up from the bench in front of me. "That *any* of this is easy? You, Gemma . . . Jax?" His hand raked roughly though his hair as he turned away, staring out towards the city skyline. "I hate being apart from you," he sighed. "I hate that you are two hours away when every instinct I have tells me that I need to be here with you—protecting you."

"Then stay with me," I pleaded. "*God*, I know I'm selfish for even asking, but I miss you."

There was a long silence between us, and his shoulders stiffened once again, defining the long muscles of his back. "I want nothing more than to stay here with you and shut the rest of the world away." He swung back around, his expression so determined. "But I owe this to Jax. After everything he's done for me . . . after everything Gemma's done . . . I need to step up and lead this coven right now because Jax can't. Can you understand that?"

Understand it? How could I argue with it? Jax had saved Caleb from a life of being controlled by a woman who would have surely tried to kill him once she found a new toy to play with. If it wasn't for Jax, I might never have found Caleb— might never have known him. *I owed* my grandfather as well. "Of course I do. But why can't I be there with you. With my training and my gifts, and you and Jax watching over me, I'll be OK."

He was shaking his head before I even finished the sentence, and it irritated me. "I can't. Don't you understand? I have the same fear for you. That if I let my guard down for even one second that Gemma could turn you—that it would all be over with, fast."

"Caleb," I sighed. "No, I can't stand here and tell you that it's not a possibility. It is. But my fate is my fate. Neither you nor Jax can control that. And you can't protect me from it."

"I can protect you! I will," he said, defiantly—and why was I surprised? The warrior inside Caleb believed he could defeat anything or anyone. And most of the time I believed it, too. He growled in frustration. "*Damn*, I'm going crazy. When you're wearing that necklace I can't *feel* you. I can't share your joy, your fear. I can't even share your anger. And, believe it or not, I *do* want it. I want to *feel* every part of you that is real."

I stood there, staring at him, clearly seeing for the first time the toll this was all taking on him. In wallowing in my own selfish pain, I hadn't stopped to think about how this was all affecting him. He was trying to save me, as well as the two people who had been his family long before I had come into the picture, and I had only made that job more difficult for him. "I'm sorry," I whispered in a choked voice, feeling the heat of several swirling emotions reddening my cheeks. "I don't mean to make this more difficult for you. You're bearing the brunt of my anger because I am insecure when it comes to family. It's just that I've lost so many . . . And now when I felt like I have it again . . . that it's OK to breathe . . ." The quivering started over my lip and tears washed into my eyes—*oh, how I hated the weakness I was showing him!* How was I supposed to prove to him that I could take care of myself if I was crying all the time? Fisting my hands at my sides, I tried to pull back my tears and keep it together. "When Jax ordered me to leave. I felt it starting again—that nagging voice in the back of my head whispering that I don't belong anywhere. But then you defended me—you fought for me. You told him my place was with you. And then . . ."

"Then I asked you to leave," he finished in a quiet voice, "and it felt as if you were losing your family all over again." The trembling started again in my lip. He reached for my hand and pulled me carefully to him, his arms wrapping around me as I leaned my head against his shoulder. For a long while we stood there in silence while he stoked my hair.

"Look at me," he finally said, breaking into the quiet. As I glanced up his fingers weaved into my hair and he palmed my cheek. "You *are* my family. Always. No matter the reason we're apart—no matter the distance. You are a part of every breath I take from now on."

I laid my head back against his shoulder. "Then prove it to me by letting me come home and help my family. Gemma and Sophie need me."

"Olivia," he said with feeling. "The moment it's safe enough for you to come home, I will be here on your doorstep ready to pack your things and begging you to come home."

I sighed and stepped back from him. "In other words, not for a while."

"I didn't say that. I said not until it's safe. I'm sorry, but you're not going to change my mind about compromising your safety."

Rubbing my hands over my tired eyes, an epiphany suddenly hit me. Gemma had been right. There needed to be consequences when Caleb made decisions without regard for how I felt. What I needed to do was get him to equate something important to me with something important to him. A smile formed behind my hands; the answer was almost too simple. "All right, then," I replied, showing him my sudden smile, which should have warned him enough. He knew I never gave up a disagreement that easily. "Since I can't seem to persuade you into seeing how important this is to me, I'll make you a deal."

"Olivia . . . ," he started, but I interrupted with my next surprising words.

"Until you let me come home, you're cut off."

His brows flattened as he stared back at me carefully. "Cut off from what, exactly?"

"No sex. None."

"*What?*" he questioned sharply, shifting in his stiff stance as if the mere thought had sent a shock straight to his balls. "That's insane. One has nothing to do with the other."

I couldn't keep back my giggle of glee now that I had figured out something substantial to bargain with him. "I don't agree. In fact, I think it's a rather brilliant idea. You said you missed me. Well . . . you're about to start missing me a whole lot more —beginning right now. So if you want to leave, then I suggest you do it now."

"Olivia!" he cried as if he was talking to a child being completely unreasonable. "You're my mate. I'm not going—"

"Oh, yes you are," I called over my shoulder as I headed inside. "See you next week."

A few minutes later, while brushing my teeth to get ready for bed, I couldn't contain my satisfied smile as I stared at my reflection in the mirror. I could still hear Caleb outside, cursing under his breath and mumbling something about me being the most stubborn woman he'd ever known as he paced back and forth across the terrace. I decided to take some pity on him, foregoing my sexiest red nightie for a much more simple midnight-blue cotton cami with matching boy shorts. But who was I kidding? I knew he adored the way the cami curved around my breast and the boy shorts cut low across my stomach. The simple truth was, I wasn't playing fair . . . and we both knew it. *Thank you, Gemma!*

I settled into the silk sheets with a soft sigh, quite sure I'd seen the last of him for the night, or even the week. So it surprised me when I woke some time later to find him scooting in behind me, pulling me against his body. "I said no sex," I mumbled sleepily against the arm he slid under my neck.

"This is not sex," he growled. "Or have you already

forgotten?" Forgotten what it felt like to make love to Caleb Wolfe? Not likely. "I want to hold you . . . lie with you tonight."

"Ok," I replied dreamily. "But no funny stuff."

"I wouldn't dream of it."

***

Monday morning, I came into the clinic in a surly mood. My own brilliant plan had somehow backfired on me. Caleb had left sometime during the night on Saturday, which was a blessing because the entire twenty-four hours beforehand had been sheer torture for both of us.

I thought it would be no problem to abstain from sex, at least for one weekend. After all, I was a woman. Our gender as a whole could be counted on in circumstances like this when required. But watching him walk around the condo with a constant 'hard as a steel pike' erection in his jeans deflated my willpower to a startling degree . . . and he knew it. The fact that I was suffering just as much as he was the one bit of satisfaction he got from this stupid idea of mine. He tried coaxing my surrender out of me several times over the course of the day— and nearly got his wish when I was doing something as simple as loading laundry into the dryer. Catching me by surprise, he hoisted me up onto the dryer and kissed me senseless until I was practically gasping for breath. I had totally melted into the feel of his body over mine, curling my legs around him as he leaned in, while the heat and motion of the dryer rumbled beneath us. Who knew a basic household appliance could be such a turn-on?

When I finally came to my senses and managed to push him back from me, he figured out I was serious about this whole abstinence thing. He then announced he would be leaving after I fell asleep. I should have been insulted by the fact that if sex was off the table, he couldn't seem to escape fast enough. But I could hardly blame him. I wanted him just as badly. And having the thing you want most dangling in front of you, like some sort of triple chocolate yumminess with raspberry topping, was clearly not helpful.

"Olivia?" Christian broke into my thoughts. "There's a woman here to see Gemma. When I told her you were filling in for her, she asked to see you."

"Did she give you a name?"

"No. She just said she was an old friend from Alberta." My face lit up with delight the same moment a puzzled frown came over Christian's. "That's Canada, right?"

"Yes!" I cheered, practically hurtling over my desk to get to the lobby. Standing there with her long ebony hair splayed over her shoulders against a brilliant sky blue blouse that matched her eyes was Maya Brunetti, my dear friend from the time I had spent training at The Oracle. She smiled brightly at me as I rushed towards her. "Maya!" I cried, throwing my arms around her. "I'm so glad to see you. Things have been so crazy around here today, I forgot you were coming."

"I can see that," she commented as she scanned the busy room. "I was coming to let Gemma know I was here so she could contact you. I wasn't expecting you would be here. When did you start working at the clinic?"

I rolled my eyes at her. "It's a long story. I've a lot to catch you up on. Do you want to get your things settled at my place and then we can go grab some lunch."

"Sounds good."

Later, we walked to a nearby Thai place on the corner, where I spent most of the meal catching Maya up on everything that had happened with Gemma, Jax and Caleb. Throughout the meal the dark-headed beauty shuffled through a mix of expressions from eyebrow-raising wonder to forehead-crinkling confusion. "So Caleb doesn't know you're working at the clinic?"

"Not yet. I'm planning on telling him when he comes down this weekend." Then I played in my head how that conversation would go between us" . . . Or maybe next weekend," I amended.

She blinked back at me in surprise. "Olivia, I'm not so sure he's going to take this news very well on either weekend."

I snorted in reply. "That's an understatement. But I can't just sit inside my condo all day doing nothing. I need to help somehow."

"I can understand that," Maya replied as she reached across the table for my hand.

"You do understand, don't you?" I said with a smile I didn't feel. "It's that . . . before the train crash I had this plan for my life—a life of music. Then it was all blown to bits the day I discovered I was a Charmer. And now, even though I was incredibly blessed to find Caleb and my grandfather, my life has become all about keeping *me* in this protected bubble. What good am I doing? What am I contributing? What makes my life meaningful?"

"Well, for one, your life is meaningful because you have people who love you, who need you, including myself, Caleb and Jax . . . and Gemma—once she's not so fixated on killing you." She then gave me an empathetic smile. "But it's only natural that you would want to have a purpose—a direction for your life."

"Exactly," I sighed. "And Caleb is very supportive of that. We have talked about me finishing my two Masters degrees in music . . . but *after* Davin is taken care of. Everything is *after.* What if Davin is still coming after me years from now? Will we still be waiting?"

"But, still, its' good Caleb recognizes what's important to you and that he wants you to have it. Is it really such a bad thing that he's worried about you? Working at the clinic—though it may be something you love doing—does put you in danger right now, especially with Davin still out there hunting you. Caleb wouldn't want you taking chances like that if he sees your living here as only a temporary situation."

"You may be right," I replied with a frown. "This has been hard on him. He hates not being able to be here with me. And I'll concede that in my anger I haven't been making anything easier. I even told him no sex until he lets me come home."

Maya's crystal-blue eyes popped wide under her dark brows. "Oh my . . . He really can't be happy about that."

I couldn't help the slightly wicked smile on my lips. "No, he's not."

"Have you had any problems with Davin or his soldiers since you've been here?"

"No, it's been fine. The necklace has been doing its job. In fact, if anything, it proves that if it wasn't for Davin, I could have a fairly normal life, aside from the occasional skirmish or two. But I've become quite the butt-kicker when I need to be.

Caleb and Jax have trained me well."

"That's good. But good training isn't a replacement for recognizing when you need help. It's about being smart too. Alec would be the first one to tell you that."

I sighed roughly at that. "I know . . . But if I ask for help then I'm never going to get either one of them to recognize that I can protect myself. I need to prove it to them."

"They see it, Olivia. They do . . . ," Maya said taking my hand. "Or there would be no way Caleb would even consider letting you stay down here by yourself. The fact that he is should tell you that he recognizes what you're capable of."

"You're a good friend, Maya."

"Just be careful while you're here," Maya replied. "And I'm sorry to hear about what's happened to Gemma. I've really grown to appreciate the vampire side of myself. But to lose the human half . . . that would be hard. Will she be all right?"

"I hope so. I pray for it every day. I truly want the sassy, happy woman we all know and love to come back to us. I want it for Jax, too. I fear if she doesn't, he will live in a place as dark and lonely as when he lost Isabeau. I may be angry with him right now, but I would *never* want that for him. Those years after my grandmother died were hell for him."

"She'll be OK," Maya said confidently. "She's a strong woman."

"I hope you're right. But can I ask a favor?"

"Of course."

"Don't say anything for now about Gemma. I promise you won't have to keep it secret for long. I want to tell Alec myself. I have a feeling this won't sit well with him at all."

"You're probably right about that. He doesn't ever talk about it, but you can tell he really cared for Gemma. Losing her to Jax and now hearing that she been turned will be hard on him."

I nodded. "That's what I'm afraid of."

Chapter Fifteen

The next night, after returning home from the clinic, I changed into my favorite super-comfy cotton pajama set while Maya set up all the makings for the perfect slumber party on the living room floor. Blankets, pillows, popcorn, and the classic chiller *The Shining* was loaded up and ready to go. Maya and I loved a good scary movie, which was a bit ironic considering that we were both well aware of the very real evil that existed in the world.

I was working on a pan of melted butter and salt while Maya was finishing up her phone conversation to her sweetheart back at The Oracle, Phin Daniels. Phin was a fierce, fast, and superbly trained Dhampir for The Brethren, and he was also fiercely in love with Maya. He had been one of the Guardians assigned to protect me by The Brethren while I stayed at The Oracle, along with Alec Lambert, Lucas Rainer, and *God help the female species*, shape-shifter Kane, who only went by one name. But as I got to know Phin better, it soon became clear he was a private man, more known for his quiet sexiness than his fighting bravado. He was also one of those men who was just beautiful to look at, with dark, smooth skin, at least where it was not covered by his perfectly shaped goatee, and the most full white smile I had ever seen on any man. Maya had been smitten practically from day one he had set foot at The Oracle, and I really couldn't blame her. "Phinneas said to say hi," she said with a red flush to her cheeks as she came back into the living room.

"Were you two having dirty-talk on the phone?"

She laughed, a hearty and healthy laugh, her bright blue eyes alight with happiness. "He's so wonderful. Do you know he's called me every night since I've been gone?"

"I would definitely say you've got him on the hook. He's crazy about you. And that's good because I want nothing but the best for my friend."

"He is the best, isn't he?" she readily agreed. "He's been strong and kind, and so patient with me. I don't know what on earths' wrong with me . . . why I'm so nervous about going to that next level with him. I know I love him."

I blinked back at her in complete surprise. Maya was only a few years younger than me. In this day and age it seemed unusual, to say the least, that she had waited this long to have sex, but there were a lot of things in Maya's past that she didn't talk about. Sometimes it made me wonder if there were reasons why she was scared to truly open herself up to an intimate relationship with a man. I wanted to ask her, but I didn't want to push. Being that she could already be a shy woman, it would be too easy for her to clam up if she felt pressed. I was her friend. I wanted her to tell me when she trusted to tell me. "I guess I kind of assumed that you had already taken that next step with Phin."

"No," she responded quietly. "Believe me—I want to . . . It's just that everything's been so great between us. I don't want that to change if we . . . you know. It's my first time. Obviously, it will be a bigger deal for me than it will be for him."

"I don't think that's true, Maya. It's a big deal to Phin too. That's why he hasn't been pushing you. He wants you to trust him completely."

"Well, first time or not," she began, "I don't think either of us can wait much longer. So I think I want to surprise him for his birthday—with me."

"Oh Maya," I cried, clapping my hands together in barely contained excitement. "I think that's wonderful! Are you sure you're ready?"

Her blue eyes rounded in question as she nodded nervously. "But what if I don't please him? He has been honest with me. You know he has . . . a lot"—she paused to clear her throat —"more experience than me."

I reached for her hands and squeezed gently. "He loves you, Maya. He wouldn't have waited this long for you if he didn't. All you need to do is allow yourself to relax and let him lead. Let your responses to him come naturally. Trust me, if you do, you won't disappoint him."

"Ooohh," she squealed, practically bouncing from her position on the floor. "I'm so nervous . . . and excited . . . and happy. I didn't know I could be this happy." She then reached for her purse beside the couch and pulled out a small box. Opening the box carefully she said, "I got this for his birthday."

I glance down to see a trading card inside a glass case, obviously valuable and important, though I had no idea who the player was. "He loves baseball," she continued, "and growing up he followed the Dodgers. His favorite player of all time was Jackie Robinson. Phin was born the year Jackie Robinson was inducted into the Baseball Hall of Fame, 1962. This was his 1956 Schedule Card and it was a doosy trying to get a hold of it."

Yes, Phin Daniels was really that old. But he was also a three quarter Dhampir who was aging very slowly and looked as if he were only in his mid-to-late twenties. Pairing up with someone in the Dhampir world was very different than dating in the human world, mostly because the age of a Dhampir was very deceiving.

"Maya," I whispered in amazement, "he's going to love it."

"You think so?"

I nodded. "It's perfect." I grabbed a handful of popcorn from the bowl she was holding and we made ourselves comfortable on the floor. "So tell me how the others are doing—Alec, Lucas, Kane . . . ?"

Maya smiled and went on about how my former guardian Alec Lambert had been doing a remarkable job taking over for his now ousted Uncle Reese as elder in charge of The Oracle, which was not surprising. He was smart, confident, and quick on his feet when it came to solving a problem, not at all the controlling tyrant his uncle had been. His biggest flaw seemed to be letting go of the fact that he wasn't a guardian anymore. He had an inherent need to save people, and sitting on the sidelines game-planning and instructing others to do so wasn't his idea of accomplishing that. I believed he just needed more time to understand how important his new role was, how much he was accomplishing, how many lives he was saving by being a leader instead of a fighter.

"Oh, and Lucas is making a serious effort to cut back on his cursing," Maya announced.

"*What?*" I said, practically stumbling over my own tongue. "The man doesn't know how to speak complete sentences without throwing in a few curse words." And that was the truth. The handsome but rough around the edges human guardian had an expletive on hand to accurately describe any given situation.

"Well, he's trying, and it's really kind of sweet because I think he's trying to clean up his 'verbal act' so to speak so he can find that special woman."

"Oh, that is sweet. It'll probably never last, but it's so sweet." Maya smiled and nodded in agreement. "And what about our favorite unrepentant shifter, Kane?"

Maya laughed. "He's the one trying to teach Lucas how to seduce the female gender without so much cursing."

We both started laughing out loud. "*God*, how I wished I could be a fly on the wall for those lessons. The sheer entertainment value alone would be gold."

"Well Kane's got bigger problems to deal with actually. I think Alec's about to lock him in the chapel in a sort of forced celibacy," Maya teased. "Kane's gotten himself in all kinds of trouble this month for causing catfights among the women."

"That's not good," I replied.

Then after a short pause we both busted up laughing again. "But it's so Kane!" we spoke in unison and then turned towards the terrace doors as I cover my hand over my heart.

"Is that—?"

"Yes!" I cheered. "He's here!"

I nearly spilled the bucket of popcorn as I bounced to my feet and headed out to the terrace. Caleb was standing on the ledge, a slow smile crossing his lips once he saw how excited I was to see him. He looked handsome as ever, dressed in jeans, heavy boots, and a casual gray shirt that accentuated his wide shoulders. "You're here!"

He dropped down light as air in front of me then reached out to snatch me firmly against his body with one arm. Before I knew what was happening his lips were crushing over mine creating a firestorm of heat. *Wow!* He kissed me as if it had been thinking about nothing else all day, his hand behind my head holding me firm in place as he nipped and teased over my lips until I felt so dizzy I had to brace my hands against his chest. When he finally lifted his lips from mine, his eyes were sparkling in the moonlight as I felt myself stumble shakily on my feet. "Easy there, sweet," he said smoothly, then glanced up and smiled at Maya. "I felt a shift in you . . . happiness. I wanted to come see for myself what had you in such a good mood. And now I see why. Hello, Maya."

"Hi," she responded shyly, obviously a little nervous around Caleb still since she did not know him very well. His height and size could be intimidating for almost anyone.

"You felt it?" I questioned him. "Does that mean you're now able to *feel* me from far away even with the necklace on?"

He smiled, though it was a barely-there kind of smile as he brushed the back of his hand over my cheek. "I was nearby," he said, "but it was nice to feel something other than your anger."

Without warning I wrapped my arms around his middle, squeezing him tight while I braced my head against his chest. "I'm sorry," I whispered. "I know I've been making things harder for you. I was just so hurt, and I've been lonely. I can't sleep as well without you.

His expression showed concern as he stroked my hair and placed a tender kiss on top of my head. "Are you having nightmares?"

"No. Just restless I guess." I then blinked up at him brightly. "But tonight we're having girl's night, complete with popcorn and a very scary movie. Will you come inside for a little while . . . let me cling to you on all the really creepy parts?"

He tapped his finger at the end of my nose as his lips pressed into a neutral smile. "That is tempting, but I think I'll let you two girls have some fun on your own. It will be good for you to have a night to catch up with your friend. You haven't got to have that as of late, have you?" I nodded at him, realizing that he was right. Gemma and I often had girl nights while Caleb and Jax were out patrolling. That might be one more thing that would change now with Gemma's transition. "And besides, I need to check in on Andie and Sophie before heading back tonight."

"You have to head back tonight?" I asked him, unable to hide my disappointment. Caleb leaned back against the terrace railing and pulled me with him. I clung to him as I sighed peacefully against his chest, staring out onto the calm lake beyond. "Is everything all right with Gemma?" Caleb remained silent continuing to stroke over my hair, and the answer in that silence broke my heart. I feared what he had been dealing with regarding Gemma's transition and Jax's despondency was even more difficult on him than I had first realized. "It will get better, Caleb . . . soon. You'll see."

"I know. And I'll be back to see you Saturday morning. I'm hoping your good mood means you've reconsidered your ultimatum."

"Oh yeah . . . the no sex thing," I smiled up at him. "Absolutely not," I laughed.

A soft frown pulled over his face. "Mmm," he sounded. "I guess I will take that as a personal challenge then."

"You can take it as whatever you want, but you'll not seduce me, Caleb Wolfe."

"We'll see about that," he murmured. "We'll see."

❋❋❋

The time with Maya had come and gone way too quickly. It felt as if she had only just gotten here and then we were packing her things for the trip back. After she left earlier in the day, I never thought I'd be so grateful to see the clock reach five on a Wednesday. The clinic had been nothing short of crazy that day, which only added to my stress that we didn't receive our delivery of syringes. Gemma was meticulous at having the ever dwindling supplies and massive amounts of paperwork perfectly organized. She knew the ins and outs of operating the clinic without having to think about it. I on the other hand was discovering that I had a lot to learn. Though mastering the day-to-day operations was a challenge, I found myself more than eager to learn. I felt useful and the reward was being able to help my family, even if they would be less than thrilled about me exposing myself like this without protection.

"Olivia?" Christian called as he walked back towards my office. "I know I'm supposed to close tonight but if it's all right, can I leave early? I have my human anatomy test."

I glanced outside, seeing I still had plenty of light left to close shop and run up and see Andie and Sophie before walking home. "No problem," I replied, "I'll shut things down."

Throwing the pack that I hadn't noticed was already in his hand over his shoulder, he smiled, "Thanks. You're the best." After turning to leave, his hand grabbed the edge of the door frame and he swung back around. "Oh—and don't worry about the syringes. They'll show up tomorrow."

"I hope so," I muttered.

Right at five, I started going through the list of closing procedures and was surprised to hear the entry bells for the clinic chime. In my rush to get everything wrapped up I had forgotten the most important step which was to *lock the front door.* "I'm sorry we're closed . . . ," I began, then my voice trailed off as I came out from the supply room. A young woman, with golden blond hair cut in a wispy bob that framed her face, had already made her way past the empty lobby and reception desk and was wandering back among the donation stations. How had she gotten there so quickly? Though the petite woman would hardly be considered threatening in her floaty little white sheath dress—something that looked more appropriate for an outdoor wedding or summer party than a blood clinic— it was odd that she would make her way to the back area as though she knew exactly where she was going. "Can I help you?" I asked.

"My mistake," she offered with a smile. "What time do you close?"

"At five. I just forgot to lock the front door."

"Oh darn," she replied with a playful lift to her voice. "I'd meant to get here earlier. But I got distracted." She then lifted one of her toned legs, motioning to her freshly groomed toes and strappy metallic sandals that wrapped up her ankles. "Is there anything more distracting than a great pedicure and new pair of sandals?" She giggled effortlessly, and there was something about her laugh that felt familiar as her pretty green eyes watched me carefully.

"No, I suppose not," I offered, more to be agreeable rather than any true feeling on the subject.

"Well, now I have a problem." She took a step closer to me,

her fingers pushing back the longer pieces of her bangs as they swept in a flirty fringe across her forehead who. "I'm afraid I'm leaving town in the morning," she explained. "Any chance you could make an exception and let me stay and donate tonight?"

OK, this seemed odd. No one was ever that excited about giving blood. "We would be grateful for the donation because we can always use them, but I'm afraid all of our blood techs have left for the evening."

Her head tilted slightly as those clear green eyes of hers looked at me curiously. "You are not able to take my blood?" *Boy was that an understatement.* Only being here a couple of weeks I was still working on how to block the cravings for the blood myself now that I could smell it all day long. I didn't know how Gemma did it, but I could only assume it was something she had gotten used to over time. Then there was the matter that I was certainly no trained blood technician. "I'm afraid I just manage the clinic," I replied. "I leave the blood draws to the professionals."

The woman's brows lifted with further interest. "Oh, so you manage the clinic? I should have guessed that. You're good with people, Olivia." I blinked back at her, wondering how on earth she knew my name when, with a delicate finger, she pointed to her own collarbone. "Your name tag . . ."

"Oh gosh that's right," I rushed out. "I'm always forgetting I have the silly thing on."

"Quite all right," she said, extending her hand. "I'm Skye Matthews."

"Skye, that's a pretty name."

"Thank you. I'm afraid my father's an ex-hippie. All my sisters are all named after mother earth."

"Mmm, sisters plural? Sounds like you're from a big family."

"You can say that. I am only one of nine."

"Nine!" I choked out. "And no brothers?"

"Not yet," she laughed."

"Is your family from around here?"

She seemed to think about that for a long moment before she replied, "We're not really from any one place. We travel around quite a bit."

There still was something different about Skye that I

couldn't quite put my finger on, but she seemed sincerely sweet, if a bit overanxious to donate blood, and I genuinely wished I could help her. "Well, Skye, I would love it if you could donate. Is there any chance you could come by in the morning before you leave? We open at eight am and I could give you a head start by having you fill out all the paperwork tonight. It would make things quick in the morning."

Her lips pursed in thought as her gaze lifted upward, as if she were ticking through all the appointments to her day. "I think I could make that work. I appreciate you helping me out." Her eyes then narrowed playfully. "I'm not keeping you from anything right now, am I? Is there a special someone waiting on you?"

I thought about Caleb for a moment and a large smile pulled at my cheeks. "There is someone special, but he's needed elsewhere tonight."

Her whole expression scrunched into a tiny frown. "Well, that's lame . . . especially because you're so obviously in love—"

She cut herself off as I blinked back at her. "I didn't say that I loved him?"

Skye chewed at her lower lip. "No, I guess you didn't. And I'm sorry if I'm being too personal, but frankly, it's written all over your face."

That certainly seemed possible as much as I found myself distracted in my thoughts about Caleb during the week when I was separated from him, but still a leap to make for someone I had just met. Skye reached for my arm and squeezed gently, her expression more . . . something . . . *Thoughtful? Concerned?* And the way it softened her features so eloquently had me utterly curious to figure out why she seemed so . . . familiar. Warmth began to spread just under my skin where she touched me, and it was strange how my thoughts went to that first night Caleb saved me at the train crash. The first time he sat reading at my bedside as I recovered from my injuries. Then the first time we kissed at the piano. It seemed the butterflies that wreaked havoc on my stomach that day and the many days since, were back. Was there ever a time I stared up into those beautiful grey eyes of his and not felt completely in love?

"You've got it bad, don't you?" she prompted as she stared

right into my eyes, her hand squeezing once again over my arm. "It's a good thing—the most important. Remember this feeling —this moment. Fate likes to play games with us . . . with our hearts . . . with what we feel. It tests us in ways we aren't always prepared for. But what you're feeling right now, is always the way back. Remember that."

I glanced away from Skye for a moment, unable to believe I was having such a personal conversation with a virtual stranger and yet somehow she wasn't. Her voice sounded like that voice of good always reassuring you in your ear. "Well, fate can't—"

I stopped suddenly and blinked hard when I turned my head back around and found that Skye Mathews was gone—as in, not standing in front of me, not in the back donation area, and nowhere to be found in the front lobby. It was as if she had vanished into thin air.

" . . . can't have my heart," I finished to the empty room.

***

Mysteriously, Skye never showed up to the clinic that next morning, and I couldn't help but be distracted throughout the day as I replayed our strange conversation from the night before in my head. "Olivia," Heather broke in over my thoughts on the phone's intercom. "There's a call for you on line two."

"OK, thanks." Clicking over to line two I answered, "Hello this is, Olivia."

"Did you happen to notice it was cloudy out today?" Andie charged ahead without any greeting.

"Well, its September," I replied, "and this is Seattle . . ." Suddenly an uncomfortable jolt ran through me that felt as if I had just been shocked by an electrical charge. "*Oh God*, Andie . . . Why are you asking me that?" But I already knew the answer. Jumping to my feet I practically pulled the phone right off the desk.

"You have to ask?"

"Caleb," I whispered while simultaneously holding my breath. "I feel him nearby. He's been here a while hasn't he? Is he there at the condo with you now?"

"Ohhh, no," Andie replied with exaggerated slowness. "Not anymore. My guess is he's skulking around on some rooftop somewhere waiting for you to get your *butt* out of that clinic."

Then she laughed almost wickedly. "I told you you're going to get caught."

Chapter Sixteen

It was Thursday! What the heck was he doing down here on Thursday? I mean . . . I wanted to see him. Every day I wanted to see him and every day I didn't wrecked havoc on my spirit. But I wasn't prepared to see him until Saturday, and now I knew I was toast!

While rehearsing in my head a calm and reasonable explanation as to why I was working at the Walker Foundation Blood Clinic, I grabbed my coat and headed for the front door, prepared to face what I suspected was a very unhappy mate. I simply told the staff I had something I had to deal with and boy that was an understatement. What had I been I thinking not telling him sooner? But I already knew the answer to that. I had been angry and hurt that he and Jax had asked me to leave, even if it was for my own protection. I wanted to rebel. At least, at first it had been about wanting to rebel. Now that I had spent time at the clinic with Christian and the rest of the staff I realized I enjoyed what I was doing. My time there had become about much more than rebelling. I felt useful and was beginning to hope if I could get myself more settled at the clinic, show Caleb how I could help him and the family continue to get the blood they all critically needed now that Gemma would no longer be able to, that he would be open to me continuing to work there.

But there would be little reasoning with him now that he found out like this.

"He loves you," I assured myself. "He will listen to reason if you explain things clearly." I took one giant step onto the sidewalk and scanned the many cascading rooftops around me but there was no sign of him. And then, as if on cue, the sun came out from behind the clouds to brighten the whole street around me. Caleb would now have to stay in the shadows, wherever he was.

I decided the smart thing to do was to head back to my

condo. That would be where he would go as soon as the sun fell back behind the clouds. After a quick twenty minute walk, I was safely standing in my entry, locking the door behind me and dropping my coat on the kitchen island. "Busy day?" his deep, familiar timbre spoke from behind me, and I swung around to see him standing there calmly . . . almost too calmly in the shadows of the hallway.

The sun shifted again from behind the clouds and the room grew increasingly brighter because of it. Well, that and the fact that I had left the curtains pulled open this morning when I left for the clinic. The bright light forced Caleb deeper into the shadows.

"Look," I began in a very rational voice while he remained completely still—like completely still . . . like it was hard to even see if he was inhaling a breath kind of still. "I realize discovering that I have been working at the clinic might be a little upsetting to you—"

"Oh, you think it might be a *little upsetting?*" he asked . . . again, way too calmly.

"Just let me explain. I have a good reason." Then I thought about that for a moment. "Well, maybe it wasn't a good or very mature reason at first, but now—"

"Why don't you start by telling me how long you've been deliberately keeping this from me."

I sighed heavily, feeling the breath deflate from my lungs along with my hope for a reasonable conversation with Caleb with it. "That's probably not a good place to start."

"And why would that not be a good place to start?" he asked. "Would it be because the first thing you did after I brought you here was to put yourself in danger by going to that clinic and appointing yourself Gemma's replacement?"

"Not exactly . . . ," I replied with an uneasy swallow. "I waited two days."

"Two days?" he repeated with clear sarcasm as he took a step deeper into the room and closer towards meet with the shuffling light of the sun. "Two *whole* days. So, in other words, I should be grateful that when I was here that first weekend— confiding to you how much it was eating at me to leave you here alone—unprotected . . . you had given the idea two *whole* days consideration."

Another step closer. This conversation was not going as I hoped.

"You had carefully considered how you were going to protect yourself from Davin and his minions if he found you there—in front of all those defenseless humans—and without getting any of them killed?"

I blinked back at him and I was sure my eyes must have been the size of saucers because the thought had not even occurred to me that I would be putting Christian's life and the other's lives in danger just by me being there.

"Ah, I can see the answer is yes," Caleb continued, but I could hear the anger growing in each word. "That would mean you also considered how you were going to let me know that you needed my help if Davin threatened you . . . before you completely exposed your supernatural abilities in front of a city of six-hundred thousand people!"

I swallowed hard a second time. "OK, so maybe I didn't have this all thought through," I admitted regrettably. "And maybe at first my intentions did come from a place of anger, but I think this could be good for the family, Caleb. With everything that has been going on you and Jax have not had time to consider your shortening blood supplies. And now Gemma's going to need it as well. I can do this job. I'm good at it. And maybe if I shared my time here and at the house like Gemma did, it would allow her a chance to get used to being around me again in smaller amounts. I could come home—"

Olivia, stop," he said, rubbing his hand over his head. "Look, I love that you want to help . . . I really do, but it doesn't change the fact that it's still too dangerous for you to be around Gemma right now."

"I want to come home!" I said miserably.

"I know you do," he said, taking another step towards me, the very last one the line of the sun would allow him, but I stepped away from him, and he did not like it. "I know you're angry with me about this. But it doesn't change the fact that putting a Charmer in front of a new vampire—who right now thinks of nothing but her thirst—is a very bad idea. I won't do it! And furthermore, I need to know *you* understand that, and stop doing these things that knowingly put your life in danger while you're staying here. That means you're gonna stop working at that clinic."

OK, so I knew Caleb Wolfe was a grade A Alpha male, but even this was a bit much. Just what the heck happened to all of the gushy warm feelings I felt for him the day before when I was talking to Skye? I knew they were still there but they were currently being overrun by the fact that he was really starting to *piss me* off. I walked right up to him and poked a sharp finger into his chest really hard. And if he were a *normal* man I'm sure it would have hurt a little. "No!" I said defiantly. "You and Jax chose to send me away, so now you can just deal with me working at the clinic."

"No, I won't *deal* with this," he argued back, thankfully still pinned to the shadows. "You're being reckless, and only to prove a point!"

"Reckless? What happened to '*Jax and I have already thought about that . . . ? Davin will be too busy dealing with Chay and your kick-ass ex-mate to be concerned with me?*"

"And they have. They have both assured me that he and his soldiers have been pushed underground well into British Columbia."

"*Both?*" I blinked back at him, hoping I had not heard what I had heard. But I could see by Caleb's expression that he was frustrated with himself for how that had just slipped out. "*Celeste* has assured you of this? Have you seen her?"

"Olivia, don't make this into a thing, because it's not," he began carefully. "She came back to give Jax and me status on what was happening—"

"Came back?" I repeated. "She's at the house? *She's* at the house? While I'm stuck down here with you refusing to even let me come home on weekends?"

"That's not—"

But I was so angry now I wouldn't let him finish. "So let me make sure I have this right. I am supposed to be your current mate—"

"You *are* my mate!" he snapped.

"—but you and Jax asked me to leave our home for my own protection while she was to be pushing Davin farther away from here. But instead, she's staying with you there while I'm here. Have I got this right?" I could feel my nails digging into my palms from the fist I was making at my sides. "Well that certainly does make things convenient for you, doesn't it? Old mate just down the hall, new mate a quick drive to on weekends."

"Olivia! You know that's not what's happening. You know it!"

"Do I? Cause I'm thinking you have no right to come down here and surprise me today when . . ." My words trailed off and I blurted out an odd sounding laugh as a new realization occurred to me. "Andie . . ." I murmured almost more to myself than him.

"What?" he questioned.

"I missed it before. You went to Jax's condo today to see Andie first," I repeated. "That's why you're here early—how you discovered I was working at the clinic." Caleb just stood there, giving nothing away and it only upset me more. "Jax has finally come out of his self-imposed hell long enough to figure out he misses his little girl."

"That's part of the good news I wanted to tell you," Caleb began calmly. "Jax has been doing better. He's been spending more time with Gem, letting her freely drink from him regularly. It's strengthening their connection, helping her recognize her mate again. This is a good sign." I threw my hands up, instantly marching towards the terrace doors to open them up to a gigantic pool of sunlight where he could not reach me . . . and he hated it. He hated being trapped in a shadowed corner, forced to stand there and watch as I moved further out of his reach. "Olivia, be reasonable here."

"Are you bringing Sophie back home with you this weekend?"

"No," Caleb replied tensely.

"But you're considering bringing her home soon?" He said nothing in response and it only infuriated me further. "Well isn't that just perfect! Soon you all can be one giant, happy family with Celeste and her coven. Should I just remain here, continuing to be a good little *mate* for you on the weekends?"

Caleb let out a fierce growl, one that I feared would shatter the terrace glass. His body was visibly shaking with anger as he came right to the edge of the shadow line. A fraction of an inch closer and what was left of the day's sun would burn him. But at the moment I was grateful for that sun, which was maintaining the fragile distance between us. "How could you think I would do that to you?" he questioned hard. "You know me! You know I love you. I would never betray you like that."

He then surprised me by reaching out for me, directly into the sunlight. As he pulled me back to him, the light burned into his flesh until his arm blackened and smoldered. "Caleb, you're burning!" I gasped as I smelled the charring of his skin. The smell of even that small amount on his forearm sickened and worried me, and I hated that it did because I wanted to remain angry at him, but I couldn't when he was in pain like that.

Caleb pulled me back into the shadows of the hall with him, pinning me between his body and the wall. I could hear how hard his breathing was just then. The pain he must have felt in that moment from his exposure to the sun had brought out the warrior side of him just that quickly. His brilliant blue eyes were right there in front of me as his chest rushed in and out like a balloon and our breaths clashed just above his fangs. He reached for me with his other hand, tenderly cupping the side of my face as he spoke. "I know being here is hard on you," he began in a rough whisper that held so much emotion. "I know you have this fear of ending up alone because you have lost so many people that you have loved. Your parents, Sarah, The Greysons . . . But Jax and I have not left you. *I* have not left you . . . and you will *never* lose me. Not to Celeste—not to anyone."

It shocked me how his words struck me with such force. It felt like someone had a physical stranglehold over me heart at that moment, and it was difficult to breathe. Often I found myself fighting my own insecurities of losing anyone else close to me—of ending up alone—and sometimes they felt too big to handle, so I chose not to face them. It had been a long time since I had thought about the night of the train crash when I failed to save my best friend Sarah from the horrific fangs of a Nightwalker. That night I believed myself to be only human. And that night I had met Caleb—for the second time—and my life started to go in a new direction with him—a wonderful direction. And when we were mated I felt wholly cared for—wholly loved. So why could I not simply trust that it would all last . . . that it wouldn't disappear . . . that I deserved it?

"Does Jax miss me?" I asked in such a small voice that it did not even sound like my own. "Has my grandfather even asked about me?"

Caleb pulled me into a full embrace against his body, leaving no part of me not wrapped tightly within him, and the contact, his strength, felt as vital to me as air. "Of course he misses you!" Caleb answered, emphatically. "I'm so sorry you have to ask because you don't already know that."

"I know it now," I said as I let my body sink a little deeper against him. Caleb's hand caressed over my side, and I realized it was the hand he had just burned. Never letting my head leave his shoulder, I reached my hand around to find his and touched ever-so-lightly over the charred flesh. "Are you all right," I murmured against his shoulder.

"It's already healing," he replied deeply as his large hands slid lower and smoothed over my hip.

"Don't do that again," I said to him and then in more of a plea, "Please don't do that again. I don't care if you can handle the pain . . . *I* can't handle seeing you in pain like that."

For several perfect minutes it felt so good to be there in his arms—it felt right. He felt strong, safe, yet his hands were gentle as he explored the curves of my body. He cupped one breast in his palm and his thumb stroked my nipple through my clothing. The sensation was heaven as his other hand reached lower and bunched the fabric of my black A-line skirt within his fingertips. He drew the fabric up on my legs, his breathing growing heavier at my ear. "Hey," I objected with my own rather breathy pant, "I thought we agreed no sex until you let me come home."

"I never agreed," he replied roughly, tearing the lacy, barely-there panty from my hips and letting it fall to the floor at my feet. "I will *never* agree to anything that keeps me from being inside you." He then cupped his hands over my bottom, effortlessly hauling me up fully against his body, my back pressing against the wall as he spread my legs around his hips until I was wrapped around him. Breathing hard, I was right there above his lips—his fangs, desperately feeling the need to kiss his mouth and I could see the same heated desire in his eyes. "I have missed you," he said. "Every day I have missed you. "I don't know if here has ever been a single moment since I met you that I have needed to be lost inside you more than I do right now." His words only pulled harder at my breath, harder at my heart as I felt him reach beneath me and start fiddling with his jean fly. My mate was preparing to take me without hesitation, without preamble, *against a wall!* And it only made my skin hotter. He braced himself with one hand and I swore I felt him shaking against me, but I knew it wasn't anything caused by weakness. He was holding himself back. "You're going to have to tell me no, Olivia. Do you understand? Say no!"

I leaned my head back against the wall, feeling almost drugged by the warmth coursing through my veins at that moment as I stared into the most luminous blue color I had ever seen in his eyes. "I can't," I replied with just a breath. "I can't say no . . ." He smiled at that as his hand slid up on my thigh, his fingers curling around its soft shape before lifting me up into position. With one rough thrust, and a hard grunt, he plunged deep inside me, taking everything he wanted without apology. "Fuck," he growled out roughly above my lips. "Your body is definitely *not* saying no. It's on fire!"

Oh, how I loved feel of him inside me. I ached for it. I felt full of him, fully taken, as my nails scraped over his shoulders. He reared back a few inches and thrust forward to the hilt, causing me to gasp against his cheek at the slight discomfort of being filled so deeply while pinned to the wall. "Are you all right?" he asked, his eyes closed with his own pleasure.

"Yes," I moaned as my head fell forward onto his shoulder, my fingers digging deep into his shirt—into his shoulders. I found it impossible to believe two people in this world fit together as well as Caleb and I did. The closeness, the intimacy every time we were joined like this—it just felt right. He thrust inside me again and again, taking me hard right there against the wall in the shadows. I was literally clinging to his body as he held my cheek in one of his hands. "God, you're beautiful when you're being taken like this," he gritted out. "You're looking at me like you know I'm the only man on earth who can make you respond this way. And I am. Make no mistake Olivia —I am."

I couldn't respond. I was breathless, lost in a euphoric haze of lust as he moved in a perfect, even rhythm inside me. My body almost slumped against him, as if to say '*take whatever you want. It's yours.*' And he did take, continuing to increase his paced, growling against my skin as my own small fangs began to press against my bottom lip, signaling my surrender was near . . . and he could *feel* it.

His next hard thrust ripped through me so fiercely I cried out with an uncontrollable gasp. The world was about to fall apart on me, an explosion to beat all explosions, but he suddenly held me still against the wall, his breaths so hard against my lips. "No!" he said. "Look at me. Do not come! I want to watch you as you try to hold it back. I want to see it in your eyes as you fight not to give in to that release you want so badly."

Oh, my God, what was he trying to do to me. "Caleb, I can't," I replied in nothing more than a plea.

"Yes you can," he said as he continued to work his body inside mine, making sure each surge forward went as deep as he possibly could go. My mouth fell slack as I stared at him through a half lidded gaze, feeling the stretch in my working inner muscles, feeling every stroke as it pushed through my flesh, feeling his smooth pace as he drove every sensation higher and higher. "Caleb," I whispered, pleading with him, begging him to finish. My nails tried to dig into his skin as my thighs tightened reflexively in his hands. The sun was completely gone now and the darkness seemed only to bring out the intensity of this moment as he continued to take me. I was shaking, my weight sagging against him, yet he held me as if barely noticing the burden of it.

"Hold it . . . *Oh God, Oh God! That's it. That feels perfect.*" I was coming apart in his arms and my legs were tightening around him as my hips lifted and his face was twisted with as much pleasure as my own. "This is yours, Olivia. I am all yours —always. Now and forever you have me. Now come!'"

"Caleb!" I screamed as my body couldn't hold back my release any longer. It seemed to lock and then release in giant waves of unbelievable pleasure as he thrust deep inside me one last time and then held still, absorbing the sensations of my muscles gripping over every inch of him. His palm slammed against the wall and he shuttered forward, his body coming hard as he growled under his breath. I fell forward, driving my fangs into his throat and drinking from my mate as if I had never known a drink in my life. Within seconds his blood energy was surging through my veins and I came around his buried flesh for a second time. I was taking his seed inside my body. I was taking his blood into my veins. He was imprinted into every part of me, into my very soul. There was no escaping it. Not that I ever wanted to try.

After I was finished drinking from him, I licked away the last drops of blood and watched his wound heal before my eyes. He straightened himself up enough to carry me into the bedroom, whispering sweet words in my ear while I rest my head against his shoulder, sated and silent. Laying me down on the bed, he began removing the rest of my clothes. When I was completely naked to him, he stood over me, his eyes touching over every inch of my skin as I lay boneless against the silk sheets. I was in a daze—a perfect haze of pleasure. I had been taken so completely I didn't think I'd be able to move again for hours, but I also understood our time was short.

"You're beautiful," he said reverently.

"You'll have to leave soon, though, won't you," I asked quietly.

He pushed down on the bed above me, wrapping my legs around him. "Not before we make up for some lost time," he smiled.

Chapter Seventeen

For the last hour I had felt a presence . . . something that was just out there, watching.

Exactly one week after Caleb had discovered I was working at the clinic, I found myself feeling restless and upset. I was worried for him, and I couldn't really explain why. It was a frightening sense that something was not quite right, and by now I had learned to trust my instincts. I understood they were a vital part of my Dhampir side that deserved my full attention when it came to keeping all of us safe.

Stepping out onto the terrace, I scanned across the twinkling lights of Lake Union and southward towards the Seattle skyline, where I could literally feel the weight of the eyes on me. Vampire energy pulled inside my chest like a giant band being stretched to its limit. This was not crossing paths. This was a vampire stalking me, and I recognized the energy. "I know you're there," I said into the clear night sky. "Show yourself."

Within seconds I heard a light click and swung around to see very long legs and very thin heels walking along a narrow ledge that may have not even been half that width with the confidence of a model owning a catwalk. "Bad time?" Celeste asked, a knowing twinkle lighting her almost luminous eyes.

"Is there ever a good time for a visit from you?" I returned, trying to appear unaffected but I was definitely bothered by the fact that Celeste knew the location of my condo. Caleb and Jax had told me it would be kept from her, and I had been wearing the necklace twenty-four-seven, so she shouldn't have been able to sense me. But then again, you didn't get to be a six-hundred-year-old Nightwalker without knowing how to overcome a few obstacles . . . probably more like annoying speed bumps insofar as she was concerned. I took a step towards her, stopping just inside the terrace doors. Celeste would not be able to cross the threshold into my condo unless she was invited, and that certainly was never going to happen. "Are you so bored, Celeste, that you've now resorted to stalking?"

"Bored? Yes . . ." she sighed, "for a couple of centuries now. All you humans bore me—and I include you in that group, since you're mostly human." She wasn't even paying attention to her next step—that if misplaced—could send her on a very long drop to the pavement below, a ten-story drop, to be exact. "As a group, you people offer me nothing new. You're so mopey and predictable. '*Oh, poor me. Why does my life suck?*' Blah, blah, blah . . . It's about as exciting as watching ants you just want to crush under your shoe."

"And yet you continue to mate with those boring humans," I replied, intentionally trying to bring the subject to Caleb without me having to directly ask about him. I wanted to know if he knew about Celeste's little visit here to me tonight, which I doubted very much.

"Yes, I do," she said, displaying an extra lift in her high step. "Although, they are no longer human once I mate them."

"I don't see why that makes you so proud. Bringing pain and misery to their lives that way . . . Why bother turning them at all?" I questioned her. "If humans are so '*boring*,' as you say, why bother mating them? Why not just mate another Nightwalker? Why Caleb?"

She watched me carefully for several long moments, then floated down from the ledge, gracefully landing on her thin heels and proceeding to walk toward me with all that platinum hair swinging across her back. "Look at you," she began—with carefully placed venom in her voice. "Staring your down your nose at me. You think you know him better than I do? Interesting . . . and so boringly human."

"I do. I love him. You may be six centuries old but I doubt you're even familiar with the concept of love."

"Oh, I love . . . And I love much more profoundly than some gawky teenage virgin he happened to cross paths with by a lake."

I blinked back at her. She was referring to the first time I had met Caleb as a teenage girl while camping with my family and my best friend, Sarah. I was sixteen at the time, and a late bloomer compared to most when it came to understanding the growing sexual feelings I had about boys and men—Caleb definitely being in the '*man*' category at twenty-nine that fateful day when Celeste had turned him. "You watched us that day?"

"You? No," she corrected. "*Him*. I could care less about you. But *him* . . . I had been watching for weeks. I bet in all your dreamy pining you didn't even realize he went fishing at that lake nearly every Sunday—God's Day, as you humans like to call it. *That lake*—nature and the sun—were like his church. He lived it . . . breathed it . . . as if it were the most important thing to him on this earth."

The breath I had been taking literally stopped in my lungs. Sarah and I had passed Caleb that day on the trail where he was fishing, but I hadn't noticed any of that. I hadn't really noticed *him*, the man underneath, at least not then. But Celeste had, and I wasn't quite sure how to reconcile that with my firm belief that I was his true mate. "Caleb Wolfe may have only been human," she continued, breaking into a victorious smile because she knew she had made a direct hit on my heart, " . . . a spectacular looking human, at that—but he had a lust and passion for life—for the sunlight—that I could only observe pinned in the dark shadows."

As I continued to try and find a way to stand there without looking affected by what she was telling me, I thought I was going to throw up. For the first time since I had met Celeste I was truly threatened by her, in a way I had never expected. She understood Caleb in the same fundamental way in which I believed I knew him—his love of nature. It was in how he saw the world. It was in his design of the tree house. It was how the man—the human inside him—expressed himself. But you had to know it about him to truly see it, and there were few of us who did, Jax and Gemma included.

Until this moment I had not believed that Celeste, a six-hundred-year-old Nightwalker who mated him for sex, could see that part of him, because it helped me feel secure in my place as his true and loving mate—his rightful mate. But right now she was tearing at the fabric of that faith, and I knew that I couldn't let her see that the effect she was having on me. "For someone who claims that humans bore you, you seem to pay an awful a lot attention to one simply fishing by a lake."

"You don't get it, do you?" she said, with an almost bored expression crossing her features. "Why does that not surprise me?" She stepped within a few feet of me, and for the life of me I couldn't get myself to move. I needed to hear her next words. I hung on them with her next breath . . . and I hated it. "He was like the sunlight I had lost all those centuries ago," she continued, " . . . something new that I could have again."

With those words, the slightest wind could have blown me over then as I watched Celeste turn her back to me, emphasizing how she saw me as no threat, and stare out onto the moonlit lake. Several of the longest, quietest moments of my life passed before she finally turned back to me with something brewing in those lavender eyes of hers. "Humans bore me . . . but Caleb Wolfe never did. And I knew it that night by the lake as I relished every possible drop of his blood I could without killing him. I knew that's what I was taking from him . . . his freedom to exist in the sunlight he loved. It would keep him tied to me. And I loved that."

"You are truly evil," I said back to her, the words crossing my lips as nothing more than a gasp. "How can you stand yourself?"

She just laughed. "Oh, I assure you, there was a moment then where I felt more charitable toward him. Then you showed up . . . a silly, sixteen-year-old girl, staring at him as if she had just come face to face with her teen idol." Celeste's whole expression seemed to snarl. "That should have been the end of it. He should have shown no interest in you. But then he squeezed your hand, and it was like watching a puppy find a new home. It was sick!"

I blinked back at her, my eyes now locked on hers, not wanting to admit I understood the implications of what she was saying.

"I could see he didn't understand it . . . That he comprehended how wrong it was to be feeling what he was feeling. You—a girl, so far short of a woman—were turning him on. But even then you were trapping him—"

"No! That's not true . . . ," was all I could manage to say back to her.

"It *is* true and you *know* it. As much as you want to pretend that you and he have some grand connection, your gift is controlling him just as it controls everyone else around you."

"It's not like that with him! What we have is real—"

"Think how much easier everyone's life would be if you were not there to manipulate it," she continued, as she began to slowly circle me on the terrace. "Caleb and Jax would no longer have to risk their lives fighting off their own kind because they are drawn to *you*. How many times have they been nearly killed while protecting you?"

"They don't blame me for—"

"Of course they do. They just won't say it. I mean . . . who else is there to blame for the attack on Jax that day but you? Davin sent those soldiers to capture you. And instead, they nearly turned a proud and dignified Jax Walker into a charcoal briquette."

She tapped the tip of her finger almost playfully against her bottom lip, while my heart began to feel as if it were being crushed in her bare hands. "Tsk, tsk, tsk," she continued. "If Davin was not after you in the first place, that attack on Jax would never have happened. Which also means you—sadly— could have prevented what happened to Gemma." Celeste then shrugged her shoulders in a calculated, cruel movement, and I felt the sting of tears wanting to wash into my eyes. "That's going to be a hard one to live with, isn't it?"

"Why are you really here, Celeste?" My voice was becoming shrill, and I hated myself for that.

"Oh, I don't know," she replied. "I just thought you would like to know that Sophie has returned home. That's right. Caleb and Jax brought a defenseless infant home, and yet you remain here. Surely you can defend yourself better than an infant. I mean . . . what does that say about them wanting you there?"

Oh, God, I now felt as if I were bracing myself for each of her verbal blows. I knew Caleb and Jax had been considering bringing Sophie back to the house, but I thought they would bring me home, as well.

"Are you *hiding* down here, little Charmer? Do you fear for your life?" Celeste moved so close I could feel her cool breath on my ear. "Because you should . . . Your mate has left you here—

unprotected. And Davin is still out there. Who's going to help you? Caleb? Your grandfather? How, exactly, are they going to do that when they have barely noticed you have been gone?"

"In case you missed it while you were bent over on your knees on that rock," I nearly hissed, "I can defend myself pretty well. Would you like an instant replay to freshen your memory?"

Without warning, Celeste was there in my face, her fangs and incredible lavender eyes warning me as much as the hiss of her next words. "It will not happen again, I assure you."

"I wouldn't take that bet, if I were you."

"Celeste!" a female voice called, and I glanced over to see Sherra, Celeste's coven sister, standing at the edge of my terrace wall. *Did the whole vampire world know the location of my condo now?* "Now is not the time for this."

Celeste looked about ready to tell her coven sister to back the hell off. But after a few moments of sucking in her obvious hatred for me, her expression calmed and the sly smile returned to her face. "Perhaps you are right, my sister."

"Unbelievable," I said with a gasp. "Are any of you tracking Davin?"

Sherra just laughed and added, "She'll remove the blinders eventually." Then she leapt onto a nearby roof and disappeared into the night as quickly as she had materialized from it.

I turned back to Celeste, who now glared at me with a wide grin. "I guess it's time to go. Caleb's waiting for me."

"Where is he?" I asked before I could stop it from slipping out.

She turned around just before she was about to drop over the edge to the roof. "He's at the house. Where else would he be?"

I stood there, speechless, as I watched her disappear into the night. What was going on? Caleb was not here, and Celeste's coven appeared to be doing everything else *but* tracking Davin! Did no one give a damn that Davin was still out there somewhere? Did they even know where?

Rubbing my hands over my upper arms, I could feel the tiny little hairs standing up from my skin. I needed to calm myself down and think rationally. Caleb would never put me in danger like this without warning me. He wanted to see Davin destroyed more than anyone. I wanted to reach out to him—to *feel* him, but there would be no way for him to feel me unless I took off the necklace, and at night like this I would exposed myself to the supernatural world—including Davin. Not to mention that I would scare Caleb half to death by taking off the necklace, something I told him I wouldn't do unless I was in trouble, on what right now was only a hunch. But I didn't trust Celeste and felt sure she was up to something. I was tired of letting her control the situation—control *my future* with Caleb. She was playing a game, dictating all the moves. And I suspected both Caleb and I were making the perfect pawns on her chessboard. It was time to make a move of my own, something that she wouldn't see coming. Then she would make a mistake, and we'd be there to catch her. Of that I was sure. Caleb was too smart not to see that his ex-mate was up to something.

Logic told me that if Celeste couldn't find me, she no longer had her chess piece to move. The solution was simple. I had to remove myself from the game.

Chapter Eighteen

The following morning, I hit the speed dials on the cell phone provided to me by The Brethren. As expected, my current Brethren Guardian, Lucas Rayner, picked up on the second ring. "Olivia?" he questioned in an impressive, half surprised, half barking tone. "Are you all right?"

"Perfectly fine," I replied. "No life-threatening vampire situations are unfolding at the moment. But I've decided to take a trip."

"Ah, fuck," he growled. "Why do I not like the sound of that?"

"Lucas!"

"What?"

I rolled my eyes. What was it with men and their cursing, anyway? Did they think the easiest way to convey what you meant was by flavoring it up with a four-letter adjective? "Never mind," I sighed. "So as I was saying . . ."

"Just tell me where the hell you are," he grumbled, "before you get yourself into all sorts of trouble."

"That's not—"

"Olivia, I don't know a single other person who gets themselves in as much trouble as you do," he interjected. "Where are you?"

"Chill out, dude. I'm on my way to you."

"*What?* You're driving here to The Oracle?"

"Should be crossing the border into Alberta in about seven hours."

A loud sigh registered over the phone, and I could imagine him shaking his head at the other end. "Don't tell me you're by yourself. I may not like that vampire you've shacked up with, but at least *he* seems to know how to keep you safe."

"Hey, I resent that," I replied. "I know perfectly well how to defend myself."

"Oh, man . . . you're high-tailing it over here on your own, aren't you?" The background sounds on the line told me that Lucas was running, then I heard a set of keys jingling. "OK, I'm coming to meet you. I'll call you in a couple hours. God knows, we've got to get you back on sacred ground before dark."

"No problem. We should make it with an hour to spare."

"Women," I heard Lucas mutter; then he hung up on me.

***

Lucas made record time meeting me, and we met before I even got out of Washington State. I didn't even want to know how many driving laws he broke to get there. Predictably, he lectured me for being *so* irresponsible as to come here alone, including a couple of curse words splashed in for extra effect. Then he instructed—no, more like *demanded*—that I get in his SUV while the fellow Guardian he must have dragged with him at the last second was elected to follow behind in my car. "What were you thinking?" he growled as we got back on the freeway. "You know you're not just in trouble with me? Alec's going to be furious at you for pulling a stunt like this."

I waved my hand through the air dismissively. "Alec's going to be fine. Nothing happened. It's was bright out today and I had the necklace on. You both need to relax."

Lucas scowled back at me as if I were a giant pain in his you-know-what. I gave him one of my best smiles and happened to catch the slightest quirk of amusement at the corner of his lips. Beneath all of his male grumbling, Lucas was nothing more than a giant softy. His willingness to try and curb his colorful second language in order to find that one woman who was right for him only proved that. "You're relying on that fucking necklace more than your common sense."

. . . Not that he was having any luck with that.

"I know this may shock you, but it just so happens that I do have a plan—a perfectly good reason for doing this."

"Oh, really. And what logical reason would you have for driving thirteen hours across the border . . . *alone* . . . without Mr. Fangs at least tagging along with you?"

"Don't call him that! Caleb's my mate."

"Whatever," he mumbled.

I shifted uncomfortably in my seat and stared out at the road ahead as Lucas's lead foot gunned our vehicle across the landscape. Darkness was falling fast and he knew it. It was the reason for his crankiness. Perhaps I could have been a little less impulsive. It certainly wasn't the first time I reacted first . . . But following my instincts had served me well so far, and my instincts were telling me that Celeste would be back now that she knew where I was staying . . . and my guess was she wouldn't be alone. "I'm trying to outsmart a vampire," I finally offered Lucas.

"Lord, help me," Lucas said shaking his head. "You think you're going to outsmart them by moving out in the open with no protection? What the hell kind of plan is that?"

"One that will work, hopefully," I snorted. "Because she definitely wants to kill me."

"*She?*" he questioned. "The vampire after you is a female?"

I nodded quickly. "She used to be mated to Caleb. Well, not technically—she tricked him. But now she wants him back, and I'm standing in the way of that."

"What is this? A bad episode of 'All My Vampires,'" he growled. "As if a vampire needed another reason to kill you!"

"Well, regardless, she's smart and has been around for quite a while. And she's definitely used to getting her way."

"What's her name?"

"Celeste . . . well actually it's Caelestis."

"Shit," Lucas bit out. "Are you kidding me? We know about Caelestis. We've been trying to destroy her for decades—but she's too damn clever. It figures you would piss off one of the most dangerous vampires around . . . like Davin wasn't enough."

"Tell me about it," I muttered.

When Lucas turned onto the long entry road to The Oracle like he was driving the final quarter-mile of a NASCAR track, we had, at most, five minutes before sunset, cutting things a little bit closer than I had estimated. After we came to a stop, Lucas looked at his watch, then back at me, with a scowl that said I owed him *big time*. And I did.

He rushed me into the enormous first floor lobby of The Oracle—The Brethren's North American home base. The onetime Bavarian-styled hotel was exactly as I remembered it, right down to the European-scale furniture that surrounded the stone fireplace, the rustic wood panels, and the elegant glass lantern chandeliers that hung from the hand-painted ceilings. Even though it was large, it was very cozy and was home to many humans and hybrids fighting against evil in the supernatural world. It was a world that I was meant to be a part of, but fate and the interference of my surrogate parents, The Greysons, took me down another path, and I was glad it did. The Oracle, though grand in purpose, was never my home.

"Let's head on up," Lucas instructed. "Alec's going to want to see you first thing."

"Alec's here?" I asked excitedly.

Nodding, Lucas added, "For tonight. He leaves for Munich tomorrow to meet with Nathanial Hawkings at his primary site, The Nave.

"Oh," I replied, unable to keep the disappointment from my voice. "This was a bad time to visit then."

"Oh, is that what you're doing?" he challenged, showing all the sarcasm he could muster. "Visiting?"

Ever since I had left The Oracle, nine months ago, I had only been back once to see Dr. Li about removing the tubal implants placed in me years ago. It was no secret that I did not consider The Oracle my home, even though it had been the home of my parents. My home was with Caleb and my grandfather . . . and, hopefully, Gemma again—someday. But I had kept in touch with Maya, as well as Lucas. Alec, however, had been so busy in his new role as Elder, one of the twelve highest positions within The Brethren, that on each one of the few times I had tried to reach him he was always away from The Oracle. I missed my former Guardian and friend and was very much looking forward to the chance to see him.

Lucas harrumphed as we walked into the special elevator that led us to the twelfth floor. I was quiet on the way up, knowing full well that Lucas was not bluffing when he said Alec would be upset at me for trying to travel here without protection. The Brethren and my Guardians still felt very responsible for me because of their connection to my mother, Eve, the original Charmer who had lived at The Oracle.

Once we reached the top, we were immediately greeted by four armed guards, all of whom had incredibly sour expressions on their faces. After a long pause, one of them finally cracked something that resembled a smile at Lucas and said, "Why can't you bloody ever follow protocol?"

"Because it's a fucking waste of time," Lucas shrugged. "I'm all about the now."

The guard scowled at him then turned to me, his thorough gaze inspecting me as if expecting to find some kind of weapon hidden under my clothes. "Is this—?"

"Olivia," I finished for him.

"Hmm . . . not what I expected. You're so—"

"Alec's expecting us, Sampson," Lucas cut in. "Can we go?"

The guard nodded and motioned down the left hall. "Go ahead. He's in the satellite conference room. Matthias will be waiting for you outside."

As we walked down the long hallway I was amazed at just how much protection Alec had as newly seated Elder of The Oracle. Oddly, I felt relieved and concerned all at the same time. I was glad his safety was being guarded so carefully, but all this protection only served as a reminder of how much danger his life was in now that he held one of the highest positions within The Brethren.

When we reached the thick, steel door, the guard gave Lucas a quick nod and punched a code into the entry keypad—not to open the door, but to signal to the occupant inside that we had arrived. After a few seconds, some sort of response was sent back, and the guard opened a small panel on the wall, entered his corneal identification and a seven or eight-digit code that opened the door.

Once we passed through the solid steel barrier into the room, there was a noticeable change in the way sound carried through the space. Quite simply, it didn't. The slightest pitch was being sucked into the acoustical material that lined the walls and ceiling. At the front of the room, a several times larger-than-life image of Sovereign Elder Joseph Davin was being streamed live on an enormous screen. As I made my way around the conference table to where Alec was seated, he was engaged in what looked to be a lengthy conversation with Joseph. "You could use his help on this, Alec," Joseph was saying. "Your success on this mission depends on being able to track the Lycan over some of the most difficult terrain there is. He is the best natural tracker The Brethren has."

"You're right, of course . . . I'll let him know to prepare, but we're not quite ready to go yet. I suspect it will still be a couple of days. And in the meantime," Alec added with a bit of a growl to his voice, "I've the perfect assignment to keep his shape-shifting ass busy."

Shape-shifting? Tracker? They were obviously talking about Kane. The man always seemed to be in trouble with Alec, and he didn't really seem to care.

Alec glanced back at both of us, giving a quick wink in welcome as an easy smile crossed his lips, pulling at the trademark dimple on his chin. He appeared to be in a good mood, despite his grumpiness regarding Kane. Perhaps Lucas had exaggerated Alec's reaction to my coming here alone? It sure was good to see him after all this time. I had missed my friend, who shortly after the age of thirty had more responsibility placed on him than I could possibly understand. As Elder, he was responsible for the loyalty, happiness and well being of everyone at The Oracle. Not to mention the priority and strategies of their missions, and keeping a productive balance with the other eleven Elders, who didn't always agree.

"Alec . . . ," Joseph warned, delivering great emphasis both with his eyes and his very mannered English accent. "I understand the need to focus him away from . . . ," he carefully cleared his throat, " . . . certain female distractions. But I prefer that you keep the peace. There are so few Natural Shifters in the world, may I remind you that we are lucky to have him— *you* are lucky to have him."

Alec sighed wistfully. "Just trying to keep peace among the women."

"More like trying to save their virtue," Lucas muttered under his breath.

I couldn't contain my loud snort in response. Evidently, Kane was still up to his habitual seducing habits when it came to the opposite sex. And why not? Everything about his '*stop you in your tracks*' good looks and stalking stride that matched the jaguar predator inside him screamed 'dare me'—hell, it screamed 'just look at me!' The opposite sex didn't stand a chance.

"Olivia," Joseph addressed me warmly, "nice to see you. Why has our resident Charmer decided to drop by for a visit? No trouble, I hope."

Joseph was actually the eldest son of Luther Davin, the vampire who was hunting me. But unlike his father, he was a kind and mild-mannered Brit who was cleaning up quite the mess left after his father's reign as Elder. As if hunting the man who used to be his father wasn't difficult enough, he was also Sovereign Elder—the highest position within all of The Brethren. He held the power of a king, yet he wielded that power with deliberation and forethought. In his mid-to-late forties, he was younger than nearly all of his council counterparts except for newly-appointed Alec and Scottish-born Owen Maberey, who ascended just last year to take the place of their corrupt relatives. In Alec's case, it was his uncle, Reese Lambert. "Somebody has to make sure you're all staying out of trouble," I teased, but when I noticed that both Elders were studying me carefully I offered the additional information they were really looking for. "Luther's soldiers have been persistent as of late . . . but it's been nothing we haven't been able to handle."

Turning to Alec, Joseph's expression stiffened. "Have you been able to locate where he's been hiding himself?"

"Not yet," Alec replied. "But it's unlikely he could've evaded us for this long without . . ." He seemed to pause as if considering what he wanted to say. "It simply doesn't make sense how he's been able to evade our trackers."

"I agree," Joseph replied. "The actual sightings of Luther have been rare as of late. That concerns me. He's up to something."

"No shit," Lucas added, and Alec immediately shot his friend a sharp look, reminding him who he was in the presence of. "Sorry," Lucas muttered sincerely.

Joseph didn't acknowledge Lucas's comment and proceeded as if it had never been spoken. "Perhaps we should bring a few more groups into Alberta to support your effort to destroy him." It was amazing how Joseph appeared completely resolved that the man they were discussing was in no way still his father.

"I'd appreciate that, Joseph," Alec replied. "I don't like just sitting back, waiting for him to make his next move."

"Agreed," Joseph finished. "Let's fill in the details when you return from Munich."

Alec nodded as the screen went to black. Then, he stood to his feet, swung around on me and in an instant his expression changed from casual to incredulous. "What the hell are you doing here?"

Chapter Nineteen

"Nice to see you, too, you brute," I scowled at him as he made his way towards me.

His brows pulled into a full grimace as he stopped in front of me and placed his hands on his hips. "You know what I mean," he continued. "You obviously didn't come with your grumpy mate or else I'd be hearing his ill-tempered beating at my wall by now."

"Caleb's not grumpy," I defended. "You set him off. And you shamelessly enjoy it."

A broad grin came to Alec's lips. "That is true," he confessed before once again straightened his expression. "Now what's this about Lucas having to break all the speed limits to go meet you in Washington?

I blinked back at Lucas, who was standing right beside me. "When the heck did you have time to call him?" Lucas just shrugged his shoulders at me while Alec continued to vent his objections.

"Never mind that! What I want to know is why would you drive here on your own without any protection? It's way too dangerous, with Davin still out there, and you know it! Lucas would have met you in Seattle if only you'd asked him."

I scowled back at Alec. His temper seemed a little quick to the mark today. Sure I understood that as Elder he now had a tremendous load to bear on his shoulders, and the last thing he needed was to worry that I might have done something to expose myself to Davin . . . *but still.* Pitching my hands on my hips, I caught Lucas rolling his eyes upward as if to say, '*Oh, here we go.*' Alec, however, couldn't have cared less. He ignored the obvious warning in my body language and continued to loom over me like the six-foot-plus, all-testosterone male that he was. "You know . . . despite what you both think, I've learned how to defend myself quite nicely, thank you."

Alec threw up his arms in exasperation. "Oh, so the woman

has had one year of training under her belt and now she thinks she's a supernatural Wonder Woman."

"Actually, more like the Sydney Bristow," I quipped and both men's brows pinched together on cue as they looked at each other. "You know . . . Jennifer Garner . . . kick-ass super-secret spy just out of college." Still not a clue as to what I was talking about, and I sighed with exasperation. "You guys really need to do a little less training and catch a TV show every once and a while. My point is that I have a perfectly good reason for coming here without Caleb. I'm setting—"

"Stop!" Alec barked as he put his hand out in front of him, then turned to Lucas. "Am I going to like this perfectly good reason?"

"Not a chance," Lucas replied with a half laugh, half snort. He then rudely went on to explain *my* plan to hide myself here in order to try and force Celeste's hand. Alec's expression shifted from merely irked to full-fledged exasperation right in front of me. He was all too aware of exactly who Caelestis was . . . and how dangerous she was.

"Lucas," Alec began with an unnatural calm, "will you please excuse us? Olivia and I have some things we need to discuss."

"What's the point? He can get the scoop later from any nearby Dhampir," I said, reminding him of our ultra-sensitive hearing.

"Not in here, sweetheart," Alec replied with a smile. "No sound penetrates these walls."

That I could believe. It felt as if I were standing in some sort of top-secret room at NASA.

"I'll be outside," Lucas said, punching in the code to release the padded, steel door.

Once he was gone, Alec lowered his head and sighed, bracing one hand at his hip as the other scratched through the back of his already tussled blond hair. "What's really going on here, Olivia? You can't convince me that Caleb would've approved of you leaving like this. In fact, I'm quite sure he'd have a big problem with it."

"I would have told him," I defended. "I wanted to tell him . . . but everything with Celeste happened so fast. I had to leave him a note."

Alec blinked back at me. "A note?"

"Well, it was more like a giant, poster-sized letter taped to the refrigerator . . ."

"*What?*"

"Caleb's not big on notes," I told him. "He wants to *feel* everything. Trust me when I say, we've had this conversation. But he couldn't feel me at the condo with the necklace on, and I couldn't risk taking it off that night, so I had to leave him something he was sure to see."

"Wait a minute. Slow down. You were at your condo. Celeste found you there?"

I nodded quickly in reply. "She wasn't supposed to know about the location of the condo—but she obviously does. I think she's up to something—or needs me for something. It's the only thing that explains why she left without trying to kill me."

"Caelestis doesn't need a reason for half the things she does," Alec replied sourly. "She simply does them because she can. She is the definition of 'Immortal thorn in the side' if ever there was one." Alec then returned his eye to look directly at me, and it was easy to see all the questions spinning in his head. "Why are you staying at the condo instead of the tree house?"

There was an exaggerated pause in my breath as I tried to work out quickly in my mind how I was going to tell him everything that had happened with Gemma, a woman he cared very much about and would probably be none too pleased to learn that he had not been informed of her condition until now. "Alec, I have something to tell you . . . Something you're not going to want to hear. But I need you to let me say it and let me finish, without going all *Alec* on me?"

"You can't start by telling me that!" he replied with a sharp blink. "And what the hell is *going all Alec?*"

"Never mind," I mumbled. "We're kind of past that point." Alec just stood there waiting for me to continue, and I could tell by his stiff stance that he needed me to continue, right then. "About a month ago, when Caleb was gone from the tree house, Davin set a trap for Jax. By the time Gemma and I got to him, he was tied to a tree with several silver chains, and he was burning under the rising sun."

"And . . . ?" Alec urged, his voice noticeably tensely.

"And everything happened so fast . . . ," I answered in a higher pitch, definitely feeling my unease of what I had to tell him next. "Gemma did what she did because she loves Jax—and knew he would die without—"

"What did she do?" he questioned hard, the tone of his voice already warning me that I needed to get to the point.

"He was dying . . . He needed blood to survive."

Alec swung his back to me, the fury he was trying to contain seeming to spark from him in little static shocks that I could feel just standing next to him. "Are you telling me he turned her?" he asked—in a voice that was much too calm for the circumstances.

"She had to do something. She couldn't just stand by and watch—"

"That son of a bitch!" Alec growled.

"Hey, that's my grandfather you're talking about."

"Yeah, and he's still a son of a bitch," he snapped angrily. "I knew something like this was going to happen. And next time it could be you! What's to stop *your grandfather*—or Caleb, for that matter—from doing the exact same thing to you?"

"Jax didn't do this *to her!* Gemma made the choice because she couldn't stand by and watch the man she loves burn to death in front of her. If it had been me in that situation, I would've done exactly the same for Caleb—and I told him that."

Alec pivoted around on his heels. "And bingo, there we have it. You're now at your condo because Caleb finally realized that eventually he or Jax would be responsible for bringing the same fate down on you. Am I right?"

"*No,* you're not right. And you don't have to sound so happy about it. They thought it was too dangerous for me to be there while Gemma was transitioning."

"Well, they're right! And I'm not happy about any of this," he barked. "After Jax destroyed Gemma's humanity, Caleb left you unprotected and opened the door for Caelestis to focus her boredom on you. It's completely irresponsible of him."

"He doesn't know Celeste found me at my condo. I came straight here today after she showed up last night. I knew I needed to go somewhere she couldn't find me."

"And that tells me just how well Caleb's been guarding you," Alec accused with a pointed finger. "You're not going back there. We'll protect you, since it seems he's incapable of it."

"Alec, don't," I replied, experiencing a slight wobble to my chin that caught me off guard. His expression seemed to stall, then calm, as if he had suddenly realized how much his words had hurt me. "Don't make this another challenge between you and Caleb. I came here because I needed a friend. Not so that you can bark at me how he's unfit to protect me. We protect each other. My home is with him. I love him as much as I ever did . . . maybe even more, now that I've been living apart from him. I will always go back to him, as long as he will have me."

Alec sat in the chair next to me, taking my hand gently in his. Though he and Caleb found little to like about each other, I knew he never wanted to see me upset. "I'm sorry," he began, in a much softer voice. "I am your friend—even when sometimes I don't act like it. But Olivia, I'm worried about you. If you protect each other, then why are you taking on six-century-old vampires like Caelestis by yourself? Why is he not there with you? Why are you having to leave him notes?"

"What happened with Gemma," I continued, shaking my head, "has shaken both him and Jax terribly. I think he's questioning what the right thing is to do for me. I worry he wants me to make a life separate from him."

"Would that be so bad?" Alec asked sincerely. "You might very well be safer."

I lifted my gaze to him, feeling as if my whole heart were pouring out on the table right there in front of him. "If your soul mate asked you to live apart from her . . . shattering your heart in the process . . . would that not feel 'so bad' to you?"

He was silent for a long while, as if he were really considering my point. "I don't know, Olivia," he finally answered. "I have no soul mate. I'm not sure I really believe in them."

I blew out a hard breath. "Someday, Alec Lambert, it's going to hit you as subtly as a freight train. And when that day comes, I want a front row seat—because I'm going to enjoy watching her turn you inside out. Only then will you understand why

Gemma did what she did for Jax that day . . . what she *had* to do."

Alec growled and sprung up from the chair, his stiff form turned away from me, his head down. Alec may not have found his soul mate in Gemma, but she was probably the closest thing he knew to it. Before Jax finally wised up and realized he was losing Gemma, she and Alec had gotten very close. It had to be tearing him up inside to think about what had happened to her. Knowing him, he would want to go to her. But he would also recognize it was no longer his place. She had made her choice. Jax was her choice. "Will she be all right?" he asked in a quiet voice.

"Eventually . . . But right now it's too early to know what might change about her. We can only let her transition run its course."

Alec's hands tightened into white-knuckled fists as he lifted them to the air as though he wanted to strike something. "*God,* I don't want to think about this right now. And I don't have any sympathy for Jax or that stubborn mate of yours. I can't get him out of my head as it is. Ever since you force-fed me his blood, it's like he's always there—at the edges somehow . . . driving me crazy."

"Hey! That blood saved your life."

"Don't remind me," he growled. "Thank God I'm not a vampire, or this connection to him would've probably freaked me the hell out by now."

I could feel the beginnings of a smile pulling at my cheeks as he turned to me with an accusing finger. "Don't laugh," he warned. "It's not funny. And it certainly won't be funny once Caleb realizes you're gone. Great," he added, massaging his thumb and index finger over his chin. "Why did you leave him a note? That's the action of someone who is running away."

"I'm not running. I told you I want to draw out Celeste—"

"I don't want to hear the story you've convinced yourself of," he interjected. "I want the truth . . . even if you're not yet admitting it to yourself."

I stared at him for a long while, not sure if I wanted the thoughts in my head to escape my lips, because then I would have to face them. "It's just that sometimes . . . Sometimes . . . I wonder if this has all been a mistake."

"What are you talking about, Olivia?" he asked sincerely.

"Look at what they've had to give up protecting me. It's not right. Jax was nearly burned alive because of Davin. And Gemma is now a vampire because of the trap he set for Jax. Caleb has become obsessed with destroying him—convinced that, until he's dead, we can't live in peace. *He* hasn't been able to live in peace. I don't want another mark on his soul."

"After what Davin has put you through this past year, Olivia, I think Caleb can handle one more mark on his soul to see the Nightwalker dead," Alec replied evenly. "It's not like he hasn't killed before. He *is* a vampire."

"You know what I mean," I pressed him. "This isn't fair to any of them."

"Did you think it was going to be easy?" Alec questioned me. "You had to know there were going to be challenges when you asked Joseph to let you live with them."

"Yes, but I didn't think it was going to be so hard on *them*. Let's face it, Alec . . . if they had not met me, they would not be fighting their own kind. Gemma would still be a Dhampir, and Jax would not be drowning himself in a self made hell about the guilt he feels over what he did."

Alec stared back at me with a sincere gaze as he squeezed my hand in his. "You can't do this to yourself. You can't take the blame for everything bad that happens around you. You never asked for any of this. And Caleb, Jax and Gemma have shown that they want this responsibility because they love you."

"It just would be easier if—"

"No, it wouldn't," Alec replied sharply, and then said into the following silence. "Look, I think you should get some rest. It's been a long day for you, and I'd really like it if you would stay here for few days while we work out a plan to deal with Caelestis. You are safest here. I can have Phin get a message to Caleb that you're here and that you're safe if you'd like."

I shook my head at him in reply. "I told Caleb I was coming here. He'll be here soon, I'm sure."

Alec blew out an exasperated breath. "The poster on the refrigerator . . . ? Great! Then you're going to have to deal with him when he shows up here pissed off and barking for my men to bring you out to him. Deal . . . ?"

I smiled and nodded. "Deal. Thanks, Alec."

Chapter Twenty

The next morning I wandered downstairs to the dining room in search of Lucas, soon finding him at a table with a heaping plate of food in front of him. He nodded for me to join him just as another man was leaving his table. A crooked smile tugged at his lips, and I couldn't help but think for all of Lucas's rough spots—and there were many—inside, he was one of the most genuine people I had ever met. He cared about the people and events happening around him, not that he would ever outwardly let it show—except when it came to Alec. His allegiance to his friend and Elder was unshakeable, and I think I admired that most about him. "Was that Dr. Li you were talking to?"

"Yeah," Lucas nodded before taking another bite of food. Dr. Arnold Li was a board certified MD, a genius, really, when it came to the specific physiology of a Dhampir . . . mostly because he was a Dhampir himself. When I first came to The Oracle last year, he had helped me to understand the chemical and physical differences in my body compared to that of a full human. Some of it scared me, like learning that I had fangs (small though they were) and that my saliva could make a human very sick if mixed with their blood. But Dr. Li made me realize that understanding those differences was the key in learning how to control them. "I tell ya, one good thing came out of that whole mess with Reese last year. Alec put the labs Reese built to good use. Dr. Li's offices are located there now. He has added staff and has the best equipment and facilities money can buy to help people here instead of using them for some crazy mission to create hybrid soldiers."

"Alec still struggles with everything his uncle has done, doesn't he?"

Lucas appeared rapt in his thoughts for a little while. "I think any of us would struggle with being betrayed by our own family. But for him—believing so fiercely in honor and truth . . . I'm not sure any of us can know what it's like for him."

"Joseph can," I replied. "He and Alec relate to each other in a way others don't. They understand that kind of betrayal. It's what drives them to do better."

Lucas nodded as he sat back in his chair. "Alec respects Joseph . . ." His voice faded as his gaze moved over my shoulder. "Damn!" he suddenly said under his breath.

I turned and followed the direction of his gaze to where Kane had entered the dining hall. Still drop-dead gorgeous with his thick, wavy black hair and silver eyes that always held a dare me twinkle to them, Kane strolled into the room just like the sleek and powerful jaguar he could shape-shift into. The man simply oozed confidence and apologized for nothing, taking in his surroundings at his own leisure.

I turned back to Lucas, who was now frantically looking at his wristwatch. "What?" I questioned, "Kane?"

"Of course," Lucas huffed. "I can't believe Phin's not here." Lucas quickly scanned the room and nodded towards two women who were seated alone at another table. "See the pretty strawberry blond?"

Pretty was an understatement. She was gorgeous, with her pale, flawless skin and rosy lips. And she seemed completely unaware that Lucas was watching her. With a small squeal of glee I turned back towards him with a huge smile. "Yes. Are you interested?"

He frowned at me as if I were being dense, causing the scar running from his temple to his cheek to wrinkle with his expression. "No. She just arrived last night. Phin and I have a bet on how long it will take Kane to make his move." He then mumbled a curse word under his breath. "It's not even been eleven hours. I think I'm going to owe Phin a twenty."

I was aghast in disbelief. "*You're betting* on how long it will take Kane to seduce that poor woman? You should be ashamed of yourself. She's new here and probably just wants to fit in. You should be warning her instead. Luckily for you, there's still time. Kane hasn't even noticed . . ." My words trailed off my lips as we both watched Kane stall in place. His focused expression appeared confused for a moment . . . until it was followed by a naughty smile. I felt my own breath catch in my chest as he appeared to inhale a full one, closing his eyes and lifting his nose to search the air. Then he turned directly towards the woman's table. *Unbelievable.* It was as if the shape-shifting jaguar within him had zeroed in on her like a big cat drawn to his prey.

"Son of a bitch," Lucas scowled. "Jaguars. What're you gonna do? Fucking Shifter can smell damn near everything."

I almost felt sorry for the woman as we watched Kane stalk towards her table with a slow, deliberate, effortless ease to his movements. What woman wouldn't be flustered at the sight of a confident, gorgeous man such as Kane making lazy strides towards her? The young woman, dumbfounded, simply blinked up at him as if she really wasn't sure she believed he was coming to their table. "We have to do something, Lucas."

"Excellent idea," he replied. "If you stall him with that Charmer thing you do, you could buy me a few more hours."

"Lucas Rayner!" I gasped. "You did not just say that!"

"OK. I didn't say it," he said sincerely.

Shooing him in disbelief, I rose from the table and headed straight towards Kane. For some strange reason I wanted to save the Shifter from himself, just as much as the woman. "Kane?"

His head lifted up, following my voice, his dark brow rising in interest as he turned to me. "Olivia." He glanced back to the women. "Excuse me, ladies. Urgent business I must attend to. Perhaps you could save me a seat this afternoon at lunch?"

"Perhaps," the woman responded coyly.

"Kane, now!" I said, yanking him away from her by his arm like some sort of crazed girlfriend. It was ridiculous!

"Easy darlin'," Kane drawled as I continued to pull him out of the dining hall, Lucas following right behind and laughing under his breath. "If you needed me that badly, all you had to do was ask."

Swinging him around to a stop, I could only imagine the incredulous expression on my face. "Are you for real? I'm mated, Kane!"

His eyes scanned the space around him as if he hoped to discover something vitally important. "What? Did you bring the vamp with you?"

"No, I didn't bring him with me," I replied with exasperation, slapping his upper arm hard enough so that it should hurt him, *should* being the operative word.

But instead he shrugged his shoulders with ease as his hands reached for each side of my hip. "Then we've got no problem here."

As my mouth fell open, Lucas sighed and stepped between us. "Give it a rest, Casanova. Olivia's trying to save the virtue of the woman you were just busting-a-move on thirty seconds ago . . . you know, the strawberry blond."

A wide, predatory grin, that so resembled the nature of his jaguar half, crept over Kane's lips. "She is a beauty, isn't she? Lord, I may need saving by the time I'm done nibbling on that lovely creature."

"Unbelievable," I blinked back at him. "I didn't think men like you really existed."

Kane splayed his arms out from his sides with an easy smile. "In the flesh, darlin' . . . in the flesh."

Stunned—though not exactly sure why, since he was acting exactly as he had the very first day I met him—I asked, "Kane, doesn't Alec need to see you?"

One brow lifted high as he stared back at me, curious. "As a matter of fact, I'm supposed to meet with him right now. Why? Is there something I should know?"

"Not at all," I fibbed, and I could hear Lucas laughing under his breath behind me. "I just think you should get up there. When I saw him yesterday he mentioned having a very important assignment that he thought only you could handle."

Kane snorted at that. "Right . . . I'm sure he does. Do me a favor, darlin'—just wait here 'til I get back. I think you and I should do a little catching up. And I have the perfect little closet to catch up in—"

"Move it, Kane!" Lucas ordered.

"All right, Grouchy," he replied with an amused smirk. "But consider yourself fortunate that you get to keep your twenty."

He winked at me and left both Lucas and me standing there in disbelief as he sauntered off, every deliberate step full of sin and naughtiness.

***

Standing outside Maya's room, I heard the feminine giggles of my friend on the other side of the door just before she opened it with a very happy Phin appearing to be tickling her from behind. When he saw me he wrapped his arms tightly around her and smiled with his chin hooked at her shoulder. "Hello, Olivia."

Phin Daniels had a beautiful smile. It was stark white against his silky-smooth chocolate skin. *God,* I knew women who would kill for that skin. Yet when Maya talked about Phin she always talked about his eyes. The blue-gray color swirled like the depths of the deep blue sea and made her want to sigh in happiness every time she looked into them.

"Hey, you two," I returned cheerfully, giving Phin a knowing glance. "I believe Lucas is looking for you in the dining room."

"Shoot!" Phin replied, glancing at his watch. "I'm late."

"Oh, don't tell me you made that stupid bet with Lucas again," Maya said.

"Again?" I echoed in surprise.

"Yes," Maya sighed. "They do it every time there's a new woman brought in to The Oracle."

I bit back another startled gasped. "Surely, Kane won't try to seduce every—" I began but was stopped short by Maya and Phin's raised brows. Shaking my head at the ridiculousness of it all, I didn't say another word, stepping past them into the room. *Good grief.* Who would blame Alec for locking Kane up in the chapel for some much needed penance?

"I gotta go, baby," Phin said, then planted a thorough kiss on Maya's lips. It was plain to see in the way Phin held her, the way his shoulders curved protectively around her as he kissed her, that Maya was not going to be a virgin for much longer. The pretty Dhampir seemed to almost melt beneath his kiss as I shuffled my gaze quickly around the room, acting as if I had just seen the most fascinating thing outside the window.

Once the door finally shut behind me, I turned to her and we smiled at each other in silence while waiting for enough time to pass to ensure that Phin was out of hearing range. I then clapped my hands together in glee. "Are you all ready for tonight?"

"Yes, but God I'm so nervous." Tonight was Phin's much-anticipated birthday, and Maya had been planning everything down to the last detail in her effort to seduce him. Of course, I had already assured her several times that Phin would need no seducing.

Grabbing her hand, I pull her farther into the room. "Don't you worry about a thing. I've got it covered." Returning to the small plastic shopping bag I had brought in with me, I reached inside and pulled out a very short, very sexy, and very translucent baby doll nightie. She stared back at me with crystal blue eyes as wide as the sky.

"Oh, my," she whispered. "I think he'll like that." With its romantic ruffled trim and whispery pleating, the effect was nothing short of perfect—romantic and feminine, just like Maya herself. She glanced at the silky fabric draping loosely from my fingertips then down to the tiny matching panty.

"Oh, my, is right," I said, holding it up to her slim figure. "But as Gemma would say, '*he's gonna have you outta that thing before you know it*'!"

"Olivia . . . I don't know what to say."

Grabbing her hand, I began to pull her from the room and headed us toward the elevator. "You don't need to say anything. Now, come on. We've got a lot to do to get this place ready. Let's go get some of those beautiful roses from the garden so it'll smell all yummy in here tonight."

Maya smiled up at me brightly. "Thanks again for helping me with all of this. I'm glad it worked out that you were here. If you weren't, I might lose my nerve."

"You'll be fine, Maya. Besides, I love helping you with this. It helps me focus on something other than how much I miss Caleb."

"You do miss him, don't you?"

"Terribly," I sighed. "I feel sick now that I just left him with a note. What was I thinking?"

"Well," Maya replied with a wide blink, "you did say it was a *big* note."

I laughed. "Poster-sized, but I doubt he'll find the humor in that."

Suddenly, we were interrupted by the sound of dozens of voices coming from the floor we were about to land on. We stepped off the elevator to utter chaos. Both men and women were running about as if they had too many things to take care of all at once. Lucas rushed in from outside with ground-eating steps and a hard glare on his face, Phin right behind him. "What's going on," Maya asked as they approached.

The two men paused and gave each other a look that said something was not right. Lucas raked his hand roughly through his hair. "It's Alec. He and his guards were ambushed this morning."

My heart lurched inside my chest. "*Oh God*, Lucas," I replied with just a breath. "What're you saying?"

"He's been captured."

Chapter Twenty-One

"Captured?" I shouted, loud enough to make the sound of my voice ring inside my own head. "Where? By whom?"

Lucas placed a reassuring hand at my shoulder. "I'm just now getting the information. I don't have all the details. So until we have them there's no reason to panic, OK?"

"Don't give me that placating crap," I snapped at him, realizing by the worried looked plastered on his face that he knew more than he was telling. "What *do* you know?"

Lucas's jaw seemed to grit against his teeth for a moment before he exhaled a rough breath and looked straight at me, his voice low and quiet. "They were ambushed as they tried to board the jet. Most of them were killed—"

"*Oh, God,*" I whispered, fearful that if I spoke any louder, somehow the news could get worse. "Alec . . . ?"

Lucas firmly gripped me at my shoulders. "Alec was alive when they took him," he added. "Sampson was able to give us that much information before he was sent down for treatment in medical."

"Will Sampson be all right?" Maya asked worriedly.

Phin nodded as he squeezed her hand reassuringly. "He's going to be fine, baby."

"Who are *they?*" I asked. "Who took him?"

"Dhampirs . . . That's all we know." Lucas watched me carefully as he imparted the information. He knew right where my thoughts would go. "That's all we know right now," he repeated. "So don't jump to any conclusions."

"You know, somehow, Davin is behind this."

"No, I don't know that." The steadiness of Lucas's voice was reassuring, but it wasn't enough. Alec was one of my dearest friends, and if anything happened to him—especially because of Davin—it would not only devastate me, but everyone at The Oracle who had grown to care for and respect him as their leader over the past year. "Listen to me," Lucas pressed. "We'll find him and bring him back. I promise you."

"You're right," I agreed. "We will find him—because I'm going with you!"

"Me, too!" I heard Maya's voice right behind me as I pushed passed both men, headed straight towards the lobby exit doors.

"Hold on!" Lucas replied roughly, grabbing my arm from behind to swing me back around to face him. "That's not a good —" He was interrupted by the angry snarl of an enormous black jaguar sounding from beside us. *Kane.*

Kane had wasted no time in shifting to his animal form, an apex predator adapted for tracking over a large territory. Lucas momentarily turned his attention to the jaguar, nodding something in a silent understanding between them. "Go. We'll be right behind you."

I wasn't sure how that was going to be possible to be right behind him. Kane responded to Lucas's command with a rough mewl that sounded more like a fierce cough, then appeared to go from zero to sixty as easily as a Maserati as he took off across The Oracle landscape. Kane obviously recognized how crucial every second was. "We're wasting time, Lucas. We need to go—now!"

Lucas's hard gaze was fierce and resolved. "You need to stay here. You have half the supernatural world after your ass! Going out in the open is not a smart idea."

"I have the necklace. It will protect me. You can't ask me to stay here when Alec's life is at stake and you know my gifts can disable the Dhampirs who have him. Besides, isn't this what The Brethren has always wanted . . ." I challenged him. "*Me* fighting with you?"

"Lucas is right this time, Olivia." Phin surprised me with his support of Lucas as he came up behind Maya and smoothed his hands down her bare arms. "You don't know if Caelestis has followed you here and is just waiting for an opportunity to snatch you once you step off sacred ground." He then turned Maya around to face him, the quiet look in his eyes sincere as he spoke. "You should stay here. I know you can handle yourself, but I will feel better if you stay behind with Olivia."

I was holding my breath the whole time Phin spoke, worried that an often-placating Maya would do as Phin asked of her.

"Phinneas, we are both trained to handle this. You don't need to worry. We're coming with you," she insisted, to my relief.

"I don't have time to debate this with you two," Lucas growled. "I know if Alec were standing right here he would say the same thing to you," he said pointedly to me, "that you need to stay on sacred ground until we understand fully what's going on."

Lucas's head shot up to meet the befuddled gaze of the middle-aged Englishmen who was approaching us. Gideon Janes was a Guide for The Brethren, sort of like a New Age know-it-all when it came to understanding the supernatural world. He was a man of stunning intellect and equally stunning social awkwardness, not to mention that he was severely fashion challenged which was evident by the truly awful plaid jacket he was wearing at the moment. "You both haven't left yet?" Gideon questioned.

"We're trying," Lucas said, clearly exasperated. "I need you to stay with Olivia and Maya."

I blinked back at Lucas. "You know Gideon can't keep us here if we want to go. He's only human."

"I'm rather afraid she's right," Gideon spoke in his formal mannered accent as he wiped his thin-framed wire glasses on his sleeve, appearing to show no effort what-so-ever that he was going to try and stop us, which made me smile. The man was smart! "There'd be little I could do to stop them."

Lucas frowned at the man with a look that said he expected more from him, but Gideon didn't really see it because he couldn't see more than three inches in front of him without his glasses on. "Fine!" Lucas barked, then motioned to the four guards posted at the entry to the lobby. They came right over at Lucas's command because he was considered Alec's second and in charge of The Oracle if Alec were unavailable—and this situation definitely qualified. "Take these two to Maya's room and post two guards outside. They're not to leave that room. Understood?" The guard nodded once to convey his understanding.

"You can't be serious?" I started to protest, but my arm was instantly seized by one of the guards at the same time Maya's was.

"Phinneas?" Maya questioned, her bright blue eyes staring back at him with disbelief.

He came up on her quickly, stroking his hands over her shoulders and pulling her in close for a gentle kiss. "Sorry, baby," he whispered above the seam of her lips. "I'll be back soon. Don't worry."

"Don't, *sorry me,*" she said as she pulled away from him and tried to pitch her small hands on her hips, but the guard's hold was restricting her movements. "You're in big trouble Mister." But without another word, both Lucas and Phin darted out of the lobby towards the army of men waiting outside.

"Let's go," the head guard commanded as they led us towards the elevators to take us back upstairs.

I was still cursing Lucas's name when the door to Maya's room closed behind us. "I can't believe him!" I complained. "He's bossier and more unreasonable than Alec."

"You can't really be surprised when it's Lucas's job as your Guardian to protect you." I blinked back at her as if to say, 'of course I can,' but she continued on before I got the chance. "Now Phinneas, on the other hand—he's in *trouble.* I have trained and have been fighting alongside all the men since long before we ever started dating. For him to start pulling this '*it'll make me feel better*' crap now is just unacceptable."

Maya was the more rational thinker of the two of us, but she looked rather cute when she was all worked up about Phin. It was obvious she loved him, but it was also evident that she wanted him to respect the fact that as a Dhampir she could handle herself and fight alongside him—the same thing I was struggling to make Caleb realize. She immediately grabbed a pen and sheet of paper, knowing that more than one of the guards was a Dhampir and would be able to hear every word we said. As she frantically scribbled on the sheet, I had an overly loud conversation with myself about what I was going to do to Lucas when he returned . . . which wasn't an exaggeration.

What do you want to do?,

Maya wrote.

I rushed over to Maya's closet, grabbed some cargo pants, several layered tops, and two warm jackets. Though it was still summer, it would be getting cold after the sun went down. We had to be prepared for anything. I nodded towards the balcony, then scribbled:

Need to get to the roof so we can see the direction they are heading. We can jump down from there and follow.

She jotted a few words and handed them back to me.

What about the guards posted at the ground?

I responded with my plan.

Good point! Once we have the tracking party's position we'll have to crawl to the backside and jump down from there. Let's go.

An inch at a time, it felt like it took forever to open the slider door while we continued our loud, meaningless banter back and forth for the benefit of the guards. Once the door was opened enough for us to slide through, Maya announced that she was going to take a shower. The sound of the water would be a good distraction and explain, at least for a little while, why the room was so quiet. It was critical that we delay the guards for enough time to let us crawl over the roof and get down before they discovered we were missing, or else they would be on us too fast.

Silently, we jumped from balcony to balcony, lucky in the fact that no one was in their rooms to spot us, given all the commotion going on downstairs. When we reached the roof we each scanned the distance from our high twelfth-story perch. "There," Maya whispered as she pointed north. The tracking party was headed north, away from the airfield and deeper into the mountains. "So now we know where they're headed . . . How do we get down?" Maya asked. "We can't jump a hundred and fifty feet, and we can't risk being spotted if we tried to crawl down."

Swallowing hard, I looked down and replied, "Yeah, I didn't really think about that. What if we go back inside, via Alec's suite, and take the elevator down? We can mix in with everyone and sneak out down there."

"Are you nuts?" she asked with wide blue eyes. "There'll be guards everywhere . . ." Her voice trailed off as she started to catch up with where I was going with this. Half of the guards went with Alec to the jet this morning, and now the rest were guarding the entries to The Oracle and Maya's currently empty room.

"All we need to do is get to a lower floor and jump from someone's balcony on the backside."

"Someone's balcony who just left with the tracking party would be preferable . . . so we don't get caught," Maya felt the need to point out.

"Another excellent point. You're really very good in a crisis situation," I commended.

She smiled and blushed. "Thanks."

"Come on. We have to hurry. The guards will fall for the shower thing for only so long."

The plan was flawless. Within minutes, we were outside The Oracle and racing at full Dhampir speed across the property towards the mountains. The only challenging part had been going through Alec's suite. As usual he kept things tidy, but just being so near the things he had touched only a few hours ago when he was safe reminded me of how much danger he was in now. As we raced to catch up with Lucas and Phin's tracking party I prayed with every step that he wasn't being tortured, turned, or even killed by the Dhampirs, and more than likely vampires, that had him.

Just before night-fall we could sense we were right on their tail. We began to fall back a little so as not to be discovered too soon, gambling on the fact that they were too distracted about Alec to sense we were there—or else they would send us packing right back the way we came. The low rumble of several off-road vehicles sounded on the rough roadways at the base of the mountain. They followed the tracking party with supplies. We made sure to avoid them, as well. If they spotted us, they would call in to Lucas.

Suddenly, Maya grabbed my arm. "They've stopped ahead. We need to wait here." She then noticed I was stroking the sapphire necklace around my throat. "Are you going to take it off so Caleb can sense where you are?" she asked. "That'll make you visible to him . . . draw him to you."

Shaking my head, I responded, "No. It would put all of us in danger if the Dhampirs and vampires who have Alec are also drawn to me without first having a plan."

"But you want to, don't you?"

"Yes," I sighed. "I miss him terribly. And by now he'll know I'm gone."

"He knows you came here. My guess is he's already on his way to The Oracle. Unfortunately, now we're heading away from it."

"I know, but it won't matter. With me gone, Caleb will be tuned in to Alec to try and find me. They are linked now, and he will sense something's wrong. He'll follow Alec's trail."

"Oh, my," Maya blinked. "It'll be like one giant collision of trouble."

"Yeah, no kidding," I snorted in reply. "And I'll be in serious trouble for leaving him a note like that when he catches up with us. I just hope he'll give me the chance to explain before he threatens to cut *me* off from sex."

Maya giggled at that. "I don't think there's anything you could do to make him threaten that. Besides, you knew exactly how upset he'd be when you left him with just a note. I don't feel the least bit sorry for you."

"Thanks a lot," I replied sourly.

"Well, you could be in my position. Phinneas's,"—she added quote marks in the air with her fingers—"'birthday surprise' is now ruined, and I'll probably be a virgin for the rest of my life."

"I doubt that," I laughed as we both sensed the party starting to move forward again in the darkness. It was obvious they were going to push themselves through the night. As we continued on through the forested thicket I reassured her, "It will happen when it's supposed to, Maya. You've waited this long. I think you can make it a few more days."

"That's easy for you to say," she complained. "You've been having blowout sex with a six-foot-four stud for a year. It's time to share the love with the rest of us."

"Why, Maya, I didn't know you were such—" My words were cut off by the burst of wind that blew right in front of us without warning. Suddenly Phin was looming over a startled Maya, who defended herself with a simple, innocent smile. There was no doubt that Phin loved Maya, but right now he looked about as happy to see her as Caleb would be when he finally caught up with me.

"What're you doing here?" he hissed in a hushed voice. "You were ordered to remain at The Oracle."

Maya just shrugged. "Well, I guess I'm not very good at taking ridiculous orders," she said with an uncharacteristic bite to her words. "How did you know we were here, anyway?"

"Are you kidding?" he replied with an exasperated exhale. "You two are chatting back here like two teenage girls on an overnight camping trip." Maya's expression suddenly looked worried, probably because she was wondering what else Phin had overheard.

"We were *whispering*," I defended weakly.

Phin just rolled his eyes at that. "I had to get back here to hush you up so you don't ring the dinner bell for the vampires who have Alec."

"So there are vampires who have him?"

"Yes," Phin answered simply.

"Is Alec nearby?" I whispered as quietly as I could considering my worry, grabbing over his arm . . . not that it moved anywhere under all that muscle.

"Kane sent a Dhampir back. They have Alec in those mountains," he said, pointing towards the rough terrain above us. "It's going to be a bit of a climb . . . but not for you two. You're headed back to The Oracle—Lucas's orders."

"What's his problem?" I muttered under my breath. "He's my Guardian. How's he supposed to guard me if I'm not with him?"

"I don't think he'll see it that way, but you can battle it out with him all you want." He then redirected his attention to Maya. "But, I want you to go back."

"No, I'm staying with you," she insisted, staring him straight in the eyes. I could see that Phin was trying to figure out how to gently inform Maya that wasn't going to happen when Lucas cleared the trees, his angry scowl warning us of his mood.

"No time," he growled. "We've got to go *now*. They're moving with Alec again. You two stay to the back. Understood?" It was unmistakable by his tone that we were not to challenge him.

Phin had been right. It was a very high climb up the mountain, especially in the dark of night and at an unyielding pace. It was easier for us Dhampirs, since we had excellent speed and night vision, but for Lucas and the other humans it was much more difficult—but they never let that slow them down. They kept up with us. I admired that about Lucas. He was tough and quick minded, relentless when it came to the pursuit of those who captured his friend, a man he had grown up alongside at The Oracle since he was a young boy. Even though Alec had been the one destined to be an Elder, making him the '*more important one*,' Lucas never let that come between them. He faithfully played the role of 'second' all his life, loyal to Alec in every way.

Maya and I did as Lucas ordered and stayed near the back so both Lucas and Phin could concentrate solely on tracking Alec. As we neared the top of the mountain, Lucas had us stop and take cover. He was waiting to hear from Kane, who soon cut through the thicket in human form, dressed only in a pair of loose fitting hiking shorts—which was more than he was wearing the first time he shape-shifted in front of me. Maya and I carefully worked our way right up behind Lucas so I could hear their barely audible conversation. "They have him tied up against a rock," Kane informed them. "Just killed his last guard."

Lucas turned to me. I hadn't even been aware how hard I was clenching his arm. "Didn't I tell you to stay in back?"

"You did, but you're going to need my help to get him out of there."

"Oh yeah . . . How do you figure?"

"Don't play stupid, Lucas Rayner. You know as well as I do that as soon as I take this necklace off I will draw the vampires to me like flies. That'll give us an advantage."

"You're suggesting we use you as bait?"

"If it saves Alec's life—use away."

"It's not a bad plan," Kane added. "Draw them into an area we control, while we send people in to get Alec. We can use the bluff to the east. Surprising them over the edge gives us a tactical advantage."

"I don't like it," Lucas growled. "Olivia, you don't know who you'll be drawing in once you remove that necklace."

"I can do this, Lucas," I assured him. "Let me help."

Lucas didn't say anything for a long while, and I thought he was about to nix the whole idea, but in fact, it was quite the opposite. "If we do this, then I want you and Phin covering her," he said to Kane. "You both can get to her faster than I can if there's a problem."

He then turned to me, his brown eyes intense. "Are you sure you want to do this?"

I nodded without hesitation.

"All right, Olivia Greyson. It's time for your first battle alongside The Brethren. Let's get to work."

Chapter Twenty-Two

Standing there in the empty field, I knew exactly what I needed to do as I pulled the sapphire necklace over my head. I was ready for this moment. All the work to understand who and what I was, what I was capable of, what I had trained for—even while being doubted at times by those closest to me—I knew I was ready. I focused on everything I had gone over with Lucas, Phin and Kane, but couldn't help wondering what my parents, Eve and James, would have thought of all of this. Both had died while I was too young to remember them—died while also fighting for The Brethren. I had declared that this was a future I didn't want, but now that I was here, faced with the situation to save Alec or not, I knew I was ready for it.

I scanned the open terrain in front of me, patiently waiting for the vampires I knew were coming to clear the tree line. They wouldn't be able to help it. They were being drawn to me, against even their strongest will. Whatever their mission at that moment, it would take a back seat to a baser need they didn't know they had—and couldn't fight against—the need to come to me. Taking one step back, I came even closer to the steep drop off at my ankles where Kane and Phin hovered on a ledge a ways below. Without question, they would protect me with their lives, but I couldn't help thinking about someone else just then, someone who was going to kick my butt to the other side of Alberta when he discovered what I was attempting to do.

In the middle of that thought, the first seriously large vampire cleared the tree line about 35 yards in front of me, clearly visible in the bright light of an almost full moon. His dark eyes focused in on me. Two others followed closely behind him. I felt like I was in the middle of a bad zombie movie rather than defending myself against a coven of vampires. They appeared almost to amble with exaggerated slowness across the open terrain between us, and it was startling to see how pale their skin appeared. It had a grayish cast that resembled ash, accentuated by dark shadows under their eyes. They looked as if they were malnourished, starving for the blood their bodies craved. Nightwalkers, for sure, but they could be mistaken for the bottom feeders of the supernatural world, truly the walking dead. Seeing them, it was clear to me how much difference there was between Daywalkers like Caleb and Jax and these lifeless, bloodthirsty creatures.

"Well, it's about time, boys," I said, as cheerfully as I could. "I thought I was going to be enjoying this party on my own." The Nightwalkers responded with sharp hisses and growls, as if trying to fight the pull of my gift to draw them in. It wasn't working. It was plain how they were locked in on me; they didn't want to come, but neither could they stop themselves. I wasn't even sure they could sense Phin and Kane there below me, they were so fixated. And in this single moment I truly understood for the first time why The Brethren had worked so hard to find me all these years, pressuring me to fight with them for their cause. When Gideon had told me stories about how powerful my mother was, I wasn't sure I believed it. The showering of adoration seemed more designed to persuade me to their goals than any real sincerity or admiration for my or my mother's gifts. But right now I believed it. I was powerful, and I felt it in every fiber of my being, in every breath. During the last year, my gift had been growing in strength, the first obvious evidence of it becoming clear to me when I held Celeste down on that rock with my touch alone.

If gaining the edge on a six-hundred-year-old vampire wasn't a sign, then I didn't know what was.

"Good thing you're here," I smiled confidently. "I wouldn't want you to miss anything."

"Didn't your mother ever teach you to avoid those things that go bump in the night?" the large one grated out. "Learning that lesson the hard way's going to be painful."

They were now only ten yards away from me, and they just kept coming. Two more emerged from the tree line, which put the count at five. Not impossible odds, but certainly challenging. "Painful for you, maybe . . . But my mother preferred to look for trouble. What're ya gonna do? It's in the genes."

"Who are you?" one of them asked.

"You don't know?" I replied with a hint of injured surprise. "Well that really hurts my feelings, boys. Seriously, you must be the last vampires in all of Alberta not to hear." Not amused by my wit, the large vampire closest to me gave no notice before he charged straight at me. I had barely enough time to lift my hands for impact, and when it came it pretty much felt like being run over by Jax's Hummer. But I was able to cling to his exposed neck. Within seconds, dozens of horrific images flashed through his mind and my own. This was one very bad vampire. My guess was, judging from the violence in his thoughts and the number of images we had only begun to crack, that he had lived for a very long time.

Immediately, he stumbled to his knees, his hands holding at his temples, while the other four Nightwalkers glanced around at each other as if some alien monster had just bested their leader. "Painful, I know," I replied. "But I did warn you. That, boys, is a personal greeting from a Charmer. I'd step back if I were you. It tends to get a little painful from here on out."

Of course, I left out the part about how it was also painful for me to see those images, though I tried to filter out as many as I could. I really shouldn't have been surprised when none of them heeded my warning and three of them charged at me all at once. Telling a vampire not to do something was the equivalent to daring them to do it. Evidently, they assumed quantity over strength would win in the end. *Not a bad plan,* I thought as they came within touching distance of me. One of them was immediately jolted back by the initial contact with my skin, and I grabbed on to the other two just as tightly as I could. Now, images from both vampires came shooting at me all at once, even though I was trying to filter most of them out. It was painful—but even more painful for them—as I focused and clamped onto their arms, forcing them both to their knees as they growled out their misery, both of them making sounds that reminded me of a whining dog.

It was strange to feel the immense strength of my special power over them. . The dominance, the security of it, was unlike anything I had ever felt before. I'm not sure I had even been aware of how quickly my gift had been growing, but now I understood. I was a force to be reckoned with—me . . . Olivia Ann Greyson, pianist and composer. It was true; I could see it, I could feel it through body and soul. But the pieces somehow didn't seem to fit together!

By then the third vampire had recovered somewhat, and he decided to come at me again as I still held on to the other two, but he was stopped short at the last second by Phin, who had emerged over the edge of the cliff with Kane. When I finally let go of the other two vampires, who were now no more that piled heaps of moaning misery on the ground, Kane was in front of me, shifting into his gigantic jaguar form as he stalked forward, warning the other two vampires with a low growl.

Normally, vampires wouldn't be the least bit threatened by a jaguar. In fact, they would ring the dinner bell . . . but Kane was different. When he was in his altered form there was a distinct odor to him that Nightwalkers and Lycans did not like. But it wasn't as simple as, say, skunk stink to a human. The scent was more subtle, masculine, with traces of something that I couldn't compare to any other scent I had ever smelled, but it made the hairs on the back of my neck stand up in fear. Their fear, combined with Kane's exaggerated size—a size that displayed he was more a creature of myth than nature—caused the vampires to hesitate just long enough for The Brethren forces to arrive through the forest from where they came.

While Phin and I handled the three that attacked me, and Kane trapped the others between him and The Brethren forces, the vampires soon realized they were severely outnumbered, and they retreated, the confused look on their faces conveying they weren't prepared for this small army that had shown up . . . which didn't make any sense. They had to have known when they took Alec that The Brethren would follow with every bit of force at their disposal to get him back. But I was focused on only one thing—getting to the other clearing, the one where Alec was being held.

Lucas and his men were already supposed to be there freeing Alec while I was drawing in the others. I ran as fast as I could until I reached the clearing and they came into view. Lucas and Maya were there, trying to revive Alec, who was sprawled out awkwardly across the ground. "*Oh, God,* please let him be all right."

By the time I reached them, I could see his eyes were blinking open in a slow haze. It took him a minute to remember where he was, but he seemed uninjured as he suddenly jerked up and scanned the area around him. Maya was tearing the chains from his wrist and ankles as Lucas laid a reassuring hand on his shoulder. "Easy, buddy. Take some water."

"Thank God, you're all right," I said with relief as I dropped to my knees beside him.

Alec shook his head, refusing the water Lucas was offering him. "Take it," Lucas ordered sharply, not in the mood for any of his friend's stubbornness.

As Alec sipped, Lucas asked, "What do you remember?"

Alec answered in a scratchy voice. "Dhampirs attacked as we boarded the jet. They killed my guards but didn't harm me. I don't believe they ever intended to."

"Then why—?" Lucas started and suddenly stopped.

Alec's eyes darted around us once again, becoming more lucid within seconds. "I'm bait," he said sharply.

"Bait for—?" Lucas didn't even finish his thought as both men's eyes widened with awareness and then turned to me.

"Get her out of here!" Alec snapped, but by then it was already too late. At least a dozen Nightwalkers descended upon us with dizzying speed. These Nightwalkers did not look sickly or starving; rather, they appeared to be full of menacing strength. We were suddenly surrounded, and one vampire shouldered past the circle that had quickly formed around us. I blinked once, unable to believe who I was staring at.

"I'm afraid Olivia isn't going anywhere," the familiar voice warned. "Except with me."

Alec tried to fight his own disbelief as he said, "Reese?" Reese Lambert, Alec's uncle, the man who had raised him after his father was killed and then betrayed him many times over with his deception and greed, now stood before him with a flat smile on his very pale face. Reese had always been a plainer man, having none of Alec's lightness or charm, but now he truly looked like the walking dead. With dirty dishwater hair that was thin on top and dark eyes that showed absolutely no warmth in their depths, his entire being and appearance confirmed only one thing . . . Reese was no longer human. He was now a Nightwalker.

Reese stood there with his small army of vampire soldiers. Alec looked as though he had been punched in the gut. Absolutely no part of the man standing in front of him resembled the uncle he had once known and loved. He was a vampire now, fully turned and functional, which meant he had been that way for a while.

"W—what the fuck?" Alec finally said, struggling with his own disbelief. "What have you done?"

"Don't look so surprised, nephew. You've only yourself to blame. After you and The Brethren tossed me aside like garbage I decided to make some changes . . . some rather permanent changes."

I could see Alec's disbelief was quickly turning to anger, and I couldn't blame him. Since I had known Reese, all he had ever done was hurt Alec. His every action had been self-serving, but he disguised everything behind a self-proclaimed faithfulness to his family. Alec never mentioned what had happened to his uncle after The Brethren refused him. I had assumed he crawled back to his family with his tail between his legs after being disgraced. Well, it now appeared he'd been busy making his own plans.

"How could you do this?" Alec demanded. "What about Aunt Judy? Antonia and Veronica? They've been frantic with worry over you. I assured them that you would eventually come to your senses and come home. Did you not give a damn about how this would affect any of them?"

Reese came toward Alec, brought his gaunt face close to Alec's, and said, with a sharp hiss. "My family will be with me soon enough."

"Over my dead body," Alec warned him.

Reese just smiled. "That's the plan, nephew. Or undead, depending how you want to look at it."

Alec blinked back at him, seemingly incapable of taking this all in. "You're insane!"

Lucas grabbed Alec and pulled him back just as he was about to lunge at Reese. "Alec, get control. You're smarter than this. He's baiting you."

"Yes, listen to Lucas," Reese added in a voice that suggested he were merely finishing a polite conversation. "Your life was never in danger, nephew. I paid those bottom feeders well in fresh kills to make sure they didn't harm you. For now I only need the woman. Give her to me and we'll be on our way."

"You won't lay one finger on her!" Alec hissed through his teeth.

Reese nodded for several of his soldiers to come forward. I stood there, stunned that this man who was supposed to be Alec's family could do this to him. Yet, why I was so surprised? Reese had only ever thought of himself, his own needs, his own obsession with power. He never cared how much his actions hurt Alec.

Alec and Lucas stepped in front of me like a human barricade, but I surprised both of them when I pushed my way between them. "Let me have a shot at this jerk," I snapped.

Lucas hauled me back behind him with a hard scowl and then shouted, "Now!" Within seconds at least a dozen Brethren fighters shot out from the forested area behind us, challenging Reese and his forces. A full-fledged war had broken out right in front of me, and Maya was one of the ones racing to join the fight. With her small frame, she seemed completely undersized among the pile of large males, but she challenged one of them with all the confidence her years of training had provided her.

I headed forward to help her, but Lucas grabbed my arm and dragged me away from the fighting. "We need to get you out of here—now!"

"But what about Maya?"

"Now!" Alec repeated as he pushed me towards Lucas. "Get her out—"

Alec's words were cut off as a lightning fast form descended upon him. Lucas and I swung around to see Reese hauling Alec up to his feet, one of Reese's hands trapping Alec's hands behind him as the other arched him back, exposing his tender throat.

I lunged forward to grab him, but Lucas wrapped an arm around my middle and yanked me back off my feet to him. "Let me go, Lucas!"

"Either you come with me, Charmer," Reese warned, "or you can have Alec's death on your conscience."

I didn't hesitate. I was going to help Alec. If I didn't, Reese would surely turn him, if not kill him, and then Lucas would be next. There was no way I would let anything happen to either one of them on account of me.

"Don't do it, Lucas!" Alec shouted. "Get her out of here. That's an order!"

"I'll do it!" I shouted back at Reese. "I'll go with you."

Lucas yanked me behind him with a force that was truly shocking for a human, as if to say 'NO' to that statement. His strength had to be coming from pure adrenaline, having to choose between his duty to me as my Guardian and his loyalty to his leader and best friend. He pulled a silver-tipped blade from his weapons belt and turned it in his palm with agile skill, displaying it in front of him. "That little blade won't stop me," he snarled.

"No," Lucas answered, but it'll be a very painful experience.

"Go with Lucas," Alec gasped at me as Reese pulled tighter on his arms.

Reese looked straight at me. "I'm running out of patience," he said as he dragged his nail along Alec's throat, creating a large gash, but not cutting quite as deep as his carotid artery. Alec's face tightened in a hard line, trying to conceal the pain as air hit the open wound. My eyes widened in terror as blood began pouring from the cut. "Very well, then," Reese said darkly, his body beginning to shake with need at smelling the fresh blood. "I think it's time for my nephew to join me on this side." He reared his head back, preparing his long fangs to slash into Alec's throat.

Instinct took over. "Alec!" I pushed off from Lucas so hard it sent him flying back to the ground, and I leapt toward Reese. Reaching for his temple with one hand, I felt the whole moment slowing down and rolling forward in super slow motion. Reese smiled and loosened his hold on Alec. My arm shoved Alec to the ground and out of his uncle's grasp. At the same moment, Reese grabbed hold of me . . . but not before my hand was able to make contact with his skin. "Damn it!" he growled as he tried to push back from me, but I continued to hold on, focusing and concentrating as hard as I could. The pain was instantly excruciating to him—and to me—but I clung to him like a mad hornet.

I heard Alec's hard grunt behind me as he hit the ground, and virtually simultaneously, both Alec and Lucas bellowed, "Olivia!"

In the confusion of the moment, I thought they were calling back in anger that I had challenged Reese alone, but their call was actually a terrible warning. Unfortunately, I figured it out just as I began to slip off the steep ridge behind me. My eyes grew wide as I plunged over the side of the forty-foot drop. A hard impact against a narrow, protruding ledge about half way down broke my fall a bit, but a second or so thereafter I collided with the hard ground below. I crashed on my side with a thud, the breath entirely forced from my lungs by the shock of it. After a few long moments, I was able to roll onto my back, and I blinked several times until my impact-clouded vision cleared. Two frantic faces stared down from high above me— Alec and Lucas. I rolled onto my side and slowly pushed myself up with my arms, but I wasn't fast enough. Reese, who had fallen with me but was better able to control his fall, loomed over me, dropping to his knees and pinning my arms to my sides as I tried to fully absorb and recover from the shock of the fall. "*Damn it,* you're a lot of trouble woman!" he spat out as he jabbed a needle into my upper arm.

Suddenly I was warm, and I lost control of my limbs. They lay there, like overcooked spaghetti, against the ground. The images of Alec and Lucas above me seemed to get smaller and smaller.

Then there was nothing.

Chapter Twenty-Three

When I opened my eyes again it felt as if I would need a crowbar to keep them open. I was someplace bitingly cold and unnaturally dark. A sharp breeze blew against my back, causing a chill to work its way up my spine, one vertebra at a time, virtually in rhythm with the soft plop of dripping water that echoed somewhere nearby.

Huddled against the ground, I tried to recall the events that had gotten me to this place, but my head pounded so hard I was having trouble focusing on much of anything. I could feel the heavy dampness, the mustiness of the space surrounding me—like wet plastic—until I felt almost suffocated. Moving my legs ever so slightly to test the damage to my body, I recoiled at the incredible pain and stiffness that resonated throughout me. The only other time I felt rocked with such shock was the night I had regained consciousness in the middle of a fiery train crash. I would have preferred to go through the rest of my life without ever having to know the fragility of that experience again, but fate had other plans for me.

A single drop of moisture splashed against my face just below my lashes and rolled down my cheek as I slowly raised my chin. My arms were numb, chained over my head to a thick post jutting up from the nearly frozen ground beneath me. I was dazed for a moment, surprised that I couldn't free myself from the chains. I had grown much stronger over the past year. Freeing myself shouldn't be a problem, except that massive amounts of solid silver chains were looped around my wrist and neck. "The silver burns, doesn't it?" a cool voice asked from the darkness. His voice echoed off the hard rock walls around us, and I realized we were within some sort of large cavern. I swung my head around just as another gust swept in from an outside entrance somewhere beyond me, causing a wrenching shiver to shoot up my limbs while Reese Lambert approached through the shadows.

But he wasn't the one who had spoken.

"You may only be one quarter vampire, but your skin burns under silver, like ours does. It may work more slowly, may just weaken you at first, but that burn you feel will grow in intensity until you are begging me to remove it."

Luther Davin.

Why was I not surprised to find these two former Elders working together once again? Both were consumed with their need for control and power. They were obsessed with it from their time with The Brethren. But at the same time, I had to wonder what was in it for Reese? Why would he resort to such measures as allowing Davin to turn him? I had seen the horrified look on Alec's face once he realized what his uncle had done. Yet again Reese had cut him deep, a betrayal that would leave scars for a very long time . . . that was, if he and the others managed to escape Reese and his soldiers unharmed. Little more than a shadowy outline of Luther appeared, the darkness seeming to wrap around him as he moved surprisingly close, considering how careful he usually was to maintain a safe distance from me with my gift. He closed his eyes and inhaled a slow, deep breath, as if taking in the bounty of scents hidden within the air. "Ah, do you feel that, Reese?" he asked. "Feel how much you want to touch her—to be near her. She casts a spell like a witch over a child . . . tempting them with the sweetest candy."

"I'll pass on that particular sweet," Reese replied dully. "She's nothing more than a devil."

"We *are* devils, Reese. What's the matter? Do you not like your own reflection now?"

I was trying to wrap my head around everything when two other male vampires approached me from behind. I couldn't see them, but the little hairs on the back of my neck stood straight up, sensing their presence just before their cold breaths blew over my ear. Next I felt their hands slide possessively over my shoulders and sides, wisely avoiding all contact with any exposed areas of my skin. I held my breath and threw them a warning glare over my shoulder as I recoiled from their touch. But it was useless, tied up as I was.

Suddenly, a whole host of Nightwalkers began to close in around me. My gift was drawing them in. Great. This was not a good situation at all. There wasn't enough training in the world to prepare me for this. *Why on earth did I ever leave Seattle? Why did I leave Caleb?*

Luckily, my gift was once again my best friend. In the vampires obsession to be close to me it didn't take long for them to make a mistake. The two touching me hissed out in anger as they felt the sharp jolt after making contact with my skin.

Davin just laughed coolly. "Careful, boys. She has the face of an angel, but the strike of a pit viper."

The vampires moved back a cautious distance from me but hovered nearby so I had to remain on guard for their advances. I was trying to find a way to stay calm and think logically about how to get myself out of this mess. I couldn't afford to let Davin know how much this situation unnerved me. "Nice accommodations you have here," I finally said with a scratchier voice than I would have liked. I was trying to draw him into more conversation, through which maybe I could learn some information that could help me.

"Yes . . ." he came back smoothly, not even affected by my attempt as sarcasm. "I'm afraid they are a bit more rustic than even the prison where I held you before." One brow arched high as he cocked his head to the right, his black eyes glittering in delight even through the darkness. "But there are small luxuries. If you follow the cavern back inside the mountain, you'll find a warm, freshwater spring. Behave yourself and I may let you soak your bruises for a while."

Ok, he had my attention there. I was tempted to be good just so I could clean all the filth from me—a filth that I knew in my head would never fully disappear as long as I remained his prisoner. "Why don't you get to the point, Davin, and tell me what you want?"

"You know what I want."

I jiggled the silver chain and shackles binding my wrist to the post. "This does feel a bit familiar, but please . . . refresh my memory."

Reese stared back at me, his lips curled into an evil snarl.

Evidently, he didn't appreciate my sarcasm.

"I'd rather let you think on it for a while," Davin replied calmly, his gaze slowly scanning the sad state of my dirty and wet clothes. "Make yourself comfortable in your new home. I'm sure it will come to you."

"This isn't my home!"

"Ahh, but it is—now. It may lack a few refinements here and there, but I'm quite sure you'll learn to appreciate its rather raw charm." Then a wondrous expression arched his brows as his fingers went to his lips. "Oops . . . that was an unfortunate play on words, now wasn't it?"

Refusing to respond to Davin's mind games, I focused instead on trying to get some circulation back into my arms. The chains binding me to the post were digging into my wrists, so I squeezed my fingers into fists while stretching my chin down over my collarbone, trying to feel for the necklace that normally hung there. "Looking for this?" Reese questioned as he dangled the sapphire from his fingers.

Inwardly I breathed a sigh of relief, knowing that with the necklace removed Caleb would be able to sense me and feel that I was in trouble. Frankly, I was surprised that Davin and Reese would make such a big mistake.

"See that glimmer of hope in those beautiful eyes, Reese?" Davin smiled. "She thinks her vampire's coming to save her."

A cold burst of air came rushing through the cavern as a familiar set of long legs and thin, high-heeled black boots landed right in front of me. "I assure you he's not," Celeste answered confidently.

I stared up at her with anger and disbelief as she stood between Davin and Reese, looking perfectly comfortable. She was obviously in part responsible for bringing me here and I just wanted to scream at how, once again, she had betrayed Caleb—a man she supposedly cared about—to take sides against him with these two Nightwalkers. It made me so mad I desperately want to pull her hair out by those platinum roots. "In fact, I'm not sure he even realizes yet that you're gone," she continued, then laughed over her shoulder to Davin. "He's been very busy obsessing over you."

"How could you betray Caleb like this?" I just couldn't keep the question from exploding out of me. "I know you don't give a damn about me, but I would have thought you'd show more loyalty to the man you are supposedly still in love with and trying to win back."

"Actually, you're wrong," she said, stepping directly in front of me. "I *didn't* give a damn about you until *my mate* took you back with him after that train crash."

I blinked back at her, absolutely stunned. "You were there the night of the train crash?"

"She was with me," Davin replied as he stepped closer to her, "waiting for Isaac to return with you. If she'd gotten anywhere near the crash site, Caleb would've sensed her immediately. After all, she is his mate." He then curled an arm around Celeste's back, his hand landing just under her breast in what appeared to be a possessive gesture.

Celeste responded by stripping Davin's hand away from her side as an ugly snarl curled her lip. "Listen, Grandpa—enough with the copping a feel! You do that again and I'll give you something to *really* feel old about."

Davin growled back at her in warning, not happy at all about the lack of respect he believed due to him. I needed to remember this. They were not one happy, evil family. There were chinks in the armor, chinks I could perhaps use to my advantage. "So that's how you've known so much about Caleb from the beginning?" I said to Davin. "Celeste fed you the information." I then turned to Celeste. "You've been betraying Caleb the whole time . . . even when he sent Jax to warn you about Davin."

"Yes, she has," Davin replied, breaking into a crookedly proud smile. "It was Isaac's suggestion to bring Annabelle and her coven into the fold once he discovered Celeste's connection to Caleb—a rather brilliant idea, at that. Of course, I couldn't have known how perfectly this would all work out with you."

Celeste snorted. "Believe me, I wanted to send that arrogant, overgrown Daywalker to whom Caleb has pledged his undying allegiance straight to hell. Jax Walker has been a thorn in my side from day one. So, of course, *he* would end up being your grandfather."

I shook my head in both denial and disbelief. "So has it all been a lie? Is Annabelle even really dead?"

Celeste laughed at that, a soft, effortless sound. "Oh, no, she's dead. A casualty I'm afraid of the greater good. Once Isaac was gone she became expendable . . . an easy victim for leading Caleb right where I needed him to go."

"I'm sure your coven doesn't know that," I challenged her. "Their anger over her death that day on the rooftop was genuine. But you were counting on that, weren't you? As well as Jax remembering seeing Annabelle with Isaac."

"Jax is a stupid, trusting bastard," she declared. "Once Caleb was otherwise occupied with me—*hunting Davin,*"—she said, making air quote with her fingers—"he walked right into that trap we set for him. And ooohh, that was so sad, what happened to Gemma."

"You are a bitch!" I snapped at her with a hatred I'm not sure I had ever felt for another person before. "How can you do these things and claim to have an ounce of feeling for Caleb at all? You don't love him! You never have!"

"This isn't about love," she came right back. "This is about sex—about mating. About that urgent, animalistic need to fuck someone's brains out and not apologize for anything. That's your problem. The human side of you believes that being mated to him is the same as marriage in the human world. Well, it's not—and the blinders he has on right now won't last. He can't commit to you the way you truly want. Beneath it all he is like an animal, driven solely by his vampire instincts. That's why he'll come back to me. As much as you want to deny it, he's a vampire. I get him. I understand him. I understand what he truly needs."

Forcing myself up fully onto my knees, I shouted at her, "You're wrong! Caleb and Jax will find me. And you'll get what's coming to you once Caleb discovers how you've betrayed him. I'll make sure of it!"

Without warning, Celeste's arm swung back and she struck me across my cheek so hard that my head was whipped against the post. I was stunned instantly. OK, so she packed a pretty mean punch, although I at least got the satisfaction of hearing her cry out at the pain she felt when her hand contacted my cheek.

"That's enough!" Davin barked as he grabbed her wrist and squeezed it hard before throwing her back against the cavern wall. I could see that his action had caught her completely off guard as she glared back at him and then turned her burning, hate-filled gaze to Reese, who seemed to be watching the scene unfold with marked interest. "Olivia is my problem to deal with now—not yours. I've gift wrapped and delivered to you what you wanted—Caleb Wolfe all to yourself. Now get back there and use those long legs of yours to keep him occupied so he stays out of my g*oddamn* way, or—so help me—I will destroy him, once and for all!"

Celeste was breathing hard, her eyes brimming with undisguised hate as she returned to her full height once again. "Oh, I'm not leaving 'til I see that little bitch get what's coming to her. Just try to make me, grandpa."

"Fine!" he snapped. "You can watch from over there. Then you will leave, before I change my mind and unleash my wrath on you!"

Celeste looked as if she was about to rip Davin's throat out, but, surprisingly, her expression smoothed to a veil of calm as she stepped back, just as Davin had commanded her. Then, with nothing more than a withering look, Davin ordered his soldiers to back away from me. They obeyed immediately, including Reese, who had been silent this whole time . . . and that concerned me. If there was one thing I could never allow myself to do, it was to underestimate Reese Lambert. I had decided the quieter he was, the more dangerous he was, because it meant he was scheming.

Davin paced in front of me, allowing the silence within the cavern to underscore how much power he had with this group. "She's right, you know," he began—in a surprisingly soft voice. "You believe they'll come for you because they care about you . . . because they love you." He stopped his pacing and surveyed all of the soldiers around him before moving his gaze back to me. "We're not capable of love. It's about thirst. It's about lust—our need for a woman to sate it, and nothing more. You see, that's the beauty of this life—gluttony. Imagine having the freedom to take everything you want . . . to feed on it . . . to claim it, and to make no apologies for it."

"Caleb and Jax are nothing like you, or her," I said, looking to Celeste. "They know how to love. They have control of their thirst—and that control will always give them the advantage over you."

Davin's gaze slowly trailed over me as he smiled. There was no doubt in my mind that this man, who to me embodied all darkness—all my worst nightmares—was truly evil. I didn't even want to guess at the thoughts currently running around in his head. "Do you think you really know what's it's like to be one of us? You have a small part of you that craves blood. For them, it's *every* part. It's a constant struggle. You have no idea . . . but you will. When I'm done with you, you will."

I felt such a shiver run through me at his words that I wasn't sure the fear would leave me anytime soon. He meant every word of what he was saying. There was no way for me to know what he had in store for me, and it was only then, as I stared back at him and Reese and Celeste, that I realized the direness of my circumstances.

Davin knelt on his haunches in front of me. "Oh, how I want to touch you," he whispered, and I recognized instantly by the softness of his voice that he was trying to use his gift to persuade me. "But first, there are things you need to learn. You'll be treated like my queen and protected by my army. I swear this to you. I will make you stronger. And you will come to accept me as your leader. No one will have the power to hurt you ever again. And no one will have the power to take you away from me."

I couldn't be sure what my expression had shown him only moments before. Was it shock or anger? But in *this* moment, I raised my chin to him defiantly and said, "*I* have the power to take myself away from you. Is that the best you've got, asshole?"

Davin blinked back and then turned to Celeste, who was snickering with delight as she leaned against the cavern wall. "I warned you, you over-aged prick. She's growing resistant to our gifts. But oh, no . . . you had it all figured out!"

It startled me when Davin responded with a smile that lit up his face and resembled something like glee. "Yes," he replied smoothly. "She's getting stronger. It seems I've underestimated her . . . but no more."

"Well, hallelujah," Celeste replied, her tone dripping with bitter sarcasm. "Now can we get on with this? I have a mate to get back to."

"He's not your mate!" I said defiantly back at her.

Davin seemed to float to his feet. "You've gotten much more powerful, little Charmer, since last I saw you. But I wasn't expecting that you would co-operate. That's where this little hideaway comes in handy," he said, winding his finger through the air.

"You're a fool if you think—"

"Actually I'm pretty brilliant," he cut in. "I certainly couldn't have your vampire or The Brethren charging in here and ruining my plans when I need time to get you to come around to my way of thinking. You tend to be a bit stubborn, even for a human. So I created a place that was undetectable. A fortress, if you will. And believe me, this has taken a while to accomplish."

"*Yes,* it has," Reese said, with obvious irritation.

Davin just humored him with a flat smile. "My gift may not be as strong on you at the moment, but it works quite well on humans. It certainly wasn't hard to persuade some—well, actually, all—of the good town-folk below to hike up here and move a little dirt for me." He caught his finger at his lips quizzically. "Well, actually not dirt . . . sacred ground. From The Oracle grounds, no less, thanks to Reese's help. You know, it can come in very handy, even for us vampires. We're sitting in the middle of a giant circle of it . . . except, of course, for one small three-foot opening for us to slip in and out of. It's like a giant wall of dead space in the middle of the Rockies. I assure you, no one will sense you're here—or us, for that matter. Gift or not, we have all the time in the world for you to learn your lessons."

Davin was undeniably insane. There was no doubt about that. If I were going to reason with anyone, it would definitely not be him or Celeste. That left just one. "How could you do this to Alec?" I pleaded with Reese, hoping that there was still some part of him that remembered his love—albeit self-serving and greedy love—for his nephew. "You were like a second father to him."

"I assure you, I'm very loyal to my family," he replied with a pressed smile. "And I intend to have them *all* in the fold very soon . . . including my stubborn little nephew."

"Alec despises you now. You saw it in his eyes at the field. He hates what you've become. There is no way he will ever join you."

"He's my family," he growled. "Part of our blood. His place will be at my side . . . just like the rest of them." In some weird way, it seemed this was what Reese had brought with him into this world, this need—no, this *obsession*—to control the family he believed he owned like a piece of property. *They* were how he identified himself. And Alec, unfortunately, seemed to be his central focus.

"You're insane, you know that? Alec will never let you *turn* your own family. He would rather die protecting them."

Reese glanced back at Davin dully. "Oh, it's going to be fun watching that smart-mouth be silenced."

"I agree," Celeste bit out. "Let's get on with it."

My gaze moved among all of them, unsure what to expect next. Davin motioned towards one of his soldiers, who disappeared deeper into the cavern and then returned, dragging an older man in chains. Looking weak with exhaustion, the man was dropped effortlessly right at Davin's feet. "This is one of those humans who was so dedicated to creating this wall around us." Davin then sighed and shook his head. "Poor soul . . . He has worked himself to the bone."

My eyes widened in trepidation for the man just as a young woman was brought forward. She also appeared thin and frail, her skin dull, but it was easy to see that underneath she was quite beautiful. The male vampire soldier's gaze met Davin's and asked a silent question.

"Oh, fine, go ahead," Davin responded as he waved his hand dismissively. Suddenly, a half-dozen male vampires swarmed the woman until they had formed a wall around her.

"No!" she pleaded, as Davin hauled the older man up from the floor with one hand.

The man's tired eyes widened in alarm. "And this is his reward for a job well done," Davin said, just before slicing a sharp nail over the man's throat. I looked away as blood began pouring from the wound and the agonized screams of the woman echoed throughout the cavern. I felt trapped in some bad nightmare, wanting to help them and feeling ashamed that I could barely move with so much silver around my neck and bound hands.

Then, without warning, my head was snapped back by a rough hand pulling at my hair. Celeste was forcing me up onto my knees in front of her as Davin filled a crude container with the man's blood. Once satisfied with the amount, Davin handed it to Celeste and drew the man against his chest, sinking his fangs into the wound and finishing him off with a savage thirst as the man could let out only a gurgled scream, but those cries were silenced in seconds.

I could still hear the woman screaming behind me and hated to even think what was being done to her as Celeste yanked my head back farther, forcing my mouth open wide. She poured the blood—all of it—down my throat so fast that I was nearly spitting it back out as I tried to prevent it from going into my lungs. "That's right. Choke on it, you slut!" While I was coughing and sputtering under her hold, I realized I had known this would happen. I had seen it—felt it when I had touched Sophie. I just hadn't wanted to examine it too closely. Jax and Gemma's precious little girl had a powerful gift—one that she was much too young to possibly handle or understand. She could see the future. Now it made sense why she cried so hard the morning Jax was burned—and why food or comfort didn't seem to help. The little girl had no other way to communicate her fear from what she was seeing.

After I finished choking down the last of the blood, Celeste shoved me back against the pole once again. I was still coughing and spitting, and my stomach began to recoil like I was about to vomit. I had never been given blood from a fresh, human kill. Just the thought of it made me sick. "Welcome to your new diet plan," Davin said brightly. "No food . . . only fresh human blood—every day. It'll make you nice and strong. And, in time, I should think you'll come around to my way of thinking."

"It won't," I gasped. "I won't do as you want."

"We'll see about that. We'll see."

Chapter Twenty-Four

A week passed, the longest week of my life. The summer was quickly edging towards fall, but I could not see any of it; I had not been allowed outside the dark cavern since I had been brought here. But I could smell the change of season in the cooler air that streamed in from the cave's entrance. The air was so thin, I knew we had to be at high altitude—which made sense if you were a group of blood thirsty vampires trying to hide yourself from the rest of the world. The thinner air and colder temperatures would make it more difficult for anyone to find you.

For seven straight days I'd had nothing to eat or drink but fresh-kill blood, and mercifully, some water. But even though my body craved the taste of things like sweet bread, nuts and vegetables, strangely enough, I felt as if I were growing stronger . . . and weaker at the same time. My muscles were responding to the blood energy, but my stomach burned with a constant hunger. I needed human food. In its absence, I felt tense and jittery—jittery because the blood seemed to amp-up my responses to even normal situations. I was alert to the slightest sound or the slightest movement, and felt less in control, less human. Of course, that human side was the part of me I desperately wanted to hold on to. I feared most now that drinking the blood of human innocents would eventually cause the darkness growing inside me to overtake whatever good I possessed.

Also, I was cold. The cavern did offer some shelter from the elements, but not nearly enough for my mostly human body. At night I would lie huddled against the post, chained and shivering, trying in vain to sleep. A couple of times each day I was allowed to walk around within the cavern—with my hands bound. But even then, Davin didn't trust me. He had me monitored by his Dhampir soldiers twenty-four hours a day, which was smart, since Dhampirs were not as affected by my gifts as the vampires. He knew I was gaining strength from the blood, which was exactly what he wanted, but that also meant that my other gifts were strengthening, as well, and because of that he had to be careful.

Under all this constant supervision, I had been waiting for the right time to try to connect with Caleb. So far, it felt as if I hadn't had a moment's peace in which I could try to concentrate. This was all very deliberate. I was sure. I had to deal constantly with the Dhampirs or vampires that were surrounding me, hovering in close, sometimes stealing touches even if it meant pain for them. I was on constant guard and unable to relax. Even when I was allowed to bathe in the spring at the center of the cavern, the guards watched me, intruding on my privacy. They couldn't help it. They were drawn to wherever I was. The last day or so, however, the incidences of them hovering over me had seemed less frequent. There was just a bit more distance. I wondered if perhaps they were getting used to me and that my gift might no longer be overpowering to them, which is something I had not considered before now.

Today I had asked to be allowed to go outside in the fresh air. I thought for sure that my request would be refused, but I was surprised when Davin agreed to it. "You see," he began. "I can be reasonable. If you continue to behave yourself, I'll give you more freedom within the cavern."

"That's a mistake," Reese warned him. "She's playing you for a fool."

"She's my concern, not yours," Davin reminded him, sharply. "You need to focus on *your* plan for *your* family. Have your men located the item?"

"I'll know soon enough."

"Then go . . . and leave me to deal with our little Charmer."

Reese seemed to suck in a potentially sharp reply as he turned and left with a small group of vampires who seemed to have pledged their allegiance to him. I was only glad I wouldn't have to look at his constantly pinched expression any more, but I was worried for Alec. How was I going to warn him of the danger headed his way?

"Take her outside for thirty minutes," Davin instructed.

"And I will personally disembowel the Dhampir who lets her get away." The Dhampirs stared back at him in abject fear, swallowing a hard knot, as if they knew Davin was not bluffing in the least about removing their organs with his own hands.

I worked hard not to give Davin an overly placating smile in reply. I needed him to believe I was being submissive, cooperative . . . but not too cooperative. That fine balance would allow him to let his guard down just a bit, and that's when I would make my move.

Once outside, it took a couple of minutes for my eyes to adjust to the clouded light, which felt a thousand times brighter than I had ever remembered. For a long while I squinted, taking carefully short strides as I made my way over the uneven ground. Inhaling slow breath of cold, thin, mountain air, I was immediately struck with how clean, how pure it was. It was so good to be outside again, and after a few minutes I began to relax, to breathe a little easier, and to notice the jitters, the anxiousness, calm a bit. This was my chance to make contact with Caleb. I scanned the terrain in front of me, trying to create a visual map in my head for as far as I could see. We were high in the Rockies, with no other peaks even close to matching the altitude around us. The surrounding area was rough, rocky, with snow interspersed with small grassy patches. In the near distance I could see the ring of sacred ground that had been constructed. Davin wasn't kidding when he said we were encircled by it. The trench was at least five feet wide, and it was roughly a circle, surrounding the cavern and located so there was a distance of several hundred feet between any point on the ring and the cavern entrance itself. The manpower it must have taken to dig it was simply unimaginable. In the last week, I had witnessed Davin killing several dozen people to feed his growing army. Somewhere, there was an entire town that must now be deserted and quiet.

"Over there," one of the Dhampirs ordered as he pushed me towards a grouping of rocks, still relatively close to the cavern entrance. "You can walk here."

I paced around for a bit and then said, "I want to sit." I said this even though it felt wonderful to move around on my stiff legs.

The Dhampir looked as if he was fully prepared to argue the point, but he decided against it and allowed me to sit atop a high grouping of nearby rocks. On contact with the rock, my skin felt as if it was being held against ice, but I had to ignore it. I needed to relax if I was going to be successful in connecting with Caleb. I prayed he was waiting for me to contact him at the other end.

I pretended to stare out ahead of me for a long while. In some ways, this place reminded me of Caleb's favorite ledge, the one that looked out over the mountain valley below our tree house. Thinking about that exact spot helped me to focus on him. I thought about the last night I saw him, after we made love. Remembering the moment alone still had the power to make my skin feel warmer. It was a good feeling—a powerful feeling—and it's what I held onto as I continued to reach out to him.

After several unsuccessful tries, my breath came in sharply when a clear vision of him finally entered my head. Remaining perfectly still, I knew I couldn't afford to alert the guards to any reaction on my part, but *oh, God,* it was good to see him. His handsome face was hardened by an anger that was accentuated by a hard slash of his brows. But as my gift touched him, those rigid lines seemed to soften and his breath caught, right along with mine. He closed his eyes and held himself tight as if he were trying to hold on with every ounce of energy he had inside him. "Caleb?" I called out to him in my head.

Usually he would call my name back, but this time he said nothing; he just focused on me, so hard I could feel it in my bones. He was somewhere outside. Just beyond his shoulder I could see the thick forest surrounding him. The skies were heavy. Wherever he was there must have been a storm moving in because the scene should look like the middle of the day, but instead it appeared to be more like dusk. I thought about where he could be, wondering if Celeste was still leading him on a useless search for Davin that would never pan out. Caleb had been so determined to destroy the Nightwalker; I feared it was distracting him from his usual highly attuned instincts and senses.

As my connection continued to hold him, Caleb's body

pitched forward just the slightest bit, his muscles seeming to flex as if he were trying to lean toward me. His breathing became harder once he appeared to take in the emptiness, the sadness, the physical hunger welling within me. And that also meant he could feel the anger lurking beneath—anger that Davin's plan had worked so perfectly to separate me from my family. Anger, that there was no way for me to warn Caleb how a woman who didn't give a damn for anyone but herself was deceiving him.

"She's hungry . . . terribly hungry," his lips mouthed, apparently directed to someone there with him. It had to be Jax. I prayed it was Jax. And then, when my grandfather stepped beside Caleb, his expression tense, like he wanted to rip the head from a bull, my heart leapt further with excitement just to be able to see them.

"Hold onto the connection," Jax mouthed in reply. "What is around her? Tell us what you see."

Us? There were others. Chay, maybe? My heart lifted at the hope that they were all trying to find me. But that hope crashed just as quickly when I saw slender, pale fingers slide over Caleb's shoulder from behind. They were clinging possessively to his shirt and I could feel an anger—no, an instant jealousy I hadn't felt until that very moment—that rolled over me and seemed to drop into the pit of my stomach. I had known she was going back to them, trying still to deceive them. I knew what her plan was, and still I struggled with the fact that Caleb had let her touch him!

My concentration—and then my connection—broke instantly as one of the Dhampirs jerked me to my feet in a hard grip. "Damn! Can't you hear, woman," he barked. "Get inside." The image of Caleb had been ripped away, and my heart felt as if it were bleeding. Celeste would do everything in her power to lead him as far away from where I was as possible, but it felt good to see him. Just having those few seconds filled me with a renewed sense of hope. I had to get back to him. I had to get outside this wall of sacred ground hiding me from him, even if it was only for a little while.

I had to escape.

***

Another week passed, and after growing tired of fighting off the advances from the vampires drawn to me and getting almost no sleep in the freezing temperatures, I was determined more than ever to make my escape. Even though I felt as if I were starving, I sensed the leaping increase in my physical strength. I was becoming stronger than I had ever known—strong enough to break through even the mass of silver chains Davin had binding me to the post. And once my hands were free, God help anyone who tried to stop my escape. I was so angry and edgy, so ready to win my freedom, I would fight anyone—even Davin himself, because if I didn't, this evil creature would succeed in slowly turning me into something as dark as him.

Patiently, I had been waiting for a day when the sun was so bright outside that the edges of it crept into the entry of the cavern. That day was today. It was perfect. Davin and his vampire soldiers would be unable to stop me once I reached the light. That left only the six Dhampirs who were in charge of watching me while the vampires slept the day away in a sort of rock-walled tomb farther inside the cave. But given the kick-ass mood I was in today, that didn't seem like a problem. Just let one of those bastards try to stop me.

I waited for the right moment, when the sun was nearly reaching its highest point inside the cave and two of the Dhampirs were making their rounds near the perimeter. That left only four to be dealt with immediately. Rising to my feet without warning, I snapped the silver chains in half in one effort and rushed towards the light that would be my salvation. Just as I reached the edge, I felt one of them blow into me, forcing me back against the wall. I swung around on him so quickly and aggressively that the angry sounds that followed made me feel more like a wild animal than a young woman. With one hard blow to his mid section, I sent the Dhampir crashing back against the wall of the cave with a force that should have stunned me, but it didn't. No sooner had I finished dealing with him than two more were on top of me. I used a lot of strength, all my training, and every ounce of my gift, to leave both of them writhing on the ground within seconds. Then I could hear the next challenge, a violent roar coming from deep within the cave.

The vampires were awake and coming for me.

With no time to think about the wave of anger barreling towards me, I dashed for the sunlight just as the last Dhampir guard collided against me at the entry to the cave. He was a Dhampir I recognized. His name was Silas, and of all my guards, he was the only one I didn't completely revile. He was an absolute giant of a man and definitely more a follower than a thinker. I had overheard Davin's harsh criticism of the Dhampir many times during my imprisonment here so far, and I had put the little pieces of conversation together and understood that Davin had saved Silas from enslavement by his Nightwalker father, only to enslave him again in servitude to himself.

Silas had never given me a reason to believe he would betray his leader. Yet there was a part of him I sensed that did not approve of what Davin was doing to me. He was a weak link in the chain, one that I could take advantage of to gain my freedom. "I can't let you leave," he said with quiet warning. Come to think of it, he was a quiet man, rarely speaking unless spoken to.

"And I can't let you stop me," I replied in a voice I did not recognize as my own. It was darker, wilder, full of desperation. Spinning away from him that moment, I thought I was in the clear. But he snagged an arm around my middle and hauled me back against him. I reached my hands up behind me and blindly dug them into his face, twisting around in his arms once I felt his strength give a little under my fierce grip. The large man bellowed out in pain, and when the anguished sound became too much for me to bear I tried to throw him back from me, but he wouldn't let go.

I continued to fight to hold on, focusing every ounce of my energy. And even as Silas slumped to his knees in front of me, I still didn't let go. It took several seconds for me to register that this huge Dhampir, a man who was strong enough to tear anyone's head off, was on his knees, defeated . . . and I wouldn't stop.

"I wanna go home," I heard myself say from somewhere deep

inside me—somewhere that had been slowly drowning in pain since the moment I had arrived here. I had to get out of this cave and away from Davin. I had to get back to Caleb, to the tree house, to Jax, Gemma and Sophie. The thoughts ran through my head over and over again until I realized Silas had fallen back motionless against the cavern floor.

I blinked back hard as I lifted my hands in front of me, trying and clear my eyes from the fog of anger that had blurred them. My breath seemed to come out with great difficulty from that point forward as a slow awareness of what I had just done began to hammer through my head. I couldn't move. I couldn't blink. I simply turned my shaking palms toward my face and stared at them as if I were looking at a stranger's hands—hands that were no longer innocent . . . hands that were evil . . . hands that had now killed.

I had taken a life. More consequently—I had chosen to take a life.

I raised my head to see all of the stunned faces—vampires and Dhampirs alike—staring at me in stone silence. Silent not because they cared whether I had killed one of their own (half the time it seemed they would have no issue with killing each other) but instead, how easily I had done it. They knew they needed to make sure I didn't run out into that sunlight, but it was almost as if they could instinctually feel that I didn't have the capacity to move my legs in that moment.

One of the vampires closest to me turned back to Davin, who was standing calmly near the back, a sly smile twisting his lips. "She killed Silas by touching him with bare hands," the vampire said, obviously surprised. "You never warned us . . ."

"That's because, until today, she couldn't," Davin replied like the proud wizard behind the curtain. "Today she had enough anger and enough strength to show all of you what a powerful queen she will make. You have been put on notice. She is the Charmer—the only one of her kind. And destroying those thought to be strongest in our world was always her fate. It's her gift."

Davin's words fell on me like an iron anchor inside my chest, hooking itself around my heart and dragging me down to the lowest point I had ever known since discovering who and what

I was. My hands started to shake uncontrollably as other rough hands clamped around my wrists and dragged me back inside the cave. And, strangely, there was not a single cry in pain from vampire who was touching me. I could have fought him, but I didn't want to. The moment I realized Silas was dead, something inside me broke. "Very good, little Charmer," Davin said as he floated towards me from the shadows. "Soon you'll be ready."

I was numb. This was what he wanted—what he had been waiting for. Some part of me recognized that from this point forward there would never be any going back. The sin I had just committed had changed me in some vital way. I didn't even fight as two Dhampirs forced me to my knees in front of Davin. The now familiar screams of one of the human prisoners echoed from somewhere deep within the cavern, and seconds later my head was being whipped back and more fresh blood was being forced down my throat.

With the image of Silas's lifeless body still fresh in my mind, I didn't fight. I understood what was happening to me. The human woman inside me was dying. I was being turned to the dark side and couldn't seem to stop it. How would I ever be able to return to Caleb and look him in the eyes, knowing what I had now done? What I had become? He was a man who fought everyday against his vampire nature so as to be worthy of walking free during the day. And I just killed a man with my bare hands who wasn't even really trying to hurt me. He only wanted to stop me.

There was no going back.

I could never take it back.

Chapter Twenty-Five

Three more weeks passed and I felt nothing. I no longer cared about the shaking in my hands from hunger, the lack of sleep, or the frigid cold. I cared about nothing. It was like floating inside a giant, black hole, void of any human sensation or emotion. Where just a few weeks ago there was anger, defiance, and a determination to escape, now there was only a calm, toneless existence, the minutes of my life passing like everyday breaths that you don't give a second thought to. I didn't want for anything, I didn't ask for anything, and didn't dare think about the future. Whether I stayed or left now made no difference to me; I was not the same person.

For three long weeks, I had not tried to connect with Caleb. I couldn't see the point. He was now part of the past, and with every day that went by, my memories of my time with him, the feelings of happiness I so cherished, seemed to be fading. In the beginning, it scared me, but now I just accepted it. I couldn't go back to him, couldn't face him, and I could never take back what I had done.

Davin no longer had me chained inside the cavern because I wasn't trying to escape. He seemed positively full of glee at the obedient prisoner I had become. Mostly, I simply tried to shut out the noise, the shrill screams as another innocent human victim was being killed somewhere deep inside the cavern. Laying my head against a rock in a darkened corner, I tried to pass the time by finding a quiet place of peace where I didn't have to think or remember a life I couldn't hope to have back. But the peace never lasted long.

"It's time," Davin smiled as he approached with my daily portion of blood. Obediently, I took the cup from his hand and shoved the contents down my throat in one shot. I was hungry —so, so, hungry—but strangely, I couldn't tell exactly what I was hungry for.

"Time for what?" I asked. He responded by handing me a

black dress that was carefully folded over his arm. As I examined it more closely, I swore it looked like a wedding dress that had been dyed a black color deeper than a crow's feathers. Three-quarters length, with a feathery-light skirt, it was pleated around the bodice and pulled tight with several long ribbons.

I blinked up at him as if he was crazy, but he simply responded, "For you to realize your potential."

That was exactly what I didn't want. I didn't want to think about how many more lives I could take with a simple touch. It was a lot easier to not think—to not care. To never have anyone touch me ever again. Could I even argue that I was any better than the Grim Reaper or a black plague, controlling the fates of others within my fingertips?

Davin's coal-colored gaze rested on me for a long while, as if he was puzzled by my mood. "If you do this for me, I promise to reward you well." He drew closer, trailing two fingers over the curve of my shoulder as the stale scent of cigars wafted on his breath. Somehow that scent, that had been a part of him when he was human, had clung to him in this life. My distaste for it only added to the cringe factor every time the man nearly forty years my senior reached out to touch me. In fact, over the last few weeks, he seemed to covet any chance to touch me, even if it caused him physical pain. It was sadomasochistic in a way, as though he received pleasure from the torture of it. "I will give you whatever you desire," he continued, " . . . within reason, of course." He caressed the length of my arm, hissing sharply at the contact with my skin, but it definitely was not hurting him as it had in the past. I couldn't tell if he was getting stronger or I was getting weaker somehow. "Perhaps you and I can learn to understand one another better."

There was no mystery in what he was implying, and I felt a bad taste on my tongue. I might seem incapable of caring about anything at the moment, but I would never accept Luther Davin as my king or lover or whatever else his sick mind wanted to call it. "Go ahead and try," I replied with cool indifference. "I promise, it'll be very painful for you."

He laughed quietly and motioned for two of his soldiers to come over. "Escort her to the spring. Watch her, but keep your distance. Understood?"

I had to laugh at that. Except for Davin, the vampires keeping their distance had not been a problem as of late. In fact, they seemed about as drawn to me as they would be a bushel of garlic, and I had no problem with that.

"Bathe like a queen," he beamed proudly, as if he were offering me the greatest gift. "When you're finished, dress in this and return to me. We'll be leaving soon."

You would think the news that I would be allowed outside the invisible wall that encircled us for the first time in five weeks would have me jumping to somehow use that to figure out my escape, but instead I simply replied, "Fine."

I hardly recognized my own voice. It had lost any change of pitch, any softness, any femininity. Instead, I sounded bored and about as un-charming as a woman could get. In fact, there was nothing about me that was even remotely attractive. I had lost weight to the point that my curves had flattened and my shoulder bones were jutting out in harsh angles. My skin had grown very pale, and my once shiny mahogany hair was now as dull as sandpaper. Thank God, vampires didn't keep any mirrors around because I was sure the reflection would show me what it looked like to be a Nightwalker—powerful, hungry, and absolutely lifeless.

"Don't be so quick to dismiss what I can offer you. After you succeed in helping me destroy the Lycans, I can give you a good life. Provide you with the finest clothing, let you savor the richest foods, build you a home, an empire—people to serve you."

"I don't want you to build me a home!" I snapped, and the force with which I said those words surprised me. I thought about why and realized I had a home—*once*. A beautiful home, built with amazing, gifted hands. But I didn't want it anymore. A home implied family, permanence, something you cared about . . . something you could lose. If I didn't care about it, then I couldn't lose it. Right now I just wanted to keep the peace so Davin would leave me the hell alone. Remembering that, I evened my tone and added, "Whatever clothes you choose for me will be fine. Food would be nice. I am hungry."

He wagged his finger in front of my nose as if to warn me

that I was already asking for too much. "First, the Lycans. Until then, I need you as strong as possible. The strength you showed me when you tried to escape was very impressive. You outmatched four Dhampir males, killing one of them. Surely you must relish the strength you have gained."

I pushed deep any feeling or memory I had of that day I killed Silas and just shrugged my shoulders at him. "It's fine."

"So easy to please these days. That's good—very good. More than I'd hoped for." He turned and nodded towards his men. "Take her back."

Since Davin was in such a giving mood, I took advantage and soaked in the warm spring for nearly an hour. My bathing time represented the only warmth I had known for the last five weeks. Yet, even after soaking for all that time I still couldn't drown away the cold. Stepping from the heat, an instant chill spread over my skin as I walked naked passed two soldiers. They might not be drawn to my overly thin shape as they were before, but they still took their eyeful. I only wanted them to keep their distance. I might not give a damn about much in life anymore, but I wasn't about to let anyone touch me. I didn't want to be touched. The thought of it sickened me, and the irony was not lost on me that it was the closest thing I had to a human emotion in a while.

The dress Davin had chosen for me hung awkwardly across my breasts and bony hips. Evidently he hadn't been paying attention to how much weight I had lost, either. The ribbons hung much longer than were intended and the tight bodice that was supposed to be tailored to my curves had about three extra inches of fabric puckering around my middle so I had to pull the ribbons as tight as they would go.

When I returned to Davin, his black gaze seemed to immediately frown in disapproval, yet he said nothing. "We leave in an hour." He then moved to me. "I hope you don't have any ill conceived notions that your vampire will find you once you step outside here. He can't feel you anymore. But then, you already know that, don't you?"

I did. I remembered the night a Rogue vampire attacked Gemma and me at the tree house. It had been my first experience fighting a Nightwalker. By the time Caleb had arrived, I had been in such shock I was completely numb inside. The numbness made him unable to read my feelings of physical pain, nor could he detect the fear that had taken over. The same was true now. There was nothing inside to feel, and that was OK with me. That wasn't my life anymore. "Can you stop wasting time blathering," I replied impatiently.

His eyes narrowed, making it clear that he didn't like that response very much. "After you," he said with false sweetness.

Once outside the cavern it felt strange to inhale the fresh air instead of the human stench of death. No, not strange . . . nice, actually. We hiked down the north side of the mountain until we came upon some vehicles parked in a small, remote little town that had only one main street and homes littered around the fringes. It appeared completely deserted. This was where Davin had gotten his trench builders.

From there it took us two nights and a difficult river crossing to get Davin's vampire army moved up into some of the most remote wilderness I had ever seen in the northeastern territory of Alberta. The land was thick with enormous spruce and aspen trees, and the temperature seemed to plummet with every mile further north that we pushed toward the sub-arctic climate. When we finally climbed to a large, open meadow that seemed to pop up out of nowhere, I sensed right away that something was off. The entire surrounding landscape felt like a giant, suffocating void, as if no life, from human to the smallest land creature, existed.

"You can't sense them, can you?" Davin asked as he stared off into the distance. "But they're here. We are standing in the middle of a Lycan Dead Zone."

I frowned at him, having no idea what he was talking about.

"When they are gathered in large numbers like this they create a dead zone around them that warns off all predators and prey. Even humans don't realize how they never enter here. It's instinctual. That's how the Lycans have remained hidden for thousands of years, growing in numbers. They feed off the bison, bears, and elk around the perimeter . . . and an occasional big game hunter I imagine. Even if the Lycans were to leave here, the dead zone they have created would remain. It makes this the perfect location."

"Location for what?" I asked.

"It's about damn time you showed up!" Reese snarled, utterly surprising me because I hadn't sensed his approach until he was right there in front of us. "You were supposed to be here a couple days ago."

"Patience," Davin warned. "Did you find what you were looking for?" Reese nodded once in reply. "Good. We'll bring your nephew into the fold soon, then. I'm sure Olivia won't mind having a familiar face around," he added with a raised brow that searched for confirmation from me. " . . . That is, if she doesn't kill him first."

I shrugged, knowing somewhere deep inside that I should care about this. I should care very much. I just didn't. Right now, all I wanted was to be done with this stupid mission so I could get some peace and quiet. Personally, I didn't care if I ever saw this place again. Despite the natural untouched beauty that surrounded it, this was a place of death.

Davin stepped forward and slowly spread his arms out in a dramatic display. "Welcome to Brahm Hill. This is what it has all been about, Olivia," he declared. "Why I needed you . . . This land—my empire will exist here. We can hunt and grow in numbers without any interference from the human world. But first I need to remove its current occupants and I need you to help me do that."

"The Lycans?" I added tonelessly. "Figures. Every useless war ever fought has been about land."

"Land is the basis for any empire," Reese replied.

"So, then, this is where you and your happy little vampire family are going to live out your bloodsucking days?"

Reese came towards me with a hard glare. "You have a smart mouth."

"Enough!" Davin warned, halting Reese. "They'll be here soon—if they haven't already sensed her." Davin turned to stare into the darkness, as if expecting a howl to cut through the moonlit forest any second. "Come get us, you hungry bastards."

"What do you want me to do?" I sighed.

"Simple. Just stand here and work your magic. Draw them in. You can probably even take out a few of them with your touch before we ambush the rest."

"Fine," I said, turning to make my way out into the center of the field.

"Uh-un," Davin replied. "Shoes."

I shot him an incredulous look. I already looked ridiculous, preparing to fight Lycans in a designer looking black dress, and now he didn't want me to wear any shoes? "It's freezing out here!"

"You won't have to put up with it for long, I assure you. You'll draw them like children to sweets." I grumbled to myself as I removed my shoes, regretting it the second my bare feet hit the frosty grass. But if I didn't get on with this I was never going to get out of here.

Davin was dividing his army, instructing them on how the ambush would proceed once I drew the Lycans in, but Davin had been wrong.

For over two hours, I stood there in the middle of the cold meadow in my bare feet, waiting for the Lycans to appear so I could get some sleep—but they never showed. Yet somehow I knew they were nearby. I could no longer sense them, but I knew they were here. They just weren't showing themselves.

Davin became incensed. "What the hell is wrong with you?" he snapped. "You should've been able to draw them out two hours ago."

"I don't know," I replied, "and I don't really care."

Davin was in front of me in an instant, backhanding me so hard I was slammed to the ground. "You will care! You want food? Then you'll make this happen, and you'll make it happen *now!*"

I sprung back up to my feet and got right in his face. "*Don't* do that again."

Reese let out a hard snort. "Shit. She's about as charming as a wart. No wonder her vampire hasn't bothered to come back for her. He's probably thinking 'good riddance.'" I could feel the snarl pulling at my lip. That comment made something inside me pull with annoyance.

Davin then studied me carefully, as if Reese had just managed to say something significant for the first time in his life. "Yes?" he questioned. "None of us seemed to be as drawn to her, do we?" He began to circle around me slowly. "Perhaps I've made a critical miscalculation. As I predicted, her ability to kill with her touch has grown by tenfold, but her gift to charm has disappeared. It must be tied to her emotions."

Reese threw his arms up and slapped them against the side of his legs. "Oh, that's just great, Luther. How the hell are we supposed to kill the Lycans if she can't draw them in to our trap?"

"I should think it's fairly obvious," Davin replied. "We need to get some emotion back in her."

"And how do you propose we do that?"

Davin's assertive gaze traced a slow trail over me, his breaths coming a little more slowly as thoughts I doubted I wanted to know filtered through his mind. "I have a couple of ideas," he smiled. "I think our Charmer just needs a little attention to soften her up."

OK. Though I hadn't had food for quite some time, I was sure I would have no trouble vomiting the contents of my stomach at that thought.

"Well you better work fast," Reese growled, "The sun will be up soon."

Davin's gaze seemed to move absently over to the horizon. "Let's move back across the river. We'll take cover there for the night . . . and fix her issues tomorrow night."

***

After darkness fell the next night, Davin made me dress up in the same ridiculous black dress and bare feet as we returned to the top of Brahm Hill where "*he was going to fix my issues.*" I couldn't wait for him to try. Unfortunately for him, an unexpected guest showed up in the form of a long-legged platinum blonde who was madder than a hornet's nest. "*We* have a problem," Celeste barked at him.

Quietly observing from a distance, I wondered how long this little drama would play out before we could get on with things. "No," Davin corrected. "If it involves your mate then *you* have a problem. I could give a rat's ass about your love life. I did my part and delivered him to you free and clear. Now you just need to keep him . . . entertained." His voice lifted on the last words as he scanned the length of her legs.

Celeste's cool gaze narrowed on him in fury. "Well then perhaps you will give "*a rat's ass*" when he shows up at your little hideaway in the mountains to kill you."

"No, I won't," he replied confidently. "Because if all goes as planned tonight, we won't be returning there—ever!"

"Listen Grandpa, you are slow to get the picture here. He will find her!" Celeste then whipped a pointed finger at me. All I could think was that she'd better keep that finger back or I would break it off. "She has been communicating with him for the past several weeks."

Celeste had apparently lost her marbles, because the only time I had communicated with Caleb was that first time outside the cave—weeks ago. Davin seemed also to question her sanity, after pinning me with a hard glare to see if I had any reaction to this news, which I didn't. "That's impossible you over-peroxided bitch! Until three days ago she'd never been outside the circle of sacred ground. He can't feel her!"

Celeste refused to back down, getting right in Davin's face, while Reese crossed his arms as if amused by this whole confrontation. "He can see her! They are connected—telepathically. It has been all I could do to send him off on a bunch of wild goose chases while I tracked your ass half way across Alberta to warn you." She then pitched her hands over her hips to stare back at him incredulously. "And this is the thanks I get?"

At that moment, I shifted a little in my stance. There was a familiar sensation . . . a tickle . . . that seemed to pull inside my chest. And with each passing second, it grew stronger and stronger and stronger until I thought the sensation would burst right through.

"Don't be stupid!" Davin continued to fume. "If he had any idea where she was, he would've come for her weeks ago. You're—"

Davin suddenly cut off his own words as both he and Celeste snapped their heads around. I followed their hard gaze into the forested area ahead of us moments before the tickle became a jarring yank inside my chest.

"You idiot!" Davin barked at her, and then whipped his head around to his soldiers. "Cover her! He's not to get near her or I will kill the man who lets it happen." Suddenly Davin's soldiers surrounded me like a caged animal, just moments before an enormous wall of air blew against us with the force of a storm. Caleb landed about ten feet in front of Davin's soldiers. He had to be moving like a bullet to create that kind of force through the air. Appearing taller than ever with his shoulders back, there was something coy about his expression, like he was primed for a battle of wits as well as strength. His gray eyes pinned me between the Nightwalkers and my stomach did an involuntary flip at the contact.

What was he doing here? He needed to leave. I didn't want to be reminded of the past. But his thorough gaze scanned me from head to toe, from my sadly pale complexion to my ill-fitting dress and freshly bruised cheek, and the tense set of his jaw revealed that he obviously didn't like what he was seeing— or *feeling*. Caleb's lips pressed into a thin line and his nostrils flared wide as full fury bloomed within his deep breaths and into those eyes. One second the shifting color was like a storm about to erupt, and the very next it was gone, harnessed under a barrage of control.

"Actually, you're the idiot, Davin," Caleb finally spoke as his gaze slice to the leader, "if you believed for one moment that I wouldn't come for her. That I would stop looking because you threw my ex-mate to me like some kind of bone." His voice then lowered to the very deepest I had ever heard it, and I knew the warrior inside him was in full control. "And you'd better believe, I'm leaving with her."

Chapter Twenty-Six

"Really?" Davin replied with clear sarcasm to Caleb's declaration. "Because you seem to be a bit outnumbered." That only brought a smile to Caleb's lips as a second wave of air blew at us and at least a dozen others suddenly flanked him on both sides. Chay stood to his left and my very ticked-off Grandfather —no, not Grandfather, just Jax, I told myself—was there on his right. Even on a good day there was never any question that Jax was not someone to be messed with. Yet, as he stood there next to Caleb, that fact was never more obvious as he glared daggers at Luther.

The pull inside my stomach tightened as I looked at him. I had not seen Jax in nearly three months, and the last time I had, he'd asked me to leave. Well . . . I left, and it was no longer his problem to worry about protecting me. So why could he not just leave things alone?

It was then that I noticed a small redhead standing right behind his shoulder, a daring twinkle to her eyes as she brushed up against Jax. The contact with him was small, unnoticed by most there, but I knew better. Gemma was standing proudly with her mate, fully aware and in control of everything happening around her, and I was having a hard time ignoring the fact that seeing all of them again was not stirring something inside me. There was the smallest bit of warmth blooming somewhere in my stomach, like a familiar buzzing under my skin.

"Are you all right, Granddaughter?" Jax asked, his tone barely containing the fury behind it. I blinked back at him uncomfortably, unsure how to answer, but I didn't have to.

"Caleb, you don't understand," Celeste began as she approached him. "Thank God you are here! Davin was about to —"

"Shut it, Celeste," Caleb replied dully. "I don't want to hear any more lies and excuses from you. I've known from the beginning that you had a hand in Olivia's disappearance." He then turned back to me, and I could see the barest hint of a smile touch the corners of his lips. "She left me a note." Something about that made the pull in my stomach tighten even more as Caleb turned back to Celeste. "I've been waiting for you to make the mistake that would lead me to her." His hands then dropped to his sides and slowly curled into tight fist as he edged closer to her. "You've no idea how badly I want to send your six–hundred-year-old ass straight to the devil."

Celeste looked startled for a moment, which was definitely uncharacteristic for her, but recovered quickly. "Oh, stop your blustering," she said, dismissively. "You know you won't hurt me. I am your mate."

"*She's my mate!*" he snapped with a sharp finger pointed at me. "And she's leaving with me. Now!" My stomach leapt again at his declaration, and I had to remind myself that Caleb was part of my old life, the life I was living before I had changed— before I had killed with my bare hands. I had no right to it anymore. The only thing I wanted was to be anywhere but here at the moment.

"*She* doesn't *want* you," Celeste snarled. "Just ask her!"

"It's true," Davin added confidently. "Olivia knows now where she belongs. And it's no longer with you."

Caleb's low growl was a lethal warning to the Nightwalker.

Davin simply countered it with a tight smile. He was baiting Caleb.

I couldn't seem to find the words to reply. My gaze moved between Celeste and Davin before returning to Caleb. Though I was now focused solely on him, I could feel the weight of dozens of expectant stares all around me as I struggled in the silence. Caleb watched me carefully, zooming in on the bruise to my cheek where Davin had struck me. For a moment, the swollen skin warmed, then tingled, as if his gray gaze literally had the power to touch me across the distance. My hands curled into fist at my sides because for the slightest second, for the barest moment in several weeks, I wanted something. I wanted to reach for something, *someone* that I believed I could no longer have, and the ache of wanting was the most alive I had felt in weeks.

Caleb's eyes released me for a moment as he glanced knowingly over his shoulder at Jax. Jax simply nodded at him once as if for confirmation. "I feel it."

Feel what? These two men knew each other so well, their monosyllabic word game was starting to irritate me. "What I want," I finally said, "is to be left the hell alone. I'm tired of all of this."

"You heard the woman," Davin practically gleamed at Caleb. "Besides, what exactly is your plan? To take on my entire army here with just the twelve of you? You're still a bit outnumbered, in case you hadn't noticed."

That was certainly true. Though caught by surprise, Davin's soldiers outnumbered Caleb's by at least two dozen.

"Actually, you have it backwards," Jax informed him with a confident stare. Suddenly, sounds seemed to close in on us from everywhere. Bursts of air, the weight of human footsteps, and snarls of anger could be heard as Davin and Reese watched Alec and his Brethren forces rise over the hill and make their way towards us. A line of armed Dhampirs guarded Alec, with Lucas right there at his side and Maya, Phin and Kane following closely behind. There were at least a half-dozen Brethren forces that eventually emerged into the clearing.

Davin appeared momentarily angry that he had been surprised by the human and hybrid forces, but you could see the acknowledgment in his eyes that the Lycan Dead Zone we were standing in—Brahm Hill—had made it impossible to detect them.

"Well, isn't this convenient, Reese?" Davin began, trying to dismiss the seriousness of the situation. "Your nephew has come to us. That saves us a trip."

Alec kept moving forward until he stood before Reese, who appeared to be drawn to his nephew like a magnet, weaving an ornate silver dagger between his fingers. Lucas was right in step beside Alec, raising his crossbow in warning, but Alec held him back with his arm, and the large scowl souring Lucas's expression made it obvious that he didn't approve of Alec taking chances like this.

Scanning over all the familiar faces, Alec, Lucas, Phin and Kane, my heart sped up before my gaze stopped on Maya. Her consoling smile across the distance seemed to reach out and hug me. Shaking my head with a long blink, I turned away from her, my hands still clenching at my sides as I felt a human hunger return to my stomach that I thought had finally been pushed away.

Caleb growled under his breath, and I swung my gaze back to meet his. I could see it there in his eyes. He could feel the moment the hunger had returned to my stomach, and he did not like it.

Still playing with knives, Uncle?" Alec asked Reese, speaking into what appeared to be an ominous silence before a storm. "I didn't realize vampires needed weapons these days. Doesn't say much for your fighting skills, now, does it?"

"Oh, my fighting skills are just fine, thank you," Reese replied.

Why were they all doing this? I wondered. *Why were they all putting themselves in danger like this?* That's when I noticed Kane tilt his head curiously as he stared at the dagger in Reese's hand. The shape-shifter never let on what he was thinking in his head . . . unless he was making an overt advance on a woman. But the fighter side of him was careful, deliberate and secretive. The fact that he was so focused on the dagger in Reese's hand meant something. Did he recognize it somehow?

Kane's hand edged slowly towards the weapon at his hip and tension seemed to fill the air just moments before all-out war erupted. Before I knew it, bodies were flying everywhere, and I was in the middle of war—literally in the middle—as Davin's soldiers surrounded me, fighting off anyone who tried to approach. I searched the chaos to find Caleb, as if possessed by some sort of ingrained response. When I found him his piercing blue eyes were already locked on me as he fought his way toward me through the mass of movement all around us.

I was inhaling a reinforcing breath, preparing myself for the meeting with him when two of Davin's soldiers suddenly charged right at Caleb, then a third. Caleb was fighting three Nightwalkers at the same time, and I felt the breath halt in my lungs. My heart pounded and my pulse raced as my feet seemed to want to move on their own. I was leaning toward him, some force inside me compelling me to go to him—to help him. But I didn't get the chance. Celeste inserted herself between Caleb and me, those lavender eyes focusing on the closest of Davin's soldiers who guarded me and they instantly split wide to let her pass. "You and I are going to finish this."

"Celeste!" Caleb snarled, while continuing to fight his way through the soldiers. "You stay away from her!"

I barely had time to worry whether he'd be all right when Celeste lunged at me, forcing me to swing low to escape her direct blow. Coming back up, I shoved a hard elbow into her side and, strangely enough, thought about how ridiculous we both must look fighting in a dress and a high skirt with boots.

At least *my ass* was covered, though.

She came at me, delivering a blow to my midsection that had me shooting like a missile to the ground. I was gasping for breath as I looked up to see Celeste above me. "Oh, I'm going to enjoy this," she hissed, falling on me and pinning my arms to the ground. "He's mine. I created him. And I'll be damned if some two-bit slut takes him away from me!"

"You don't get it," I snapped back at her as I pushed my arms free from her grip then rolled over on my side. "He was never yours." When she followed, I kicked her to shove her back instead of choosing to use my touch to send her writhing in pain to the ground. Six hundred years old or not, I wanted to fight her one-on-one, with no gift, proving I could kick her ass without it. When she went down, I wanted her to know exactly who had defeated her.

Ironically, the blood she and Davin repeatedly forced down my throat was pumping through my veins at warp speed, sending energy to every muscle. I was fighting for something, moving faster, striking harder, and defending myself with perfect technique. "Face it. You've never had him," I said as we circled each other carefully. "That's the only reason you want him. If he'd fallen over you like the others, you would've moved on to the next mate by now."

"True," she smiled. "But I'm still going to make sure you don't get him."

Suddenly, we both paused as an ominous howl cut through the thicket that surrounded the open meadow. I recognized that howl like an echo from the past. I knew the unrelenting hunger behind it. But I was hoping I was wrong.

As we both turned our heads in the moonlit darkness, I blinked back when long, hair-covered limbs tipped with ferocious three-inch claws reached out and snagged a Nightwalker that had been battling near the edge of the tree line. The Nightwalker hissed and turned to deal with the enormous Lycan who was dragging him into the trees . . . but it was too late. After they disappeared from sight, a brutal snarl and then a horrid cry of pain shot out into the night. The unmistakably ferocious sounds of a Lycan gnashing on its prey rumbled through the dense forest. A quick scan of the tree line then revealed the eye shine of at least a dozen other Lycan's, hungrily waiting for the opportunity to grab easy prey. Lycanthropes were notoriously opportunistic hunters, and the ongoing chaos of battle allowed them to feed in the cover of the trees with minimal effort. At the moment, they weren't too worried about Davin's plan to take over Brahm Hill—their territory. They just saw dinner.

Another vampire disappeared into the tree line, and for the brief second I had, I tried to find Caleb. I needed to know it wasn't him who was being dragged into a Lycan's jaws, but I couldn't find him, and then Celeste was on me again, diving at me, pushing me to the ground. I rolled her on the grass until I was clear to jump back to my feet. My foot smacked against her jaw and sent her flying back. While she was down, I heard another low howl from a Lycan over by where Alec and Lucas were fighting Reese.

Reese lunged at Alec with the dagger, forcing him back to the ground as he was about to drive the blade into his chest when Lucas threw himself in front of Alec at the last second, and the blade went instead straight into Lucas's chest.

A sharp pain pulled through my own heart as if I could feel the sharp sting of the blade myself. Even through all the numbness I had felt for the last few weeks, I was not immune to this. I couldn't pretend any longer that I didn't feel anything. "Lucas?" I whispered; at the exact same moment Alec shouted out his name. Kane was there in an instant, before Reese had a chance to come at Alec again. Alec, meanwhile, protectively covered an unmoving Lucas.

With his hand he put pressure in the Guardian's wound but left the knife in his chest, knowing that Lucas could bleed out too fast if he removed it. "Damn you!" I heard him curse, miserably. "Why did you do this?" But already it appeared to be too late. Lucas wasn't moving.

Instinctively, I wanted to go to them, but Celeste had already returned to her feet, blocking my view of both of them. "I'm sick of playing with you," she hissed. "This ends now!"

She shot towards me with the speed of a bullet, crashing with such force that there was no controlling the impact. The breath was whooshed from my lungs, momentarily stunning me, before I managed to come back at her in relentless pursuit. Any semblance of time disappeared as the next combination of kicks, punches and evasive maneuvers seemed to unfold in slow motion, but in reality it all happened within a few seconds. For weeks, I had sworn to myself that Celeste would regret the day she had forced that blood down my throat, and that day was here. With one final blow to her side, my leg swept her feet out from under her, sending her crashing back to the ground. I dropped over her, bracing my arm at her neck. She tried to push me off her but I didn't move. I was too strong. "This is over!" I snapped. "You come at me again and I'll show no mercy. I promise you, you don't want that much pain."

"You're dead!" she snarled as she jerked and fought to come at me again. I held her down with one arm while my other hand locked over her temple. Within seconds she was screaming, writhing in pain. It only took me a second to decide what to do next.

I let her go.

She rolled away from, her hands clawing at her temples. "You were saying?"

Celeste remained down while I came to my feet to find Alec and Lucas. Several Brethren soldiers were circled around them in a protective force as Alec slumped over Lucas's unmoving body, his fingers closing the lids over his still eyes. My chest started to ache; my mind was spiraling with thoughts of our past together, wanting to go back in time somehow to change the outcome of this moment.

"No, Lucas . . ." Suddenly, I felt something akin to fire rise up inside of me. And it was painful. The same feeling appeared to hit Alec as he leapt to his feet and charged at Reese, who was still battling Kane. With more anger than sense, Alec pushed Kane out of the way and came at Reese with one of the silver-tipped crossbow arrows on the ground, plunging it straight into his heart. The vampire, who had at one time been like a father to Alec, fell, frozen to the ground with a shocked look grotesquely distorting his face. Alec seemed to pause for a moment, as if reconciling in his own mind what he was about to do. That split second of hesitation was all it took for fate to swipe the decision from his hands. The loud howl of the Lycan came just before the creature darted out through the trees and snatched Reese's frozen body, yanking him back into the cover of the woods.

"Olivia?" Caleb's voice called from somewhere behind me. I swung around to find him, my chest rising and falling so hard I thought my lungs would explode. He was all right. "Come," he said simply.

I wanted to go to him. The notion was instinctual, somewhere deep inside me. But I fought it. "No," I said in a low voice more to myself than anyone, still shocked about Lucas. "I can't go back. This is who I am now . . . I can't change what I've done." Confusion, anger, and sadness seemed to press on me until it felt as though I was suffocating from a sudden wave of emotions. Turning away from Caleb, I ran smack into Chay. He carefully looked at me, his eyes not missing the shaking in my hands. I squeezed them tight, trying to get back the steely control I had grown comfortable with over the past few weeks. That control was eroding, and it was the only thing that would get me out of here, get me away from all of these emotions I no longer wanted to feel.

Chay then tried to reach for me, but I pulled away, lowering into an aggressive attack stance. I wasn't quite sure what I was thinking, but I had to get this energy . . . these thoughts . . . whatever it was that was upsetting me, out of my head. "I will not fight you, Olivia," Chay said, calmly, extending his hands, palms toward me, in a gesture of peace.

"I'm not giving you a choice," I answered, pressing towards him, but before I even had a chance to strike, Caleb dropped in front of him, his arm held out from his side to signal to Chay that he would be dealing with me.

"You want to fight, Olivia?" Caleb asked with dark challenge, but I could still here the concerned edge to his voice underneath. "Then you'll fight me."

"No," I said, shaking my head, trying to move around him to challenge Chay again. Something about fighting *him* definitely wasn't right.

Caleb cut off my path, stepping in front of me a second time. "Yes," he came back sharply, moving towards me, crowding me. "I'm challenging you. You have to deal with me." He was forcing me back from the battle but at the same time keeping me away from the Lycan death trap that waited at the fringes of the tree line. I couldn't afford to let him isolate me like this. "You've trained for this," he continued to push. "Now do it!"

"Let me go!" I cried. "I can't go back."

"Do it!" he yelled again.

I let out an angry cry and charged him with everything I had. I pounded my elbow against his side and heard his loud grunt just before I moved to trip him to his knees. But Caleb was ready, blocking me and trying to hold me still by my arms. I managed to get away, coming back at him even harder, throwing my hands up in preparation to use my gift. He surprised me by leaving himself open for me to latch onto his temples. Once there, I focused all the energy I had through my fingertips, but he wasn't fighting me. At all! Instead he almost seemed to relax with me against him. Soon images started rolling through my mind. But they were good images—images of us . . . memories. I saw the night he saved me at the train crash, when he had squeezed my hand that first time and told me he didn't want to hurt me. I saw our first kiss at the piano, felt his cool lips brushing over mine and it seemed so real it was almost as if I were back in that moment for a split second. In fact, I was shaking beneath the memory of it. Then I saw the first time we made love at the piano, the sapphire eyes of the warrior staring back at me with such need—and yet with such gentleness. That was the first moment in which I knew I never wanted to be separated from him.

A strange sound welled up in my throat, something between

a cry and a whimper as I pulled my hands from his temples and allowed myself to collapse right there against his body. He wrapped his arm around me, supporting my weight against him. Somehow, even in the middle of a horrific battle scene, this was right. We were right. This was where I was supposed to be.

"You're still in there, my sweet," he murmured above the shell of my ear. "I feel it. Now come back to me."

It was strange how in a single instant I could feel so at peace against his body, like I was safe, home again for just a moment. I blinked slowly as I turned my head against his chest, wanting to hold onto this for as long as I could, because I knew it couldn't last. I would have to walk away from him again, which seemed nearly impossible, but I was no longer the same innocent woman I could feel in those memories.

As the battle continued around us, I glanced over to see a Nightwalker pull Maya off her feet, slamming her back against his ferocious chest, about to sink his claws and teeth into her small body. Words tried to come out of my mouth but were caught in my throat for one long, tense second. Then I saw Phin pushed his way through the chaos, ripping the vampire away from Maya. She fell hard to the ground, while Phin thrust a wooden stake straight through the Nightwalker's heart, freezing him instantly.

As Phin followed him to the ground, another Lycan came, fast as a striking cobra, from the cover of the woods. Hearing the grumbling sound behind him, Phin turned to respond, but everything happened too fast. The Lycan grabbed him and bit into his shoulder, gnashing the flesh and holding him pinned between his powerful jaws. Phin's face twisted in agony as Maya screamed out his name, and inexorably he was being dragged back towards the tree line, where he would be unable to escape.

Grabbing a nearby silver-tipped lance, Maya charged the Lycan, burying the lance deep into the creature's back. The Lycan turned on her, dwarfing her as it rose to its full height, at least eight feet.

"Maya, no!" I called, while Caleb pulled his arms tighter around me. "I have to help her!"

Caleb swung around to see what was happening. At that moment a fierce growl erupted behind me. I turned my head just in time to see Davin thrust a silver-tipped lance straight into my side. "She's mine!" he roared, sounding half mad with the volume of each word.

The red-hot pain that followed was immediate—and unlike anything I had ever experienced. It felt like a volcanic fire had instantly ignited inside my body, seizing every muscle in my limbs. I was helpless and could not move.

I slumped in Caleb's arms, the strength of them the only thing that stopped me from crumbling to my knees. Then, as Davin yanked the lance back with no regard for how much flesh he was tearing in the process, I screamed out, shaking uncontrollably. "*Goddamn you!*" Caleb roared, while Davin prepared to sink the lance into me again. Caleb swung me away from Davin just in time to take the slice of the blade through his own side. With one hand he grabbed onto the lance and held it still so it couldn't sink any deeper into his flesh. He then let me slide down his side as gently as he could. "You son of a bitch!" he hissed back at Davin as he pulled the lance out of his side and swung it back around on the vampire.

No longer able to see them because I was huddled against the ground as they fought behind me, the vampires' growling fury could be heard as they clawed and pounded against each other like two pride lions. All the warmth I had only started to feel again had begun to leave my body as my eyes slowly scanned the war still going on all around me. Kane was helping Maya fight off the Lycan who had attacked Phin, sending a second lance into the creature's body. Badly wounded, the Lycan stumbled back into the safety of the trees.

Maya fell to her knees, inconsolable, as she cried over Phin, who was now shaking violently against the ground in reaction to the Lycans poisonous bite. As she tried to protectively cover his large body with hers, he pushed her away. "Get back, Maya!"

Maya's formerly strong battle face was dissolving from so much pain. Being an Empath, she was feeling every bit of Phin's suffering as well as trying to deal with her own. "Phinneas . . . I love you," she sobbed. "You're going to be OK. You have to be . . ."

My heart ached for her as its rhythm slowed. I felt strangely numb from my chest down.

Phin shook his head, "It's too late."

"Take it!" Kane snarled, practically forcing the contents of a small vial in his hand down Phin's throat.

Maya screamed in protest, reaching her arms out desperately for Phin as Alec turned her head against his shoulder. Phin stared up knowingly at Alec, his expression almost pleading in some way. "I'll take care of her," Alec murmured, trying to hold a nearly hysterical Maya back as Phin crawled to his feet and stumbled away from all of them.

Kane seemed almost frozen in place as he watched Phin leave. "I know what I should do," he rasped in a broken voice, "but I just can't do it."

Maya screamed, nearly crumbling to her knees in Alec's arms. The shrill sound pulled Kane from his distant thought, and he swung around to come over and help Alec.

"Don't kill him, Kane," Maya pleaded. "Please! Please, don't kill him!"

"Olivia!" Jax called from somewhere close to me, pulling my tired eyes away from a heartbroken Maya. Glancing up slowly, I watched as he came towards me from across the field. "Chay!" he bit out sharply, "Stay with Gemma!"

Chay nodded at him once as my eyes found a very confident Gemma battling toe-to-toe with one of Davin's last remaining soldiers. She moved expertly but with grace, her gift to levitate still a part of her repertoire, as she seemed to almost float in the air before landing another kick directly to the vampire's jaw.

Jax stopped just short of me; the scent of the blood pouring from my wound was soaking into his senses, preventing him from getting any closer. "Hold on, Granddaughter," he almost growled, sounding angry with himself that he had to keep his distance. "I will get help."

Meanwhile, Caleb and Davin's battle caught my attention again, since it had shifted to the middle of the field. The raw rage pouring from Caleb summoned the warrior from deep within him. That part of himself was so primal, so elemental in his need to conquer, that no man or creature stood a chance against him when he was in that frame of mind. He was quicker, stronger, and unrelenting, but true madness seemed to be keeping Luther one step ahead of him.

"Alec!" Jax called, but it was Celeste who zoomed in on me while Alec still tried to calm a distraught Maya. Her fierce expression burst into unmistakable delight as she discovered me huddled there against the ground. She swung around and locked her lavender gaze on her two Brethren challengers. Within a split second she had them looking completely lost, and then she snapped their necks, one right after the other, without a second thought.

She turned back to me and shot me a look that said she intended to silence me the exact same way . . . but Jax saw her, too. A low, harsh growl of warning lashed at her just before Jax charged, sending Celeste crashing to her back against the ground. He reached for a rough stick and drove it powerfully, dead center, through her heart, freezing her in place.

Even helpless, Celeste's lavender eyes still brightened, trying to trap him in her gaze, but he avoided her direct stare. "You have no idea had badly I want to finish this," he hissed. "But I will not let your death stand between me and Caleb. It has to be his choice to take your life." Jax's fangs came within a hairsbreadth of her face, and even though she was frozen beneath him, it wasn't hard to imagine her fear at seeing an enraged Jax in such complete control above her. "But if you ever come anywhere near my Granddaughter again," he snarled, "I will not give a damn about the consequences. Understood?"

With that he yanked the impaling stick out of her heart. Sucking in a hard gasp, her chest heaved and she sat up. Jax didn't even give her time to recover before he gripped her chin in his large hand. "Are we clear?" he asked in a violent whisper.

Celeste nodded stiffly, still trying to gather her breath as he tossed her twenty feet, as though she weighed no more than a tennis ball. "Alec!" Jax bellowed a second time, and this time Alec heard him, his eyes going wide as he saw me lying there, still, on the grass.

Alec quickly transferred Maya into Kane's arms. "Get her out of here," he said to Kane as he raced towards me.

The world around me continued to slow down along with

my heartbeat. It was strangely silent, even though all of this commotion was still going on all around me. I felt sure that the numbness running throughout my entire body was a sign that death was near. That, plus the fact that I saw something so strange, something so completely out of place, I believed that I had to be imagining it. I wasn't sure where she had come from, but a young woman appeared at the edge of the bloody battlefield. She looked completely out of place, like an angel dressed in soft flowing white, although I couldn't for the life of me tell you the details of what she was wearing. It was like she was just an image—just there. I decided she had to be an angel. Fate had caught up with me, and she was there to take me away . . . but she didn't come to me. She went to Lucas.

Kneeling over my Guardian's lifeless body, she stroked her open palm over his forehead and then turned to catch my bewildered stare of her. I gasped in a weak breath when her face came into clear focus. It was Skye Matthews, the mysterious woman who had come into the clinic while I was closing up. She smiled softly, her pretty eyes filled with empathy, and suddenly the last words she had spoken to me that day at the clinic popped into my head—at the exact same moment she mouthed the word, "*Remember.*" And I could hear her voice so clearly back at the clinic that day. "Fate likes to play games with us . . . But what you're feeling right now is always the way back. Remember that."

"Caleb," I whispered as tears began to fill my eyes, needing to find him, needing to touch him just one last time.

Kane caught my stare and followed it across the field. He did a double-take when he saw the woman who was clearly out of place and whispering in Lucas's ear, the chaos of battle continuing to die down around her.

"Hey, you there?" Kane yelled, still holding onto Maya. "Stop!"

I wondered why Kane would be yelling at an angel? Then it further occurred to me. *How could Kane see the angel?*

"Olivia," Alec said, blocking my view. "Just hold on. You're going to be OK."

"Lucas?" I murmured. "He's with the angels now."

"Take it easy." He spoke gently, but I could hear the slight break in the pitch of his voice. There was no doubt he was hurting at the loss of his best friend.

"I'm cold, Alec."

"She's dying," I heard Davin laugh in the distance as he and Caleb continued their fierce battle. "You can feel it, can't you? I warned you that you wouldn't leave here with her."

Caleb released a bellowing roar as he deflected Davin's charge and his attacker's lance upward and to one side. Grabbing the lance at its middle, he whipped it back across Davin's ribcage, sending his enemy roughly to the ground, and then immobilized him by driving the silver lance into his chest. "Save a place for me in hell, Luther," Caleb snarled, then he pitched up Davin's immobilized body by the lance and shot it into the barn size fire that had already been started to destroy the Nightwalkers.

As I watched Davin's body shrivel and burn in the flames, I sighed softly, unable to believe it was finally over. I was finally free of the man who had been chasing me non-stop for the last year. Somehow, knowing that Caleb would also be free of him —would be able to find peace again someday—seemed to make it OK for me to let go of the lingering feeling that I should have been the one to finally kill this evil, evil man and spare Caleb the new mark on his soul.

"Olivia! Olivia!" Caleb tried to come to me, but there was too much blood.

"Stay back, Caleb!" Jax warned, halting him with his braced arm.

"Here," Alec said, throwing a plastic container towards Caleb. "Hurry!"

After a few lost blinks, Alec was trying to tilt my chin up to pour vampire blood into my mouth, but I didn't want it. "Swallow it, Olivia," he ordered. "Now!"

"No more blood," I said weakly.

"Olivia, don't you do this," Caleb pleaded in nothing more than a rough growl. "Don't you dare leave me!"

Alec's hand was patting my cheek, trying to keep me awake, his light brown eyes glossed with a fear I had not seen in him before.

"Damn it! Force her!" Caleb shouted and I saw Alec bring the container back to my lips . . . but I shook my head at him.

"It's OK, Caleb. Lucas and I will be OK," I whispered, just as the darkness came for me.

Chapter Twenty-Seven

I was surprised to feel warmth surrounding me.

I wondered if I was with the angels now, where I no longer had to suffer the bone-deep chill beneath my skin. Yet glimpses of the familiar seemed to seep in, reminding me what it felt like to be alive—to be human. I didn't know how much time had passed before I began to recognize the slow in and out of my breathing, the steady rhythm of my heart, or the tingles over my skin . . . but they were definitely there. *I could feel!* At one point, the warmth grew to a fiery heat, but it was calmed by a coolness that surrounded me, overtaking the heat until my skin felt comfortable again. Then a chill followed, taking over until I was blanketed in soft warmth and my shivers eased. Now I was thirsty, and a cup was being pressed to my lips, but I pushed back instantly from it. "No," my croaky voice spoke as I tried to bring my heavy hand up. "No more blood . . . please."

"It's all right," a familiar deep voice whispered over my ear. "It's just tea mixed with some dandelion and eucalyptus for your fever. Please drink it, sweetheart." It didn't matter how dazed or out of it I felt. I would have known that voice anywhere. Caleb was with me, taking care of me. That much I understood, even in all the fuzziness. He pressed the cup to my lips a second time. I sipped slowly while his other hand stroked over my hair. "That's good. I also have some broth here. Can you drink some of this for me?"

The salty chicken broth slid into me, creating a warm trail all the way to my empty stomach, and the elation I felt at finally having some human food was tempered by my absolute exhaustion. As I fell in and out for sleep I continued to feel Caleb's presence there beside me, his familiar body pressing against mine while soft kisses were tickling my warm cheeks and neck. I reached blindly for his hand, and when I found it he squeezed mine gently in return. "Caleb, where are we?"

There was a steady exhale above me that sounded like relief, then a palm brushed across my temple. "You're someplace safe, Olivia." Immediately, my mind flashed back to another day when he said those exact words to me. The first day Caleb had brought me back to the tree house after the train crash. At that time I didn't know his voice, didn't trust the man saying the words . . . but now I knew better. This man always made me feel safe, always surrounded me with both strength and security—but was my mind playing tricks on me?

"Am I dreaming? Am I still in the cave?"

"No, sweet girl. You're here with me. No one's going to hurt you anymore, I promise." His thumb continued to brush back and forth over my cheek. "Can you open those beautiful eyes for me?" As if the silkiness of his voice had the power to dictate my actions, I slowly fluttered my lashes open. At first my eyes struggled to adjust to the brightness of the fire coming from a large stone hearth, even though the light throughout the room was low because every window to the outside was covered. We were in some sort of small cabin, the whole place not much bigger than an average size living room. It was so barren; it looked as if no one had been there in years, like some sort of hunting cabin.

Caleb was just above me, his long body leaning over mine as he sprawled over the floor on his side, the light from the fire reflecting in his eyes. He reached over my head and grabbed an old tin cup, bringing it to my lips. After taking a small sip I wrapped both of my hands around the warm cup and greedily drank more. Once I was finished he set the cup down, and his fingers skimmed over my bony shoulder, and I could see his teeth clench slightly against his jaw. "You're nothing but skin and bones."

"Davin fed me blood, just blood, no human food—"

"I know," Caleb cut in quietly, turning his head away to hide the angry grimace that tightened his features. "I can *feel* your hunger. When you think your stomach can handle something solid, I have some bread and a little cooked meat here for you."

I nodded and then felt a pain in my side. I reached down by my hip, where I remembered Davin had struck the lance through me, but Caleb stretched his hand for mine and stopped me. "You need to lie still. Your wound is still healing." He ran his fingers gently over the swollen skin, shaking his head, and there was so much pain in his expression. "I thought I was losing you," he said quietly. "I never want to know that feeling again."

I stared up at him blankly, unsure about how to process the sudden swell of emotion that was blooming inside me after I had felt so little during the past few weeks. Instead, my hand felt around me to the soft pelt of animal fur beneath me—like a bear's—cushioning me from the hard floor. I had no clothes on beneath the blanket covering me, and beside me there was a small pile of bloody gauze and bandages that looked as if Caleb had just finished changing. "The blood . . . ?" I questioned him, worried the scent of my blood would be too much for him.

Shaking his head, he quickly put my mind at ease. "It's all right. I'm not thirsty."

"Where are we?"

"We're still in Northern Alberta. We found this old hunter's cabin within a few miles of the battle site. Jax and I didn't want to move you very far and we could smell that no one had been here for quite a while."

"Jax is here?"

Caleb nodded, his eyes brimming with concern. "He and Gem are not far away. It's still too soon for her to be around your gift, but she has been asking about you."

My eyes slid away from him sadly. I wasn't sure if Gemma would ever be able to handle the effects of my gift now that she was a full vampire. The thought of never being able to be around her again made me remember how lonely I had been for the last five weeks in the cave. "Is she doing all right?"

"Much better . . . but I'll let Jax fill you in. He's anxious to see you."

As Caleb said those words I tried to squelch the pain that pulled inside my chest. I couldn't get comfortable around Caleb and Jax again because I had to remember what I had done to Silas, what I was capable of doing. "I . . . I . . . I'm still very tired."

Caleb's expression was neutral, but I could tell he was disappointed by my response. But for the past five weeks I'd had no life, no family, no home, outside of that dark cave. I had seen things of the Nightwalker's world that would always be with me. I had killed with my own bare hands. I would never be the same innocent woman they had all known when I made the fateful decision to leave Seattle because of Celeste. So how could I expect to step back into the life I knew as if nothing had ever happened? How I could ever be the same woman in Caleb's eyes?

"Get some rest," he murmured in reply. "I'll wake you later so you can try and eat a little more."

✱✱✱

Caleb did wake me later, but it wasn't to eat. Instead I was greeted by the slight scowl pulling across his brows as he said, "Alec's here. He's insisting on seeing you. Do you feel up to a visitor?"

I nodded eagerly, and my enthusiasm to see Alec didn't seem to please Caleb. I didn't want to hurt Caleb. To the contrary, I wanted to throw myself around him and beg for him to take me back to Seattle, no matter what I had done.

Caleb moved to the cabin door, his tall frame, with its spine stiffened, appearing very awkward. As the door cracked open I could see the cloudy daylight trying to squeeze through, which was the only time that made sense for Alec to risk himself to come see me. As the Elder entered the cabin his concerned expression immediately fixed on me even before he knelt on the floor beside the makeshift bed. He offered a relaxed smile as he quickly glanced back over his shoulder at Caleb. "Try to not kill my guards."

"She needs rest," Caleb said to him, not appearing amused by Alec's humor. "I'll be back in a few minutes." He then shut the door firmly behind him.

"Grumpy as the day I met him," Alec muttered, then sighed heavily. "But I can't deny that he loves you." He took my hand with a gentle squeeze. "It's good to see you awake. You scared me there for a minute, little Charmer. All that talk of angels . . ."

His smile then seemed to fade as if he had guessed my next question even before I asked it. "Lucas . . . ?" Alec shook his head, and I could see the incredible energy it took to hold back the well of grief that showed itself for only a brief moment before being pulled back. "I'm so sorry, Alec," I murmured in a quiet voice. "We will all miss him very much . . . but I know for you it's like losing a brother."

He nodded, the emotion trapped in his throat until finally he managed to say, "He saved me. The dumb bastard threw himself in front of the blade meant for me. He was always doing stupid stuff like that." Alec turned his head away and I could see he didn't want to continue with this subject.

"And Maya . . . ?"

Alec's expression didn't lighten any. In fact, it pinched into a tight grimace. "She's inconsolable. Hasn't eaten . . . hasn't left her room. She was already worn down from the search to find you. Now with Phin . . ." He paused for a long moment, seeming to consider his words before he continued. "Her gift to *feel* is gone."

I inhaled sharply. Maya's Empathic gift to feel was as integral part to who she was, just as Caleb's was to him. She would be lost without it. "Oh, Alec, she's in so much pain. Give her time."

Alec shook his head. "I promised Phin I would take care of her, and so far I'm doing a lousy job."

Squeezing his hand, I said, "Phin knew he could trust you. That's why he asked you. Don't give up on her. If anyone understands loss, it's you." Alec looked at me, seeming to appreciate my words. "I want to see her. I'll try to come as soon as I can."

"Hmm," he sounded. "I suppose that means I'm going to be having Daywalkers camped outside The Oracle for a couple of days."

"Oh, stop your blustering," I teased him. "You know what I think. I think you've actually grown to respect Caleb in your own way. You just don't want to admit it."

"Good God, that can't be true. I have that guy stuck in my head enough as it is. It's much easier to detest him."

I laughed. "Whatever you say, Alec."

Alec's responding laugh faded into a soft smile. "Seriously, though . . . You're free of Davin . . . and I am free of Reese. Whatever are we going to do with all of this free time we have now?"

"We're going to stay in touch," I replied confidently. "Just because you're ruling this mini-empire doesn't give you an excuse to not call or see me."

I could see the sarcastic retort lined up and ready to go, but I stopped him with my fingers to his lips. "Seriously. You are the truest friend I could ever have, and I expect both of us to make an effort to stay in touch."

He smiled against my fingers. "I was going to ask . . . if you would let me finish . . . if Caleb could build me a little guest house in a nearby tree." My responding laughter caught me completely by surprise and it felt good. It had been so long since I had something to laugh about. "That way it's always ready for me to drop by. I might need a few extra rooms though for my guards."

Holding my side, I said, "OK, stop. Do you want me to get better here?"

"I do, little Charmer," he said, leaning forward to place a soft kiss on my forehead. "I do. But I better keep this short before old blue-eyes comes snarling back in here."

"Alec . . . ," I warned him.

"All right, fine. I suppose they're gray most of the time," he acknowledged with half-hearted enthusiasm. "Will you be returning to Seattle with Caleb soon?"

I blinked at him, almost caught off guard by the question. "I don't know."

Alec appeared to want to ask more questions, but then he seemed to think better of it. "I'll tell Maya that you'll be by to see her." I nodded as he came back to his feet as Caleb re-entered the cabin, his not-so-subtle signal that time was up. As he walked towards the door, Alec stopped short and asked with a taunting smirk, "Did you kill any of them?"

"Would you notice?" Caleb growled back. "There's like twenty of them out there."

"True," he replied, then turned to me and gave me one of his trademark winks before disappearing into the daylight.

As Caleb shut the door behind him he grumbled under his breath, "Of all people to have connected to me."

***

Several more days passed and I was feeling much stronger.

My appetite had returned with full force, my wound from the lance was healed, and it seemed that Caleb had not left my side for a moment. But this morning I opened my eyes to see Jax sitting there, quietly, beside me. His long, dark hair was pulled back tidily at his nape with a leather strap, and his amber eyes appeared thoughtful, soft, the color seeming to almost swirl like brandy. "Caleb?" I questioned him in a hoarse morning voice as I sat up.

"He is feeding. I reminded him that if he was going to take care of you, he also needed to take care of himself." I nodded quickly, letting him know I wholeheartedly agreed. "It is good to see color in your cheeks again, Granddaughter . . . though you are still much too thin. We will have to fatten you up a bit," he smiled, trying to lighten the tense air between us, but I lay there in silence. This man was my grandfather, and aside from Sophie, the only blood family I had. But he had hurt me so deeply when he asked me to leave the tree house, despite the fact that I understood the pain he was in over Gemma. "I know you are still angry with me," he finally continued as if able to read my thoughts, "and I deserve it. I simply could not face what I had done. And I needed to protect you—from *me*." He sighed heavily. "But I never should have forced Caleb to choose to send you to the city. It was wrong."

"I'm not angry anymore," I replied, and I could hear the sadness in my own voice. "I understand that you were trying to protect me . . . but you hurt me, Jax. You sent me away from the only family that I have—you, Gemma, and Caleb—at a time when we needed each other most. And now things are different —I'm different." I could see the emotion and regret in his eyes. It was obvious he wanted to say something, but he remained silent, letting me finish. "I haven't yet decided where I'm going to—"

Jax's silence ended abruptly as a hard line drew over his brows. "You are not going anywhere. You have a home—a family—a mate who loves you. And you will stay here with him until you are well. Then you will come home to us where you are needed."

It irritated me that he said that as if I should know better. "You didn't need me—"

"I have needed you in my life every day since I learned you were my flesh and blood. And I needed you most of all on that horrible day with Gemma," he returned with such feeling. "You handled things so well that day—as well as anyone could have, considering the circumstances you were faced with. I have never thanked you for saving my life. I am doing so now."

"How is Gemma?" I asked.

A relaxed smile came over his lips that seemed to animate his whole body. "She is well. She remembers much of her life and our beautiful little Sophie. She forgave me," he continued. "Her heart is capable of an unconditional love that has truly humbled me. That is what she brought with her into this life, and I love her all the more for it."

At the mention of Sophie's name, I was suddenly reminded of his daughter's very special gift. "Jax, there is something I need to tell you about Sophie," I began carefully. "She has a gift —one that is very difficult for her to understand while she is so young."

"Tell me," he replied.

"She can see the future. When I touched her that day I could see the images she was seeing of me—of my time in the cave with Davin. She was upset because the images frightened her."

"Those must have been some frightening images for you too, Granddaughter. I wish you had told us. ."

"I know," I acknowledged. "But I didn't understand what I was seeing at the time."

"My poor little girl," Jax whispered in a worried voice. "How do I help her with this?"

I squeezed my hand gently around his arm. "I don't believe Dhampirs receive gifts that they cannot handle. Each one is unique to the individual. She'll be all right, now that you and Gemma understand what is happening—and as long as she knows she is loved, that she is safe and secure."

Jax smiled. "Gemma asks about you . . . when she can see you . . . if you will be coming home with us."

An unexpected tear slipped from the corner of my eye as I shook my head at him. "I'm not the same person I was when I left. I've seen things, done things . . . I don't know if I can be the woman Caleb fell in love with anymore."

"Is that why you are trying to keep such distance between you and him since you woke?" I blinked back at him. "He can feel it," Jax answered to my silent question.

I lowered my head and nodded.

"When Caleb learned that you had been forced to leave Seattle because of Celeste he was devastated—furious with both himself and *me* for being so stubborn, for leaving you unprotected . . . and rightfully so."

"I had planned to return in a few days . . ."

"It would not have mattered. Caleb was already on his way to you at The Oracle." Jax's expression then pulled into a tight grimace. "But once he felt what happened to Alec he knew it was a trap meant to get to you. He followed Alec but got there too late. Reese had already disappeared with you, leaving no trail for us to follow."

Caleb had come for me just as he always did. Knowing that created a warmth inside of me that would be strong enough to defeat any cold.

"He was furious . . . and scared. He told Alec he had to return to Seattle to play the clueless mate with Celeste in order to trick her into revealing what she knew." Jax paused, turning his head and remaining silent for a long while. "But he never expected it would take this long for her to slip up. That first moment Caleb saw you again . . . felt the physical hunger you suffered . . . the emotional void . . . he was ripped in half. I know because I felt it in him."

The warmth inside me grew as Jax spoke. I loved Caleb. I *still* loved him. There simply was no choice for me in the matter.

Jax then captured my face in his hands. "Let him help you with whatever is holding you back . . . then come home. I do not want to miss another day of being able to know my beautiful granddaughter."

I hugged my arms around him and Jax was careful not to squeeze too hard, but the enthusiasm of his embrace left no doubt how much he treasured this moment. Both Jax and I looked up as we heard Caleb enter back through the cabin door. Though he tried not to show it, I could see the hurt in his eyes that I was currently showering affection on Jax when I had been so guarded with him. "Has she eaten?" he asked.

Jax released me, shaking his head. "I will leave that for you to take care of," he smiled. "I need to be getting back to Gemma. We will be returning to Seattle tonight." He then placed a reassuring hand over the taller man's shoulder, silently communicating his expectation that we would follow soon. The two men understood each other's silent gestures better than their verbal ones, it seemed.

Caleb nodded in reply, and then watched as Jax left through the open door. There was a long silence between us while I watched him bring a pan of heated water over from the barely workable cook top. His very attentiveness as he carried out this simple task made me realize what awful conditions he had been putting up with to take care of me in this crude cabin. He sat down beside me and asked me to lie back so he could check the side that had been pierced by the lance. His fingers prodded gently over the skin that was now fully healed. "I'm better—in no pain. You don't need to worry."

His gaze met mine and I couldn't tell what he was thinking. He reached for a clean washcloth, taking his time soaking the cloth in the warm water before drawing the sheet that was covering me away from my body and wiping the cloth along my skin. And I let him. I couldn't stop myself from letting him. In fact, I could barely breathe, the simple gesture of cleaning my body feeling so private, yet so familiar between us. He was thorough, gentle, massaging in slow circles over the edges of my shoulders, the curves of my breast, and the soft arc of my thighs. It felt so wonderful to be touched by him. I had felt sure I'd lost the ability to feel anything deeply after the last six weeks of captivity, but Caleb's touch never failed to stir that part of me so deep, so responsive to him, so impossible to deny.

"We can leave here tomorrow if the clouds hold up," his deep voice broke into the quiet. "I'd prefer moving you during the day, since there might be a few of Davin's stragglers about. But I don't expect them to be a problem for—"

I stopped him by placing my hand over his. "Caleb . . . we need to talk."

He was quiet for a long moment, his gray gaze staring into me thoughtfully. There was no mistaking that he had guessed where I was going with this conversation. "You're coming home with me, Olivia." He didn't say it as a command, but from a place of pain, as if he couldn't believe it was an option for me not to return with him.

Shaking my head at him, I replied, "I want to . . . but things are different now."

"You keep saying that. Of course you can return. It's your home. It's where you belong. I never should have asked you to leave it in the first place. I should've found a way . . ."

My throat tightened and I could feel the unspent tears wanting to break through, but I needed to be strong so I could make him understand that I wasn't doing this to hurt him but to do what was best for him. "It's not about that, Caleb. I've changed. I've seen things and done things now that I can't ever take back."

He speared his long fingers into my hair, his hand cupping my cheek in his palm so he could lift my eyes to face him. "Tell me what you've done that you believe is so unforgivable," he intoned softly. "Because I feel the same woman I have always felt, except that she is pushing away from me—and I *hate* it."

My cheeks suddenly felt hot and my hands began to shake as Caleb pulled me into his arms. He had such strength, and he offered that strength to me without hesitation, letting me curl against his hard body and just breathe easier. "I . . . I killed one of Davin's soldiers with my bare hands," I murmured against his throat so low it was barely audible. "I've known for a while now that my touch was getting stronger. Even that day when I fought Celeste I sensed that if I held on when I had her head in my hands I would've killed her. But I didn't think I was capable of not having control—of not letting go. I didn't believe . . ."

Caleb remained silent, intently listening while I spoke, continuing to hold me securely against him. That silence was a bit unnerving. What was he thinking? Could he ever possibly look at me the same way again? Shaking my head as if somehow I could erase the painful memories, I continued on. "I was trying to escape . . . I had managed to fight off several of Davin's soldiers, but—"

"Stop," he said, dropping his cheek to rest on top of my head. Just stop. You can't blame yourself for this—for wanting to escape a madman who was starving you. Who was hurting you. I won't let you."

"But Caleb, I—"

"No!" He silenced me by pulling back and covering my lips with a needy, almost desperate kiss that caught me off guard. My heart lurched inside my chest in one hard thump. His kiss was trying to take away the pain while at the same time reminding me who I belonged to, unconditionally. It felt amazing to be touching him again, accepting his kiss, to be held within his strong embrace. He was filled with such gentleness, passion, and most of all—love. "I would've wanted you to do whatever was necessary to survive," he spoke over the seam of my lips, " . . . to gain your freedom. I can't take away the monstrous things that you saw, or were forced to do, but I can help you remember the good and beautiful woman that you are. No one can take that from you. It's a part of you. And I will remind you of it every single day, and how much I love you."

I stared back at him in amazement, my eyes becoming blurry with tears.

"Don't you see, Olivia? I don't want this life, Daywalker or otherwise, without you . . . every part of you. Not just the good stuff—the easy stuff."

Suddenly, the breath was whooshed from my lungs as his lips locked with mine for a second time. All coherent thoughts vanished from my head as his kiss drew my breath into his body in one sweet rush. The world was spinning around me, but in a good way. "You're coming home with me," he breathed, "and you'll not be taken away from me ever again. You're my mate, my other half. You belong with me."

At those words, the rest of the emotion, the fear, bottled up inside me since I had come face to face with him again released like a giant dam. I curled my arms around him and tucked my head into his shoulder, my body shaking with tears I had no hope of pulling back or stopping.

He laid me back against the makeshift bed, pushing the blankets back as his lips kissed away the tears falling over my cheeks. "Shhh, it's OK, my sweet," he whispered. "You've nothing to be fearful of anymore—nothing to be ashamed of. You are finally free."

I blinked up at him as if remembering what he was saying was true. *I was free!*

His kisses continued to feather and coax as he moved lower over my throat and the valley between my breasts, his rough bristle tickling me as it dragged over my skin. I was completely bared to him, every part of me exposed both outside and in. A cool breeze filtered through the room, sending the good kind of shivers through my body as Caleb worked a not-so-direct line of kisses down to my bellybutton where he licked his tongue playfully around the edges.

Oh, God, his kisses felt really, really good. All I could manage to do was gasp a breathy reply, my fingers sinking into the thickness of his hair. His own breathing was becoming harder as he moved back up my body and his large hands massage over my hips then held them in a firm grip. I sighed as one hand swept to the outside of my thigh and curled one of my legs around his waist, opening my body to him. "It's time for my sweet to feel something again," he rumbled against my skin just before his cool mouth dropped over my breast and he suckled the rose colored tip between his lips. With a soft groan he took hold, his tongue lashing back and forth until I thought it was possible to jump right out of my own skin.

"I'm free," I whispered with a smile, feeling soft and warm beneath him. He made me believe I could have everything I ever wanted if I would just take it, all while being subjected to incredible, pulse pounding pleasure. I had missed this, feared I would never know this kind of warmth again.

Caleb licked in small circles, placing little nibbling love bites in a trail down my body as his fingers descended between my thighs, stroking my intimate flesh there until I heard my own gasp. Instinctively, my back arched, straining higher the more his touch excited me. "Can you feel this sweet girl?" he murmured over my skin.

Feel it? My toes were curling into the fur beneath me. *Dear God,* this had to stop or I was sure anyone within a ten mile radius would soon hear my screaming beyond all limits of my control. I was already on the edge of exploding, panting hard, and he hadn't even removed his jeans, the only article of clothing he had left after slipping effortlessly out of his shirt.

That problem would soon be rectified as the sound of him shuffling through his button-fly was bliss to my ears. He took only enough time to push his jeans down his hips, and then leveraging himself above me on one elbow. "I need you," he breathily declared as his hands held my hips firmly in place and he pushed his thick flesh inside, impaling me with one hard movement. I moaned helplessly, arching my back to try and draw him even deeper, savoring every incredible sensation of being taken by this man I loved so completely. It had been too long since I had been a part of him, connected to him in this way.

"Caleb," I murmured, rolling my head back and then blinking up at him in surprise. I was staring into the most beautiful eyes—*not electric blue, but gray*—their color dark, smoky, swirling with heat and raw need. They held me in their grip as he began to thrust forward in a slow, even rhythm. Somehow he had found the secret to controlling his change, calming the warrior inside him so his more human side could experience this moment like a normal man.

His hands curled beneath my thighs, his fingers digging into my soft flesh as he wrapped my legs high around his waist, then braced his arms at each side of me and began thrusting deeper, maintaining his thread of control. "*God,* you feel amazing," he rasped.

My breathing came out in broken, hard gasps that pressed against my lungs. Heat was coiling low in my belly and I knew it wouldn't take long for me to fall apart in his arms.

Caleb locked his lips to mine, keeping them together as he drove in one last push, burying himself to the hilt, filling me until I exploded. I cried and moaned into his kiss, going off like a firecracker around him while his hands held the sides of my face and he swallowed my cries as if they were the greatest gift in the world. There wasn't one part of me that wasn't touching him—one part that wasn't connected to him in every way a person could be connected as he drank in my orgasm with a wide smile against my lips. This was his fantasy . . . and mine.

"Beautiful," he whispered, lifting his head just above my lips. "Now again," he instructed, turning his head and coming back down over my lips with hard, urgent kisses, thrusting once again inside my body with no mercy. He wasn't even going to give me a chance to catch my wits about me. My nostrils were flaring to try and take in enough air. And even though my head said there was no way I could release again so soon, my body was responding to him in every way, revving up like a car engine with each new drive forward.

I gripped Caleb's shoulders, lifting my curled legs higher, trying to trap him deeper inside me, to hold him in place, even though the feel of his flesh against mine as he moved within me was the most beautiful thing I had ever felt. But I had to hold onto him. I needed something to ground me when the world threatened to fall away. He groaned into our kiss. "Come with me," he breathed.

"Caleb!" My strangled cry was loud as my hips began to rise and my walls clenched around him.

"Yes, that's it . . . *Oh, God* that feels good . . ." His mouth covered mine once again with a fierce intensity that he might never have the chance to kiss me again in this life. My fingers clawed into his back while I moaned into his kiss. He inhaled every breath, every passionate whimper, every rippling quiver, until he couldn't hold back any longer. He thrust forward one final time, his lips lifting just off mine for a moment so I could watch as his eyes transformed into the most amazing shade of blue and his fangs punched forward. His body shuddered out his release in an explosion so powerful it had all my limbs shaking around him.

Sometime later the world stopped spinning and I started to see clearly again. I was breathing hard through my open mouth, while Caleb's head was dropped into the curve of my neck, his weight lifted from me on his elbows. The moment I had come around him while he was kissing me was so intimate, so intense, I wanted the warm feeling inside to never go away. It symbolized life, emotion, love. I was home. Home for me now was not a condo in the bustling city or even a spectacularly remote tree house in the mountains. It was wherever he was.

He was home.

"Caleb, look at me," I requested, softly. He lifted his head just above mine, his eyes still swirling with heat but now having returned to their many different shades of gray. Without doubt, he was the most beautiful man in the world to me, a true gift from God. With a slightly unsteady hand I touched his cheek and stared back at him with all the amazement I felt in my heart. "I'm free."

"You're free," he repeated with a beaming smile.

I laughed lightly, all the heaviness gone from my heart. "You're going to have to think of a new sexual fantasy," I said quietly, "since I'd say we truly did an excellent job of fulfilling your last one."

His cheeks split wide in an almost boyish smile, full of mischief and youth. "Actually, I'd like to give that fantasy another go. I think I might've blacked out there for a moment." We both laughed, his a deep, throaty rumble against my neck that reached deep inside me as he rolled me onto my side. "Did I hurt you?" When I stared at him blankly, he added, "Your side I mean."

I shook my head and continued to smile at him. It sure did feel good to smile.

Still semi-soft inside me, he slipped from my hold as he twisted himself awkwardly and reached between our curled bodies down to his pants, which were bunched up around his knees.

"What're you doing?" I giggled.

"I've something I want to give you," he said. "I've been carrying this around with me for a while."

I kissed his forehead and cheeks, wanting to convey every ounce of love I felt in my heart at that moment. "You don't need to give me any more gifts Caleb. I just want—" *You*, was how I was going to finish that sentence, but my eyes blinked incredulously as he held up a diamond ring between his thumb and forefinger. "Caleb," I gasped with barely any sound coming out.

The ring was stunning. An elegant white gold band with brilliant, round cut diamonds set in a channel around the entire circumference. It was perfect. No matter how you turned it, the diamonds were caught by the light. Their sparkle could be seen even through the happy tears washing my eyes. "I intended to give this to you before you disappeared. I know this wouldn't have fixed the fact that you were angry with me for asking you to leave our home, but at the very least I wanted to assure you that you've never been second to Celeste . . . and you never will be."

I looked up at him, distantly remembering Jax's last words of warning to Celeste at Brahm Hill. "Do you think she'll be back?"

He shook his head. "If I know anything about Celeste, it's that she didn't get to be six hundred years old by being stupid. She and her coven have already moved on. I can feel it."

"And if she does, we will face her together," I said confidently.

"Together," he promised, and then gently pulled my hand towards him, slipping the ring down my finger until it was rooted comfortably in place. "When I saw this I thought it symbolized our love. There's no break, no change, anywhere in the ring. It's eternal."

"No end, no beginning," I murmured. "Caleb, it's beautiful. Really, I don't know if I've ever seen anything so perfect. But you don't have to do this—"

"I do," he said, stroking his hand along the side of my cheek from ear to jaw. "I want our union to be recognized by your world as well as mine. I want to be committed to you as my mate and my wife. Committed to you, just you, only you." He stared at me with a hopeful smile, and I was speechless. I honestly didn't know how I could be any happier. "Will you marry me, my beautiful mate?"

Swinging my arms around his shoulders, my happy tears fell down his neck. "Yes, Caleb, I will marry you. I love you. I love you."

"Hmmm," he hummed. "There's my sweet girl's fluttering heart."

EPILOGUE

Two years later

"Olivia! Over here," an excited voice called, and I turned to see a bright-eyed Gemma standing with Jax beneath the hot backstage lights of the performance hall. She looked gorgeous in a gold-sequined cocktail dress that was cut to flatter her slight frame. Her red hair was pulled up in a loose twist that left a few dangling pieces along the line of her jaw, and the twist itself was decorated with an emerald clip Jax had bought for her last Christmas.

At her side, Jax looked equally as handsome, with his formal three-piece tuxedo—black, of course. I had never seen my grandfather look so happy. He had an enchanting little green-eyed brunette tucked safely into his arms. Now two, Sophie smiled in her lavender-colored ballerina dress and lifted her hands excitedly into the air as she cried out in a happy little chirp. Jax had all three of his angels, as he liked to call us, around him, and to him that was heaven.

Over the last two years, Jax had found a true peace to his life that he had never known before. He accepted his mistakes in this world, put to rest his past, and—most importantly—forgave himself for turning Gemma, though I doubted he would ever truly forget.

As I approached, he nuzzled softly at Gemma's ear and whispered his intent to take advantage of her later, which of course I could hear even above the noise of the quickly filling auditorium. She giggled lightly and returned a look of challenge with her lifted brow.

Gemma had accepted her fate as a Daywalker remarkably well. That was because she loved my grandfather more than she missed her human life. Aside from the fact that she no longer enjoyed some of her most favorite human foods, Gemma seemed to be as happy with her current life with Jax as she had been before. And she was a devoted mother. Both she and Jax showered their little girl with love and attention, just as Jax had always done with Gemma.

It had been a long road to get here, though, one that at times, had not been easy on any of us. Gemma, like other vampires was drawn to me. And even two years later it was something she had to constantly work at, but over time she was gaining more control. By maintaining her Daywalker life—and never having taken that first human kill—she had a purity about her that was unheard of for a vampire. That purity gave her a foundation of control around my gift that other vampires simply couldn't possess. I liked to think that my gift could recognize that goodness in her. Therefore it didn't feel the need to protect myself against her like it did with other vampires.

Still, there had to be changes to make it work. I sold my downtown condo, and Caleb and I moved in to the Walker condo after we had returned from Alberta. We visited Jax, Gemma and Sophie every weekend to give Gemma the time to gain control before we tried to move back full time. That was something we were all still working on, but all of us believed it could happen, perhaps sooner rather than later. We were a coven—a family. We were stronger together than we would be apart. I firmly believed that.

And Caleb had even agreed to let me work part-time at the blood clinic, since he was able to be close by in case I needed him. Together we had actually gotten pretty good at fighting off any threats to me. Caleb, though still always concerned for my safety, trusted in my abilities and my gift to fight alongside of him. And in return, I had learned that I didn't have to try and do it all myself to prove something. Together we had each other's backs, so to speak, and it was a nice, respectful balance.

Working at the clinic also allowed the family to continue getting the critical blood they needed to feed, and it gave me the opportunity to work and go back to school to finish my Masters degree in Music Composition and Musical Performing Arts. I loved getting to study music again. I realized I just felt more fulfilled as a person when music was at the forefront of my life. I guess, in a way, I had chosen music over the supernatural world. I could never escape my supernatural destiny, and I would always be a part of that world, but my time with Davin in the cave made it clear to me where I wanted to focus my life—with my music and my family. I guess that clarity was one thing I could be grateful for with respect to Luther Davin.

"Thank you for coming," I said with a sigh of relief. "I can use all the support I can get tonight."

Gemma waved a dismissive hand through the air. "Are you kidding? We wouldn't miss this. You're gonna do great!" I couldn't help but laugh. It was truly amazing to see how much of her irresistible combination of fun and sass Gemma had brought with her into her Daywalker life. "Olivia, you look stunning in that dress. I certainly hope Caleb doesn't destroy it later."

"Gemma," Jax scowled.

She just laughed at him. "Honey, it's no secret why I'm having to drag Olivia to the stores every other month."

Positive that a full-blown blush swarmed over my cheeks at the memory of the last dress he tore from my body before he made mad, passionate love to me, I tried to not let it affect my already blooming nerves. I did love this dress though. It was a vibrant red, his favorite color. The length of it reached my toes and floated on the air like a feather. The shoulderless confection made me feel pretty. "Caleb saw the dress earlier and very much approved," I smiled.

Gemma loudly snorted at that. "I'm sure he did. Where is the overgrown tower of brawn anyway?"

"He has the best seat in the house," I replied with a coy smile that faded as I glanced out over the packed performance auditorium within Benaroya Hall. The majesty and magnificence of this great hall, the building taking up one full city block, was truly amazing to behold from the vantage point of the stage. Tonight would be my very first live performance as a featured solo pianist with the Seattle Symphony Orchestra. "I wish he were down here, though," I added. "I'm so nervous. I don't know what possessed me to agree to this."

"You did it because you have a gift that needs to be shared," Jax said, kissing the top of my head. Since I had returned, Jax and I had become so close we were more like father and daughter than grandfather and granddaughter—though, admittedly, a father and daughter appearing remarkably close in age. I had forgiven him for making me leave my family and my home, and in that forgiveness came a newfound trust that I felt assured would never be broken between us again.

The symphony runner nodded to me to take my mark. "We're ready to start."

"Ooohhh," Gemma clapped. "This is so exciting! Come on, honey," she said, tugging at Jax's sleeve, "we have to take our seat."

"I am right behind you, angel," he replied, giving me a quick wink. "I am proud of you, Granddaughter."

I felt the threat of tears coming to my eyes and I swatted my hands at him. "Oh, go now, or you'll make me cry, Jax. I'm nervous enough as it is." His soft, rumbling laugh echoed around him as he and Sophie followed Gemma from behind the stage to their box just above and to the right of the stage.

Minutes later, standing just off the stage floor in preparation for being introduced to the lively crowd, I glanced up to the high bowed ceiling above me and smiled as I rubbed my hand over my flat stomach. "You think we should tell him about you tonight," I whispered, "now that we know for sure? It is a night for celebrations all around, isn't it?"

"Ladies and gentleman," the announcer began. "Welcome to our winter Concerto Series at Benaroya Hall. We begin tonight with an accomplished pianist who is as truly charming as she is talented. Performing Tchaikovsky's Piano Concerto No. 1, please join me in welcoming the very lovely *Olivia Greyson-Wolfe*."

The roar of loud applause in response seemed to come up through the floor. As I made my way into the bright lights and took my seat in front of the keys, I realized how truly special this moment was for me. This was my dream. Ever since finding out I was a Dhampir and a Charmer, I had focused on training and survival, on keeping myself safe from Davin. Once Davin had been destroyed, I was able to live in peace with Caleb, just as he promised we would. Aside from occasional skirmish every now and then, I was truly happy, and living the life I had always wanted for myself through my music.

And more . . .

I was living with my mate, my husband, and now soon-to-be father. Somehow, God had seen to it to give Caleb and me our miracle child. Odds were that the little boy I sensed growing inside me would probably be the only child we would ever have. But I would cherish this gift—our child—with every breath of life in me.

As the conductor signaled with three waves of his baton, my fingers began to move over the keys and the notes filled the sparkling auditorium around me. I closed my eyes and played each note for the man who was listening above—the man who had changed my life, who had saved me in so many ways. But most of all, he had saved my spirit so that I could be free to love him completely. "I love you, Caleb Wolfe," I whispered inaudibly, knowing he would hear me.

From the spectacularly high rooftop above us, under the crisp, winter moonlight and night stars, Caleb's deep voice replied, "Yes, that's it. Play for me, my sweet. Play for me."

Here is a preview of Christine Wenrick's
exciting new series . . .

THE MEN OF BRAHM HILL

COMING IN FALL 2013 . . . BOOK ONE:

SOMEONE ELSE'S SKYE

Chapter One

"Umm . . . Do you think we should be doing this . . . here?"

A deep, male groan rumbled through the breath-heavy air around them as Kane drew his lips from the chestnut-haired beauty who had just managed to interrupt the paradise he'd found in her arms. Perfectly curved, perfectly lovely, and perfectly willing, this woman had all the assets to make a man's blood boil with lust. Then again, most women could make Kane's blood boil, given the right setting. And this small, dark and absurdly archaic phone booth they were crammed into was, in his opinion, the perfect setting for stirring a man's blood.

But damn if he didn't just draw a blank on her name. *Was it Laurie? No Lucy?*

"Oh screw it," he thought. That was the problem with being a full time playboy, seducer, rake, philanderer, or whatever label might fit a man who lived and breathed almost solely for finding pleasure from women's bodies . . . forgetting their names. In this case, though, he was pretty sure there was an 'L' in there somewhere. *Linda?*

Kane's fingers dug into her wonderfully soft, fleshy thighs, drawing them snug around his hips as the thought struck him that he should just call her Lemon, because her skin smelled of the temptingly tart citrus, mixed maybe with a little lavender. Lemon, he decided, was a perfectly nice scent that reminded him of lounging with lemonade on a hot summer's day, or . . . unfortunately, the cleanest kitchen.

Frowning inwardly, Kane decided he had the sudden, inexplicable need to sneeze, causing him to wonder if—on some level—he might be allergic to lemons. He hadn't considered that until now. Though, they had never seemed to bother him before.

"I mean, maybe . . . ," she continued, the pink blush to her cheeks and the shy quality of her voice really quite charming, "we could go back to your room, where we could have some privacy and talk. Someone might catch us in here, and . . . I kind of wanted this to be more special."

Kane couldn't prevent his shoulders from visibly slumping a bit. There was almost nothing he wouldn't do to accommodate such a lovely creature for the privilege of sinking himself deep within the lush warmth of her body. But this playboy had two rules (actually he had, like, ten, but the other eight were generally enforced more on an as-needed basis).

One: never, *ever*, have sex without a condom.

And two: never, *ever*, in a bed.

Admittedly, the second one could be inconvenient, to say the least, but sex in a bed was just *way* too personal. It gave the woman the wrong idea right off the bat, and he always tried to be clear up front about what he wanted—and it wasn't a commitment. Hell, it wasn't even a relationship. He always liked to think of it more like a vacation. Some he regarded as overnight fly-overs, while others might stretch into a long weekend getaway . . . but still minus the bed. The bed was *his* space, his domain, whether his own or a borrowed one. It was the one place where he could relax and sleep without worrying about anything other than just that—sleeping.

Was he a selfish bastard? Of course. But he was also a fitful sleeper, so he needed the least possible amount of disruption in order to even hope for a few good hours of shuteye. And that meant separating the place where he slept from the places where he had sex.

Instead, Kane preferred his sexual adventures a little more public—of course, without being, well, *too* public. He decided it must be the '*chance*' of being caught that charged his blood so. For example, a lusty midnight tryst on one of the dining hall's serving tables, a setting in which anyone suffering from their own bout of sleeplessness could walk in on them, would be an exhilarating way to start the day. What dish could possibly be displayed as perfectly as a woman's curved body stretched over starch-white linen?

He contemplated the decadence of it all while palming Lemon's lush hips under her skirt, the heat of their mingled breathing hovering in the darkness around them as their bodies contorted into all sorts of deliciously bendy positions within the tight, wall-to-wall carpeted booth. *God, was there anything better?*

Perhaps one thing, he thought wickedly. He loved the sensual rawness of taking a woman from behind. As in the stretched-over-her-back—stroking-into-her-warm-body-to-the-rhythm-of-her-own-moans-in-front-of-floor-to-ceiling-mirrors kind of behind. The very thought of it had his fingers kneading impatiently into Lemon's thighs, imagining what she would look like at the very moment she hit the highest point of her pleasure. *Beautiful,* he thought.

Luckily, he had a lot of floor-to-ceiling mirrors available to him to enjoy just such a rendezvous. There were several in the on-site training rooms at the century-old former hotel he called home—The Oracle.

The Oracle was converted to a sort of dorm-styled home for Kane and the other members of the secretive group he belonged, an organization known simply as The Brethren. The Brethren owned and operated twelve such properties around the world. They were a place for the hybrid offspring of humans and supernatural beings—such as vampires, shape-shifters, witches and warlocks—to live year-round, to train for combat, and to work to protect humans from the supernatural world that unknowingly surrounded them.

The North American Oracle site, with its mountainous Chalet feel, magnificent high gables, and wooden bargeboards, was nestled between a pristine glacial lake and the base of the Canadian Rockies in the southwestern corner of Alberta, Canada. Simply put, it was spectacular, and had truly felt like a home to Kane for well over a decade.

Kane had no illusions that The Brethren's motives as a whole were entirely pure. When you take in the hybrid offspring of those you are fighting against, innocent or not, lines tend to get blurred, to say the least. And after two centuries of war with some of the darkest denizens of the supernatural world, The Brethren had managed to amass more resources, power and wealth than any one organization should rightfully have. But Kane was happy here. He'd found a home after feeling like he didn't belong anywhere for most of his thirty-four years. He had friends he would give his life for, innocents he genuinely wanted to save . . . and he *loved* the fringe benefits, such as sneaking into a curtain-fronted phone booth with one of the scorchingly-hot women he cohabitated with.

How did a man get this lucky?

As Kane stared back at the aforementioned Lemon, his lids drew lower and he licked his bottom lip, savoring the orange taste she had left there before offering her his sexiest smile. "I think this is the —— place," he drawled before capturing her mouth once again in a playful kiss, nibbling at the corners with the practiced skill of a man who could make a woman forget her own name . . . just as he had forgotten hers. "We're comfortable," he added between kisses, "and you are simply too irresistible in this short skirt." His long fingers, already exploring under said skirt, twined around her bikini strings. "Very irresistible," he added.

Soon, Lemon was melting beneath his kisses, her breath hot and heavy as she sagged against him, hopefully forgetting any notion of stepping one foot from this delightful little phone booth. "No one's gonna find—"

"Kane?" The sound of a familiar male voice calling his name at that exact moment had to be some kind of karmic joke. *Had the planets all aligned just then?* His pretty Lemon screeched and squiggled out from under him as she straightened from the bench seat he'd had her firmly pressed into. She frantically adjusted her clothes, re-hooking the lacey yellow confection he had just managed to get open.

No. No. No! This was all wrong. "What?" Kane growled as he drew the velvet drape back over his shoulder just enough to poke his head through to the other side. There stood his longtime friend, Aiden Rowan, standing with his facial expression pulled into an easy smirk. Aiden knew damn well what Kane had been up to. It was obvious just from the fact Kane was looking up at the six-foot-five mountain of a man from his knees.

"Am I interrupting?" Aiden asked, his brows lifting curiously while his chin stretched in an effort to peek through the curtain.

Kane didn't even get a chance to answer him because Lemon suddenly burst through the curtain as though her skirt was on fire. A startled gasp escaped her the moment she ran smack into the wall in front of her that was, unfortunately, Aiden's chest. She probably would have bounced right from it if it weren't for the fact he caught her in his long arms. Their eyes met with equal disbelief. His ambered-browns seeming to collide with her golden-greens, green orbs that had grown to the size of saucers after realizing who it was that held her in his grip.

"Lily," Aiden said with a thick swallow.

Lily . . . That was it! Thank God! Kane knew there was an 'L' in their somewhere!

"I'm sorry," Aiden continued, "I—I didn't know it was you . . ."

Kane noticed that his friend appeared truly and thoroughly flustered by the whole event, a behavior completely unlike him. Aiden was always very careful about what he let show on the outside, always had been. But right now he looked as transparent as a glass pane. Just what the hell did he have to be flustered about? He wasn't the one still ridiculously on his knees with a raging hard-on in his pants. "This had better be good, buddy," Kane grumbled when he finally rose to his feet, straightening his shirt over his jeans to cover the evidence of just exactly how *un*flustered he was.

"Excuse me," Lily said, quietly, dropping her head and running off like someone was chasing her . . . who, at the moment, wasn't Kane.

"Well, hell. Look at that," Kane said, staring after her. "You scared her off."

Aiden swung back on him with a fierce scowl. "Perhaps she's a bit embarrassed at getting caught in a phone booth with the hotel gigolo after being here only three weeks."

Kane's gaze narrowed on his friend carefully. *Had he missed something here?* A signal that Aiden was interested in the lovely Lemon? It wouldn't be hard, since Aiden kept his feelings regarding the fairer sex close to his chest, especially lately— which in itself was a good clue. But Aiden knew him well enough to know that if a man had staked a claim on a woman, then Kane would back off, no questions asked. He would never poach on his friend's woman. There were simply too many other fish in the sea to risk ruining a good man's friendship.

"That's a bit harsh," Kane declared. "If I didn't know any better, I'd say you had a thing for the fair Lem—,"—he quickly cleared his throat—"I mean, *Lily,* yourself."

When Aiden just continued to scowl at him without a reply, Kane went on. "No? Of course not. That would be ridiculous. You're far too tall for her. What's the rule? Never date someone who's less than half your height plus seven inches? . . . Or maybe that's never date someone younger than half your age plus seven years. Either way, you've got a good foot on her, buddy. It won't work. You'd need to be an even six feet, like me. Not too tall or too short."

"You're an asshole," Aiden replied flatly as he turned and started down the hall. Then he looked back over his shoulder and said, "Come on. Alec wants to see us."

Kane hitched his hands at his hips and shook his head with a silent groan. Alec Lambert was an Elder, the highest position within The Brethren, and he was also a direct human descendant of one of the original twelve men who founded the movement more than two centuries ago. Each Elder was responsible for a Brethren site around the world, and The Oracle was Alec's baby. "Shit," he murmured under his breath. "What've I done now?"

Minutes later, Kane and Aiden followed Alec's security detail into his private suites on the top floor. For Kane, it was always a trip to visit the Elder's office because it was an utterly pretentious and overblown space. Not that any of that was Alec's doing. He didn't give a damn about pleated drapes, nail head trim, or tufted leathers. This was the office he inherited from his uncle, Reese Lambert, who had it decorated a few years ago to fit *his* personal taste, which evidently resembled an old English library that someone vomited jacquard print all over. It was in complete contrast to the dark, wood-paneled wainscoting and simple, clean, old-European feel of the rest of the floor. And considering that Alec couldn't even stand to be reminded of his deceased uncle these days, it was a wonder he could work in these offices at all.

Not surprisingly, Alec was standing at a large, gabled

window overlooking the incredible property before him, a wide grassy plateau that rolled into a lake a couple of hundred yards out. He appeared to be considering something quite intensely —but then, Alec always appeared to be considering something. At only thirty-two, it seemed he had more responsibility than God, but he bore it well. It had come with some adjustments, though, such as trading in the comfortable jeans and tee shirts everyone had seen him in since he was a boy for Italian, wool-lined slacks, silk shirts, and even more expensive leather shoes.

Kane had no idea whether Alec liked his new clothing or not, but he wore them well, as though he was comfortable with the man underneath the clothing. And Kane figured, that's what was really important.

The Elder's hands were tucked into his pockets until he removed one to rake stiffly through his short, spiky, blond hair, almost as if he were trying to excise some tension that wasn't outwardly on display. But Kane knew Alec too well. They were friends . . . though it hadn't initially started out that way. They had been Guardians first, men brought in and trained by The Brethren to watch over and protect humans that were in danger from the supernatural world. Alec himself was human, which meant he had to work ten times harder than almost everyone else around him. His accomplishments as a former Guardian, team leader, and eventual Elder were all the more impressive considering he was at such a disadvantage speed- and strength-wise when compared with a Shifter like Kane. It took time, but he and Alec eventually forged a bond that on the best days could be as close as any friends, and on the worst could be like chest-thumping boys.

By Alec's current serious expression, today looked liked it was leaning toward a worse (or worst) day. "That's all, gentlemen. Thank you," Alec said, dismissing his guards but never moving his eyes from Kane. Deciding he needed to get comfortable because he was in for a long lecture, Kane settled into one of the tufted leather arm chairs in front of Alec's desk, a position that by now he was very familiar with. In the three weeks since the bloody battle of Brahm Hill, where they had lost two of their team to their vampire and Lycan enemies, it seemed a particularly insufferable amount. Kane had tried to give the Elder some slack, knowing that the outcome of the battle had been particularly difficult on him, but it was getting harder and harder, as his moods were becoming increasingly sharp.

Alec's former uncle, Reese Lambert, had killed Lucas Rayner, a man who had been like a brother to Alec. They all missed Lucas, but for Alec it was more than that. He and Lucas had grown up together at The Oracle since they were boys—trained together. They shared everything. And to his credit, Lucas had never once been jealous or resentful of the ruler Alec was destined to become. Instead, he embraced it, always standing beside Alec, protecting him from those who would try to hurt him, even from his own family in his very last breath.

Lucas's death truly seemed to stun Alec, because he never imagined ruling without his best friend beside him. The realization of it over the past three weeks had changed Alec. Kane could see it, though Alec tried hard not let it show. But the betrayal the Elder must have felt over his uncle turning to the immortal dark side and then taking the life of his best friend would leave scars. Lucas's life had been the last thing Reese had taken from Alec before Reese himself was killed by a Lycan.

Unfortunately, it was also the biggest.

"So . . . ," Alec began slowly, the large dimple in his chin stretching a bit as he observed Kane dangling his legs casually over the arm of the ridiculously expensive leather chair. "I'll get right to the point. It appears that our head kitchen mistress no longer wants to serve you in the dining hall."

Unfortunately, Alec hadn't directed that statement at Aiden, who was standing at respectful attention beside him with his hands clasped behind his back. The man was a kiss-ass, Kane decided, as he rolled his eyes—but he smiled inwardly. No one would ever hear a bad word said about Aiden from him, and vice versa (other than their common affinity for referring to each other as assholes). Aiden was, quite simply, his closest friend. "Does she plan on bringing my meals directly to my room?" Kane replied easily.

"No," Alec said slowly, obviously trying to keep those sharp edges in check. "If she had her way, she wouldn't feed you at all.

Two of her top servers mysteriously can't seem to get along anymore. In fact, they are engaging in cat fights not only with each other but also with the rest of the staff." Alec took a deep breath and thinned his lips as he slowly leaned forward. "Any guesses why?"

"Competing recipes?" Kane quipped with an innocence that impressed even him. But beside him, Aiden—the traitorous bastard—snorted with laughter. That certainly didn't help the situation. Still, Kane worried when his flip response only managed to elicit a gleam in the Elder's light brown eyes, rather like he had just watched a mouse walk into a trap full of cheese. Kane understood he was the mouse, and he was officially concerned.

"No, not recipes," Alec continued, now speaking more slowly. "Mrs. Stippich proceeded to explain to me"—he stopped and lifted a sharp finger—"in much more detail than I cared to know, mind you, how one of these women walked in on a certain man and the other woman in . . . shall we say . . . a compromising position on top of Mrs. Stippich's butcher block."

Aiden stifled another snort, and Kane very much wanted to reach out and smack him upside the head just then. He was *not* helping!

As Alec waited for him to respond, Kane thought back to the particular incident. It had been well before sunrise and he hadn't been able to sleep a wink. So he'd been wandering the halls when he came across the slightly plain but wonderfully curved Serena in the kitchen. A little while later, admittedly, things hadn't ended as he planned when Candy had walked in on them at *exactly* the wrong moment. I mean, who knew the breakfast shift started so early, anyway?

Fortunately, he had just come so hard his brain had been in the midst of a sexual freeze, so he had been fairly out of it when the shouting had begun. Instead, he gathered himself and concentrated on disposing of the condom. He'd been unable to avoid the messy scene altogether, though, once the nails had come out . . . literally.

Kane remained relaxed in his chair even though he felt like squirming, because he refused to let Alec see him flinch.

Although he couldn't be sure a bead of sweat wasn't about to break over his brow.

"Well, I told Mrs. Stippich," Alec continued as he walked around his large mahogany desk and leaned back against it with his arms crossed, "that I couldn't believe any of my Guardians—men trained and trusted with other people's protection—would ever do something so irresponsible."

Kane wanted to roll his eyes at that. Alec might be an Elder and have more responsibility than God, but he was young, good-looking, fit, and most definitely sexual in nature. He loved his indiscretions just as much as the next guy. In fact, rumor was that Alec had a special fondness for female Dhampirs drinking from him. Kane could go along with that, he supposed, if the woman initiated it, but it wasn't his thing—a little *too* much pain for his taste. Now, granted, this was an unsubstantiated rumor because Alec had the good fortune of an entire floor of a hotel to provide discretion. *So unfair.*

"Nonetheless," Alec continued, seeming to read his next thought, "I promised her that I would give it my fullest attention." The Elder then smiled and Kane finally fidgeted perceptibly in his chair. Alec was starting to enjoy himself way too much over this whole, tiny, misunderstanding. "Her request was that I ban you from the dining hall altogether while either of the two women in question is on duty. But since their schedules have now been separated and at least one of them is there from sun up to sun down—that would be a bit inconvenient for you as far as eating's concerned."

"You think?" Kane grumbled as Aiden bust into full-fledged laughter behind his hands, unable to retain what little control he had maintained so far.

Alec simply clasped his hands behind his back and began to walk the room. "No worries. I would never be so cruel as to deny you basic food . . . although you may deserve it."

"That's good to—"

"But I do think it's good for you to stay out of the dining hall and out of Mrs. Stippich's sight for a while. So I have a better solution in mind. One that keeps you fed and occupied so I don't have to waste my time dealing with any more crap like this any time soon."

"I don't suppose I'm going to like this idea," Kane said dully.

Alec gave him the knowing smile of someone who just watched the mouse go for the cheese. "You're leaving for the Trek outpost—"

"The Northwest Territories?" Kane blurted before Alec could finish. "It's nearly winter up there now. It'll be like five degrees and about five hours of daylight this time of year."

"You exaggerate," Alec countered. "It's October. You've got some time before winter fully hits. And I'm afraid this can't wait. It appears we have an Unidentified roaming around up there."

Unidentified, was the term for 'unknown supernatural being.' They didn't get those very often, since they were aware of just about every type of being and where they were located these days. But a new being had to be evaluated as to whether it posed a threat to humans. Not every supernatural being was a threat, but many were, and that got onto Alec's radar every time.

"Lucky and his team have spotted him as close as the southeast corner of Wood Buffalo National Park."

Aiden raised a brow. "Near the Lycan Dead Zone . . . That's a quick way to become extinct. Why not just let the Lycans take care of the problem . . . because they will."

The Lycan Dead Zone was to be avoided at all cost unless you had a really good plan. When gathered in large groups, the Lycans collectively emitted a scent that warned off all other creatures. From the smallest squirrel to the largest grizzly, everything within a five-mile radius was gone, creating a dead zone powerful enough to render even a Dhampir's gifted senses practically useless. And for humans, there's no warning at all till it's far, far too late. "Lucky's telling me this thing's too fast for the Dhampirs to catch."

"What?" Aiden blurted. "That's impossible—unless this thing's faster than a vampire."

Alec leaned back against the front edge of his desk, while Kane remained quiet in his chair. "I agree," he said. "But when the Dhampirs try to get close enough to see what we're dealing with here, it apparently vanishes into thin air."

"Vanishes?" Kane questioned. "Where?"

Alec seemed to light up at Kane's interest, as if he'd been waiting for it. "That's one of the questions I need you to answer for me."

Kane snorted. "So you're saying we have a Lycan-stalking phantom causing a ruckus up north—the very same Lycans *we* are also trying to take out. And you want me to go up there and do what, exactly? Make sure he *only* takes out Lycans? For Pete's sake, Alec, you could send anyone up there to babysit this thing."

Alec inhaled slowly, looking completely at ease with the power he knew he held over Kane at that moment, but he never used that power lightly. Alec had learned the lessons of his uncle's mistakes. He never abused his power with either deception or an iron fist. "Not true. If we're going to be able to identify this thing we need to be able to find it first. That sounds like a job for my best tracker, does it not?" When Kane didn't look convinced, Alec sighed and added, "I need your jaguar's gift of smell on this."

There it was. He needed Kane's Shifter abilities. And considering he was one of only about a handful of Natural shape-shifters left in the world, of course Alec would send him. As a natural born Shifter, the jaguar was Kane's inner animal, the token form with which he was most comfortable and shifted into regularly. He could also shift into other living, breathing forms as long as they were somewhat similar in size or could be projected larger, but it was much more painful to shift into forms his body was not readily familiar with.

"And it's a bonus," Alec continued, "that I'm killing two birds with one stone. I get the information I need on our mysterious phantom while also satisfying Mrs. Stippich's request that you stay off of her butcher block."

"I wasn't the one on her—"

Alec waved his hand. "Never mind, I don't need details. I just need to hear you say you'll do this for me."

"Do I have a choice?" Alec didn't even bother with a reply, his eyes saying, *'not at all.'* "Fine, I'll do it," Kane sighed. "As long as I know that when I get back there'll be no ban from the dining hall."

"Elder's honor," Alec replied with a smile.

Aiden just continued to chuckle under his breath. "Dude . . . babysitting duty in a sub-arctic climate? That'll teach you to be a little more discrete."

Before Kane could hiss out a blistering reply, Alec added, "I'm glad you're so amused by this, Aiden. Because you're going with him."

Acknowledgments

It's funny how after navigating the long, exhaustive road to publishing your first series, you reach the end of the journey and feel a bit sad. These first characters are the ones that lifted my imagination and kept it soaring. I will always be grateful to them and hope to honor them by creating new characters just as challenged, flawed and complex.

I am so grateful to all of you fans. As lovers of stories and books, you make this wonderfully descript world of reading and writing possible.

And of course, none of this would be possible without help from a lot of people. Paul, Sam and Kevin, thank you for your efforts and for seeing me through this journey.

About the Author

Christine is a graduate of Washington State University where she received a BA in Interior Design. And true to form of using mostly her 'right brain', she splits her time between her commercial design career and her imaginary world of writing. She lives in the scenic Pacific Northwest where she enjoys hiking, camping and photographing many of the wonderful places that serve as inspiration for her Charmed Trilogy. Her biggest reward in life is any given day when one of books connects with a reader, because she herself is such a lover of reading.

Made in the USA
Charleston, SC
13 July 2013